FURTHER PRAISE FOR *CONGRESS OF SECRETS*:

"A sumptuous and romantic tale of two ordinary people caught at the confluence of history, politics, and dark alchemy, *Congress of Secrets* will have you turning pages late at night."
—Aliette de Bodard, Nebula Award–winning author of *The House of Shattered Wings*

"A heady mix of politics and alchemy, friendship and betrayal, set against the grand sweep of nineteenth-century Vienna and the aftermath of Napoleon's downfall. This is historical fantasy at its best."
—Beth Bernobich, author of *The Time Roads*

"Reading Stephanie Burgis's *Congress of Secrets* is like eating a piece of rich, decadent chocolate. Filed with intriguing characters in a vivid and alluring setting, *Congress of Secrets* weaves its own brand of alchemy, drawing you in to 1800s Vienna. I couldn't put it down!"
—Sarah Beth Durst, author of *The Queen of Blood*

"Intense, vivid, and romantic. A compelling story of intrigue and dark magic in a richly drawn historical setting. Recommended!"
—Laura Florand, bestselling author of *The Chocolate Kiss*

"Intrigue and romance, history and magic, all blended with a deft touch. Stephanie Burgis writes with the heart of a poet and the eye for detail of a scholar. Recommended!"
—D. B. Jackson, author of the Thieftaker Chronicles

"A keen sense of adventure and a sparkling wit combine to make Burgis among the best in the business. She's my go-to writer for pure delight."
—Justina Robson, author of *Glorious Angels* and the Quantum Gravity series

"This is a gripping and enjoyable historical fantasy thriller, with engaging characters scheming for survival and revenge, fighting addictive alchemical magic against the lush background of the 1814 Congress of Vienna."

—Martha Wells, author of The Books of the Raksura series

"Napoleon has been defeated, and the Great Powers have gathered for the Congress of Vienna in order to decide the fate of a war-ravished Europe. In *Congress of Secrets*, Stephanie Burgis paints a vivid picture of Emperor Francis's court, its glittering balls and scheming royals, and the dark secrets behind the emperor's rule that no one is meant to know. After more than twenty years away, Michael and Caroline return to the city where they were born, transformed and hiding secrets of their own.

Burgis has created an alternate Vienna shrouded in fear and dark alchemy, political unrest, courage and love. A stunning historical fantasy—highly recommended."

—Jaime Lee Moyer, author of *Against a Brightening Sky*

"*Congress of Secrets* is an alchemical concoction of Vienna, secrets, beautiful prose, and the dark side of the royal court. Highly recommended."

—Laura Lam, author of the Micah Grey series

CONGRESS OF SECRETS

ALSO BY STEPHANIE BURGIS

Masks and Shadows

CONGRESS OF SECRETS

STEPHANIE BURGIS

an imprint of Prometheus Books
Amherst, NY

Published 2016 by Pyr Books®, an imprint of Prometheus Books

This is a work of fiction. Characters, organizations, products, locales, and events portrayed in this novel either are products of the author's imagination or are used fictitiously.

Cover images © Shutterstock
Cover design by Nicole Sommer-Lecht
Cover © Prometheus Books

Inquiries should be addressed to
Pyr
59 John Glenn Drive
Amherst, New York 14228
VOICE: 716–691–0133 • FAX: 716–691–0137
WWW.PYRSF.COM

20 19 18 17 16 • 5 4 3 2 1

Library of Congress Cataloging-in-Publication Data

Names: Burgis, Stephanie, author.
Title: Congress of Secrets / by Stephanie Burgis.
Description: Amherst, NY : Pyr, an imprint of Prometheus Books, 2016.
Identifiers: LCCN 2016019178 (print) | LCCN 2016025475 (ebook) |
    ISBN 9781633881990 (paperback) | ISBN 9781633882003 (ebook)
Subjects: | BISAC: FICTION / Fantasy / Historical. | FICTION / Alternative
    History. | GSAFD: Fantasy fiction. | Love stories.
Classification: LCC PR6102. U72 C66 2016 (print) | LCC PR6102. U72 (ebook) |
    DDC 823/.92—dc23
LC record available at https://lccn. loc. gov/2016019178

Printed in the United States of America

For my brothers—my lifelong co-conspirators!—with love and thanks.

CHAPTER ONE

1814

"Of course, I could never go back to Vienna," Michael Steinhüller said.

It took a fine art to pitch his voice to wistful melancholy over the sound of three dozen carousing actors in Prague's tiniest and most crowded tavern. But Michael had chosen this tavern, and this moment, carefully—and the notorious Count Cagliostro himself, the greatest trickster of all time, had taught Michael the art of successful vocal control.

"You've been to Vienna before, then?" Michael's drinking companion, Peter Riesenbeck, smiled at him from a face flushed with elation and alcohol, looking far too young to be the director of a theatrical troupe. "Did you think it the most beautiful city in the world? The tales I've heard—"

"I was born there," Michael said. *Honesty, for once.* The thought was bittersweet; he let it linger, to lend sincerity to his wistful smile. "And I can tell you, every tale you heard was true. The lilacs in spring—the Stefansdom cathedral by evening light . . ." He sighed.

"You miss it, then," Riesenbeck said. "Why did you leave?"

"I? Oh, never mind my history. Star-crossed love, disinheritance, disasters, tragedies . . . . We should drink to your good fortune instead. To the Riesenbeck theatrical troupe! And to your Grand Tour. May you take Vienna by storm and dazzle every member of the Congress."

"From your lips to the Almighty's ear!" Riesenbeck laughed and chinked clay cups with him by the guttering candlelight. "But there's no need to trust to fortune, my friend. I've been preparing for this moment for years."

So have I, Michael thought.

Skating from one gamble to the next, from one disguise to another, from deposed French nobleman to earnest Russian mine-owner . . . for the past four-and-twenty years, whatever role the moment called for, Michael had willingly played, and Fortune had smiled on him as warmly as if to make up for the shattering of his former life and shining ideals. He'd never waited too long to flee when a game went sour, never picked a dupe who couldn't afford their losses, and always won enough to keep himself until the next game paid off.

But even his run of luck could not continue forever, and at eight-and-thirty years of age, Michael was ready to aim at higher stakes than mere survival. It was time to play the gamble of his life. Every instinct in his body told him that the Congress of Vienna was the chance he'd been waiting for: the moment he could finally play the cards he'd held hidden in his sleeve for the past four years.

Within a week at most, the city would be full of the wealthiest and most influential men and women in all of Europe, gathered together to waltz, gossip, and be witnessed in glorious celebration of Napoleon Bonaparte's defeat. Even now, diplomats were preparing themselves to barter the fate of the Continent, aristocrats to display their finery, and the city of Vienna to become the beating heart of Europe.

Michael couldn't possibly miss it.

But first, he had to find a way back through the Vienna city walls.

As they downed their beers, Michael glanced out of the corner of his eye at the rest of the actors from the Riesenbeck troupe, busy lording it over their less-fortunate colleagues on this, their last night in the eastern backwaters of the Austrian Empire.

Please God let them be fêted with as many drinks as possible, and let their moods rise as high as their fortunes had with their invitation to the empire's capital.

Michael signaled to the tavern keeper, and more beer arrived at their own crowded corner. Riesenbeck reached for his purse, but Michael forestalled him.

"Allow me, please." He paid the waitress and shrugged, smiling crookedly. "Fate may have left me little, but I can still afford some pleasures."

"Forgive my curiosity." Riesenbeck leaned forward, gesturing expansively with his beer. "I'm an actor and a playwright; I love stories. I have to know. Why did you leave Vienna? Why can you not go back?" He grinned infectiously. "Feel free to bash in my nose if I'm too impertinent—but I'd rather you aimed for some part that wouldn't show up so well on stage."

"I'll keep that in mind," Michael said dryly. "But you're too young to waste your time with tragedy stories like mine, surely."

"Why, what old stories is our director drawing out of you?" Marta Dujic, the Riesenbeck troupe's gloriously curvaceous leading lady, purred the words directly into Michael's ear. "Herr Riesenbeck is a veritable fiend for stories, you know. He'll pull every last one from you as fodder for his plays, if you aren't careful." She smiled at his blink of surprise and slid into the seat beside him, smelling of sweet perfume as well as sweat.

Michael didn't begrudge her either scent. She'd fallen all across the stage that night in the company's final Prague performance, showing an impressive athleticism that mingled oddly with her current demeanor of limpid femininity. He was neither deceived nor offended by the intimate smile she aimed at him now from her position of enticing closeness; he could see her husband, Karl, watching them carefully from a safe distance away. Actresses, like fraudsters, had to learn to play many games to succeed.

"Marta, this is Herr . . ." Riesenbeck frowned. "Damn it, I've forgotten—what did you say your surname is?"

"It was Von Helmannsdorf when I was born," Michael said. He gazed into his beer, swirling the dark liquid in its cup. "My father was the first count of that name, raised up by the old empress of blessed memory; I was his eldest son. Still, I've gone by the name of Neumann for so long now, I sometimes forget I ever had any other name."

"But how mysterious," Marta breathed, leaning closer. "Why—?"

"You mentioned earlier: disinheritance, disasters, and tragedies?" Peter Riesenbeck was smiling outright, his blue eyes gleaming with sheer enjoyment. Did he believe what he was hearing? Michael couldn't tell. But at least he was listening.

"And star-crossed love," Michael finished for him, nodding. "That was the cause of all the rest. You see, my father, being the first count, had high hopes for all of us. So, when I married an actress from the emperor's Burgtheater . . ."

"The Burgtheater." Riesenbeck's face smoothed into near-religious bliss. "She must have been accomplished indeed. Which troupe did she play in?"

"Ah . . ." Michael blinked and took a stab in the dark. "She was Italian—an opera singer, in fact, hired by Emperor Joseph himself. The first time ever I heard her sing—"

"She stole your heart, of course," Riesenbeck finished for him. "But—naturally—your father did not approve?" He took a swig from his beer. "Let me guess the rest. The disinheritance came next, followed by her death from—oh, a wasting disease, I suppose? Very romantic, very tragic. And then, of course—"

"Peter!" Marta said. "Do remember you are speaking to her widower."

"I beg your pardon, Michael. Herr von Helmannsdorf, I should say." Riesenbeck looked genuinely abashed. "I was carried away, I'm afraid. It's only that it sounded so much like a play, I—"

"Never mind." Michael smiled tightly. "It has been a long time since I lost my Gabriela. I could hardly expect you to understand." There was a short, uncomfortable silence before Michael took pity on the director. "But you were quite correct. I did lose Gabriela. By then, my father had cut me out of his will. I left Vienna—I could no longer bear the memories—and I heard the news of my father's death only a year later."

"But why can you not go back?" Riesenbeck asked. "Surely after so long, even the most tragic of memories—"

"Ah, but the memories themselves are not the difficulty," Michael said. "Not anymore. Now we come to the true mystery. You see, my brother inherited the title as well as the entirety of my father's fortune. And yet..."

"And yet?" Marta raised perfectly arched eyebrows.

"And *yet*," Michael said, drawing the word out, "my mother always claimed in her letters that a second will had been written by my father, after I'd left Vienna."

"Brilliant." Riesenbeck grinned. "Hidden, of course—they're always hidden. But you must return to Vienna, man! Rip up the floorboards! Search the secret passageways! Hunt—"

"I would care for nothing more," Michael said. "Unfortunately..." He paused, moistening his lips, as he prepared for the climax of the piece.

Like a play, Riesenbeck had called his story—and so it was. Michael had chosen it precisely for his current audience, and he could only pray that they applauded it. The truth... The truth was something rather different.

Although Michael had abandoned his own ideals years ago, as the price of survival, he'd never lost his cursed status as an enemy of the state. If he was discovered by the customs guards at Vienna's city walls, he would be taken to Vienna's notorious secret police for interrogation—and whether they arrested him as the idealistic boy radical he once had been or as the wickedly accomplished fraudster he had become after his escape... well, Michael knew better than most just how bitterly his own story would end.

As it had ended for the two people he had loved most, on the night he'd fled Vienna, twenty-four years earlier.

Curse it. He hadn't thought of them in years. He had sworn never to let himself—and he had succeeded, until now. It was the thought of Vienna that brought back his former life to him, the one he had discarded and forsworn decades ago. Michael gritted his teeth against the memories. Still they rose to fill his vision with a vivid intensity that the years had done nothing to diminish: *her* face, tear-streaked but gazing at him through the flames. As if he were her only chance for salvation . . .

He would not remember what had happened next. He couldn't let himself. If he did, he could never return to Vienna. And if he didn't return to Vienna, he would miss the greatest opportunity of his life: the chance for true security at last.

"Let me tell you about my younger brother and his ploys," Michael said, and shook aside the disquieting sheen of memory. "You see, he could hardly take the risk that I might return and claim my true inheritance. So . . ."

Michael told his invented story with all the color and excitement of an epic drama, and in the telling of it and the creation of a dozen confirming details, he almost managed to forget his moment of unaccustomed weakness. He ordered a third round of drinks for the entire theatrical troupe, and then a fourth. And when, in the middle of the celebrations, Peter Riesenbeck suddenly looked up with an expression of delighted inspiration, Michael felt the delicious frisson in his chest that marked the moment of success.

"Do you know," Riesenbeck said, "I may have a solution to your dilemma!"

"Impossible," Michael said. "Ever since my brother arranged the theft of my identification papers, I cannot pass the walls, and—as I cannot enter the city—"

"Ah, but we can pass through the walls, can we not?" Riesenbeck said. He winked knowingly at the little group of his actors that had gathered around them as the evening progressed. He drew them closer, as his voice dropped to a stealthy undertone. "You wouldn't know this, of course, not being an actor yourself . . . but there's a bit of a trade secret to our traveling carriages. You see, we haven't always got all the spare money one could hope for . . . and customs inspections are so damned heartless and thorough . . ."

"Yes?" Michael said. He had to grip his cup of beer in both hands, to keep his tone innocently curious. *Almost there . . . only say the words . . .*

"The fact of the matter is, your old family home isn't the only spot with secret hiding places," Riesenbeck said. "Of course, it would be a tight squeeze for you, fitting into the compartment under the floor-boards of our carriage . . ."

"We'd have to pack him in with some food," Marta said. "He could hardly go seeking his inheritance without any sustenance, after all."

"Apples should be enough for the trip," her husband said judi-ciously, narrowing his eyes at Michael's lean frame. "At any rate, he'll only need to be hidden down there for an hour or two at most, for the passage through the walls. We'll have to poke some holes into the floor-boards, though, to be safe. We wouldn't want him suffocating during the customs inspection."

"Well, Michael?" Riesenbeck raised his clay cup in salute. "What do you say? Are you ready to join us for an adventure?"

"Am I ready?" Michael shook his head in true wonderment, trying to control the excitement that wanted to overwhelm him. To return back to Vienna, after four-and-twenty years of exile—to begin the greatest adventure of his life . . .

He couldn't hold it back after all. Exhilaration rushed through Michael's chest, as irrepressible as air. He let it break out in a grin that took in all the beaming faces that surrounded him. "My friends," he said. "You have my deepest gratitude. I would be honored to make use of your secret compartment."

Sabers flashed in the early morning sunlight, signaling the arrival of the emperors, princes, and archdukes of Europe at the Congress of Vienna's opening ceremonies. Battalions of infantry, regiments of cavalry, and all the cuirassiers of the Viceroy of Poland joined ranks to honor them. As Europe's highest rulers crossed the flower-strewn grass to the open tent in the center of the field, bright sunlight lit the golden orders of distinction on their military-styled jackets until they too seemed to blaze with triumph.

"My, my," murmured Caroline, Countess of Wyndham, in French

to her companion. "What a distinguished company indeed. I had no notion that so many of our kings were so very martial." She widened her eyes innocently, dropping her voice. "Do you think they defeated the great Napoleon by blinding him with their medals in the sun?"

Her companion, the Prince de Ligne, turned stifled laughter into a cough, his shoulders shaking. His blue eyes twinkled in his weathered face, still handsome even in great old age. "Why, Lady Wyndham," he murmured back, "I would be astonished to learn that you, of all people, haven't heard yet of the finest entertainment in this Congress."

"Your Grace?" She tilted her head closer, ignoring the neighbors around them.

They sat in the front row of seats, facing the sovereigns' tent—a coup indeed in the battle of social grasping that already ruled the newborn Congress. The Prince de Ligne breathed his words directly into Caroline's ear.

"Why, the finest and most popular form of entertainment among our serene rulers, madam, is to gift each other with the highest of honors. Distinctions that men used to fight and die for are now handed out like baubles between friends. Indeed, they've already been reduced to awarding each other mere military ranks. Emperor Francis is now a colonel in Tsar Alexander's Imperial Guard, I believe, and Tsar Alexander a colonel in our own Hiller regiment."

"But what a distressing turn of fortune for their wives," Caroline said. "Do you think the emperor shall care much for his new life in a humble colonel's tent camped somewhere in the Crimea? Next time the tsar decides to mount another war of invasion, I hope the emperor is not, at least, given a tent that leaks. It would detract so sadly from the glory of war for him."

She bit her tongue abruptly, wondering—had she gone too far? No, surely not, judging by the twinkling amusement in the prince's eyes.

The old prince was as wily a diplomat—in both courtly and political life—as she had ever met. Born a prince of the Holy Roman Empire, he had made his name across the Continent for his glittering epigrams, his famous—and infamous—letters to all the greatest personages of Europe, his books on military history, and his own dramatic military exploits as a field marshal of the Austrian Empire. In short, he was a very master of self-publicity, and if he did not penetrate her disguise, no one ever would.

Of course, it would have been a joy to befriend the Prince de Ligne for nothing more than his keen wit and open-minded intelligence—both qualities more precious to Caroline than gold or jewels, after years of vapid high society—but she did not have the luxury of acting for pleasure now. The Prince de Ligne had been a great man of the Austrian court for at least the past half century. She had worked and planned to achieve her introduction to him three nights ago, and this seat beside him today.

Now that she had it, and had his undivided attention as well . . . She moistened her lips and kept her tone as light as if she hadn't been maneuvering toward this goal ever since they'd met.

"Of course, I've never met the emperor himself, so perhaps I am unjust. Perhaps he would care for nothing better than a tent that leaks."

"Life *au naturel*?" The Prince de Ligne laughed. "I hardly think so, my dear. You're thinking of the grand old days of Versailles and his aunt the Queen, who used to hold such charming picnics there. I fear our current emperor is not a follower of Rousseau's philosophies."

"What a pity."

"Perhaps, and yet . . ." The prince narrowed his eyes at the tall, stooped figure across the field. "I think, on the whole, we must be grateful, Lady Wyndham. For I must confess, I shudder at the very idea of His Majesty in a simple shepherd's outfit."

Following the Prince de Ligne's gaze across the field, Caroline spotted the signs of preparation as the last of the royals settled into position. Only a few minutes left to achieve her first goal; no time left for maneuverings. She smiled up at her companion and abandoned all subtlety. "Will you indulge an unfashionable urge in me, Your Highness? I find myself oddly curious to meet the emperor."

The prince studied her a moment, his eyes narrowed in thinly veiled speculation. Caroline felt as if a hot light were being held to her face.

She kept her smile open and held his gaze without flinching. She was the Countess of Wyndham, a wealthy British visitor. Why shouldn't she desire to meet the Austrian emperor, to brag about the event to all her friends back home?

She felt uncomfortably certain that she wasn't fooling her companion in the slightest.

The prince finally shrugged. "But of course. I would be delighted to assist you, my dear, just as soon as this ceremony is over." He raised one eyebrow, his gaze still speculative. "I'm afraid the field may become a trifle crowded if we aren't quick about it, though—would you mind very much if we met His Majesty before seeking out any refreshment?"

"Not at all," Caroline said lightly. "Why should we wait?"

Her voice hadn't even trembled—it was nigh-on miraculous. Caroline kept her smile fixed as she raised her fan to hide the quickness of her breaths. Her heartbeat thrummed in her ears.

Her own long wait was almost over . . . and she could not, *would not* be too late.

"Aha. And now, I believe, the ceremony is finally ready to begin." The prince indicated a white-haired old man rising to his feet within the tent, by the grand altar. "The Archbishop of Vienna, my dear. I hope you can bear with us for some time. Your own Church of England believes in, ah, short services, does it not? Have you ever had the opportunity to sit through a ritual in the true faith?"

"Not in England," Caroline said, with scrupulous honesty. Her tone dismissed the subject, but she cursed herself for weakness. Why hadn't she simply lied, and said, "*No, never*"?

Open-minded the Prince de Ligne might be, but if he knew her true identity she would be ruined in an instant. Caroline knew better than to put her trust in any man. She'd learned that lesson four-and-twenty years ago, scarcely six miles from where she sat now.

Gold sparkled from the ornaments on the altar, and wax candles lost their battle with the sun as the Archbishop intoned the Latin Mass. Caroline tried to distract herself from the nervous thrum of her pulse by watching the varying expressions on the rulers' faces as they all waited through the ceremony. Protestants, Catholics, and Orthodox Russians had all united against Napoleon Bonaparte—and indeed, here in this glittering array of thanksgiving, one would never guess that Bonaparte had ruled the Austrian empire itself in all but name, holding it as a tribute state until less than eight months ago. Emperor Francis had even given the invader his own Habsburg daughter as a second bride, to buy an illusion of autonomy.

But then, Emperor Francis, as Caroline knew, had never been one to let his conscience interfere with his pleasures.

Guns thundered out a salute as the archbishop blessed the bread and wine. Swords clashed in honor. Incense filled the open air. And with the glory of the noise and the dizzying scent and the holy benediction—

No, Caroline thought. *No. Not again!*

A tingling thrill shot through her body and seized her. Inescapably, it bore her to her knees. She was barely conscious, through the confusion, of the rest of the assembled thousands dropping to their knees around her. The noise of the guns and swords ceased abruptly as the soldiers themselves fell prostrate.

Did the others take it for real religious fervor, the gratitude and grandeur of the moment, that overwhelmed them, stole all energy from their bodies, and tossed them onto the ground, half-conscious?

Caroline knew better.

It had been twenty years since she had felt this invasion. She could fight it—she had learned so many techniques of resistance by the time she was fifteen, though none of them had worked well enough in the end . . . but she was five-and-thirty now, a girl no longer, and her life had granted her a will of steel. She had sworn that no one else would ever use her so again.

She could force herself to her feet and spit in the face of the man who did this—

But if she did, and so revealed herself, she would lose everything she had waited and planned for so long.

Caroline forced herself to breathe deeply, fighting down the panic that thundered in her ears as she felt the energy bleed from her body. Funneled into . . . where, this time? She forced her eyelids open to peer across the field.

Even the sovereigns had prostrated themselves on the ground. All of them seemed lost in the moment, except . . .

Aha. Francis II, Emperor of Austria-Hungary, looked up with a small smile, surveying the field around him. She could almost see the glow of reception around his prone body. It was he who benefited from all of them this day, receiving the glory of a thousand.

And the man who gave it to him . . .

Caroline knotted her nearly numb hands into fists on the grass. She did not need to see Count Pergen to know that he was here, somewhere, manipulating all.

It had been four-and-twenty years since her life had been ripped into shreds around her. But she was ready, now, at last.

She would not leave Vienna again until she had rescued her father from the men who had destroyed her childhood.

CHAPTER TWO

"**R**evenge!" Peter Riesenbeck declaimed. He leaped to the top of a sturdy, wooden table, waving his wine glass threateningly at the inn patrons in the courtyard around him. "For the murder of my father, the theft of my inheritance—"

"What madness is this?" Marta cried. Fluttering an imaginary fan, she flung her free hand to her brow. "Oh, heavens, say my dear lord's wits are not o'ercome!"

A third actor shouldered his way through the crowd of spectators who'd gathered around the impromptu rehearsal. "A messenger, my lord! The count, your father-in-law, approaches."

"Ha!" Peter bellowed. "Now I have him at my mercy."

Marta fell to her knees. "Husband, I beg you—"

"And you will all learn what comes of it tomorrow night, good people!" Peter said. He jumped down from the table and swept a bow to the gathering. "Behold the Riesenbeck company at your service, summoned from Prague for the noble Congress of Peace, for which only the finest theatrical companies are desired. Marta Dujic, my leading lady"—he lifted his wine glass to her, and she swept into a graceful curtsy—"Rudolf Griesinger, playing the messenger"—a bow—"and myself, Peter Riesenbeck, director of the company. Come see us at the Theater an der Wien any night of the week for theater performed in good honest German!"

A bevy of young men converged on Marta, and Peter stepped back, draining his wine glass. As he wiped the sweat from his brow, Marta's husband, Karl, spoke grudgingly behind him.

"It went well."

"Of course it did." Peter pasted a smile on his face as he turned to face the older man. Even now, he saw, Karl was scowling—Good God, had the man no heart?

"Look at them all," Peter said. "They're in town for the Congress but too poor for the balls and royal entertainment. They know this city's the center of Europe right now, but it's all going on above their heads. What better time for theater? Much less our theater, eh?" He slapped Karl's broad shoulder. "The best small company in Prague, isn't that what the *Wiener Diarium* called us? The best acting, best direction—"

"Best acting." Karl's eyes, still focused on Marta as she flirtatiously accepted the accolades of the men who surrounded her, narrowed thoughtfully. "I think we should all have pay rises now that we've reached Vienna."

"Pay—?" Peter nearly choked. "My friend, perchance we might wait on a ticket sale or two for that? All my funds went into our trip and the inn roof above our heads."

Karl shrugged off his protest. "The Theater an der Wien should pay for that. They would, if you knew what you were about in dealing with them. They were desperate enough to get us, after all."

"Well, naturally, and yet . . ." Peter took a breath. *Desperate*, he'd called the theater agents, to the rest of the company. In truth, it would have been a better description for himself.

With debts mounting up in Prague all around them, he'd fought and scrambled for the invitation to Vienna, and then only managed it by scraping his requirements so low it would be a wonder if they made any money from the theater at all. He could hardly have told the actors the truth of that, though—for the predictable effect on their performances, if nothing else. And they would never have understood. The looks of betrayal that he would see on their faces, if he ever told them the truth . . .

And the look he could imagine on his old mentor's face, if he heard that Peter's young, hopeful theater troupe had fallen apart after less than three years in existence . . .

"You're no hero, boy, only a minor bit player."

No. Peter drew a deep breath, forcing back the too-often remembered words. *I'll prove you wrong yet, Master Périgord. This is my chance.*

Vienna was the center of the whole world just now, not only of the Austrian empire. If their performances went well—no, *when* they went well and achieved the success he'd always dreamed of—why, then they'd be offered contracts from every theater in the empire, even the Habsburgs' Burgtheater itself, and Peter would only have to choose the top-paying offer to gift them all with infinite luxury.

Every dramatic hero took a few risks before gaining everything in the end. This trip was an investment for their future.

For their *survival.*

Peter forced his grin to hold. "Why, Karl, I do believe you have a point," he said. "And I promise sincerely that I'll think on it. Only let us play our first week in Vienna first."

At five-and-twenty, Peter was one of the youngest theatrical directors in the empire. He'd pulled all of the actors into his company on the strength of his energy and dreams. He would not fail them now.

Peter turned away from Karl, ignoring the mutinous expression on the older actor's face, and started back through the crowd toward the inn's entrance, in search of a waitress. A tug on his sleeve stopped him just before the door.

"Herr Riesenbeck?" The man was about his own age, with a pleasant smile and unobtrusive air. If Peter hadn't been hailed, he might never have noticed this fellow in a crowd, so sober was his dress and so quiet his voice. "An excellent performance, sir."

"I thank you, sir!" Peter bowed. "Are you a keen theatergoer?"

"Not as much as I should like." The man smiled ruefully. "I run errands for my employer, who often makes me work at night. I do have a friend who serves as theater critic for one of the local newspapers, though."

"Really?" Peter brightened.

"Indeed." The man pointed to the empty seats at the nearby table. "Won't you join me, Herr Riesenbeck? I've already ordered more wine for both of us."

"I'd be honored." Peter sat down, relief flowing through him. The other patrons at the table were all engaged in a heated conversation on the new tariffs, which he was happy to ignore.

It was his first stroke of luck, and less than an hour since they had arrived. A good omen if he'd ever seen one.

"May I ask where you've performed in the past?" the man asked. "Your style is quite distinctive—I could have sworn I'd seen it before— yet I'm afraid I didn't recognize the name of your company. As I said, I don't spend nearly enough time in the theaters, so . . ."

"Unless you've been to Prague, I doubt you've ever had the chance to see us before," Peter said. "Thus far, we've only toured in the provinces. But as for the style . . ." He paused, debating within himself, and then gave in to practical honesty. "I apprenticed to the director Paul Périgord."

"Ah. Now that name I do know." Peter recognized, with resignation, the sudden spark of real admiration in the man's widened eyes and genuine smile. "You were fortunate indeed to have so distinguished a mentor."

"Indeed," Peter said, and stifled a groan. How Périgord would laugh if he overheard this conversation. Still, he would make himself known for his own achievements, and not only for his too-famous mentor. *Soon*.

"Might I have the pleasure of your name, sir?" he asked his new companion.

"Vaçlav Grünemann."

"Aha. Another Bohemian, then." Peter leaned one arm against the table. Through the inn door, the smells of roasting meat floated temptingly. Should he—could he—pay for Grünemann's meal as well as his own? He had watched Périgord feast the reviewers and theater managers in Prague so many times. If Peter thought of it as an investment . . .

"Originally Bohemian," Grünemann said. "But my family moved to Vienna a long time ago."

"I understand." A plump waitress arrived at the table, bringing a jug of wine and two cups, and Peter smiled at her as he spoke. "My family has been in Prague three generations now, but we're of Austrian stock."

"I wondered, actually . . ." As the waitress moved away, Grünemann leaned closer, still smiling. "I thought I might have recognized an old friend, when you first arrived."

"Sir?"

"Another man rode with you, did he not? A man who wasn't a member of your excellent troupe."

"Ah . . ." Peter blinked. Michael had slipped away almost the moment they'd arrived in the busy inn yard, too worried about being sighted by one of his scheming brother's acquaintances to linger. Grünemann didn't look the sort to spread rumors, and yet . . . "I'm afraid I don't know what you're talking about," Peter lied smoothly.

"No? I could have sworn I saw you help another man from your carriage—and not from any of the usual seats." Grünemann sat back and began to pour wine. He handed Peter a full glass. "I only ask because he looked so familiar. I thought it might have been a game with him, to ride undetected through the city gates."

"Mm." Peter accepted his wine glass, thinking furiously. If Grünemann really wanted to know, what damage could it do? Yet, they'd sworn secrecy to their illicit guest, and Michael had seemed a good fellow. Moreover, if word came out that the Riesenbeck company had thwarted the customs checkpoint, even as a game . . .

No, continued secrecy was the best, as well as the most honorable, option. And after all, no matter how influential a friend he might be, Grünemann would hardly take offense at that. It couldn't mean so much to him just to learn the truth of one small adventure.

"I'm afraid it must have been a trick of the light, my friend," Peter said. "Only members of my own troupe traveled with me. We do cram ourselves within the carriages, you know, to save on space. Perhaps you saw me helping Karl."

Grünemann's gray eyes remained disconcertingly intent upon his face for a long moment. The guests around them continued their deafening hum of talk, and brassy music sounded from inside the inn, yet Grünemann was ominously silent.

"I do apologize for any confusion," Peter said. "Is he a good friend of yours, this man you thought you saw?"

"Not particularly," Grünemann said. "Ah well." He toasted Peter with his wine glass. "Your health, sir." He smiled again, yet Peter thought the smile had taken a wry turn. "You may be certain that we shall meet again."

Twenty blocks away, Michael turned into a crowded tavern in the sixteenth district, smiling and confident but careful not to make eye contact with any of the other guests. His satchel swung in his hand as he strode through the haze of smoke and laughter to the back door. Two outhouses stood hidden behind the tavern. He ducked into the first, holding his satchel high above the filth.

Five minutes later, he stepped out remade. He'd removed the close black wig to reveal his own short, thick brown hair, styled with his fingers into waving disorder—last year's style, alas, but still the only fashion he could manage acceptably on his own, without the aid of a mirror.

Far better, he'd changed his plain, dark-colored overgarments for a deep blue tailcoat and tight, fawn-colored breeches in the fashionable, English style. A carefully tied cravat around his throat, gleaming silver buttons on his butter-yellow waistcoat, a walking stick beneath his arm, top boots on his feet, and a great seal ring on his left hand completed the picture of a wealthy European royal in search of expensive amusement.

Not just the picture, Michael thought, as he slipped on the ring. *The man himself.* He closed his eyes and arranged his features, letting them gradually slide into the expression that felt most natural in this outfit, this new cloak of identity. The man who wore these clothes—the prince who wore these clothes—would wear them without a thought as to their cost, or to the reactions of those around him. When he walked through these familiar streets, he would expect others to make way for him.

He must look as far removed from a grimy printmaker's apprentice as any creature on Earth could be. If anyone from Michael's past saw him now . . .

But there was no one left to recognize, or to mourn. His beloved first master was gone. That much was certain. And the only other person who had ever known him well enough to recognize him in any disguise, the only person he had ever been foolish enough to let himself care too much for . . .

Michael took a deep, steadying breath. It had been twenty-four years, and he would never know what had happened to Karolina, for good or for ill. There was no purpose in torturing himself over possibilities, even as he walked the streets of the city that he'd shared with her.

The man he played now would never even speak to anyone from her class of society, let alone care about her fate. And in the gamble that lay ahead, that truth was all that Michael could allow to matter.

He set his shoulders and drew a deep breath.

His satchel, abandoned, sat in the back corner of the outhouse as Michael strode briskly back through the tavern, gratified at the careful berth the other men drew around him, now. A beggar approached him on the street—one of the few, perhaps, who had escaped the police purges during preparations for the Congress—and Michael flipped the man one of his few spare coins with an expansive gesture.

He couldn't change the past and save the people he had once loved. But he could do his best now with what he had.

Why not be generous, after all? He was about to play the greatest gamble of his life, to win a fortune, a title, and a future. He could hardly quibble at mere florins now.

Caroline was still shaking as the crowd around her, freed from paralysis, rose to their feet and broke into a German hymn of thanks. Thank Heaven for her disguise; she wasn't meant to be able to speak German. It had been a sensible precaution: French, the official language of the Vienna Congress, was a language she'd only learned after moving to England, so her French, at least, was inflected with a suitably British accent. Whereas her German . . .

Even if Caroline had been willing to admit to speaking Austrian German, one airing of her native accent—the Viennese inner-city tones of a printmaker's daughter—would have ruined her disguise forever.

Now, though, the ruse served a different purpose. As the men and women around her, even the cynical Prince de Ligne himself, raised their voices in the German prayer, she gained a breathing space to calm herself in near-private. She clenched the thin skirts of her muslin dress as she waited for her hands to stop shaking. Steeling herself, she endured the chills that flooded her body, chills that felt only too familiar: she'd been eleven years of age the first time she'd felt this aftereffect.

Eleven and terrified, in a windowless room. And even after it had happened, leaving her shivering and weeping, she'd still begged the man who'd done it: *Where is my father? When is he coming back?* Worse yet, she'd even believed his promises: *Soon. Only be a good girl...*

Caroline's teeth nearly pierced her bottom lip. She forced her lips open and made her shivering fingers relax their grip on her dress.

She was Lady Wyndham now, not helpless Karolina. She wouldn't let herself break down in fear before her plots had even begun. She would not give her old jailers that satisfaction.

The ceremony came to a close with the ending of the hymn. As the archbishop signed a perfunctory blessing before the restive crowd of royals, the Prince de Ligne turned to Caroline.

"Well, my dear. Now that you've seen the Austrian way of celebrating peace, what do you think of it?"

Caroline's smile cut like a knife through her face. "I found it most . . . enlightening, sir."

"An interesting choice of words." He cocked one eyebrow at her. "I must admit, I found it surprisingly moving at the end. It may have been my first taste of true religious fervor since, oh . . . 1752, perhaps?"

"And what happened then?"

"Oh, that was when I first read Voltaire. We were all very enlightened back then, you know. Even you might have been startled by our salons, I think—each of us trying to outdo the others in our heresy and freethinking. Not like these modern days." The prince sighed faintly as he looked across the crowd. "It's become fashionable now to act terribly moral. I fear I find it rather tiring."

He did look tired, although Caroline would not insult him by pointing it out. No, more than tired . . . *drained*. Earlier, in his sparkling company, Caroline had nearly forgotten that the Prince de Ligne was eighty years of age already. But it could not be healthy to have so much energy sucked out of him now. And for such an object . . .

"But I'd almost forgotten—you desired an introduction to the emperor," said the prince. "Will you take my arm?"

"Of course," Caroline said.

The prince held out his thin arm and Caroline took it, careful not to lean any of her own weight on it. She felt it taut with suppressed exhaustion under her hand, but the prince's face was clear and good-humored.

"I must warn you, my dear, that I am no favorite of the emperor these days. I made the mistake of publishing a series of letters a few years ago that debated some few points of public policy . . . forgetting, you see, that over the last few decades the criticism of the emperor's peers has turned into a crime."

"A brave move indeed," Caroline murmured.

"I'm afraid our admired emperor did not find it so. I am too much of a public figure, even these days, to be openly punished for such an act, and yet . . ." The prince shrugged. "The atmosphere at court turned notably cold for quite some time."

"A loss indeed. And yet . . ." Caroline aimed a slanted smile at her escort. "Might I hazard an impudent guess, Your Highness? When you attended the court functions anyway, did not you gather more friends and admirers around you than the emperor himself? And were not at least a few of them drawn by the scandal you'd provoked?"

The Prince de Ligne broke into laughter as infectious as that of a boy. "You are far too perceptive, my dear. And, of course, you are entirely correct. I could have eaten ten suppers a day for the next six months if I'd accepted a quarter of the invitations that suddenly came flooding in upon me." He shook his head, his eyes gleaming with amusement. "But now that you've guessed so much, I have another riddle for you to solve.

"You remember how we spoke earlier of our new Robinson Crusoe out on his island Elba? Well, perhaps you may guess my secret name for our honored emperor, too, once we've spoken to him."

Caroline laughed and answered and tried, as they walked across the field, to subtly support the prince's weight herself as much as possible, without embarrassing him. As she saw the new lines on his cheeks and the fever-bright gleam of his blue eyes, though, rage seethed inside her. She forced it down. *Not now*, she told herself. *But soon . . .*

Silently, she added one more point to the list of misdeeds that needed accounting before she left Vienna.

CHAPTER THREE

The emperor of Austria, Hungary, and much of Italy and the Balkans stood surrounded by his fellow rulers in the royal tent, chatting and laughing. From a distance, at the beginning of the ceremony, Caroline had thought his long, thin, sunken face looked hard and wary—closed off from those around him, as if suspicious of all the world. Now, though, he positively glowed with good humor. Even his normally stooped posture had straightened with the influx of energy.

She hadn't thought it possible to hate him more than she already did.

"Your Majesty," said the Prince de Ligne, bowing. "May I present a charming English visitor? Caroline, Countess of Wyndham, of Sussex."

Caroline swept a deep curtsy. *Breathe in . . . out . . .* She timed her breaths, using them to control her anger. *Be charming*, she told herself. *Be British. And remember he holds your father's life in his hands.*

"Lady Wyndham."

Emperor Francis lifted her hand to his mouth. His lips felt moist and cool, brushing against her skin. Caroline repressed a shiver.

"Your Majesty," she murmured. "A great honor."

"Is this your first time in Vienna?"

"It is." She rose from her curtsy, leaving her hand in his narrow grip. The scent of incense still drifted through the tent, mingling with the fragrances of freshly cut grass and flowers. "You rule a beautiful nation."

"That I do." His thin lips compressed into a smile. "And your countrymen seem finally to have realized as much. We have many English visitors this year."

"Vienna is the center of the world just now." *Enough pleasant-*

ries. She'd planned this meeting for days, yet now she found she could hardly bear it.

Francis had taken his place as emperor in 1792, when Caroline was thirteen years old and had already been a prisoner for two years. Even under the reign of his first, enthusiastic patron, Emperor Joseph II, Pergen had never dared keep Caroline and the others in so official a prison as the underground cells used by the secret police. Until 1792, Pergen had kept Caroline and the others hidden in his own house on the outskirts of Vienna, secret even from Austria's highest rulers—and as minister of the secret police under both Joseph and Francis, he had had the power to keep as many secrets as he chose.

Upon Francis's ascension, though, Pergen had brought his private prisoners into the Hofburg Palace itself. Caroline still remembered the young emperor's first visit of inspection and the fascination on his face as he had studied her from all angles and then stayed to watch the alchemical ritual.

"Amazing," he had said afterward as Caroline had wept, furious at herself for her lack of control. She would have done anything to restrain the humiliating tears, but the new emperor never even noticed them. *"You must show me how to do this,"* he'd said.

And, *"Certainly, Your Majesty,"* Count Pergen had replied.

Caroline wasn't surprised that Emperor Francis did not recognize her now. How could he? The pale, weakened girl with the tangle of black hair and an orphan's clothes had become a grown woman in the height of fashion.

Unexpectedly, though, she found that she had to bite down on her tongue to keep herself from reminding him. She should have been triumphant at the success of her disguise. Instead, she wanted to tell him exactly who she was and see the light of horrified recognition dawn on his face. She wanted to tell everyone who stood around him, fawning over him, who and what he really was, and which master he followed.

Instead, she forced herself to say her prepared lines. "These are truly magnificent festivities, Your Majesty. No wonder all Europe flocks to see them." Lowering her eyelashes demurely, she added in a near-whisper, "The cost must be truly staggering."

"Well . . ." His grip tightened—involuntarily, she hoped—around her hand. "No more than we all deserve after twenty years of the Corsican Monster, eh? And certainly no more than the chancellery can stand."

And *that*, she knew, was an outright lie. Austria's treasury was nearly empty from the long decades of war, and Francis's festival of self-congratulation—it was an open secret—cost fifty thousand florins per royal visitor every day. The head of the treasury, she'd heard, was in none-too-secret agonies about the cost and the question of how the poverty-stricken empire could ever meet it. And yet . . .

"I wonder—could I help?" She looked up, blinking innocently, into the emperor's hard blue gaze. "We are all so very grateful for the part Austria played in the late war, you know. We all saw how you stood as buffer against the Monster for the rest of Europe. The sacrifices you made . . ." The words tasted like poison on her tongue, but she saw the emperor's smirk deepen. "I would so love to do what I could to support the Congress," she finished in a rush.

"My dear Lady Wyndham . . ." The emperor considered her narrowly for a moment. "We must speak further."

"Oh, yes," Caroline murmured. *Not now.* She would have to play the very image of a proper lady and pretend to swoon from the heat if she were held here in conversation with him much longer.

"Will you be at the masked ball tonight, in the Hofburg?"

"I hadn't received an invitation . . ."

"Nonsense." The emperor squeezed her fingers and, finally, released them. "I look forward to meeting you there, Lady Wyndham."

"Then I shall not disguise myself too carefully," she said.

He turned away, and she had to stop herself from sagging with relief. She looked up at the Prince de Ligne, whose expression was quite blank beneath his watchful gaze.

"Your pardon, Highness. I fear the heat has been too much for me. I believe I must retire for an hour or two, to rest."

"I'll escort you to your carriage, then." As they walked across the grass, away from the incense and the emperor, the Prince de Ligne breathed his next words into her ear. "I do look forward, dear lady, to finding out exactly what you are intending. I don't believe for an instant that you feel any romantic loyalty to the Habsburg emperor."

"My dear sir . . ." Caroline let herself, for just a moment, lean against his arm as belated reaction made her legs weak. "I hope you would never think so badly of me as that." She risked a mischievous grin as she glanced up at him. "But would you force me to disclose all my secrets to you on first acquaintance?"

"I should never be so ungallant." The prince smiled back, but wariness mingled with the amusement in his eyes. "I shall look forward to watching events develop. I have a feeling, Lady Wyndham, that life at this Congress will become more intriguing by the day."

❧

The emperor of Austria waited until Lady Wyndham and the elderly Prince de Ligne had disappeared from view before he beckoned to his former minister of the secret police.

"Your Majesty?" Count Pergen slid through the crowd on the field and slipped into position at his side.

In his seventy-ninth year, shadows seemed to leak from the lines in Pergen's face. And his eyes . . .

The emperor winced and looked away from the vast chasms of emptiness in his most trusted minister's eyes. He kept his expression cheerful for the sake of the guests around him as he spoke under his breath.

"One of our latest visitors to Vienna, Pergen. Caroline, Countess of Wyndham, from England."

"Your Majesty?" Pergen stepped closer. He carried a chill with him these days, seeping through the warm air. It brushed against the emperor's skin, making him shiver.

It will not happen to me, Francis told himself, not for the first time.

Pergen had consulted dark powers for decades before Francis had ever taken the throne. Pergen stood as buffer for his emperor, loyal protection against the powers that Francis himself drew upon.

Lately, the physical effects of Pergen's work had become all too obvious. Francis had given him honorable official retirement that he might not be exposed to public notice. In private, though, Pergen ruled the secret police as he ever had and served his emperor . . . as he always had.

The taint, he'd promised, would not spread to his master.

"Find out who she is," the emperor said. "What she does here, what her resources are . . ." He took a deep breath, fighting the irrational impulse to run. That had been growing lately, every time Pergen approached him. Childish fears, truly, and yet . . .

He tipped his face back to absorb the warm, reassuring sunlight. Still, his shoulders would not relax.

"My men will look into it," Pergen promised smoothly. "As shall I."

"Do," said the emperor. "She may be useful. And if she is not . . ." He shook his head tightly as he finally gave in and began to move away. "Discover it. I want to know everything about her."

He did not need to add the corollary.

If Lady Wyndham had anything but an honest desire to aid the empire, Pergen would know exactly what to do about it.

He always did.

❧

Michael was perspiring by the time he reached the inner city, after an hour of walking in the heat. But some sights, even after four-and-twenty years away, were worth the wait. Emerging from a narrow, winding side street onto the *Graben* itself—the main thoroughfare of Vienna's first district—Michael let out a sigh of pure appreciation.

Rising before him, a spiraling plague column swarmed with stone figures, all striving toward an upraised gold crucifix, a tribute to Vienna's salvation from that historic horror. At the far end of the broad,

curving, cobblestoned street, the colored roof slats of the great Stefansdom cathedral slanted high in the air, displaying the Habsburgs'
proud double-headed eagle in its triumph. And between those two
points . . .

Michael took a deep, ecstatic breath and stepped into it: the breath
and life's blood of the city, all packed into two crowded blocks of
Vienna's first district. Carriages were not permitted here; everyone on
these streets traveled by foot and mixed shoulder-to-shoulder, from all
branches of society. Scantily clad *Graben-nymphen* fluttered their eyelashes at packs of strolling gentlemen and uniformed soldiers; ladies
of fashion walked arm-in-arm to the elegant *Konditoreis* that lined the
street for cakes, window seats, and gossip; middle-class women in sober
dress shooed their families in and out of the side doors that led to their
own apartments above the busy shops, situated well below the upper-
level apartments owned by the nobility; street children darted through
the crowd, hawking newspapers or picking pockets.

Michael had been one of those children once. He knew, if he closed
his eyes, he could summon up the buzzing nerves and exhilaration of
it as if he were six years old again: the smell of packed humanity all
around him as he dove through groups of adults, his head at the level of
their waists, his legs running too fast to ever be caught . . .

Of course, if he did close his eyes, he'd undoubtedly have his own
pockets picked by one of his honorary descendants. Grinning, Michael
abandoned the lure of nostalgia and strode toward a familiar side street,
swinging his walking stick nonchalantly.

Ladies of fashion might go to the Konditoreis on the Graben for
cakes and elegant conversation, but men of all classes went to the *Kaffeehäuser* on the branching side streets for newspapers and tobacco, billiards, wine and strong, dark coffee. In Michael's early apprenticeship
to a printmaker, he'd made a good living at the Kaffeehäuser of the first
district, hawking political brochures of all stripes. The coffeehouse had
been the home and heart of political debate then, and every new pamphlet had been seized upon with shouts of eager anticipation, all sides
preparing delightedly for a new outrage.

All that had changed, of course. Emperor Joseph II had instituted strict censorship laws when Michael was eleven years old; two years later, in 1789, when the hated Turkish war began, Michael's employer had to circulate all his leaflets of protest in deepest secret. All debate had disappeared from the coffeehouses by then, with the onset of political informers. When any man beside you could be in the pay of Count Pergen's secret police, only waiting to report your words, who would dare to speak of politics?

But one thing had remained constant throughout: if a man wanted to know what was happening in the city, if he wanted to hear the latest gossip and keep abreast of the wagers and the news, there was only one place to go.

CHAPTER FOUR

C afé Rothmann took up two levels of a narrow, stone town-house on the Dorotheergasse, one and a half blocks away from the Graben. Bright, merciless sunlight revealed the peeling of its sky-blue paint and the crumbling of the elaborate plastered curlicues that decorated the façade of the old building, but none of those ravages of time affected the crowd flowing in and out through its hallowed doors. Carriages rattled past on the Dorotheergasse, both local and foreign; from the dark opening to the coffeehouse, Michael heard fragments of French, Russian, and English mixed in with the local *Wienerisch* German. Dogs nosed around the street outside, searching for any remnants of food left on the cobblestones with the muck from the carriage horses and the refuse from the apartments overhead.

Michael tucked his walking stick underneath his arm and stepped through the coffeehouse door into smoky darkness.

"Sir!" An eager voice hailed him in German before his eyes even adjusted to the gloom. A hand grasped his elbow. "Tell me: was Tsar Alexander wearing fur at the ceremonies this morning or was he not?"

Michael blinked and found a crowd of eager young men confronting him, their black university robes carelessly split open above more fashionable dress. Their cheeks were flushed with more than wine, and their eyes were fixed upon him. A wager, evidently, hung upon the question.

"Alas, I cannot help you," Michael said, and allowed a regal hauteur to reveal itself in his disapprovingly raised eyebrows, as well as in his faintly accented drawl. No prince, after all, took well to being imposed upon by strangers. "I have only just arrived in Vienna this day."

With an impatient sigh, his interrogator released his arm and turned away. "I'm telling you fellows, he always wears fur! It's in the Russian blood. They can't be warmed."

"Nonsense!" Across from him, another young man let out a derisive snort. "If you'd ever been further east than Pressburg, you would know . . ."

Michael slipped past them, nodding, and scooped up one of the newspapers that hung from a rack by the door. In his day, the students had kept to their own cafés in the ninth district, but perhaps the arrival of so many foreign visitors had skewed the normal social balance. If Tsar Alexander himself walked into the café—or any of his aristocratic entourage—their wager would certainly be decided soon enough.

He slid into an empty table and spread the newspaper before him. The *Wiener Diarium* sat well under the imperial thumb, like every other newspaper in Vienna these past seventeen years, but it should be reliable enough for his purposes. In his day, at least, it had offered scintillating social gossip to offset its bland political reportage. Now he scanned the social pages for names and events. The English Lords Castlereagh and Kelvinhaugh had attended Princess Bagration's salon two nights before . . . the king of Prussia had been observed there as well . . . another masked ball was planned for the royal entertainment at the Hofburg tonight, with only the most distinguished foreign visitors in attendance . . .

Michael flipped through the pages with lessening interest. Discretion, it seemed, was the order of the journalistic day.

Not so, however, for the group of students at the front of the Kaffeehaus. As Michael ordered a strong *Melange* from a stiff-backed waiter, he caught more and more fragments of the students' wrangling conversation, which grew louder with every shouted boast. The other patrons, older, wealthier, and far better bred, shot glances of veiled dislike across the room.

Discretion might well rule Vienna's newspapers, but seated just a few feet away from him . . .

Perhaps this prince could unbend himself, after all.

Michael rose and crossed the distance, leaving his newspaper behind him.

"Pardon me." He tapped the closest student on the shoulder. "I couldn't help overhearing..." As they all turned to stare at him, Michael smiled with gracious condescension. "Perhaps we ought to make our introductions."

As the waiter glided up with Michael's drink balanced perfectly on a tiny porcelain saucer, Michael bowed politely to the group. "I am Prince Stefan Kalishnikoff and am myself half-Russian by blood," he said, in the broadest, richest Eastern accent he could summon. "I would, of course, be more than happy to answer any questions about my countrymen. And perhaps in exchange..."

Michael accepted his Melange from the waiter and paused just long enough to take a deep, appreciative sip of dark espresso and whipped cream. "...I can see that you are gentlemen of wit and experience," he finished. "Might I have the honor of ordering more drinks for all of you? And then perhaps you can tell me a bit about your own city, as well, and what you know of my fellow visitors."

Caroline breathed a sigh of relief as her chaise finally reached Vienna's inner city, after an hour of tooth-grindingly slow travel. The narrow streets were clogged to the brim with phaetons, chaises, and more exotic styles of carriages, all returning from the ceremony of thanksgiving, and her head was throbbing as much from the long, tedious trip as from reaction to the ritual itself.

In the middle of the ninth district, she directed her coachman to stop and wait in front of a nondescript bookshop. A young man, bespectacled and dressed in plain, dark clothing, left the shop a moment later and swung himself into the chaise and onto the padded seat across from her.

"I hope I didn't try your patience by too long, Charles," said Caroline, as he closed the door behind him. "The traffic was abominable."

Her secretary, now doubling as her man of affairs during their time in Vienna, shrugged her apology aside. "I was well-occupied, my lady."

"I see." Caroline eyed his bulging satchel. "And did you find any books of interest today? Or is it foolish of me to even inquire?"

"I did make one discovery," he said. "But what of your ladyship's own quest?" He drew a writing tablet and pencil from the inner pocket of his coat. "Did it succeed?"

Caroline smiled wryly. "I am honored beyond measure. The emperor wishes to meet me tonight at the masked ball."

"You'll need a disguise, then." He made a note in the commonplace book.

"Another one?"

"Your ladyship?"

"Never mind." Caroline glanced through the glass windows, feeling the pressure in her aching head increase. The weather outside was only pleasantly warm, but inside the carriage, the mixture of bright sunlight and still, stale air had stultified over the past hour into unbearable stuffiness. "What I would give for a bit of fresh air . . ."

She caught the infinitesimal blink of the man across from her and relaxed into a more natural smile. "Dear Charles. You are a gem among secretaries. Yes, I know I sat outside for two hours and more this morning, but the air was full of incense, perfume . . ." She paused. "And alchemy."

"Alchemy!" He sat forward, his gaze sharpening. "I had no inkling of that."

"How should you? None spread beyond the field itself."

"I should have attended the ceremony, or at least waited in the carriage."

"You would have been insufferably bored until then."

"Still . . ." He compressed his lips. "Of what sort was it?"

"A transfer of energies." She kept her face smooth as she said it, watching him. She'd never been certain how much he knew, or guessed . . .

His expression gave away nothing but his frustration. "I would have given a great deal to see it. Theoretical knowledge is all very well, but . . . oh, next to a practical demonstration, my new book is nothing."

She raised her eyebrows as he showed her the book he'd bought. "Isaac Newton? Had you not read it before, back in England?"

"One can still learn from an old book," Charles said stiffly.

"I'm certain of it. While we're in Vienna, though, you may want to take advantage of the local knowledge. This city was a veritable hub for alchemists in the last century. Ignaz von Born, Count von Thun, Count Radamowsky, an entire nest of Rosicrucians . . ."

And Count Pergen, Caroline added silently to herself. But she did not say the words out loud.

She might have grown easy enough with her secretary, over the course of their long journey across the Continent, to address him with more familiarity than she had offered any other man in years. But she did not share all of her secrets with anyone, no matter how trusted an employee.

"Of course," Charles murmured. "I have much still to learn."

His voice was submissive, but Caroline saw the glint in his eyes, behind the round spectacles. She'd found him young, only at the beginning of his career. But was he still young enough?

Caroline quelled her nerves with an effort. Better an alchemist in her employ than one working against her. Particularly in Vienna.

"Do let me know if you need more funds for books while we're here," she said. "I should hate to let you lose any chances for advancement."

"Thank you, Lady Wyndham." Charles's pen hovered above his commonplace book. "Shall I procure a costume for you this afternoon, for tonight's ball?"

"If you would."

"And perhaps you might be so good as to give me more details, later, of the ritual you observed?" His tone was bland.

Caroline's breath caught in her throat. Her vision blurred. For a moment, she couldn't see her secretary's face in front of her. She was caught again, trapped in that tiny stone room that had held her for years, tied down by ropes and hemmed in by candles, and all she could see . . .

Caroline blinked back into the present with an effort that left her breathing quickly. She met her secretary's speculative gaze with an even stare.

"Perhaps," she murmured, as lightly as she could. "I shall do my best to remember it for you."

As if she could ever forget. The words were burned into her mind. They still haunted her dreams, even after all these years—the nightmares she could never escape, no matter how many miles she traveled away from Vienna.

But if she truly needed to . . .

Caroline took a deep breath as the chaise turned into the first district, rattling toward her apartment on the Dorotheergasse. If necessary, she would tell Charles exactly what she had seen. In detail, and with instructions.

Her hands clenched with the repulsion that swept through her at the thought, but her resolve still held.

She would do anything to save her father.

". . . And everyone knows that the Countess von Hedermann is already Tsar Alexander's mistress," the youngest student told Michael. As he leaned across the table to share the gossip, Herr Hüberl's face glistened with a heady combination of excitement and wine. "Oh, he brought a few ladies with him, of course—besides the tsarina—but he's been seen with the countess everywhere. I saw them myself, riding together in the *Prater* just the other day, and he had six different Russian soldiers in full uniform in his entourage!"

"Well, the countess *is* very religious, just like him," added a second student. "Everyone knows how devout the tsar is, and ever since they met, she's been acting terribly mystical and holy, too, so it only makes sense that he would want her."

"And Countess von Hedermann's husband is looking for advancement in the Russian court," another student piped in, "so . . ."

"If I were the tsar of all the Russias, I wouldn't content myself with acquiring mistresses and attending Mass." A fourth student, Herr Stultz, gave a sniff of disapproval. "When you consider that his grandmother was Catherine the Great . . ."

"The Prince de Ligne is the greatest of the diplomats *and* soldiers here," young Hüberl said worshipfully. "Do you know he refers to Bonaparte himself as 'our Robinson Crusoe'? Every day he has thirty or forty guests at least, all gathered only to listen to his sayings and—"

"And how many battles has he won recently?" Stultz demanded. "The Duke of Wellington—"

"—Isn't here for comparison," Herr Hüberl said impatiently. "And as for the tsar of all the Russias—"

"But you must know more about all that than we do," said the oldest of the students. Herr von Alxinger raised his wine glass to Michael. "Do you know the tsar well, Prince Kalishnikoff?"

"Not intimately," Michael said, "but I may say that we are distantly related."

And why not? Surely every member of the human race was related in some fashion.

The look in Von Alxinger's eye, though, was distinctly wary. Michael leaned back in his chair and exerted himself to smile charmingly. "I may tell you, though," he said, "of one particular incident . . ."

He didn't take his leave for another half hour, by the end of which even Von Alxinger was laughing along with the rest of them. As Michael stepped back out onto the street, he heard young Hüberl's voice raised high above all the rest.

"—And if Prince Kalishnikoff himself, who's half-Russian, says so—!"

Michael smiled and let the door swing closed behind him. With luck, the students would continue as merry and boisterous for the whole of the next few weeks, spreading his stories and his name with them.

Nor had his time with the newspapers been wasted. His next step, clearly, was to find a concealing domino as soon as possible. As to which of the "most distinguished guests" he would approach at that night's masked ball—well, he had all afternoon to make that decision. And in the meantime . . .

An English-styled chaise drew up ten feet ahead of him, in front of a light-pink building embellished with freshly painted cream curlicues. A footman leaped down nimbly from the top of the carriage to open the door and lay down steps. A dainty foot emerged, shod in a high-heeled boot, and Michael paused to admire the glimpse of ankle beneath the raised skirt.

As the footman reached inside to help his mistress out, Michael's brain worked busily. Apartments on the Dorotheergasse had been expensive even when Michael had been young. Now, with inflation from the war combined with the sudden influx of wealthy foreign visitors, the landlords' prices must be very near astronomical. His new young friends at the coffeehouse had told him that half the Prussian king's own retinue had been forced to stay in inns outside town. To afford an apartment on the elegant Dorotheergasse itself, this lady visitor must be wealthy indeed.

Michael tipped his hat politely, already fashioning introductory phrases in his head.

Clinging muslin skirts swung into view, followed by a slender but strong arm, its gloved hand supported by the footman. Next, glossy black curls that peeked out from beneath a fashionable poke bonnet, the head still tipped away from Michael's vision. Michael noted, with appreciation, the delightful curves beneath the fashionably thin dress. No slip of a girl, this, but a grown woman in all the glory of maturity and experience. The lady stepped onto the pavement, neatly avoiding the pile of horse manure only a few steps away, and released her footman's hand.

"Thank you, Henry," she said in English.

An Englishwoman indeed, then. Michael smiled. This should hardly even be a challenge.

He cleared his throat and stepped forward.

"Pardon me, Madam," he began, in English, "but—"

She turned to face him, and all his carefully chosen phrases dried up in his throat.

"No," he breathed.

It wasn't possible . . .

The warm color drained from her cheeks. Her mouth fell open.

"*Karolina*," Michael whispered.

Her pale face was strongly defined in clean, square lines now, where it had been round and chubby before. Her black hair, which she had always worn in a tangle around her dirty neck, was dressed high and smooth in a fashionable style, with only a few careful ringlets hanging curled around her face. She was—what? She must be at least five-and-thirty, and he could see her age in the faint lines around her eyes. But her face was the female version of her father's. It was unmistakable. And those dark eyes . . .

The memory of her eyes had haunted him for years . . . especially in his worst nightmares. More than that: he'd been thinking of her ever since he'd set foot in Vienna, no matter how hard he'd tried to repress the memories.

He would have known her in any disguise.

She opened her mouth as if to speak, then stopped.

"It *is* you," Michael said. He found himself reverting to German, the quick Viennese patter of his youth. "What are you doing here? How—?"

"Forgive me," the woman said hastily, in French. "I'm afraid there must be some mistake." She lifted her strong chin in a poignantly familiar gesture. "I've never seen you before in my life."

"But—"

"Henry!" she said sharply, and the footman hurried to open the house door for her.

Without a further glance, she disappeared into the building.

Michael stared after her, reeling. He hardly noticed, at first, that a young man in plain dark clothing—a secretary, perhaps?—had followed her out of the chaise and was walking toward the same door.

"Wait!" Michael said. He started forward, trying to regain his former air of dignity. "Sir," he said in French. "I fear that I've offended that lady with my foolish error. Would you do me the honor of telling me your mistress's name?"

The man blinked behind his spectacles and gave Michael a searching look. "My mistress," he said at last, in careful German, "is Caroline, Countess of Wyndham, widow of Lord Wyndham of Sussex." He stepped closer. "You thought that you had recognized her, sir?"

"A misunderstanding, no more," Michael said. "I thank you, sir. I am sorry to say I have never met Lady Wyndham before."

He stepped back and watched the younger man walk into the house. As the yellow door swung closed, Michael fixed the house number in his memory.

Caroline, Countess of Wyndham, indeed.

The door closed with a solid thud.

"Karolina," Michael murmured. He shook his head as emotions whirled disconcertingly within him.

She was alive.

She was here.

And she had somehow, unbelievably, transformed herself into an English noblewoman.

He didn't know if he was more shocked, relieved . . . or, unexpectedly, amused.

A smile quirked at the corner of Michael's mouth as he walked down the street, twirling his polished walking stick.

One dilemma, at any rate, had been resolved.

He knew exactly whom he would approach that night, and how.

CHAPTER FIVE

Caroline's hand shook as she brushed rouge across her cheeks. With a hiss of frustration, she dropped the brush and let her hovering maid dab away the misshapen pink smear.

Impossible.

Of all the outrageous ill fortune, to meet the one person she would have paid most dearly to avoid . . .

"Milady?" Caroline's maid coughed discreetly. "Shall I finish for you?"

"No, thank you, Johnson. I can manage it myself." Caroline took a deep breath and met her own gaze in the mirror. Her face looked unnaturally pale against her black curls, her eyes dark and wide. She looked frightened.

Don't be a fool. Caroline set her jaw and dipped her brush into the pot of rouge to begin again. As she raised the brush under her servant's watchful gaze, she took care to smooth out her expression.

It wasn't safe to show fear, even here. And more importantly . . .

I have nothing to fear.

So she had been recognized. What of it? Michael Steinhüller—regardless of the clothes he'd worn—had been nobody as a child. He would be nobody of consequence still. For all that she'd once idolized him . . .

Her lips twisted, despite herself, at the bitter memory.

Of course she'd recognized him, even after all this time. The memory of his face had taunted her, as fresh as last night's frantic dreams, ever since she'd set foot back in this cursed city.

But perhaps she should count herself lucky to have had the reminder of his presence today as she began her work. After all, he had taught her a valuable lesson twenty-four years ago . . . and she had never been foolish enough to trust anyone again. No matter how charming or how well-intentioned the people she met here might seem—the Prince de Ligne, for only one such example—she would know better than to ever reveal her true self to them, or to expect any help unless it benefited them, too.

And as for the man who had taught her that lesson . . . well, Caroline was no weak-willed miss to let such a freak coincidence turn her resolve to trembling.

Yet the look on his face as he'd recognized her . . .

She tightened her fingers around the cosmetics brush.

Tonight she would dance and flirt with the emperor of Austria. She would set her plot in motion, as she'd planned for the past two years, ever since Bonaparte's retreat from the snows of Russia had signaled a first hint of his coming defeat. She wouldn't let mere nerves upset her now.

And if any ghost from the past should appear in the midst of it?

Caroline sucked her cheeks into grim hollows as she ran the brush along her cheekbones. Her deep-pink half-mask sat on the dressing table before her, waiting for her to assume the night's disguise.

She had brewed her plans for far too long to let *anyone* stand in the way of them.

Inside the Hofburg Palace, cold, dank air wafted against the emperor of Austria's neck. He felt Pergen's approach even before he turned.

"Well?"

In Francis's lush, red-and-gold dressing room, his minister looked like a dark scarecrow, ragged and bony despite the rich black satin of his tailcoat and the many gold orders pinned to his silk waistcoat.

"Your Majesty." Count Pergen bowed deeply. "May I say how well your outfit suits you?"

"I thank you." Francis inclined his chin slightly, mindful of the thin gold band balanced atop his head. His valet hovered nearby, adding the finishing touches; Francis waved the man away and waited until he had left the room before speaking again. "Well?" He stepped away from the heavy, gilt-framed mirror and waved Pergen to one of the crimson settees. "What have you discovered?"

Pergen sank down onto the settee, his posture ramrod-straight, and placed his hands flat against one another, his usual pose of deliberation. "Lady Wyndham is well-known at the English embassy. She is one of the wealthiest independent ladies of London society, with large estates in Sussex. Her late husband was a man of fortune. Both of her late husbands, I should say; she was married first to an elderly and"—he coughed—"rather eccentric marquis, according to reports, who seemed fond enough of her and yet did not remember her in his will; and then to the late Earl of Wyndham, who bequeathed all of his non-entailed properties to her. Nothing disreputable is known of her."

"But rumors say…?" Francis frowned down at his manicured nails. God forbid he should refuse such an unexpected gift—the Star Chamber would drive him mad with their dire plaints of bankruptcy otherwise—and yet… Something felt strangely off-kilter about the English lady and her so-generous offer.

"My men have had only one day to search," Pergen murmured, "and yet… they could find no trace of any history for Lady Wyndham before her marriage to the marquis. No parentage, no origin…"

"A commoner, then."

"No mere daughter of a tradesman, either, or secrecy would not have been so scrupulously preserved. Only a scandal could account for it. In other words…"

"A whore. The man married his mistress." Francis shook his head as the puzzle pieces clicked into place. That would explain it, certainly.

He remembered the look in her eyes as she'd taken her leave of him. *"I shall not disguise myself too carefully…"* A pleasurable tingle rippled through him at the memory. He should have known she was no true English aristocrat when she'd looked at him that way. Cold fish, those highbred women, for all that one had to admire them. But this one…

"Such was my inference, Your Majesty."

Francis's lips twitched as he saw the distaste on his minister's face. "Thank you, Pergen. Excellent work, as always." He turned back to the mirror and straightened the collar on his costume robes. The candle-branches to each side of the mirror filled his reflection with soft light; above the glass, a winged horse soared high and triumphant. Francis smiled. "Will you be attending tonight's festivities?" he asked.

"I think not. My own work . . ."

"I understand." Francis reached for his half-mask and hesitated. Perhaps he ought to take some time tonight to observe Pergen in his experiments, even offer to take part . . .

But no. He still felt vastly refreshed from this morning's ritual, with no need of excess energy. Moreover, tonight he had rulers from every country in Europe waiting for the honor of his company. He had the tsar of Russia and the king of Prussia to compliment and reassure, he had political schemes of his own to pursue whenever their backs were turned . . .

And, it seemed, he also had a meeting with a courtesan to conduct in full view of his own damnably celibate wife and her retinue. Not that he could ever allow himself to blame Ludovica for her poor health, of course, but still . . .

Francis slipped the mask over his face. Through the slits in the mask, the candlelight sparkled with odd intensity, and darkness seemed to boil around his most trusted minister's face. He laughed aloud with rare satisfaction.

An excellent night awaited him.

Peter Riesenbeck strode through the darkened streets of Vienna, drinking the cool evening air like sparkling white wine. Deep blue twilight merged with the descending black of night to blur the tall spires of the churches and the towering buildings that lined the narrow warren of streets. His wandering had taken him deep into the first district, miles from his company's humble inn. Though Peter had never visited Vienna before, he'd studied maps so closely that his legs led him straight toward his goal.

He emerged from the cluster of high buildings onto a busy street—and blinked, blinded by sudden light.

Before him, carriages filled the Herrengasse, preceded by runners holding out flambeaux to light their way, filling the dark air with flaring light, heat, and smoke. Beyond them, he glimpsed an open square. *There.* He could barely breathe as he crossed the last few meters.

The square—his lips moved silently to name it, *the Michaelerplatz*—was filled with fashionably dressed people, mostly crowding through the archway that led to the Hofburg palace, on Peter's left. He ignored it and them without compunction. All he cared about was the plain, short building that stood across from the archway, beside the church.

Peter let out the breath he'd been holding as he finally saw it with his own eyes.

The Burgtheater, the court theater for all the Habsburg Empire, could have been any other nondescript building in inner-city Vienna if it hadn't been so short and squat—a broad stepping-stool beside the tall, thin palaces of the nobility that surrounded it. Even its sculpted stone pediments were less ornate than those of the buildings behind it. And yet . . .

Peter stepped forward, drawn by irresistible force. Once past the church, he left behind the main force of the crowd of high nobility and entered the crowds that led to the Burgtheater itself. The emperor himself would often attend performances here, surrounded by his courtiers, but tonight, with the Hofburg open to imperial festivities, the Burgtheater would be left to the lower nobility and the eager middle classes.

The heat of the crowd reached out to him through the cool evening air as he approached. A sign, located discreetly apart from the drive, set out the night's program; Peter read it slowly, savoring it.

Tonight the Burgtheater presented a musical evening: "Wellington's Victory," a novelty piece for orchestra by the great Beethoven; the

Andante from a piano concerto by a composer Peter had never heard of; a rare return appearance made by Annamaria Dommayer, one of the past century's most acclaimed sopranos . . .

A body shoved past him through the crowd, pushing Peter off-balance. Automatically, he reached with one hand for his pocket, and with the other he grabbed his assailant's arm.

"If you've snatched my purse, my lad," he began—then stopped, staggered.

A heart-shaped face, pale with fear and surrounded by wildly curling brown ringlets, blinked out at him from beneath an old-fashioned hooded cloak. Peter felt his purse safe and solid within his pocket. His question changed, insensibly, in his throat. as he met the girl's dark-eyed gaze.

"What's amiss?" he asked softly, and stepped closer. "Can I help?"

"Let me go!" she hissed. "Quickly! Or—" She glanced back, let out a moan of frustration, then set her jaw. "Oh! Blame yourself—it's your own fault."

She leaned closer for a dizzying second, filling his senses with warmth and an unexpectedly fresh, spicy scent. Then she kneed him between the legs, with piercing precision.

Peter yelped and doubled over. Her arm pulled free of his grasp.

Through the haze of pain, he heard her footsteps racing away across the cobblestones.

"Stupid," Peter groaned. "Oh, stupid, stupid . . ."

He stayed bent over, cursing himself, for another minute after her slim, cloaked figure had disappeared from view.

Hard footsteps pounded to a stop beside him a moment later. Peter glimpsed high, stained boots and heard the jingle of a chain.

The police. Oh, what a memorable first evening in Vienna, after all.

Peter prepared his story as the gruff voice spoke, in such a strong Viennese accent that he could barely understand it.

"A girl—running hard—did you see which direction she went?"

Peter sighed and straightened, setting his teeth against the pain.

"No girl," he said, to the heavyset man who confronted him. "Only a pickpocket boy who attacked me. Don't you gentlemen bother to control thievery in this city?"

The policeman grunted and set off running...

In the wrong direction, Peter noted. He felt less enthusiasm than he might have at the observation a minute or two earlier.

"Don't confuse yourself with those heroes you play onstage." How many times had Périgord snarled that at him, when they had argued? Perhaps there was a grain of truth in his old master's taunts, after all. Peter winced at the thought.

Even as he turned away, though, damning his own taste for melodrama, Peter's neck prickled with a sudden and irrefutable awareness: he was being watched.

He turned back quickly. The crowd pressing toward the archway of the Hofburg was full of the highest aristocracy of Europe, chattering and preening and wearing clothing that cost more than Peter would ever earn and jewels that were only muted by the smoking light of the flambeaux. Peter could never mix in such a crowd, nor would he want to.

But for a moment, he was certain he saw familiar features, set disconcertingly above a gentleman's luxuriant finery.

The next moment, he knew it to be impossible. Vaçlav Grünemann, a nobleman's servant, could hardly be part of such a crowd, much less dressed in clothing that would befit his own master. And when Peter looked again, more closely, the face he'd thought he recognized had already disappeared from the crowd.

Too much melodrama for one evening, indeed. He was glad to be distracted from his own folly by the sound of a child's rough voice, hailing him.

"Sir?" A street urchin approached him, holding a sheaf of tickets in his grubby hand. "For tonight's performance"—his gaze swept across Peter with disconcerting frankness—"the cheapest seats in the back of the stalls, sir—"

"Not tonight," Peter said. He smiled ruefully and tipped his hat to the boy.

He finished the thought only to himself as he turned and limped away across the cobblestones.

Not tonight . . . but soon. And he wouldn't be buying the tickets, but standing on the Burgtheater's wooden boards, with all eyes on him and his company. Not even Périgord himself had ever reached such dizzying heights. If—no, *when*—Peter achieved that glory, even his old master would have to admit that he had proven himself at last.

Now that Peter was here, at the heart of the empire, everything would fall into place. He was certain of it.

But he promised himself, as he limped, that he would save his next set of heroics for the stage.

Michael arranged his cravat with meticulous precision—no mean feat when standing in the deepest shadows of the alley behind the Eszterházy town palace, without the benefit of a looking glass. It was worth the extra effort, though. All the rooms in the finest hotels were reserved already, and Michael knew better than to settle for any but the best. To be witnessed emerging from a scruffy, middle-class inn in the suburbs would be to announce immediate defeat in the war of confidence and appearances that ruled this game.

As to where he would sleep tonight . . .?

He would know the answer to that question, for better or worse, by the end of this evening.

Michael realized, with a start, that he was actually nervous. It was, of course, ridiculous. Hadn't he played dozens of games like this over the past two decades? Hadn't he fooled men and women of all ranks in life, winning nearly every gamble and always exiting just in time to escape the losing hands? This should be a grand adventure—his greatest game and his most thrilling challenge.

And yet . . .

His fingers hesitated on his cravat and stilled.

This was not Prague nor Budapest nor Krakow, where he'd carried no identity but those he'd invented, as free and unburdened as a swallow in flight. This was Vienna, where he'd grown and lived his first fourteen years. It was, whether he cared to admit it or not, his history.

And the look on Karolina's face when she'd recognized him . . .

Michael couldn't remember, anymore, a time when he hadn't known her. Even before he'd turned apprentice to her father at the ripe old age of eight, he'd seen her peering out the window of the print shop or rolling about with the other infants of the neighborhood with gloriously uninhibited energy. And once he'd begun to work with her father in earnest . . .

No. This wasn't what he wished to remember.

He should think of how he'd teased her as she ran after him, gazing worshipfully up at him from her chubby five-year-old face when he was all of eight years old and a proud new apprentice. He should summon up gratifying memories of how he'd treated her to luxuriant ices at the *Prater* on her eleventh birthday, and how he'd let her fall asleep against his shoulder afterward, with his arm wrapped protectively around her.

Anything but the last time he saw her through the flames, only two months later, and heard her high, agonized shrieks of terror as the fire blazed around her and the policemen dragged her father away.

There was nothing he could have done for her. Nothing.

Michael set his teeth with a snap. He'd been a fugitive himself, hunted out of the city at only fourteen, hiding in a butcher's cart. What could he have offered to a helpless eleven-year-old girl? He could only have put her in more danger. Even Vienna's grim orphanages must have been an improvement over that.

And at any rate, she certainly hadn't suffered for his decision. "Caroline, Countess of Wyndham," indeed. Michael relaxed into a rueful smile as he remembered it. He could hardly wait to hear that story.

He had been haunted for years by the memory of Karolina, but he quite looked forward to becoming better acquainted with Lady Wyndham.

A footstep sounded in the darkness behind him, almost too softly to be heard.

Michael spun around, reaching for the hidden pocket in his coat.

Before the man behind him had the chance to speak, Michael's dagger was at his throat.

"Drop—your—knife," Michael snarled.

The thief's eyes met Michael's from a hard, emaciated face that showed disappointment but no real fear. His knife clattered to the cobblestones. It was a butcher's knife, heavy and broad, designed to hack through animal flesh. *Or human.* It could have slit Michael's own throat with swift and final certainty.

"Now back away," Michael said. He kept his voice to a low growl. He had to, to hide how hard it was to breathe.

The man stepped slowly backward, his hands held high. He was dressed in an outfit Michael recognized from every city in Europe—a ragtag collection of cast-offs rescued from the rubbish of the wealthy, mended to its last breath and beyond.

It was the outfit Michael himself could have worn by now, with only too much ease. In the darkness, he felt a sudden involuntary kinship with the other man.

A few feet away, the thief lowered his hands and nodded to the butcher's knife that lay by Michael's feet.

"Not tonight," Michael said, and stepped down hard on the flat of the blade.

He could see the man measuring him, guessing at the probable outcome of a fight. Michael kept his own expression harsh and unyielding and his dagger held high.

The man shrugged and turned away. But Michael kept his dagger raised long after the other man's footsteps had faded into the distance.

There but for Fortune...

He sheathed the weapon in his pocket, breathing hard as the aftereffects of danger rippled through him. He hadn't lost his street instincts yet, thank God. But in another year or two...

As he aged and his hearing grew less sharp...

Michael straightened, his back creaking, as an unpalatable truth forced its way into view.

A man could survive on his wits for only so long. And when they, or simple Fortune, finally ran out . . . would he become another such desperate knave, surviving only by robbing or murdering passing strangers? Or would he be dead in another alley long beforehand?

Michael scooped up his new black domino from the pile of clothing and swept the cloak around him, twitching the shimmering black silk into a commanding swirl. He set his glittering half-mask into place and straightened his shoulders beneath the disguise.

No. He was no hapless fool trapped in poverty's desperate, inescapable spiral, nor yet a mere rogue forced to live on sheer luck. Not anymore. He was Stefan, Prince Kalishnikoff, now. He would play that game for all it was worth.

It was the best chance he would ever have to win himself a future.

CHAPTER SIX

The angel above the *Michaelerkirche* gazed down with cool marble eyes, its wings raised high in either benediction or the preparation for flight. Caroline hesitated beside the church, her stomach clenching with sudden panic as her carriage drove away from her. Across the square, the Hofburg Palace rose in massive stone grandeur, immense and sickeningly familiar.

She took a deep breath, fighting down the memories.

The night air smelled of fire from the smoke of many torches. Through their flaring, leaping light, Caroline watched the other masked guests stream past her toward the great stone arch that led into the grounds of the palace. Laughing and flirting, they passed in glittering array through the entryway and disappeared, couple by couple, from view.

She had disappeared into this palace once before, and it had swallowed her childhood.

Caroline lifted her chin and crossed the square, following the others. As she passed underneath the double-headed Habsburg eagle that topped the stone archway, she had to tighten her hands on the satin trim of her pelisse to hide their trembling.

It had been twenty years since she had escaped her imprisonment here. She would no longer be afraid.

Inside the first stone court, servants in imperial uniforms waited to direct the crowd. Caroline followed their lead to the ladies' cloakroom, where she dispensed of her warm pelisse and smiled greetings to faces familiar behind their masks.

"Caro, my love." A warm arm slipped into hers, and Caroline

inhaled musky perfume with resigned familiarity. "It's been an age! But what a delicious costume you've chosen. Ottoman pink—really daring! But it does suit you, despite everything. There aren't many women willing to take such risks."

"Thank you, Marie." Caroline smiled warily at the woman beside her, Lady Rothmere. "I hadn't heard that you'd come to Vienna."

"Oh, well, I could hardly miss the most fashionable event of the decade, could I? And poor George—he's aiding Lord Kelvinhaugh now, you know—was simply driving me mad with his attempts at reporting the balls here—he's absolutely useless at remembering any of the most interesting gossip—so here I am at last!" Marie opened her rouged mouth wide in laughter behind her glittering cat-mask as the two women stepped out into the great hall. She raised her voice to be heard above the sudden roar of noise. "And I must say, the gentlemen here are far more delectable than in London, don't you agree?"

Caroline looked around, less to consider the question than to gain herself a moment of breathing space. Crystal chandeliers blazed light across the waltzing couples who filled the great hall. A circular gallery ran along the sides of the hall, with open doors leading into more rooms. An orchestra sat at the back of the great hall, playing waltzes for the dancers in the center, while the tunes of different minuets and polonaises streamed in from the other side rooms to create a deafening confusion.

Before Caroline could even formulate an answer, Marie pulled her forward. "Just look at Emmaline Kelvinhaugh! Oh, what a terrible outfit she's chosen. Poor dear, she's never had any real taste, has she? But we must be kind and visit with her anyway. After all, she hasn't much else to fall back on, does she, with a husband as stuffy as hers? No wonder she acts like such a lack-wit . . ."

Resigned, Caroline followed Marie through the crowd at the edge of the room. It was just as well, she told herself, to have a moment or two to adjust to the glittering chaos—and better yet not to seek out the emperor with too-obvious eagerness. She'd set her lures already this afternoon; best to let him reel himself in with no visible help from her.

A group of women sat along the gallery on raised chairs disposed like an amphitheater, watching the dancers circle past them. Marie led Caroline to one of the closest chairs, where a plain, plump woman in a nun's loose habit sat with two women wearing black silk dominoes, the simplicity of their own disguises offset by their glittering diamond necklaces and towering tiaras.

"Emmie, my dear, I don't need to present Caro to you, do I?" Marie smiled brilliantly at the woman dressed as a nun before turning to the other women. "But your friends . . .?"

"Oh, of course." Lady Kelvinhaugh's naturally soft voice was nearly lost in the din. She smiled nervously at Caroline and turned to the masked women beside her. In careful French, she said, "May I present Lady Rothmere and Lady Wyndham, good friends from London, Your Majesties? And Marie, Caroline"—she turned back, lowering her voice still further—"you may give your deepest respects to the empress of Austria and the tsarina of Russia."

"A great honor, Your Majesties." Caroline curtsied deeply.

Poor Lady Kelvinhaugh. Caroline had seen her tongue-tied and miserable often enough in London society, where she'd lived all her life. Here in Vienna, Sir Edmund Kelvinhaugh was now one of the top diplomats working to divide up the conquered territories of Europe, and he would expect his wife to play her part in his work—thus, her enforced intimacy with the greatest ladies of the Continent.

"No need to curtsy tonight, Lady Wyndham," the Austrian empress murmured. "There can be no crowns when all are masked, after all." But her voice was rich with satisfaction as she tilted her chin in a condescending nod.

"Have you had any supper yet?" Lady Kelvinhaugh asked, with a visible effort at sociability. "The food here really is delicious. Especially the—" She caught herself and stumbled to a halt, giving the young empress beside her a panicked look. "That is, my husband always says that *everything* in Vienna is of the finest quality, without exception. Perhaps—?"

"I'm sure it is," Caroline murmured. "But I fear I really must move on—I've promised to meet a friend, and I see him now."

Leaving Marie to settle in for a solid round of poisonous gossip and ingratiating flattery, Caroline curtsied again and slipped away. The crowd around the edge of the ballroom was so packed that she had to turn to squeeze herself through, protecting her gown with her elbows pointed out, and aiming for one of the side salons. A familiar voice hailed her after only a few steps.

"Lady Wyndham!" The Prince de Ligne stopped her with a light touch on her arm. "Well met, my dear."

"And you, Your Highness." Caroline smiled sincerely at the old man, who stood unmasked in ordinary dark finery. "You've saved my manners, too—I swore I'd seen a friend in the crowd, to escape a tedious conversation. I'm glad you've made an honest woman of me."

"Oh, never that, I hope!" The prince glanced behind her. "Whom—? No, let me guess. But first, let me introduce you to my young friend." He gestured to the young man beside him, who wore a domino but no mask. "The Comte de la Garde-Chambonas, a delightful young friend from Moscow, Paris . . . oh, every great city in Europe, surely! And Augustin, let me present the charming Lady Wyndham, one of our favorite new English guests."

"A pleasure," said the comte. His plump face shone with excitement. He glanced rapidly about the room as he spoke, with apparently involuntary distraction. "I am writing a book of memoirs about the Congress, you know, Lady Wyndham."

"What, so soon? You can hardly have collected material enough, surely—the Congress is only a few days old."

"Oh, no! I meant to write it later, and—"

"I understand, my dear sir." Caroline smiled at the young man's discomfiture and set herself to placate him. "If you wish to gather stories for your future memoirs, then you've certainly come to the right place. Our friend De Ligne knows more people, and more clever stories about them, than anyone else I know."

The prince arched one eyebrow. "Indeed? You set me on my mettle, Lady Wyndham. Let me see . . ." He pivoted slowly, peering through the crowd. "Aha!" He took the young comte's arm. "There! You see the fellow in that extraordinary mask? There goes Tsar Alexander—without, for once, the charming Countess von Hedermann. Her poor husband must be so disappointed. Perhaps she's at home practicing her religious fervor for the tsar's benefit. And there . . ."

His lips twitched as he turned, the comte following his gaze with earnest attention. "Do you recognize that tall and noble-looking personage whom that beautiful Neapolitan girl is holding around the waist? No? Well, that is the king of Prussia." The prince nodded, his eyes sparkling. "He seems well pleased by his captivity, does he not? And for all that the clever mask on that lady *may* disguise an empress, it is quite on the cards that she is merely—forgive me, Lady Wyndham—a member of the *demimonde* who has been smuggled in for the night."

"Much more likely, from stories I've heard of the Prussian king," Caroline murmured dryly.

"Oh. Well." The comte swallowed, flushing. "But surely . . . with such a collection of noble personages, all in one room, there must be—"

"You desire a more romantic tale? I understand." The prince shrugged and turned back to the search. "That colossus in the black domino over there is the king of Württemberg, and the man close to him is his son, the crown prince. His love for the Duchesse d'Oldenbourg, Tsar Alexander's sister, is the cause of his stay at the Congress, rather than any concern for the grave interests which one day will be his." He tightened his lips into prim delicacy. "It is a romantic story, the *dénouement* of which we may witness before long."

"Ahh," sighed the comte, with satisfaction.

Caroline met the prince's eyes for a long, poignant look. *Ahh*, indeed.

"Ah, youth," the prince sighed. He brushed a speck of dust off the lace at his cuffs. His attention sharpened; he spoke again, more softly, aiming his words at Caroline.

"And here is the person you have been waiting for, have you not, my dear? Do endeavor not to look too pleased—or, perhaps, even to notice?"

Caroline smiled wryly at the advice but followed it nonetheless,

turning to gaze in a different direction and waving her fan softly to
relieve the heat. She didn't have to look to know who was coming. In
the emperor of Austria's own palace, the crowds drew apart to let him
through even when he wore a disguise.

Her fingers tightened on the delicate fan. The prince kept up a stream
of inconsequential chatter, which the comte did his best to accompany.
Caroline kept her fan moving slowly, casually, back and forth . . .

"Your Majesty," said the prince. "What a delightful ball indeed."

Caroline turned, assuming a look of startled pleasure, as she finally
allowed herself to notice their new companion.

Emperor Francis stood clothed in black silk monk's robes. A
golden chain was wrapped about his narrow waist, a narrow black half-
mask covered the top of his face, and a thin gold crown took the place
of a tonsure around his silvering fair hair. His eyes went straight to her,
she noted, but he spoke courteously to the prince.

"I'm pleased that you're enjoying it, De Ligne. And . . .?" He
glanced briefly at the comte, before his gaze returned to Caroline.

But not to her face. Caroline had to resist the impulse to nervous
laughter. The neckline of her dress was fashionably low, to be sure, but
not so low as to account for any irresistible magnetism. She began to
raise her fan to cover her chest, but halted herself in mid-action. It
suited no part of her plan to discourage the emperor's attention . . . no
matter how surprising or unpleasant that attention might feel.

As the comte finished his enthusiastic response, the emperor
moved forward. "And Lady Wyndham." He reached for her hand and
leaned over it. "Enchanting, Madam. A very *odalisque*, to the life."

"I thank you, Your Majesty." Caroline kept her smile cool as she restrained
the question that desperately wanted to be asked: how the emperor
would have ever had the chance to see a sultan's concubine in person.

. . . Or, on the other hand, perhaps not. There were some answers,
after all, that she had no wish to hear.

Charles had certainly chosen her costume well, though, judging by
the emperor's smile.

The orchestra swept to the end of one waltz and paused.

"May I have the honor of this dance?" the emperor asked.

"Of course," Caroline murmured, and snapped shut her fan.

She slipped its loop around her wrist and nodded a smiling fare-well to the prince and his companion. The prince nodded back with a small, mischievous salute.

The emperor wrapped his long, dry fingers around hers and drew her through the crowd to the dance floor, just as the orchestra struck up a new waltz.

One-two-three, one-two-three...

For a moment, Caroline was swept back to disconcerting recollections of her first dancing lessons, at seventeen. Already once a widow and remarried, she'd twitched at the unexpected intimacy of the dance-tutor's close embrace, while her forty-five-year-old new husband had watched with sharp attention from the corner of the room in his rambling country house, far from any other observers. Wyndham's gaze had felt critical but not unkind as he'd prepared her to enter high society, to win the high-stakes wager he had set with his closest circle of friends upon her first widowhood.

"She's bright enough, despite that atrocious accent. What a waste it was for Morham to hide her away! With a few good tutors and all the right gowns, I'll wager I could turn her into a true English lady."

It was a wager she had chosen to accept, as had the drunken, reckless men who'd surrounded the two of them in her first husband's house after his wake. Clothed in black, vibrating with tension, and with nothing to her name, Caroline had looked into the cool, calculating gaze of her soon-to-be second husband and seen her chance, at last, to rise from the ashes of her past into something new and powerful.

A month later, she and her tutor had danced around two-hundred-year-old furniture wrapped in dust cloths, dancing her first tentative steps toward a real future...

It was an age and a world away from the glittering Hofburg hall tonight, filled with color and light and the overwhelming hectic gaiety of circling masks and costumes and people doing what they would never dare to do without disguise.

I can dare anything, Caroline told herself, and closed her eyes behind the mask. *Oh, Father . . .*

"I do hope you are enjoying yourself tonight, Lady Wyndham," the emperor said.

He was holding her no closer than the dance demanded, but that was close and intimate enough that he could breathe the words into her ear. Caroline kept her body supple within his grasp, holding at bay the tension that wanted to stiffen her back or push away his hands.

She'd come planning to charm him and bribe him, in that order. And she knew enough about men, after all the long years of her marriages, to understand exactly what that might have to entail.

"How could I not?" she murmured, glancing up at him from beneath her eyelashes.

His eyes glittered behind his mask as he turned her in the patterns of the dance, his hand firm against her back. "I have thought upon your words from earlier."

"Your Majesty?"

"Generous indeed, Lady Wyndham. Your sense of . . . gratitude is admirable, as you must know."

"We must all be grateful to you, mustn't we?" She glanced up at the chandeliers above them, blazing ornate glory across the room. "If the Monster had conquered all Europe and moved to England . . ." She gave a careful shudder, without moving any closer.

His grasp tightened. "I do admire your principles, Lady Wyndham. But perhaps . . . Might I not wonder, at what you might desire in return?"

She blinked, innocently. "I?"

"You," the emperor murmured. "Lady Wyndham." His smile was not altogether pleasant. "You see . . ." His voice lowered to a whisper. "I know your secret."

She stiffened involuntarily, took a breath, and released it, still following the rhythms of the dance. "Your Majesty?"

"My men looked into your history today."

"And?" Her voice sounded too breathy. But he couldn't possibly— she had worked so carefully, for so many years—

"I know who you really are," he murmured, "or rather, who you were. You had to transform yourself, did you not?"

"I'm afraid I don't—"

"Have no fear, Lady Wyndham." The emperor's gaze dropped to her chest. It felt exposed beneath his hot stare. "I'm no prude," he whispered. "If the marquis chose to marry his mistress, it can make no difference to me."

"No?" Caroline fought down helpless laughter as she relaxed within his grasp. Her head whirled with calculations—better? Worse? Or only different?

"If you wish to move forward in your own society, I'm only too glad to help. Perhaps we can aid each other after all."

"I'm glad you think so." Caroline drew a deep breath and watched him track its progress. "What I truly want . . . what I most desire . . ."

"Mm?" The emperor's gaze didn't move, even as they circled.

"Information," Caroline breathed. Exhilaration made her feel giddy and light as air. *Finally.*

The emperor frowned. "Pardon me?"

"No one knows my secret but you," Caroline whispered, "but still . . . they all suspect there's something missing. Something odd. Now is my chance. Can you understand that?" Steeling herself inwardly, she moved closer in his embrace until their clothes brushed against each other with shocking intimacy, just as he'd clearly been angling for from the beginning of their dance. Her voice dropped to a scant whisper against his skin. "All my friends are here with their husbands for diplomatic work. If I could only have some hint—some hope of what might lie ahead—?"

The emperor's frown hadn't faded, but he was breathing more quickly. "You wish to stay one step ahead of them?"

"Nothing too dangerous," she murmured. "Nothing too deep. If I could but know more than they . . ." She met his eyes, scant inches from her own. "Perhaps we might consider exchanging some of our secrets?"

The strings of the orchestra hit a final cadence, and the waltz slid to a halt, along with the dancers. The emperor released Caroline's hands slowly, still standing close to her on the floor.

"A most intriguing conversation, Madam. I do thank you."

"I was honored," Caroline said, and dipped a curtsy.

"I will think on what you've said. And perhaps . . ." The emperor drew a breath. "Perhaps I shall see you again. Very soon."

Caroline smiled and lowered her head. "I do hope so."

"Indeed." The emperor paused. She felt his wary, measuring gaze upon her. "Tell me," he said abruptly. "Your friends came with their husbands, but you . . ." His voice dropped to a whisper. "Surely you must have companionship here as well, Lady Wyndham."

"I?" Caroline looked up and met his gaze with wide open eyes. "I came alone, Your Majesty. As you see me."

His lips curved into a hard, satisfied smile. "I am pleased to hear it."

He bent to kiss her hand, and she curtsied deeply, glad for an excuse to drop her gaze. When she looked up again, he was gone. Caroline straightened, smoothing down her narrow skirts. Triumph battled with revulsion in her chest . . . and won.

She had done it. She hadn't known if she'd be able to, even after so much planning, even during the long carriage trip across the Continent to come here.

When the moment came, though, she had managed it, for her father's sake. For the first time in twenty-four years, she was actually one step closer to saving him. She could feel every muscle in her body relaxing with the relief of it.

She couldn't leave yet, of course, but at least she was finished with her work for the night. Perhaps—

A warm hand slipped into the crook of her arm for the second time that evening. But it was a man's hand this time, taking her arm into a firm grip and turning her inexorably around to face a tall figure cloaked in a black domino.

Caroline's breath froze in her throat as she recognized the eyes behind the glittering half-mask.

"Lady Wyndham," Michael Steinhüller said. Beneath the mask, his face broke into an all-too-familiar cocky grin. "I cannot begin to express how pleased I am to meet you."

CHAPTER SEVEN

The orchestra struck up another waltz behind them, and Michael took advantage of his companion's shock to draw her forward onto the dance floor.

She struggled for a brief moment, then stopped, glancing covertly at the couples around them.

"Very sensible," Michael said affably in German, as he took her into the embrace that the waltz required. "You wouldn't wish to create a scandal, would you? Not when so many awkward questions might arise." He couldn't stop the bubble of delighted laughter that broke out of his throat, as he swept her around in a wide, exuberant turn. "*Karolina*. I can't believe you're truly here! If you only knew how many nights of sleep I'd lost worrying about you over the years . . . and now here you are! Could you even imagine it, the two of us here, together again?"

Her feet followed the steps of the dance, but no answering laugh came from her throat. Instead, she said in English-accented French, "I'm afraid I don't speak German, sir. There must have been some mistake."

"Oh, indeed, a great mistake. I'd never reckoned that I might find you at this Congress. At the very center of high society, no less!" Michael turned her in the dance, holding her close. "Karolina," he breathed into her ear. "I never stopped wondering what had happened to you. Now see how well you've come about! You have to tell me everything."

"Perhaps the mask has misled you," she said evenly, "but—"

"That mask barely covers your eyes, as you well know, and the disguise . . ." Michael grinned as he glanced down at the low-cut rose damask gown, covered in sheer gauze. "The disguise is outstanding. To say the least. How on earth have you managed to pass yourself off as an

English noblewoman here, surrounded by the true article? Even I'm impressed. If—"

"Keep your voice down!" she hissed. She'd gone pale when he'd first greeted her, but now her face flushed with anger, in attractive complement to her black ringlets and Ottoman-pink mask. "I *am* an English noblewoman," she added in a fierce whisper. "I have every right to be here. What excuse do you have?"

He laughed out loud. "Why, I outrank even you now, my dear. I've turned pureblood royalty, myself. Prince Stefan Kalishnikoff, at your service. Half-Russian, half-French, disenfranchised heir to a godforsaken little Balkan republic in the middle of a chain of mountains."

"You must be mad!" She stared at him. "You'll never convince anyone of that."

"You think not?" Michael arched one eyebrow, maneuvering them neatly around the other couples on the dance floor. "I have proof. A signet ring, a deed of signatory—and better yet . . ." He drew her in to murmur the words in her ear. She'd turned out tall, barely four inches shorter than him—who would have guessed it, all those years ago? "Now, of course," Michael whispered, "I have you."

Focus, Francis told himself. He strode through the crowd, smiling and nodding as he passed familiar faces. Politics must be his quarry now, not pleasure. Yet he could still smell the lingering traces of Lady Wyndham's light perfume clinging to his hand where it had touched hers in the waltz. He had to force himself not to lift it to his face, to breathe in the scent. *Later.* Later, when the night's intrigues were over, he would let himself remember the feel of her in his arms and the promise in her eyes.

"I came alone . . ." Warmth pooled pleasantly within him as he heard again her murmured words.

Tomorrow afternoon, perhaps, he would slip away from his public schedule of appointments, if only for an hour. Oh, indeed, this Congress was to be his great public monument, the moment when he led Austria, through charm, deception, and intrigue, to her proper place in the forefront of the new world order. But why should he not pursue his own pleasures in the midst of it . . . especially when they landed so neatly in his lap?

He had been forced to give up so much over these last decades, and suffer so much public humiliation. That upstart Corsican had left nothing great and noble on the Continent untouched, not even the Holy Roman Empire that should have lasted for a thousand years. Only for the sake of survival, only to be granted the right to cling onto what power he had left, Francis had been forced to formally abdicate his family's ancient throne after Bonaparte had declared the Holy Roman Empire—and the German nation as a whole—dissolved forever.

How his uncle Joseph would have raged at that sacrilege if he'd still been alive. But then, it was just the sort of thing he had predicted for Francis, the nephew he had held in such contempt. And if Joseph had witnessed Francis, now a mere emperor of Austria, handing over his own pure, Habsburg daughter as a bride to the Corsican abomination . . .

If it weren't for Pergen's supernatural assistance, bearing him up throughout the worst of it, Francis could never have survived the humiliation, much less smiled, with gritted teeth, while doing so.

But the long nightmare was finally over. Pergen and Metternich had both been right: by biding his time, by smiling in public even as his gut burned with poison, Francis had triumphed over Bonaparte in the end.

This was finally his moment. And he deserved every luxuriant reward he could imagine for achieving it.

As the crowd shifted about him, Francis caught sight of the tsar of Russia with his cheeks flushed and mouth wide open, entrenched in one of his endless monologues as usual. This time, his captive audience seemed to be the Prussian king and that poor little courtesan Friedrich Wilhelm had found somewhere. Rehashing the dispute over Poland, no doubt, Francis thought, and sighed at the blatancy of it.

Alexander was so determined to be named the new spiritual overseer of Polish liberty, he was quite incapable of imagining that Austria and Prussia would not simply give in to his demands and release their two-thirds of the partitioned kingdom to him. Indeed, Friedrich Wilhelm, the Prussian king, was only too ready to be intimidated into submission. With an effort, Francis kept his lips from twisting into an open sneer as he approached them.

He was neither such a weakling as Friedrich Wilhelm nor so unsubtle as the tsar.

The English ambassadors, Castlereagh and Kelvinhaugh, stood ten feet away, speaking in low voices. Alexander shot them venomous looks as he talked—still sulking over Castlereagh's latest attempts at rational persuasion, no doubt. The blustering fool truly couldn't understand why England's supposedly liberty-loving representatives wouldn't choose to support a new Polish republic under Alexander's guiding patronage.

No, to understand *that*, one required a balanced perception of the world and an intelligence capable of analyzing the raw economic basis beneath the public principles that a nation might choose to present to the outer world.

No matter what Alexander thought, success in politics did not depend on six hundred thousand soldiers in the field, nor on an ability to shout louder than anybody else and fly into public rages when one's will was thwarted. Success in politics, as in every other aspect of life, lay in the ability to wear a mask in every situation, no matter how seemingly intimate . . . and in the determination never to let your enemies guess your aims until your trap had already closed around them.

Francis stepped up to the tsar and the Prussian king and nodded with friendly courtesy. "My friends." He inclined his head ever-so-slightly to the courtesan, who curtsied deeply, wide-eyed behind her mask. "I trust you are all enjoying my little entertainment?"

"Oh, well . . ." Friedrich Wilhelm looked frankly miserable, trapped beside the tsar. All he wanted, poor man, was to be allowed to dally with his little plaything in peace. "Marvelous, of course, no doubt. That is . . ."

"But what do you think of this new absurdity of Castlereagh's?" Alexander turned on Francis, his face flushed, his voice booming far too loud. "Claiming this Congress should have the power to decide whether or not I make Poland into a republic, as if I were no more than a—"

"My dear Alexander." Francis laughed gently as he shook his head.

Past Alexander's bulky body, he could see his own foreign minister, Metternich, approaching Castlereagh and Kelvinhaugh through the crowd. Metternich met Francis's eyes and nodded slightly as he joined the British ambassadors. Satisfaction settled deep in Francis's chest as he saw his plan take perfect launch.

Castlereagh's face might show all the emotion of a weeks-dead Irish haddock, but Francis knew the man was shaking in his polished boots at the thought of Alexander becoming the next Bonaparte and disrupting the all-important flow of English trade. A twittering race of accountants, the British, but their gold cast every other country in Europe into the shade—and the guiding motto of the British diplomatic service was *Maintain the balance of power at all costs.*

All that the British ambassadors needed now was a hint of direction as to which Continental nation should be the proper recipient of their financial support.

Giving in to temptation, Francis finally let himself turn to the dance floor and rest his eyes on Lady Wyndham's graceful figure as he worked.

"There's really no point asking me about such matters," he said to Alexander. "Metternich makes all of those decisions, you know. I take no personal interest in politics."

He coughed slightly, lowering his voice so that Alexander and Friedrich Wilhelm both had to lean toward him to listen. "But I should perhaps tell you, for our friendship's sake," he murmured to Alexander, "what the French foreign minister said of your armies' showing in the field this morning . . ."

Francis bit back a smile of deep satisfaction as the tsar's face turned purple with rage, and the Polish scheme was forgotten for an entire evening.

Caroline fought down the urge to scream. From the corner of her vision, she could see the emperor watching them across the crowd. She schooled her features into smooth placidity and spoke in a strained whisper.

"*Now you have me*?" she repeated. "What, precisely, is that supposed to mean?"

"What do you think?" Michael grinned down at her. "Come now," he said. "You were always the cleverest girl I knew. Don't you remember how we outwitted that sweetshop owner together? We made a perfect partnership."

As a young girl, Caroline remembered, she'd found that grin dazzlingly attractive and his overwhelming confidence addictive. But now . . .

Well, he was still attractive, unfortunately. His eyes were the same warm hazel she remembered, and even the new specks of silver in his thick brown hair were not unappealing. His soft, youthful good looks had hardened into a strong, lean handsomeness that might even have been compelling, mingled with the sharp intelligence and humor in his face—if she hadn't felt so tempted to kick him.

Kick him?

Caroline gritted her teeth at the recognition of her own weakness. Only a few minutes with her father's old apprentice, and she had already regressed into rowdy adolescence. It was exactly what he'd intended with his oh-so-innocent childhood references.

She didn't only want to kick him. She wanted to kick him *hard*.

Caroline took a deep breath and released it without answering him. *Calm*, she told herself. She was five-and-thirty now, not a gape-struck eleven-year-old. She knew perfectly well how to manage a grown man, no matter how enraging or unreasonable he might be.

"Forgive me," she murmured. "I was so surprised, I fear I forgot my manners for a moment." She relaxed into his embrace, releasing the tension in her spine that had held her distant. "Truly, I am glad to see you again." She smiled warmly at him. "Michael."

He raised his eyebrows. "And I am delighted to hear it—but my name is Stefan, now. *Caroline.*"

"Of course." She set her teeth but held her smile. "We must talk more, one day, about the past."

Only in a thousand years, when her corpse was long-rotted, would Caroline ever consent to discuss her past with anyone, much less with Michael Steinhüller. Michael's murmur of assent, though, was her reward for the small gambit.

Emboldened, she continued, "My late husband left me a great estate in Sussex. Perhaps, once this tiresome Congress is ended, you might visit me there?" She lowered her eyes demurely. "We have so much to talk about, after all."

"And, fortunately, we have absolutely no need to wait." Michael gathered her close as they turned, and he whispered, his breath warm on her face: "Believe me when I say I am not complaining, but you needn't waste your charms on me, *Lady Wyndham.* I'm far too old a hand to be moved by them—and I am fairly certain you're alarming the poor emperor."

Caroline jerked away from him. For the first time in years, she felt her cheeks flame with humiliation. "Why, you—"

"No, no, don't apologize!" He pulled her smoothly back into his arms. "I was impressed, I assure you. But you don't want to waste all the effort you spent on your last partner, do you? You wouldn't want the emperor to think you found any other poor fool attractive."

Caroline gritted her teeth. "Trust me, I do not."

"I didn't think so," he said cheerfully. "So let's abandon the usual nonsense and be honest with each other, shall we? I don't know what game you're playing now, but—"

"I am playing no games." She glared at him. "Unlike you, I have every right to be here! And—"

"Which is, of course, why the emperor knows all about your past and who you truly are?" He smiled down blandly as she simmered. "As I said . . . I have no desire to interfere with your schemes. In fact, I wish you the best of luck with them. Just as I'm sure you have only the warmest feelings toward mine. Yes?"

"Mm," Caroline said noncommittally.

"Don't you? Well, at least you are far too wise a woman to choose to injure me in mine." His smile hardened as he swept her through another wide turn. "Especially as it would suit neither of us for me to become . . . forgetful . . . about which name to call you. And to whom."

She sucked in a sharp breath. "Are you by any chance daring to threaten me?"

His eyes glittered dangerously in the candlelight. "Why should I? We can help each other. Whatever it is you want from the emperor, I'd be delighted to assist you in gaining it. And you—"

"I have no desire to assist you in *anything*," she snarled. "Do not even consider asking me for help. Not tonight, and not ever!"

"No?" His eyebrows rose, and he blinked. "That is unkind. After all these years, aren't you even a little bit pleased to see me again?" He shook his head. "Don't you have any loyalty left from childhood? Any—"

"Loyalty?" Caroline stared at him. "You? Speaking of *loyalty*?"

"And why not?" For the first time, he looked truly shaken. "Do you feel so little for the past? The girl I knew . . . Are you so arrogant that now you've reached the top, you haven't even any sympathy for those of us without your luck?"

"My *luck*?" Caroline spat the word. "If you had any idea what you were talking about . . ."

"Then enlighten me!" he snapped. "The last time we saw one another, we were good friends. I was genuinely glad to find you alive and well, whether you choose to believe that or not. And now . . ."

"I found out precisely what your friendship and sense of loyalty were worth twenty-four years ago," Caroline said, enunciating every word with sharp precision. "Do not insult my intelligence by pretending any claim on that score."

The waltz drew to a close. Michael's face shut against her, turning hard and cold.

"I did what I had to do, that night," he said, as they came to a halt at the edge of the dance floor. "Would you pretend you've never been forced to make a painful choice?"

"A painful . . .?" Caroline shut her mouth, swallowing the venom that wanted to rise out of her. The shriek.

I saw you! she wanted to scream. *Through the flames! I was so relieved. I thought you would save us . . .*

It had taken her years afterward to finally understand.

Michael had always treated her with the careless affection of an older brother, but Karolina, by the time she was eleven years old . . . Caroline cringed now at the memories. She had adored him completely.

She had learned a valuable lesson that night. Yet she found that the pain was still fresh at hand when confronted with her first teacher.

"Save your speeches," Caroline said, through a tight throat, as she stepped out of his embrace. All around them, couples separated and dissolved into the shifting crowd. "I preferred it when you spoke of honest blackmail."

"Well, then." His voice was clipped and soft as he leaned forward. To an outsider, it might have looked as if he were whispering endearments into her ear. "I need your patronage and your social acceptance. I wish to be introduced as your old friend. And at the moment, I also urgently need a room to stay in."

At that, she almost laughed. "You couldn't possibly stay with me! I'm a widow."

"And a dashing one at that." His smile held no humor. "Where does your secretary stay? A separate apartment beneath your own, am I not correct? I've made some enquiries, you see."

Caroline gritted her teeth. "My secretary is an entirely different matter."

"Quite. Unlike him, I'll be out of your vicinity as soon as I can, for both of our sakes. You'll hardly even know I was there."

"Until you're exposed and ruin both of us."

"Caro!" Marie's voice rang out behind Caroline with practiced pleasure. "My goodness, I've come across you again in this crush. What a delightful coincidence!" She regarded them both with bright surmise as Caroline took a too-hasty step away from Michael. "May I be introduced to your friend?"

Caroline swallowed bitterness and gave an equally false smile in return. "But of course. Marie, Lady Rothmere, may I introduce *Prince Kalishnikoff*?" She pronounced the name with venomously dramatic rolling accents. "My very old friend," she added.

"Very old indeed," Michael murmured.

The satisfaction in his voice was almost too much for her to bear.

CHAPTER EIGHT

Michael woke to the sound of soft footsteps approaching. Automatically, he tensed, fisting his hands beneath his covers. He slitted his eyes barely open . . .

Oh. A figure in a lace cap and apron passed through his narrow line of vision, and Michael relaxed. He almost laughed out loud in relief.

A maidservant. Come to pull open his curtains, set a newspaper and breakfast within his reach, and possibly even—? *Yes.* Michael heard the rich, comforting crackle of a fire being lit in the woodstove across the room. Luxury, indeed, to match the deep, soft mattress he lay upon and the silk sheets that surrounded him.

Feigning sleep, he waited until the door had closed behind the girl before opening his eyes. Alone, he pushed himself up in bed to survey the room for the first time in full light.

Wallpaper in shining green and gold covered the high walls. Here in the crowded center of Vienna, rooms in even such a richly appointed house as this were forced into narrow proportions, but the high, gilded ceiling gave a false impression of space. A silhouette of the Duke of Wellington hung above the washstand, beside the zebra-wood secretaire; Michael's lips twitched as he looked at the iconic picture. Karolina—no, he should keep to the rules of the game and call her Caroline now, even in private—was playing the part of a loyal Englishwoman all too well.

The tall clock in the far corner of the room set the time at eleven o'clock. Michael tugged the bell cord and swung his legs out of bed, luxuriating in the comfort. No flea-infested inn mattress this time. He swiped a fresh, crescent-shaped *Kipferl* from the breakfast tray and licked its golden crumbs off his hands as he waited for a servant to arrive. A bath—yes, he'd take a long, hot bath to refresh and prepare himself for the day, and then . . . why, then, there would be no socially acceptable option but to pay a courtesy call upon his hostess and old friend in the apartment upstairs.

The shadow of last night's anger intruded, darkening his glow of well-being as he remembered.

"I found out precisely what your friendship and sense of loyalty were worth twenty-four years ago."

Had she really thought that of him, all these years? Even as he'd looked back on her as one of only two people who'd truly known him in his life, two people whose opinions had meant everything to him for that brief, halcyon period when they'd given him his first and last true home . . . and she'd thought of him with bitterness, as an enemy, all the while?

Michael leaped to his feet, driven by sudden restlessness. The look in her eyes as she'd accused him with the unmistakable sincerity of long-held, simmering rage . . .

He didn't know how to shrug aside rage from Karolina. All the armor he'd built over the years had been inexplicably pierced at her first blow. *"You, speaking of loyalty?"*

He'd been drawn into saying far more than he'd meant in the way of threats, in return. Oh, it made little difference in the end—she must know, quite as well as he, how impossible it would be for him to ever reveal her true identity without hopelessly exposing his own—but still, the whole experience left a sour taste in his mouth.

And her accusations . . .

They were, of course, ridiculous. If Michael hadn't been so taken aback, he could have argued and debated her into rationality.

"I was fourteen years old. What did you expect of me, against the full force of the secret police? What else could I possibly have done?"

Perhaps he might even have persuaded her. But he had been angry and surprised, and the force of her words had slammed directly into the one weak spot he'd never manage to shield, in all these years.

For once, his wits had failed him.

Michael paced the narrow room, battling down his emotions with the tools he'd mastered over decades. What did it matter if the adult Caroline had taken a dislike to him? He'd made a career of charming distrustful strangers in the worst of circumstances. He could certainly work this game to his own advantage, whether Caroline chose to cling onto irrational past grudges or not.

But the knowledge of her anger pricked at him, more unnerving than any mere setback in a game. The wrongness of it was a nearly physical irritation. He let out a sigh of sheer frustration. Karolina had been almost a sister to him in childhood. Caroline should not be an enemy now.

A respectful knock sounded on the door—a servant responding to his summons.

"Come in," Michael called. Tension drained out of his shoulders as he relaxed.

Thank God for well-timed distractions from useless *feelings*.

An hour later, his hair still damp from the bathwater and his shaven cheeks freshened with lavender water, he finally started for the door. His cravat was freshly tied, its creases carefully hidden, and yesterday's clothes looked as impeccable as he could make them with the aid of an unsmiling but respectful footman-turned-valet.

Later, he would visit a tailor to replenish his royal wardrobe, but for now, Prince Kalishnikoff was ready for the day . . . and it was time to confront his gracious hostess.

Michael opened his bedroom door and stepped into the narrow corridor just as the opposite door opened. Caroline's English secretary stepped out, tucking a book into his light brown jacket.

"Sir." Michael nodded slightly, with distant courtesy. Prince Kalishnikoff would do no more.

"Your . . . Highness." The younger man regarded him coolly for a long moment before he bowed. "I am honored."

Michael stilled, brought up short by the look in the man's eye. He calculated rapidly and settled on a thin smile. "I don't believe I know your name, sir."

"Charles Weston. Secretary to Lady Wyndham. We met yesterday afternoon, you may recall, when you approached me to ask my employer's name." Weston raised his eyebrows. "I take it that you were acquainted with Lady Wyndham, after all?"

"You assume correctly." Michael darkened his voice with a rolling Eastern burr—Prince Kalishnikoff's underlying accent creeping through, in the height of offence. "Is it customary for servants in England to make such *assumptions* about their employers' guests, Mr. Weston?"

A flush rose behind Weston's pale skin. "Not customary, perhaps, Your Highness. But only to be expected in odd circumstances."

Michael narrowed his eyes. "And do you consider these circumstances to be odd, Mr. Weston?"

"I, sir? How could I? After all . . ." The secretary's voice was bland as butter. "You have only just informed me that it would be impertinent."

Michael glared at him with regal hauteur. "I must go and make my duty to my hostess. I am certain you must have duties of your own to perform elsewhere, Mr. Weston."

"Naturally," said the secretary. "Lady Wyndham expects me to wait upon her at this hour." He smiled tightly. "I will show you the way to her apartments."

By the time the clocks in her drawing room struck noon, Caroline had been sitting surrounded by unread newspapers, letters, and notes of invitation for over an hour. All of them were of pressing importance and would have to be dealt with that day. Normally, she would have worked her way through the entire pile in less than forty minutes. Today, she found herself completely unable to focus on any of them.

All that she saw, when she looked at the words, was Michael Steinhüller's familiar-unfamiliar adult face inches away from hers. When she closed her eyes, she felt his arms around her again, leading her through the dance. Worse, she heard his maddeningly confident voice in her ears, speaking without an ounce of guilt.

"Would you pretend you've never been forced to make a painful choice?"

The quill pen snapped in her right hand. Caroline released it with a gasp and let the two pieces fall onto the desk before her. *Damn him.* The situation was impossible. And now, as she worked—or attempted to work—he was only one floor beneath her. Perhaps directly below her feet. The knowledge felt like an itch flaming just beneath her skin, filling her with restless, turbulent energy that wouldn't allow her to settle into any task.

Michael Steinhüller was in her building.

She had been the elegant Caroline, Countess of Wyndham, for so many years. But it was Karolina Vogl, unruly and prickling beneath her skin, who couldn't stop listening for his step now.

By the time Caroline finally heard a knock on the outer door of her apartment, it came as nothing but relief. *Just as well.* She took a deep breath and released it, smoothing an expression of fashionable boredom onto her face.

Far better to see Michael in this sunlit room and be done with it than to waste another hour or more in useless anticipation.

This time, she would not be taken off guard. And this time, he would *not* walk away the winner.

"Your Ladyship." Michael stepped into the drawing room and swept a flourishing bow. Behind him, she glimpsed Charles, his face set in unreadable lines. "May I congratulate you on your fine apartments?"

Caroline gave him a cool smile, conscious of her secretary's watchful gaze. "I trust your room is adequate, Your Highness?"

"Charming, Lady Wyndham. But of course." Michael crossed the room to take her hand and brushed a warm kiss across her knuckles, a mischievous glint in his eyes. "Entirely charming," he breathed.

Caroline fought down the urge to slap him. Instead, she said calmly, "Do sit down, Prince Kalishnikoff, and allow me to order tea. Charles, you may find the accounting books open in the study, but first…" She waited until he had closed the door behind him, then lowered her voice as she spoke again. "The housekeeper tells me that one of the maids has left her post."

"Ah." Charles took his pencil and writing tablet from his jacket. "Shall I arrange a replacement?"

"No need." She kept half her attention on Michael's bland, abstracted expression. He was absorbing every word, she knew. "It seems that we've been fortunate enough to have a replacement appear already this morning. The first maid's cousin . . . or so I'm told."

"Her cousin." Charles's pen stilled above the notepad. He looked up at her. "Do you think—"

"I believe," Caroline said evenly, "that I have attracted His Majesty's attention. And it would be most unwise to turn away this new maid, regardless of how well or badly she might choose to perform her duties." She took a deep breath, still carefully not looking in Michael's direction. "Even more unwise to write any letters or notes which might cause discomfort. Even if they were left in the fireplace and thought to be illegible."

"I understand." Breath hissed out through Charles's teeth. "Lady Wyndham . . ." He glanced quickly at Michael and then back to Caroline.

"You may speak freely in front of Prince Kalishnikoff, Charles," said Caroline. "He is an old friend, of course." *And you have not half the wits I credit in you if you take me at my word and loosen your tongue before him.* She smiled serenely at Charles, trusting him to read her hidden message without help.

Infuriating and untrustworthy Michael Steinhüller might be, but he was far too intelligent to miss any hints dropped clumsily in his vicinity.

"Thank you, Your Ladyship." Charles bowed first to Caroline, then, more stiffly, to Michael. "Would you excuse me? The accounts are waiting."

"Of course."

Caroline nodded dismissal. It took no particular wit to guess that he would be doing those accounts not in her study but in his own room in the apartment below . . . and only after carefully hiding every alchemical document he possessed. Thank God for a discreet secretary, she thought. If the emperor—or, worse yet, Count Pergen—were to suspect that she had brought a tame alchemist in tow . . .

"Clever man," Michael said as the door closed behind Charles. He sank down onto the cream-colored settee and grinned at her. "Too clever to be a comfortable neighbor, I must say."

"If you aren't pleased with your living arrangements, I beg you won't stay on my account."

"Spoken like a true aristocrat." He shook his head, looking around the elegant drawing room, filled with light from the tall windows. "A beautiful apartment, too—both of the apartments you hired. It was an extraordinary expense to rent your secretary an apartment of his own in this district."

"I'm a wealthy woman, now." Caroline aimed a smile without warmth in his direction. "A busy one, too. It's best to have my secretary within easy reach."

"Mm. To do your accounts and the like." A smile twitched at Michael's mouth as he shook his head. "Give over, Karolina. I'm not such a dunce that I can't tell a game when I see one."

Caroline's jaw clenched. "I told you last night: I don't play games!"

He gave a shout of laughter, leaning back in his seat. "And you're astonishingly easy to rouse with teasing, too. *Just* like when we were children."

Caroline forced her breath out in a shuddering sigh. "Let me order drinks, *Prince* Kalishnikoff." She rose to her feet and pulled the bell cord. "I take it you drink tea now? As a half-Russian royal?"

"Me? Not hardly. I'll have you know, I spent all the melancholy years after my poor kingdom's invasion visiting the stately homes of Bohemia, Moravia, and even Turkey, learning the tastes of all their national brews." His eyebrows rose. "My poor girl. Are you telling me that now you're an English noblewoman, you aren't even allowed to drink coffee? Here in the first coffee capital of Europe?"

"I bear the pain well enough, somehow," Caroline said dryly.

She'd made the coffee for Michael and her father in the old days, as they'd raced to put out their latest pamphlets, but of course she'd been too young, then, to drink it herself . . . or to share in any of the real work with them.

"*Soon*," her father had promised her, on one of their final mornings together. He'd turned away from the massive printing press to rub Karolina's hair with rough affection after she'd carried their cups into the dark, windowless back room where he'd moved his most important work, for safety, after the laws had changed.

She'd had to sidestep around the tall, neatly piled stacks of paper that were waiting to be bound and duck her head to avoid the fresh-printed sheets that hung from a clothesline above her to dry, but she had taken infinite care not to spill a single drop of the precious beverage she was bringing them as fuel for their great battle against injustice.

"*Just a few more years and you'll be ready to join us, Lina . . .*"

The drawing room door opened, and the new maid entered, ducking her head in a curtsy.

"One tea, with milk on the side, and a Melange for the gentleman," Caroline told her. "And . . ." She paused, as another knock sounded on the outer door. "It sounds as though we have company," she finished lightly. Sensible relief mixed with an unaccountable pang of disappointment.

They wouldn't be speaking any more of the past today, after all.

A moment later, she heard familiar tones rising above her butler's muted greetings. Caroline smiled wryly, glancing at her uninvited guest, who had an expression of bright interest on his face. *And now the ruse truly begins.*

"Lady Wyndham!" The Prince de Ligne nearly bounced into the room, followed closely by his companion of the night before.

"Your Highness. Comte." Caroline stepped forward to offer her hand with real warmth. "I'm delighted to see you both. May I make you known to an old friend of mine? Prince Kalishnikoff, the Comte de La Garde-Chambonas and the Prince de Ligne."

"The general who traveled with Catherine the Great when she took the Tauride!" Michael said. "I am truly honored, sir."

"Ah, you have a long memory, Your Highness. A charming trait indeed, to such ancient relics as myself." The Prince de Ligne bobbed a bow. "You'll have much in common with my young friend the memoirist here, then."

"Two more coffees, please, Bettina," Caroline said to the maid, as she sat back in her chair. "And pastries, too, to fortify us if we're to speak of battlefields."

"I would never be so ungallant as to do so in front of a lady. Particularly when her own battles are so much more engaging." The prince swept back his coattails and sat on the elegant, high-backed chair next to Caroline, his eyes sparkling. "I've had no chance yet to compliment you on your victory of last night, Lady Wyndham."

Feeling her new maid's eyes upon her, Caroline gave a light laugh. "What a pity," she said. "Particularly as I haven't any idea what you might mean. It's always infinitely more satisfying to be praised for accomplishments one knows about, don't you think, Your Highness?"

Out of the corner of her eye, Caroline saw Bettina turn and slip quietly from the room . . . without closing the door behind her.

The prince raised his eyebrows. "But my dear, have you not heard? You were the toast of last night's ball. The emperor could barely take his eyes off you, according to all the gossips. Nor could the empress, for that matter, when she saw what interest the emperor took in you."

"A compliment indeed." Caroline smiled, shrugged delicately, and turned the subject. "But tell me what other appointments you have today. According to *my* gossips, your house has become the meeting place for half of Vienna."

The Prince de Ligne waved one hand in graceful dismissal. "Half the most tedious company of Vienna, certainly."

"We had to resort to a ruse simply to escape them last night so that we might attend the ball," the young comte put in. "Forty men gathered in his salon, only to listen to his sayings—"

"And then to laugh inanely and repeat them in garbled form, as bearish nonsense credited to myself. An honor indeed. Pah." The prince shook his head. "I go nowhere near my own house today. I slipped out too early for any of them this morning, and in an hour I shall lunch at the Palais Palm." His lips twitched. "Although I have not yet decided whether to dine on the right or on the left."

"Your Highness?" Caroline raised her eyebrows in enquiry.

"Well, you must know, my dear, that the two apartments on opposite sides of the grand staircase are rented by Princess Bagration and the Duchesse de Sagan separately."

Caroline frowned. "But those two ladies, I thought—"

"Exactly!" The prince's eyes sparkled with mischievous delight. "They loathe each other with a passion—particularly now that the duchess has stolen our honored Prince Metternich from Bagration every bit as neatly as she stole Armfelt from her own mother thirteen years ago."

Michael said, "Was it choice or only a happy accident that put them in the same palais?"

"An accident?" De Ligne snorted. "My dear Prince Kalishnikoff, do consider: these ladies have hated each other for years! How better could they indulge their enmity than by taking rooms close enough to note all of each other's comings and goings, pay each other's servants for damning information, and thereby spite their rival at every turn? But now whenever anyone speaks of visiting the palais, one must always refer to which apartment one is visiting—the right or the left. And, in my happy case, they have both issued invitations to me for the very same hour."

"A dilemma indeed," Caroline murmured. "Alas that I cannot attend to observe your performance."

"No?" Michael tilted his head. "Why ever not? Don't you enjoy a good performance, Lady Wyndham?"

Caroline's smile cut her face. "I am a respectable widow, Prince Kalishnikoff . . . as you well know. And the salons of both Princess Bagration and the Duchesse de Sagan—"

"Are no place for respectable widows, no matter how charming," the Prince de Ligne finished for her, with mock sorrow. "It is their only flaw."

"And it is precisely the reason why you make a point of attending them," Caroline added tartly. "So, Your Highness. Which shall you choose?"

"I have not yet decided. And, most distressingly, my young friend De Garde-Chambonas cannot accompany me to either."

"I have another appointment," the comte murmured. "A friend from Sweden who wishes to tell me the story of his experiences on the battlefield."

"I've only just arrived in Vienna myself," Michael said. "So I must confess to envying your busy schedules. After so many years of fruitless wandering..."

He sighed.

It was well done, she had to admit; neither melodramatic nor soulful. Still, Caroline had to fight the impulse to roll her eyes. She glimpsed a momentary gleam of mischief in his own eyes as he slipped a glance at her, but his face revealed nothing but solemn sincerity as he turned to face the rest of the company.

"And where have you come from, Prince Kalishnikoff?" asked the Prince de Ligne.

"Most recently? Since Bonaparte took my principality and I was forced to flee, I've visited half of central Europe, at least, and even spent time in the East." A grin broke across Michael's face, dispelling the melancholy. "Which can hardly be counted as a disadvantage! Had I not lost my rule, I might never have had time nor opportunity to see more of the world. Instead of which, I've spent the last ten years learning all the languages of Europe and being a guest at both palaces and hovels in the most extraordinary places, meeting half the nobles and scoundrels of the Continent."

"Many of them the same people, no doubt," said Caroline.

"But of course," Michael said, smiling directly at her.

"I have a charming idea," said the Prince de Ligne. "Lady Wyndham, might you possibly spare me your friend's company? Prince Kalishnikoff, if you'd care to accompany me to the Palais Palm, we may take our choice of feasts together and you may seize the opportunity to be introduced to Viennese society at ... er ... one or another of the most fashionable salons in the city."

"What a marvelous idea," Michael said. "Don't you agree, Lady Wyndham?"

"Oh, yes," Caroline murmured, through gritted teeth. Through the doorway, she glimpsed the flutter of a lace cap—the new maid, finally moving away from her position by the door. Apparently, she'd heard enough to make her first report. "Marvelous."

Within the Hofburg Palace, Emperor Francis sipped espresso and nibbled at a still-warm Kipferl, listening to the morning report with only half of his attention. If he pleaded a headache that afternoon, perhaps he could beg off riding in the Agate with the tsar and the Prussian king. If he had a note delivered to the charming Lady Wyndham first, to ensure that she would be waiting in her apartment for him without receiving any other guests . . .

The young officer who'd been sent to Francis's private sitting room that morning recited the news in a numbing monotone.

". . . And the king of Prussia went out last night after the ball, dressed in civilian clothes with a hat pulled over his face, and didn't return until seven o'clock this morning . . ."

Francis forced himself into a show of interest. "Did he leave or return with anyone else?"

"Ah . . ." The officer checked his notes, flushing. "Only with his grand chamberlain, Your Majesty. Prince Wittgenstein."

"Mm. Out looking for prostitutes, then, as usual. Carry on."

"The Russian guests brought back several Graben-nymphen to their rooms last night—"

"Again." Francis sighed. "At least the Prussians have some sense of discretion in their favor, even if poor Friedrich Wilhelm's disguises never work. And?"

"The Prince de Ligne has taken Sophie Morel under his protection—"

"Excellent taste. As usual." Francis brushed off his hands carefully, scattering flaky crumbs across the Oriental table. He'd worked hard enough for the morning. It was time to move on to the news that actually interested him. "What of Lady Wyndham, from England? Any new reports on that lady?"

"Yes, Your Majesty. Let me find—ah. Yes. Last night, a gentleman she met at the ball traveled back with her in her carriage. Our informant reports he is staying in the same building as Lady Wyndham, in the apartment below hers—"

"No very strange coincidence that they shared a carriage, then."

"He is staying in an apartment for which Lady Wyndham herself holds the lease."

Francis's hands paused in midair. He looked up and met the officer's neutral gaze.

"Ah," Francis said. "Is he indeed?"

He took a breath. *Concentrate.* She had danced with another man directly after him, and Francis had watched them circling across the floor. Had it been that one, or—?

His long fingers closed into a fist around his Kipferl. Golden crumbs scattered between his fingers. It didn't matter who the man was. All that mattered was that the bitch had lied.

"I came alone, Your Majesty. As you see me."

How many people in his life would try to use him?

How many people *still* saw him as the weakling his uncle had named him, even now? *A man who could be lied to with impunity.*

He had offered her the chance to be frank with him. He had asked her outright if she had come with a companion to the Congress! He wasn't an unreasonable man. He wouldn't have held it against her if the answer had been yes. He wouldn't even have let that hold him back from a discreet connection, had she made the possibility tempting enough.

But she had looked him in the eye and smiled and lied.

She had treated him as a fool, and he had let her.

"Bring all new reports on her to me," Francis said, "as swiftly as possible." He rose, wiping off his hands and smoothing down the folds of his crimson dressing gown.

"Don't you wish to hear the rest of my report, Your Majesty?"

"Not at the moment," Francis said. "You may pass it all to Prince Metternich without reserve today, but I . . ." He paused to control his tone, as rage coalesced into a hard ball in his chest. "I find I have quite enough to consider already."

CHAPTER NINE

Peter Riesenbeck stood in the auditorium of the Theater an der Wien and fought to summon up his patience after a night without sleep. Shrieks of rage mingled with melodramatic gasps and groans on the crowded stage and echoed around the empty theater.

In less than twenty-four hours of life in the capital, Peter's proud troupe of actors had become a tooth-jarringly shrill nest of prima donnas. He could happily have banged all their heads together.

Instead, he jumped up onto the stage and forced an innocent smile. "Ladies! Gentlemen!"

There was no cessation in the noise. Peter took a deep lungful of air and bellowed.

"*Actors!*"

They turned as one to look at him. But only for a moment.

"I will not be asked to share a dressing room!" Marta declared, glaring at the second lady of the troupe, Josephine Weiss. "And particularly not with this—this—"

"These conditions are intolerable!" Her husband, Karl, planted his hands on his hips and glared menacingly at Peter. "Does no one understand the reputation of this company?"

Only too well, Peter thought with grim humor. Sighing, he moved forward and assumed an expression of grave sympathy.

"Marta, my dear—Josephine . . ." He caught one hand from each of them. "My dear ladies. I'm horrified that this has been asked of you. Of *both* of you," he added, as he saw the mutinous expression on Josephine's thin, sharply pretty face. "You deserve to be housed in the finest rooms in the city. And you shall be! But first . . ."

He stepped back, releasing their hands and stretching out his arms to encompass the whole of the company. "First we must prove ourselves. And we shall! To Vienna, to the empire, and to all the honored visitors who've come from across the Continent. Everyone will know our company's name . . . *your* names," he added, aiming the amendment at Karl's glower. "You will be famed and admired. But first we must give our debut performance! Is that not worth a minor sacrifice or two?"

He knew he had lost them even as the last words left his mouth. Faces that had been smoothing into placidity erupted into new and greater outrage.

"Minor?" Marta demanded. "*Minor?!* Your leading lady is being forced to receive her admirers in the tiniest of cramped, little moldy rooms, and to share it with the smelly costumes of a minor player, and you say—"

"A minor player?" Josephine flung her head back. "According to the critics in Prague after our last performance—"

Karl stepped forward, raising one hand to silence the rest. "When exactly are we to see our pay rise?"

Peter's head began to throb.

Behind him, he heard a cough. He turned.

"Herr Riesenbeck. And honored company." His new acquaintance of the day before stood in the first row of the stalls, every bit as neatly and soberly dressed as Peter had remembered. He smiled slightly and bowed, extending his gesture to include the company as a whole. "Vaçlav Grünemann. We met yesterday at the inn, but perhaps you don't remember . . ."

"On the contrary." Peter jumped down from the stage, grateful for the sudden interested silence that enveloped the watching company. "It's a pleasure to see you again, my dear sir." As he took Grünemann's hand, Peter scrutinized his face as discreetly as he could. It was similar, truly, to the face he'd thought he'd glimpsed in the aristocratic crowd the night before . . . but what of it? There must be a thousand men in Vienna of whom the same could be said. This man, at least, would never stand out in a crowd.

"In fact, I was hoping to see you again, sir," Peter said, as he released

Grünemann's hand. "If you'd do me the honor of accepting free tickets for both yourself and your friend to tonight's premiere performance . . ."

"I wish I could accept, but my employer keeps me far too busy." Grünemann smiled dryly. "The life of a nobleman's attendant is not always an easy sinecure. I've come with an invitation for you, however. My employer was most intrigued by the reports he read of your company's prowess. He hopes that perhaps early this evening, before your performance, you might do him the honor of visiting his town palace for three quarters of an hour to describe your play to himself and his company? It will be a small group, but distinguished, I think you'll find. Of course, if you are already engaged . . ."

"On the contrary. I would be delighted to accept his invitation." Peter took a deep breath, struggling to keep outright elation from showing on his face. "Your employer's name and address—"

Grünemann shrugged uncomfortably. "He is a very private gentleman, I'm afraid. He requested me not to give any information"— he glanced meaningfully at the listening actors, before meeting Peter's gaze—"until we are entirely alone."

"I understand." Peter kept his voice as bland as Grünemann's own, as if he received such invitations every day of the week. In Vienna, the nobility ran their own private theaters, as well as helping to subsidize the national Burgtheater itself. To attract the favor of an aristocrat of wealth and influence was an event of miraculous proportions. "How shall I find him tonight?"

"If it please you, I can meet you behind the theater at twenty past six this evening and escort you myself."

"Excellent. Most excellent!" And if ever he had been granted a perfect deus ex machina to save him from a certain disaster . . . Peter waited in bubbling impatience for Grünemann's small figure to exit the auditorium, then turned back to his gaping company. *Now.* He jumped back up onto the stage before any questions or disputes could be remembered. "Ladies! Gentlemen!" He clapped his hands together. "You heard what honors may lie ahead of us. Now let the rehearsal begin. First scene!"

The cries of the street sellers and the dull roar of the passing crowd pressed against the glass windows of the Prince de Ligne's carriage as it rattled through the packed and heaving city center. Despite the gilded crest on the doors, it was not a luxurious carriage. It might perhaps have been well-sprung in the past but not since the last century. The cushions were covered with detailed embroidery that must once have glittered brightly with gold thread, but the colors had dulled and the cloth had worn thin without repair.

Still, when Michael considered how his travels through Vienna had risen, from smuggling himself through the city gates to walking straight across the city the day before, he was well contented with his current elevation. After all, the carriage looked vastly impressive to outside observers . . . and, as any gamester knew, appearances were everything.

"So, Prince Kalishnikoff." The Prince de Ligne leaned forward in the small carriage, his eyes gleaming with interest. "Tell me. How did you come to know our entrancing friend?"

"Lady Wyndham, you mean?" Michael let his lips quirk into a fraction of the mad grin that wanted to be released. "To be truthful, Your Highness, I can hardly remember a time I didn't know her."

"Truly? I'm surprised she traveled so far in her youth. These English aristocratic families are so insular. And then the wars . . ."

"Ah, but my father sent me to England as a boy, to study at Eton for a year. It was my one glimpse of life abroad."

Had Caroline invented brothers or sisters for herself? Michael was tempted to spin a tale of five mischievous older brothers, each with their own singular trials and travails—all of which Caroline would be forced to remember for her own future conversations with the prince—but he regretfully gave up the plan as flawed, this late in the others' acquaintance. *Ah well.* Best to remain simple, as always.

"Lady Wyndham's father was an old friend of my own father, from the days of his Grand Tour through Europe. He was kind enough to have me stay for the school holidays during my year in England."

"Ah. And then later . . ."

"I met her again by the happiest chance at last night's ball, only hours after I arrived in this city. Good fortune indeed."

"Indeed." The Prince de Ligne narrowed his bright eyes, his gaze still fixed on Michael's face. "May I be so importunate as to ask, Your Highness, what it is, exactly, that you hope to accomplish at this Congress? For I cannot imagine that you came to Vienna merely to renew old friendships, charming though they may have been."

"Need you even ask?" Michael met the old man's gaze steadily, even as his pulse sped up. The game had begun. "I've come like every other ruler whose possessions were stolen and annexed by the Corsican monster. The treaty of the Peace of Paris issued an invitation to this Congress to all the Powers engaged in Bonaparte's long wars. How could I not accept that invitation, after ten years of exile? Bonaparte took everything from me."

"Mm . . ." De Ligne leaned back into the thin cushions, looking pained. "Forgive me, my friend, but I feel I really ought to drop a word of warning in your ear. You see . . ." He paused. "One article of the treaty did indeed issue such an invitation, and all Europe can bear witness to it. But that was not the only article of the treaty. And there were other articles that were never publically witnessed."

"I beg your pardon?"

"I, of course, was not there." De Ligne shrugged delicately. "And yet, rumors say, and the behavior of the delegates confirms . . . that there was a secret article included in that treaty. *That* article confined all decisions on the disposal of Bonaparte's conquered territory to the four Great Powers alone: Russia, Austria, Prussia, Great Britain . . . and none other."

Michael's eyebrows rose. "And the rulers of the conquered territories?"

"Must petition the Great Powers for the gift of their own lands' return, apparently. But a power does not become Great by listening to subtle moral misgivings, you know, or by indulging in open-handed acts of generosity."

"I . . . take your meaning." Michael drew a deep, steadying breath.

It was going too perfectly to be believed.

He'd imagined it would be a challenge to assert his right to monetary compensation for his "loss" without accepting the "return" of his land and powers—a gift that he could never dare accept. Kernova might be a tiny and distant principality, but it was filled, after all, with people who had met the real Prince Kalishnikoff before that drunken sot had safely left the Continent.

But if the Prince de Ligne was correct . . .

Michael hardened his face into melancholy fortitude. "Might I ask you for one more piece of advice, Your Highness? Among the many politicians gathered here, who would be the best to approach with my dilemma?"

"Well . . ."

"I do understand that perhaps nothing can be done. I may never see my home again." Michael gave his lips a bitter twist. "Perhaps the Great Powers of the Congress will find it best, in their wisdom, to barter my homeland to the highest bidder . . . and I have no armies or funds to spend in my defense. And yet . . ." He set his jaw. "I find I cannot quite give up without a fight."

"Of course not." The prince regarded him, frowning, for another moment, then nodded abruptly. "Very well. I shall introduce you to Monsieur le Baron de Talleyrand, the French foreign minister."

Michael tilted his head, as the ill-sprung carriage bounced and jolted beneath him. "But France was not on your list of the Great Powers."

"Indeed not. Therefore, Talleyrand is all the more amenable to the breaking of that secret pact—and all the more interested in finding moral high grounds from which to forcibly lever it open. Better yet, he's bound to be at luncheon today . . . but whether on the right- or the left-hand side of the staircase, I cannot tell you." A boyish grin broke across the prince's elfin face, setting it alight with sudden glee. "Have courage, Your Highness, and harden your stomach—if the worst comes to pass, we can always eat luncheon twice and listen to each hostess pass judgment on the next!"

Michael leaned back into the thin cushions of his seat as a vast contentment rose within him. "I can hardly wait."

＊

Caroline was midway through her letter writing when the drawing room door opened. A discreet cough captured her attention, and she looked up.

"Charles."

She smiled and lowered her quill pen as her secretary walked into the room. He closed the door so carefully behind himself that Caroline raised her eyebrows.

"Yes?"

He crossed the room in silence, lips pursed. Only when he stood beside her did he finally speak, in a low tone. "Lady Wyndham..."

Caroline gestured to the chair beside her. "Do sit down."

"Thank you." Charles sat and regarded her gravely, blinking behind his spectacles. "I've made my room safe for any inspection, I think. And your study as well."

"Excellent." She smiled encouragingly. "And...?"

"Lady Wyndham..." His hands clenched into a knot of tension on one knee. "I must ask you to forgive me for what I am about to say."

"Good God, Charles, what's amiss to inspire such an ominous tone from you? Have half my housekeeping accounts gone astray?" Caroline forced a laugh into her tone. "Did one of Vienna's ominous secret policemen take you out drinking last night and force you to reveal all your darkest secrets?"

"Of course not!" He flushed. "I hope your Ladyship knows me better than that."

"Of course I do." Caroline restrained a secret sigh of relief. "Forgive me my levity. You may speak freely, of course."

"In that case..." He paused a moment, then met her gaze. "Would it be too impertinent to ask what Prince Kalishnikoff is truly doing here?"

Ah. Caroline sighed inwardly. Of course, she should have expected this.

She widened her eyes in innocent surprise. "My dear Charles. Have I forgotten to explain? His Highness is an old friend from many, many years ago. I hadn't realized he would be here in Vienna—in fact, I didn't even recognize him at first glance, as you may recall. So many years had passed that his appearance had quite altered—and of course, he did not know my married name. But once we renewed our acquaintance at the ball last night . . ."

She shrugged. "You know how difficult it was to find available apartments in this district even when you reserved this one for me months ago. It's almost impossible to find any accommodation in the whole of Vienna at the moment. How could I refuse the pressing request of such an old friend?"

"Naturally. And yet . . ." Charles looked down at his clenched hands and drew a deep breath. "I shall be truly impertinent, now. I did witness your meeting, yesterday, and it led me to think—if you were not, in fact, old friends . . . if there was any other tie that bound you and forced you into sheltering a man you held in distaste, a man who was threatening you in any way . . ."

"Charles!" Caroline forced a gurgle of laughter into her tone. "I fancy you've been reading Mrs. Radcliffe's Gothic novels. What's put these follies in your head?"

"*If* any of that were true," her secretary continued, inexorably, "I hope you would have confidence enough in my discretion to confide in me. And I would do all that was in my power to aid you, without reserve." He looked up and met her eyes. "I would do anything for you," he added softly.

Caroline stared at him. The light response that she'd prepared withered and faded away, unspoken, as she met her secretary's steady gaze. His expression was intent . . . and unmistakable.

She drew a deep, careful breath. "I thank you. Sincerely, I do."

For the first time in the conversation, she was aware of how close they sat to one another. His knee rested only inches away from hers,

though she had thought nothing of it until now. He was—she calculated rapidly—twenty-four? Or twenty-five? At least ten years younger
than her, certainly. A boy, no more. It was absurd to even consider him
in that way. But he was a boy looking at her with all the force of a compelling first attachment.

Unmistakable danger hung in the air.

Caroline smiled. In all the masquerading of her past years, she did
not remember ever having to judge a smile quite so carefully, imbuing
it with friendly warmth . . . but nothing more.

"I do trust you," she said. "I'm very grateful to know I can rely on
your assistance so completely." She made a rueful face. "And of course,
you are correct. I wasn't pleased when I first saw Prince Kalishnikoff.
The last time we saw each other, we parted . . . badly."

To say the least. Michael's face through the flames, distorted by
smoke; the police surrounding Caroline, holding down her arms . . .

She swallowed and forced sincerity into her tone. "But all of that
was resolved at last night's ball. Truly, there is nothing for you to fear
for me. I am genuinely delighted to have him here as my guest from
now until he chooses to move on."

Charles looked at her steadily, without speaking. The muscles in
his shoulders bunched beneath his coat as if he were bracing himself
for action . . . or barely restraining himself from it. Caroline eased a
fraction of an inch further away on her seat, endeavoring to make the
movement look casual.

"But of course," she finished pleasantly, "I do appreciate your
kindness."

Inwardly, she winced at the banality of her own words. But what
else was there to say?

"I am glad," Charles said, his voice as colorless as water. "And
relieved. Of course." He straightened his shoulders. "In that case . . ."

"Yes?" Caroline felt her heart beating uncomfortably quickly. Of
all the unexpected and unwelcome complications . . .

"If you'd allow me, Lady Wyndham, I would like to remind you
of an offer you made when you first hired me. You said then that you

would aid me with my alchemical research." She could read no trace of emotion on his face. "I would be most grateful if you would help me now by showing me how yesterday's ritual was accomplished, as you did agree when we spoke yesterday."

"So I did," Caroline said. "I remember. But, Charles . . ." She drew a breath, suppressing a flare of sudden panic, and forced her voice to remain mild. "I would beg you to reconsider. A transfer of energy may sound fascinating to a man of scientific bent, but the aftereffects—"

Lying limp and weeping on the cold stone floor, incapable of movement, helpless to struggle—

"I don't fear the effects," Charles said.

"But—"

"Please, my lady." He stood with a sudden jerk, only barely maintaining a submissive edge to his posture. His eyes glinted with the ominous beginnings of impatience. "Let me decide for myself what is too dangerous. This was, after all, part of our agreement when you hired me."

"I understand," Caroline said evenly. She fought to keep her expression impassive as panic gibbered silently within her. *I can't, I can't, I can't . . .*

But what other option did she have? She breathed a silent curse and gave in.

"I will show you, then," she said. "Of course."

Cold fear seeped through Caroline's chest at her own words, but she kept her smile firm.

She'd promised to do anything to bring her father back, and she would hold to that promise. No matter what it cost her.

CHAPTER TEN

"**H**is Highness the Prince de Ligne and His Highness Prince Kalishnikoff!"

Accompanied by the resonant, Russian-accented tones of Princess Bagration's butler, Michael stepped into a long, narrow salon, hot as midsummer, stinking of perfume, and filled with bodies.

No, he corrected himself, as he took it all in. This hothouse room, wallpapered in rich gold and deep pink, was filled not with mere bodies but with *power*, palpable as steel. Princess Bagration herself might scandalize all the proper ladies of Vienna, but all the most influential gentlemen of Europe gathered here nonetheless to eat, drink, and keep a wary eye on each other in the enticing company of charming and far-less-than-proper females.

Any of these men might help him on his way if they chose; any of them might yet discover his ruse by chance and denounce him to the world as an imposter and a rogue.

Exhilaration filled Michael's chest as he stepped forward to join them.

"De Ligne!" A weary, Russian-accented voice spoke from the depths of a great chair at the end of the room, cutting off the glittering, swirling conversations. A blonde woman wearing a diaphanous, clinging gown of white muslin, which showcased every one of her exquisite proportions, uncoiled herself from her seat and swept across the carpeted floor toward the new arrivals. Jewels sparkled on her outstretched hands; a select few diamonds glinted in her upswept golden hair, above porcelain-white skin. "You've deigned to attend my little luncheon after all. I can scarcely believe it."

"Could you doubt that I would come?" De Ligne kissed both hands, then turned to Michael. "Your Highness, may I present the ineffably enchanting Princess Bagration? And, Princess, my companion— Prince Kalishnikoff."

"At your service," Michael murmured, leaning over her hands. Her skin was warm, perfectly soft, and fragranced. "I do apologize for intruding without invitation, Your Highness."

"In this company?" Her eyebrows arched. "Heavens, De Ligne, you've found one gentleman with manners in this dreadful city. We are in luck, after all." She left her hands in Michael's grasp, but stepped back to openly appraise him. "And where do you hail from, Prince Kalishnikoff?"

"Kernova, Your Highness." He shook his head to forestall her. "You would never have heard of it, I'm afraid. A mere principality, but a beloved home to me—until Bonaparte decided to add it to his private collection, that is."

"Ah." She sighed. "But of course. The old story. And have you, too, come to Vienna to talk over dreary political woes with every other poor victim of the Monster?"

"I?" Michael smiled and pressed her hands gently as he released them. "Why, this city is filled with the greatest beauties and wits of Europe, and I"—he met her eyes—"have found myself at their center, I believe. How could politics take forefront in my mind?"

"Indeed?" She looked consideringly at him a moment and then at De Ligne, who was nearly vibrating in his determined silence. Her full lips twitched. "Well, I do appreciate a man with charm. Come sit by me, Prince Kalishnikoff. De Ligne . . . you are as much a rascal as ever, I see. Are you stirring up mischief again?"

"I can but try, my dear," the Prince de Ligne murmured, bowing his head modestly.

Michael followed Princess Bagration to her seat, while De Ligne glided to the opposite corner of the room to kiss the hand of a lushly endowed young woman and murmur a remark, *sotto voce*, that made her laugh.

Princess Bagration sank back into her seat with a deep sigh and gestured limply at the men gathered around her. "His Highness Prince Kalishnikoff, of Kernova-that-was; Monsieur le Baron de Talleyrand, foreign minister to His Majesty of France; the Marquis de Noailles, also of France; Lord Kelvinhaugh, ambassador of His Majesty of England . . ." She smiled, lowering her eyelashes. "Surely you gentlemen must be able to find *something* of interest to talk about."

Michael saw the glint in her hooded eyes, and his lips twitched appreciatively. He schooled his face to sober receptivity, though, as the English ambassador began to speak.

"Kernova," Lord Kelvinhaugh said thoughtfully. "Ah, now. Kernova. That would be at the edge of Poland and Galicia, am I correct?"

"You've an excellent grasp of geography, my lord." Michael sat down on an unoccupied seat and laced his hands around his knee. "Few people recognize even the name of my poor principality, anymore."

Lord Kelvinhaugh's lips curved into a humorless smile. "It is the business of this Congress to recognize such names, Your Highness. As the Prince Regent's representative, I could hardly fail to study European history."

Talleyrand laughed, a dry bark. "The business of this Congress? Kelvinhaugh, you haven't studied long enough if you truly think so. Only ask our friend De Ligne, across the room. What new epigram of his did I hear repeated, only the other night?—ah, yes: 'The Congress dances, but it does not advance.' Your own superior, Lord Castlereagh, was seen to crack a rare smile at the truth of it."

Lord Kelvinhaugh's craggy face chilled into distant hauteur. "I like to think our work here is greater than that."

"So would we all like to believe," Talleyrand murmured. "My own most aggrieved government most of all, I think."

In the momentary silence that followed, Michael studied the Frenchman's face as discreetly as he could. He had heard of the man before, of course—one could hardly have followed European politics for the past twenty-five years without having heard the name of Talleyrand.

But how had Bonaparte's top minister—the man who had orchestrated Bonaparte's original seizure of power—become the closely trusted foreign minister of the newly restored Bourbon king? That must have taken wit and agility indeed . . . and even, from the rumors Michael had heard, a fair amount of outright, treasonous cunning.

Then again, as Talleyrand himself was rumored to have said: *Treason is a matter of dates.* Talleyrand's own dates had been carefully chosen. It argued a wily intelligence indeed to have prophesied the great Bonaparte's downfall in time to make the most of it.

It was not what one might have guessed from the man's appearance. Less dapper than the Prince de Ligne or even the Marquis de Noailles, who sat beside him, Monsieur le Baron de Talleyrand presented no more than a minimally respectable appearance for the minister of such a great—if fallen—kingdom. His clothes were notably sober compared to the other Continental gentlemen in the salon, though still more bejeweled and colorful than those of the English Lord Kelvinhaugh beside him. Talleyrand's face sagged with deep, distorting wrinkles, and a cane lay propped against his chair for the sake of his twisted feet. And yet . . .

Michael had not won so many gambles in his life by misjudging men's appearances. The gleam in Monsieur le Baron de Talleyrand's eyes was as alert as it was disconcertingly intelligent. If the Prince de Ligne was the most charmingly distinguished courtier of their shared era, Talleyrand was surely the most dangerous. If Michael was to succeed in his gamble, he could not afford to make a single false move before this man.

Even as the realization crystallized in Michael's mind, the Frenchman spoke again.

"Kernova . . . the name is familiar indeed. Did I not meet your honored father once in Paris, Prince Kalishnikoff?"

Damnation. "I'd be astonished if you had, Your Excellency. My father was a man of the old school, not prone to speak the name of France after the revolution . . . nor to allow any of the rest of us to speak it, either." Michael shrugged, his expression open and frank. "Still, I suppose that stranger events have come to pass . . . and a father does not share all his trips or secrets with his son."

"No? I suppose not." A smile played on Talleyrand's lips as he considered Michael. "Still . . . the edge of Poland, my English colleague says? My, how often we have heard the name of Poland uttered in these past few weeks."

"Indeed?" Michael blinked with genuine uncertainty. If only the students in the Kaffeehaus had been foolish enough to speak publicly of politics . . .

"The great tsar of Russia himself is all ablaze to build a new model kingdom there, with liberty and democracy abounding . . . all held safe beneath his imperial protection, of course." Talleyrand's tone was uninflected to the point of monotony, and his expression remained bland, even as his words caused Lord Kelvinhaugh to stiffen and the other Frenchman to purse his lips with disapproval.

Then Talleyrand's eyebrows rose in apparent surprise. "Ah! And now I come to think on it, Kernova would be one of the territories amalgamated."

"Into a kingdom of Poland?" Michael said, with genuine startlement. "But surely, Your Excellency . . ."

"An intriguing thought, is it not?" Talleyrand sat back in his chair, smiling gently, as the English ambassador visibly simmered nearby. "It is always so instructive for the rest of us to observe the way the Great Powers think."

"And it is well for others of us, from time to time, to take some nourishment to fuel our own thinking." Princess Bagration gave a most improper—and attractive—stretch, and rose gracefully from her seat. "We'll wait no longer to eat, I think. You have fine broad shoulders, Prince Kalishnikoff—will you be gallant enough to lead me in to luncheon today?"

"But, of course. I should be delighted."

Michael stood and offered her his arm. With a murmur of pleasure, she slid her hand into the curve of it, as sleek and soft as any cat; he was nearly tempted into petting her.

Nearly, but not quite. Princess Bagration was no tame house pet but a sharp-witted politician in her own right. She would not take kindly to any man foolish enough to fall for her pretense at pliability. And even if that were not the case . . .

He looked down at the top of her piled golden hair, which brushed lightly against his arm. Caroline had stood beside him in nearly the same position last night at the conclusion of their dance. Where Princess Bagration leaned into him now, her perfume twining around him in invitation, Caroline had stood vibrating with outrage. The difference between the two was striking. And yet . . .

And yet, somehow, he found himself irrationally disappointed by the contrast. Incandescent with frustration and rage, Caroline had felt like a line of flame against him—and all of her fury, maddening though it had been, had been aimed at *him*, not at any charmingly assumed persona. It was the first time in years that he had felt so frustrated . . . and so deeply engaged, at every level of his being.

Princess Bagration said, apparently idly, "Talleyrand, do sit by me today." Her sweet smile deepened into a smirk as she glanced back up at Michael. "I believe this luncheon may hold some real interest after all."

By the time Caroline returned from her afternoon of paying social calls and driving in the Augarten, she was seething with suppressed tension. She stripped off her gloves as she stepped into her apartment building, her back teeth grinding together. She'd barely made it through her last requisite afternoon visit—with Marie Rothmere, full of poisonous gossip and prying questions—without missing a dozen social cues and shattering the disguise she'd worked so many years to build.

Her second husband might never have cared to learn anything of what he'd termed her "disreputable past," but he had been both firm and exact about how to build her future, for both of their sakes. *"Don't humiliate me, Caroline."* She never had. She hadn't broken any of his social guidelines in years. After memorizing them so carefully at seventeen, she'd absorbed them until they were nearly second nature by now.

But in the drawing rooms of Vienna that afternoon, all of her years of training seemed to have abandoned her, leaving only a brittle veneer of custom to defend her. All that Caroline had been able to focus on, as gossip swirled and eddied around her, was what lay ahead of her that night. Her foolish, impossible, unbreakable promise to Charles . . . and her damnable, creeping, inescapable fear.

She felt as fragile and ready to shatter as a pane of glass threatened by a bullet.

You knew this was coming, her reason reminded her, with cool censure.

Of course she had. Caroline had calmly planned her own reintroduction to alchemy as a necessary step in her scheme, as she'd sat alone in her elegant London drawing room that spring, far from Austria and the past. Sitting comfortably there in her favorite chair, surrounded by all the trappings of her new identity, she'd imagined herself cool and collected and far too adult to be frightened by old nightmares.

More fool she.

It did nothing to aid her mood when she heard the door open behind her and feet run up the twisting staircase in her wake. She knew that confident step, even after all these years.

Still, the sight of Michael Steinhüller, no longer a ghost from her long-lost past but vividly real and all grown up, was a shock against her senses when he came into view a moment later.

"My lady Wyndham!" He caught up with her on the first landing, smiling broadly. His scent, fresh and unfamiliar and a world away from his old boyish musk, brushed her with unnerving warmth as he swept a bow. His very presence seemed to vibrate with energy. "May I tell you how charming you look today? Quite the grand lady indeed, I must say."

"Must you? Really?" Caroline swiveled to face him, giving up even the pretense of cool composure. He looked flushed, happy, handsome, and confident. It was unbearable. "You would be far kinder to leave me in peace. But I suppose there's no purpose in asking for impossibilities, is there?"

His smile faded as he stepped back. "Perhaps not. I had intended to thank you, though, for the introduction you granted me this morning."

Caroline stared at him. "I could hardly do otherwise under threat of blackmail."

"Nonetheless . . ." He drew a breath through his teeth and nodded stiffly. "Believe it or not, I am still grateful."

"Grateful? If you only knew what it had led to—"

"The introduction?" Michael shook his head, impatience creeping into his tone. "I hardly think—"

"Not the introduction," Caroline said. "The—oh, never mind." It was nonsensical to blame him, anyway, for Charles's request. That would have come sooner or later, regardless of this new complication. But that it must come at all . . .

Michael stepped forward, frowning. "You're weeping."

"I am not." She dashed away the brimming tears, hardening herself. She hated the vulnerability in her chest . . . and the sudden, inescapable memory of how she'd carried all her worries to him in the past.

She'd wept on his shoulder more than once, in the old days, and felt blissfully safe and comforted by doing it.

Unbearable.

She closed her teeth with a snap. "I'm only weary."

"And melancholy. Or . . ." His face softened in sudden concern. "Frightened?"

He reached forward, as if to touch her cheek. She put her hand out to stop him . . . and found their hands touching.

The heat of sudden, unexpected awareness sparked against her skin, shocking the breath from her.

Caroline stepped back as abruptly as if she'd been slapped. Her hand tingled, unnervingly, against her side. Michael's warm hazel eyes were wide and startled in his lean face.

"Forgive me," Caroline said. She winced at the sound of her voice, husky and unfamiliar, as if it belonged to someone else. *A weakling.* Steeling herself, she brought it under control. "I am in no state for company, I'm afraid."

She broke away from Michael's gaze, forcing a thin smile. "Not even the company of such old . . . friends." He was standing between her and the stairs up to her apartment. Worse yet, he was looking at her as if he knew her. As if she was still Karolina instead of Caroline . . . and as if he actually cared.

She had to escape. "Move aside, please, *Prince* Kalishnikoff."

He didn't move. Instead, he asked softly, "What happened to you all those years ago? After the fire, after—"

She shook her head tightly, refusing to meet his gaze. "That can have no significance for you."

"Orphanages can be . . . harsh. I've heard—"

She laughed, and almost choked on it. "Have no fear, then, Prince Kalishnikoff. I wasn't in an orphanage." No orphanage locked its charges in tiny rooms to be food for monsters.

And now, to willingly repeat it again . . .

"Karolina." Michael caught her wrist, his grip warm and compelling. "What's amiss? You can tell me."

"Oh, yes, indeed. Of course I can. After all, how could I possibly fail to trust you, of all people?" The impulse to bitter laughter subsided into sheer exhaustion. Caroline looked up and met his eyes, only inches away, with a flat, impenetrable stare. "Release me," she said with icy clarity. "Now."

His hand fell away. As light from the windows faded, shadows flung themselves across the narrow stairwell and cast his face into darkness. Caroline was glad that she couldn't see it clearly.

"Enjoy your evening," she said briskly, as she might have spoken to a stranger. "Do you go tonight to a ball, or to the theater, or—"

He shifted aside to let her past. "I've been invited to the Hôtel de Ligne for supper and an evening party. As have you, I believe. If—"

"Pray convey my apologies," Caroline said as she brushed past him. She picked up the skirts of her pelisse and dress, the better to run the rest of the way up the stairs. It was a cowardly maneuver, but then, at heart, she was a coward. "I have a previous engagement."

That evening, at a quarter past six, Peter abandoned the stage of the Theater an der Wien at long last. He'd instructed every stagehand twice and insisted on hearing back their catechism of orders for the evening's performance. He'd inspected the stage from every angle of the audience, gauging half a dozen last-minute adjustments that needed to be made to their flexible touring set. He'd tested every floorboard on the wooden stage itself.

It was time. Peter slipped down the narrow corridor that led to the back entrance. High and increasingly aggravated voices floated out through the closed door of the dressing room that Marta and Josephine shared; thank Heaven for his urgent appointment, which called him away from such volatile territory. A grin twitched Peter's mouth at the thought. He hurried past, lest his footsteps be heard and he be called in to settle some new dispute.

But it was a different door that opened as he passed.

"Riesenbeck." Karl's broad shoulders filled the doorway of the men's communal dressing room. He crossed his arms and regarded Peter steadily. "On your way?"

"As you see." Peter paused but didn't turn. "Wish me luck, my friend."

"It's a fine time to be gallivanting off, with less than two hours left before our first performance."

Peter let out his breath in a sigh. "Would you have had me turn down such an invitation? Such a chance, for all of us?"

"It wasn't necessary to turn it down. Had you only asked for a different time—"

"Oh, indeed I could have done. But if another time had not happened to suit our prospective patron . . ."

"How would we know, when you didn't bother to ask? Meantime, if our first night's audience is held waiting while you dally—"

"Karl . . ." Peter gritted his teeth and closed his eyes, praying for patience.

He'd known from the very first month of the company's existence that Marta's husband seethed with impatience for his own company.

Peter had hoped that the trip to Vienna would calm Karl's ambitions, but instead it seemed to have kindled the lurking flames. He would challenge Peter for control at every turn if Peter let him.

But only if Peter let him. Peter forced himself to tamp down the flaring irritation in his chest. He summoned up a cheerful smile as he relaxed his shoulders and turned to face the other man. "The attention of a nobleman is rich and fleeting, I'm afraid, and their whims, if not fulfilled upon the instant, may pass just as quickly and leave us grasping for a lost opportunity." He clapped Karl on the shoulder. "Have no fear, though. I've a head for timing, even if my host does not. I'll make a case for our company and be back in plenty of time."

"That's what you say now."

"It is indeed," Peter agreed genially. "And so I'd best be off now, with no further ado, or else find myself eating my own words."

"Ha." Karl glowered but didn't move to stop Peter as he started down the corridor. "We'll be waiting for you."

"Excellent." Safely out of view, Peter rolled his eyes and called back, "If I'm not back in time, my friend, feel free to begin the play without me."

Karl's answer followed him down the corridor. "We might at that."

Peter escaped through the back door into the fresh, cold air of early evening. The bite in the air tingled against his skin as he shook off the encounter. No time for fretting: the evening's first performance had already begun. The sky was already blue with gathering twilight, and the narrow alleyway behind the theater was unlit. Still, Peter had no difficulty in recognizing the figure waiting in the shadows.

"Herr Riesenbeck." Vaçlav Grünemann's quiet voice purred with satisfaction as he stepped forward. "My employer awaits you."

CHAPTER ELEVEN

Caroline dismissed the servants at half past six for an evening's holiday. Spies or no, not one of them stepped forward to complain. She heard their muffled voices through the drawing room door, talking in excited whispers as they left the apartment.

And none too soon.

She drew a shuddering breath as the outer apartment door closed with a thud behind the last of them. She'd been pretending concentration on her embroidery for the past half hour. Her frozen fingers hadn't managed to set more than a dozen stitches.

When she heard that door reopen, only shortly after it had closed, Caroline dropped her embroidery and hurried forward to open the drawing room door herself. Anything to keep from thinking of what was about to happen.

The door opened before she could reach it. Charles stepped inside, glowing with barely suppressed excitement.

"They've all safely left the building," he said. "I watched the last of the maids turn the street corner before I came up."

"And the apartment door?" Caroline asked. Her voice sounded steady, she thought. *How odd.*

"Locked." Charles lifted the books and candles he'd brought. "We should move to—that is . . ." He took a deep breath. "My lady, where would you recommend that we begin?"

Caroline found a thin smile at the forced submission in her secretary's voice. "Here will do as well as any spot, I think. They're bound to notice the smell of smoke tomorrow morning, but we can bring in several candelabras afterward and burn the candles down to create an explanation."

"Well thought, Your Ladyship."

Caroline looked away from Charles's eager face to the windows at the far end of the room. Outside, the night sky was a deep, dense blue, shading into black. Candles lit the windows of the opposite apartment in the building across the street, creating a rectangle of light within the curlicued façade. Through the windows, Caroline could see a party assembling for the theater, slipping on greatcoats and pelisses and passing around opera glasses.

"Pull the curtains," Caroline said, in a voice she barely recognized as her own. "We want no observers for this."

Peter Riesenbeck matched his footsteps to those of his companion and forced himself not to chatter. Excitement pressed against his chest, but he remained as silent as Vaçlav Grünemann, beside him, as they crossed through the dark, crowded streets bustling with pedestrian and carriage traffic. Music filtered out of the taverns and restaurants they passed, brass bands mingling in the concatenation with Hungarian violins, full chamber orchestras, and lilting female voices. The Kaffeehäuser burst to overflowing, spilling customers to sit out on the streets despite the deepening darkness and the chill in the evening air.

How many of them would move on to one of Vienna's many theaters afterward? Perhaps some of the men Peter saw drinking now would be sitting in the Theater an der Wien in less than two hours' time to watch the Riesenbeck troupe's first Viennese performance. And perhaps, just perhaps, they might be startled and impressed as well by a public announcement of the company's new patron . . .

Peter's feet quickened, despite himself. Even Karl wouldn't be able to mutter about his management when he brought back such a prize. And once Peter was freed of his financial terrors . . .

Well, he wouldn't be able to give the actors their pay rise quite yet, unfortunately; he'd raised too many debts with this trip, all of which needed to be paid off before the company could feel the change in their circumstances. But the compliment, the glory of it, mixed with the promise of far greater rewards to come . . .

"This way, Herr Riesenbeck," Grünemann said, and touched Peter's elbow softly to turn him.

Peter blinked, taking in the darkened façade before him. No torches were set outside this entrance. Half-hidden by shadows, a small wooden door was set, nearly hidden, in a plain stone wall. It was the same wall that ran all along this side of the Herrengasse, surrounding . . .

"My God." It came out in a whisper of reverential terror. "It's part of the Hofburg!"

"You are observant." Grünemann's small, prim mouth curved into a smile.

"But then . . ." Peter's head whirled as he stared, his feet frozen into lead, at the door.

If Grünemann's employer lived here . . .

Well, half the crowned heads of Europe, at least, were staying as honored guests in Emperor Francis's Hofburg Palace, as well as three courts in exile.

But Grünemann was no mere visitor to Vienna nor foreign equerry. And only one family claimed ownership of the Hofburg palace.

"Will you not enter, Herr Riesenbeck?"

Peter took a grip on himself. *Don't be a coward. It's only stage fright.* He'd presented himself to noble patrons before—he'd had audience with a visiting French count, even, once in Prague.

But the emperor himself . . .

Just think of how Périgord will curse at the news, Peter thought. So much for all his old mentor's warnings of certain failure, eh?

He licked his lips and straightened his shoulders. "Ready." His voice boomed out, sounding as confident and easy as when he stepped onstage.

He'd always known that coming to Vienna was the right thing to do. But he'd never imagined such an opportunity as this could unfold before him.

Was it possible to feel more fright than joy at such news, so sudden and unexpected? He'd never thought so before.

The door handle turned beneath his hand.

"It's unlit," Peter said. He peered into the unremitting darkness. "Do you think we've come to the wrong door?"

"There's no need to worry," Grünemann said. "It's the first door on the right—you need no light for that. I'll guide you, have no fear."

"Of course." The emperor was spending fifty thousand florins a day on each of his royal guests, by all reports. That had to strain even the grandest treasury to its breaking point. Why waste candles on a servants' entrance?

Peter took a deep breath and stepped into the blackness. He heard the door swing closed behind him.

But Grünemann hadn't followed him.

Ahead of him he heard a sudden scuffle of feet.

"Hello?" he called softly.

There was no answer.

But suddenly, he knew.

Blinded in the darkness, Peter spun around. He threw himself at the door, landing hard against it. He fumbled desperately along the smooth wood, searching for the inside handle. It was hidden in the darkness. Before he could find it, strong hands fastened on both his arms, pinning them behind his back.

A hood dropped over his head. Gasping for breath, Peter jerked his head back. It crashed against a taller man's face. A curse sounded behind him, and the grip on his arms loosened.

Peter lunged forward, pulling away. Somewhere before him, he heard the door open. If he could only get there fast enough, find his way out into the busy street—

He ran straight into another man's chest.

Vaçlav Grünemann's sigh sounded in his ears. Small hands pushed Peter firmly backward, into the waiting grip of his attackers.

"Do calm yourself, Herr Riesenbeck." Grünemann's voice was as dry and emotionless as ever.

The door fell closed again as Grünemann pushed past Peter in the pitch-black corridor.

"I told you my employer was expecting you."

It wasn't what Michael had expected.

The Hôtel de Ligne was an unprepossessing, unusually short building set on the Mölker Bastei, the sloping, cobbled street built on top of the old walls that had once encircled Vienna's inner city. When Michael was a boy, this street had been full of the noise and flurry of building works, as the middle classes competed in building new homes to match the grand palaces in the city below. Now, with the building works long gone, the narrow street possessed an air of quiet but modern elegance. The houses that surrounded the Hôtel de Ligne might be modestly sized and painted in tastefully muted colors, but each one glistened with fresh paint and visible pride of place—except for the Hôtel de Ligne.

The best that could be said of the Prince de Ligne's own home was that the house itself looked . . . not ill-built. In the shadows, it even hinted at an atmosphere of past grandeur, albeit faded and long-distant. Only dim lights shone in the windows, though music and laughter sounded through the door.

The Prince de Ligne's name and lineage were known across Europe; his military exploits, published letters, and memoirs would have made him a force to be reckoned with in high society, even had he not been by birth a prince of the former Holy Roman Empire. From his clothes and manner, one would expect him to be a gentleman of vast wealth. Even if his own resources had run out over the years, considering his military and political distinction, it would be nigh-on unthinkable for the imperial government not to have stepped in to fill the gap. At the very least, they would surely have created an official post for him to act as excuse for an elegant state pension, to comfortably support him through his grand old age.

And yet . . . the shabby interior of De Ligne's carriage had offered the hint of another possibility, had it not?

Michael studied the faded paint on the knocker and the scratched and crumbling stone above the door and wondered if De Ligne might not be, in truth, as much of an adventurer and illusionist as Michael himself.

"Ah, my dear Prince Kalishnikoff."

A dry voice spoke in French behind him, and Michael turned, his hand dropping away from the untouched door knocker.

The French foreign minister stood on the pavement below, leaning on his cane while his carriage drove away.

"Monsieur de Talleyrand." Michael bowed. "What a pleasure to meet you again."

"A pleasure indeed." Talleyrand's disconcertingly flat, uninflected manner of speaking shaded the phrase into ambiguity. He smiled, though, tilting his head. "A lovely evening, is it not? Perhaps you'd do me the honor of taking a turn with me around the neighborhood before we venture inside."

"But of course." Michael ran lightly down the steps to the pavement, feeling his pulse quicken.

So he had succeeded, after all, in catching the man's attention that afternoon. Satisfaction mingled with a tinge of nerves at the thought of it. The attention of Monsieur le Baron de Talleyrand could be a double-edged sword for a professional deceiver.

Michael fell into step with the older man, slowing his pace to match the ambassador's lopsided steps. Lights glittered along the street, sparkling within the houses, but this far from the center of town, only one solitary carriage rattled by as they walked.

"Is this your first visit to the Hôtel de Ligne, Your Highness?" Talleyrand asked. He leaned heavily on his cane as he walked, his attention apparently focused solely on the bumpy paving stones beneath his feet.

"It is," Michael said. "I haven't been to Vienna at all since I was a boy, I'm afraid—I've spent most of the past decade wandering about Bohemia and Moravia."

"Have you indeed?" Talleyrand's lips twitched, as if appreciating a private jest. "Prepare yourself for a true delight. Not in the atmosphere nor the food, I fear—furniture made nearly out of straw, you understand, and meals of the same consistency—but the company, ah, the company . . ."

He paused, balancing on his cane, and gazed contemplatively up at the closest house, which flooded brilliant light from its broad first-floor windows. "Ah, now the company cannot be bettered. A school for conversation, we've always called it. Between the prince, his daughters—marvelous women, all of them, their wits as sharp as daggers—and the guests he always manages to gather around them . . . whether despite or because of the shortness of their memories . . ." He bent his glittering gaze on Michael.

"Your Excellency?"

"I'm intrigued by your mention of early visits to Vienna," Talleyrand said. "Do you remember much, if anything, about them?"

"As much as could be expected, I suppose, after a full thirty-year gap."

"Indeed? You astonish me."

Michael met the other man's gaze steadily. "I'm afraid I don't catch your meaning."

"No?" Talleyrand shook his head. "What a pity. You seem such a bright young man. And yet, you took a misstep today. You see . . ."

In the same flat, dry tone of elegant disinterest, the French minister continued, "I'm afraid you made the wrong guess at luncheon this afternoon. You see, I did meet the former Prince Kalishnikoff in Paris, twenty years ago. But the prince did not travel alone."

"Ah." Michael moistened suddenly dry lips. "Your Excellency, perhaps I ought to say—"

"No, Monsieur, I believe you ought not. For the old prince traveled with his son as companion. His only son, who was a full twenty years of age at the time . . . and looked, I'm afraid, nothing at all like you. Therefore . . ." Talleyrand smiled thinly and looked at Michael, who stood fully exposed in the light from the window above.

"I do not know who you may truly be, Monsieur, but of one thing I am certain: you are not Prince Kalishnikoff of Kernova. And I imagine the Viennese secret police would be most interested to learn that."

CHAPTER TWELVE

Rough hands pushed Peter down into a chair. It was wooden, he could feel that much; wooden and bare of any cushion. They tied his hands to the back of the chair with thick cloth.

He didn't struggle. He was working too hard.

Use all of your senses. That had been one of Peter's first lessons, when Paul Périgord had plucked him as a seven-year-old off the streets of Prague and transformed him into an actor. Hard to do, though, when your head was swathed in a hood of coarse sacking. The material smelled of rank sweat and . . . what was that bitter scent that mixed with it?

Peter fought down panic. It made his breath come too fast and loud; made it impossible to listen. He took slow, deep breaths and forced himself to focus. If he could focus on the clues around him, he could reason out where he was and why this was happening. Then, if he worked hard enough, he could think up some clever way to escape. That was how these situations worked, wasn't it?

In plays, things like this often happened. Heroes were taken prisoner for no known reason. They were held captive by villains, but they always used their wits to escape. In plays . . .

Peter didn't remember any hero on the stage ever expressing the raw terror he felt thrumming against his skin—the panic of a captured animal. Heroes gave noble speeches of defiance in these situations, didn't they? He didn't think he would be able to form a single coherent word through the choking knot that filled his throat . . . much less come up with a brilliantly cunning plan to escape the harsh ropes that bound his wrists.

Things like this happened in plays, not in real life. In real life, he had to be back in the Theater an der Wien in less than an hour. He couldn't miss the premiere of his own play. It wasn't possible. This, now, *was not possible.*

The world spun like a Catherine wheel around him, filling his head with sick dizziness, realigning what was possible and what was not.

Through the sack, Peter could hear voices and heavy footsteps moving around him. The voices were of no help at all. They only muttered directions without explanations—"Here" and "Leave that."

The door was somewhere behind him, of that at least Peter was certain—

Oh. Another door opening, in front of him. And, more telling than that, the sudden and absolute silence of his attackers.

The new door closed. Soft footsteps moved toward Peter and stopped only a foot or so away.

A sensation of cold, seeping toward him . . .

No. That was just weakness, an actor's taste for melodrama. He couldn't let himself give into it, not now.

Peter's breath hurt his chest.

Several sets of heavy footsteps shuffled backward, toward the first door. It opened with a creak and closed again.

Soft footsteps moved closer. Cold air brushed against Peter's skin.

Peter's fingers fumbled against the wooden chair. He strained to turn his wrists within their tight bindings. Finally, he managed to grip the back of the chair.

Don't cry out. Don't lose control. Stay sharp, no matter what happens.

The footsteps circled him slowly, consideringly. Peter's muscles tightened as he squeezed the wooden chair, keeping his breathing even.

Cold seeped through his back, up his arms, into his chest. He gritted his teeth, suppressing a shiver.

The footsteps came to a halt in front of him once more.

"Well," said a cold, dry male voice. "Peter Riesenbeck. Actor. Director." It paused, then drew the word out like a delicacy. "*Revolutionary.*"

"No!" Peter said. The hood muffled his words; he spoke on anyway, projecting his voice as much as he could. "Someone's told you a lie. I care nothing for politics! That is..." He stumbled, caught himself. "I'm a loyal citizen to His Majesty and always have been. I would never betray the empire."

"Never?" Cold blew into Peter's face as the voice came closer, lowering to a hiss. "You were observed."

Peter kept his voice steady. "Who accuses me?" Cold prickled across his skin. No use telling himself it was imaginary anymore. No use torturing himself by imagining added horrors, though, either. Not yet. He'd wait until later, until he was warm and safe and free . . .

"You aided an enemy of the state," the voice whispered. "You and your entire company hid him and helped him into the country. You tricked the loyal guards at the border. You lied to protect a spy."

Oh, God. Michael. Peter recalled his arrival in Vienna with sudden, horrible clarity. Michael tipping his hat, smiling, and disappearing from view—and then Grünemann entering into conversation so casually. Handing him a glass of wine. *"I could have sworn I saw you help another man from your carriage."* It had all begun so quickly, and he hadn't even known it . . .

Peter moistened his lips. No use making excuses now. "I'll tell you everything I know. He said he was the son of a count, and he'd been disinherited for marrying an opera singer, years ago, but now—"

"Don't waste my time with lies, Herr Riesenbeck!" The voice snapped out now, loud and angry, hurting his ears even through the muffling bag. "You knew exactly who you were aiding, and why."

"I didn't—"

"You'll admit it soon enough, under torture. Even if you don't, other members of your company surely will."

Torture. The shock of it took Peter's breath away.

"There's no point in trying to fool us, you see." Footsteps sounded as the voice moved away. "You were witnessed again that night. Aiding another traitor to escape the police."

"I don't know what you're talking about."

"Don't attempt to act any more, Herr Riesenbeck. Your Bohemian reviews . . . led me to expect a more impressive set of skills."

Pain blossomed in Peter's skull, beneath the cold, as panic threatened to overwhelm him. "I'm telling the truth, as God is my witness. I swear. I helped no—" Sudden realization stopped his voice.

He had. He had helped that brown-haired girl escape from the policeman who'd been chasing her. And—oh, sweet Christ—Grünemann had seen him do it. Peter had recognized his face in that crowd, after all.

And he'd thought he was being such a hero . . .

"I didn't know," Peter said, but he heard the helplessness in his own voice as it failed him for the first time in his life. "I swear, I didn't know. I thought she was only a pickpocket."

"A charming excuse for breaking the law. And yet"—the voice sighed—"another lie, I'm afraid."

Caroline clenched her hands in her skirts as she watched Charles rearrange the drawing room, pushing all the delicate small tables out of the way, against the wall. *Out of harm's way.*

She fought aside her mounting dread. She could do this. She had to do this.

She had failed her father once already.

Caroline closed her eyes, torn by memory.

Father . . .

They'd been eating together, in the small kitchen above their shop, when the knock came on the door below. Caroline hadn't known to be afraid until she saw the look on her father's face.

Her calm, competent father, who took care of everything and everybody and worked so tirelessly against injustice.

She'd never seen him afraid before.

"Who—?" she began, but he silenced her by putting his hand on hers. His solid body stilled, listening . . . listening . . .

"*Polizei!*" a voice barked, in the darkness outside their house. It sounded like the voice of God, commanding and impossible to resist. "Open the door!"

"Go, Karolina," her father said. He strode across the small room to the narrow stairway, his face pale and set. "Get under your bed and stay there, no matter what you hear. Go now!"

She heard the crash of the door breaking in the shop below, even as her father ran down the staircase. She hovered, frozen in indecision, between the stairs and the narrow doorway that led to the bedroom.

Then her father cried out in pain, and her feet made the decision for her.

She arrived just as the first blows of the clubs fell upon her father's cherished printing press, smashing it to fragments. Just as her father slumped unconscious in the arms of two policemen. Arrived at the bottom of the staircase just in time to catch the eye of the man who stood behind the policemen, watching as they destroyed her father's shop.

In time, also, to see the impossible, spiraling column of darkness that lurked behind him in the shadows, and to watch both figures—the man and the nightmare—turn as one to meet her gaze.

It would be four more years before she was released. Four years before she was traded as useless—too weak, too broken—to one of the rare, honored observers who had been allowed into Pergen's experimental chambers. Then sent, at fifteen years of age, to a foreign country, not even sharing a language with the fifty-year-old man who had bought her.

That was twenty years ago. Caroline forced her fingers to unclench and gritted her teeth to hold back the shivers.

No one could ever send her back. She would never be a prisoner again to an alchemist, a government, or a man.

I survived. And I won, against all odds.

So why was she still afraid?

Charles straightened, breathless, after shoving the last heavy sofa against the wall. His brown hair had fallen into disarray. His eyes gleamed behind his spectacles.

"I've brought all my books—"

"No need," Caroline said. She smiled, and the gesture stretched her skin until she thought it might crack. "I have it all by heart."

"I don't know!" Peter repeated. He'd said that phrase so many times now that the hateful words sounded false even to himself.

"You don't know?" The voice hissed so close to Peter's ears that he felt the cold chill of breath through the hood. *So cold . . .* Wasn't breath supposed to be warm? Unless—

Don't imagine. Don't let yourself.

"How could you not know who told you to come to Vienna? Who hired you to pass him secrets?"

"His name . . ." Peter fought down the hysterical laughter that wanted to bubble up. *You're an actor. Just act!* But his mind wouldn't cooperate. It kept stubbornly flinging up images of horrors, of monstrous impossibilities, when it should be working to come up with a good story. *Pretend that it's a play . . .*

"I have a feeling that the rest of your company will be more helpful—and have better memories. Perhaps the leading lady—"

"No!" Peter said. He clenched his hands behind his back. *My mistake. My responsibility.*

He'd been the youngest theatrical director in Prague, even younger than Périgord had been when he'd started his own company. He'd been so proud of his abilities, his charm, his success in persuading so many mature and talented actors to leave more established sinecures, believing in his promises of security . . .

He'd been so determined to prove himself to his own old master, he'd never even thought to question whether he had a right to the other actors' trust, until now.

The most the others could hope for now was to make their own way back to Prague somehow, without money, patronage, or reputation, and even—he confronted the truth, even as his teeth began to chatter from sheer panic—without Peter himself. But if he could at least convince this creature that he, alone, had been the traitor—that no others in the company were at fault . . .

Peter drew a shivering breath, forcing his jaw to still. "He hired me in Prague," he said. "After one of our performances. He took me out to—to the Himmelsreich tavern. He offered me money, promised great rewards..."

"...If?" the voice prompted.

"If I would smuggle him into Vienna." Peter's swallow hurt his throat. "We arranged to meet the day my company left, as if by accident. He would come up with a story of mistaken identity, lost inheritance—"

"Romantic nonsense."

"Absolute nonsense," Peter agreed, numbly. *Only a fool*... But no. No time for self-torment now. Not in the middle of the second act. "My actors all believed it. I didn't take them into my confidence because I wanted to keep the money for myself."

The snort that sounded in his ears was almost a hiss. Peter shuddered, despite himself. "And then?"

"And then... when we arrived in Vienna, he disappeared. Without even giving me the money." Peter forced a tone of injured surprise. "I didn't know what to do."

"And you did not think to report it to the proper authorities?"

And end up here even faster? He would have had to be a fool indeed to take such a course. Peter almost laughed. Instead, he plowed onward. "I heard from him that night—only a note. He said, if I would meet him and bring any news..."

"News? News of what?"

Good question. Peter shut his eyes, hidden by the hood. He prayed, with true fervor, for the first time in years. Inspiration, cliché, anything...

"News of rebellion," the voice finished for him.

Peter's eyes shot open within the hood. "Pardon?"

"That's why you met with that girl. Aloysia Hoffman." The voice pronounced her name with sharp precision. "You wanted to use her contacts—collect leaflets. We know they're being printed somewhere. Fomenting dissent, rabble-rousing..." Each syllable shot out like a bullet made of ice.

"Perhaps," Peter said weakly. He licked his dry lips. "That is to say . . ."

A hand clamped down on his shoulder. "Confess and be done with it! Do you think your lies will be believed?"

I hope so.

For a moment, Peter remembered Michael's face—the good humor he'd seen in it, the genuine friendliness of the man. He'd seemed so damned likeable . . .

Easy enough to be friendly when he was using us for fools. And it didn't matter, anyway. Even if Michael had told nothing but the honest truth, Peter would still have no choice. Not anymore.

If he wanted the rest of the company to survive . . .

"Yes," Peter whispered, and gave up. "I confess."

CHAPTER THIRTEEN

Michael's chest ached. He hadn't released a breath since the French foreign minister had spoken.

It was too early. For God's sake, he'd only been back in Vienna for a day and a half. How could he have lost the game already?

Not too early. Too late, too late... The words drummed in his ears, as if spoken by a ghost. Or by the man who'd tried to rob him in the alley last night, as Michael had prepared for the masked ball with such purpose and confidence. Even then, it had already been too late, and he hadn't even known it.

When had he fallen from the grace of Fortune? Had it been over-confidence that toppled him? Or was he simply too old to run a gamble anymore? He was only thirty-eight...

Old enough. Old enough and experienced enough to know what a thin and fragile surface he had always skated upon. He'd found one true home in his life, but never again ... and that first home had lasted for only six years. Once his luck finally disappeared, there would be nothing left.

Destitution, desperation...

Michael forced down the panic, sweeping it out of his mind. It could hide in the locked back rooms of his soul, with the memories of fire and loss from his youth, and with everything else it did no good to remember anymore. He released his breath with a shudder, releasing his scattered thoughts with it. *Control.*

Monsieur le Baron de Talleyrand was watching him with a faint smile. He hadn't turned away, nor had he shouted out a cry for help. Clearly, he was not afraid of an attack ... but still, why hadn't he left, having delivered his damning judgment? Was it merely curiosity that held him? Or . . .

Or perhaps the game hadn't ended yet, after all.

Michael forced a rueful smile. "*Touché*," he said. "You have me at sword's point, Your Excellency."

"I'm glad you have the wit to recognize it." Talleyrand's mocking gaze did not waver. "But have you the stubbornness to continue?"

Michael raised his eyebrows. "That . . . would entirely depend on what was being offered."

"I rather thought so. Take my arm, Prince Kalishnikoff."

Talleyrand offered his arm, and Michael took it without allowing himself to hesitate.

He might have lost the first hand, but he was still in the game.

At least, for now.

Caroline blew out all but five candles. Charles watched her, wide-eyed, from his position at the center of the carpet. There was no sign of fear in his face.

Not yet.

Caroline set one candle above Charles, one to his left, and one to his right. He shifted, but only with impatience, as she finished forming the star pattern around him.

They'd had to tie her down for this every time. Even after years of imprisonment. Pergen had tsk'd over the necessity.

"Aren't you tired of your little rebellions yet?"

She never had been, though. They were all that she had had left. If she had ever sat still and let it happen without protest or even the feeblest attempt at escape, then none of her memories of warmth and love would have been enough to save her anymore. Without that stubborn ember of independence glowing inside her chest, she would no longer have been worthy of escape.

Caroline focused on it now as she set down the sixth candle. She imagined the ember of rage and pride glowing within her, a reminder of her true self. Imagined it glowing constant. No matter what she did . . .

She tasted bile. For a moment, she faltered.

Her father's voice spoke in her ear. *"Go now!"*

She would never know if it would have changed anything. If she hadn't disobeyed—hadn't run down the steps, against her father's warning and direct orders—Pergen might never have seen her. And if he had not . . .

Every other printer and pamphleteer of that era had been released years ago, freed after five or eight years in prison, at most. Their imprisonment had been an open record.

Only her father had not been released. Only her father remained hidden in one of the empire's scattered prisons, unnamed and unpardoned. How could they ever release him when his first act would be to search for his daughter? And if, by any trick of fate, he ever actually discovered the truth of her treatment—with a known history of publishing to the Viennese populace what their rulers did not want them to know . . .

Because of Caroline, they could never set him free.

My fault.

How could she fail him again, now, after all these years? Just when she was finally on the cusp of success?

Caroline circled the star figure, blowing out the candles one by one. She heard Charles's quick breath in the darkness. She clenched her fists until her nails bit into her own flesh, as she took up her position at the peak of the five-pointed star.

I will not abandon you, Father.

She spoke a single word, and all six candles burst into flame.

Charles's breath sucked in between his teeth. His face shone with excitement in the candlelight.

Caroline spoke and heard Pergen's words coming out of her mouth.

She'd heard them so many times that she'd memorized them despite herself. She'd dreamed them at night and woken up sobbing. Sometimes she still did, even now.

She spoke the stream of words that had sucked her childhood out from her.

Power surged through her body, cold and overwhelming as a flood.

Caroline doubled over at the shock of it, but her voice didn't stop. It couldn't. Syllables streamed out of her mouth, as sharp and clear as icicles. Her vision blurred as she fought to control the rush of energy, to keep herself upright and whole.

Then something else broke through.

The emperor of Austria pressed a secret panel, and the door to the interrogation room swung open.

He smelled rank sweat even before he stepped inside. Sweat and something less tangible . . . *Fear.*

Pleasure uncoiled through Francis's stomach as he walked into the room.

The man tied to the chair was hooded, but his head swung around with the jerky speed of panic as Francis closed the door. Francis walked softly across the room, balancing lightly to make minimal noise. He watched the man's head track him, cocked to listen to every sound.

I could make him scream before Pergen even touched him. Francis stepped down sharply with the heel of his boot and saw the man flinch at the sudden clatter. He held back a laugh but felt his chest relax as the day's tension flooded out of him.

Oh, yes, this had been the right decision. He'd spent enough evenings at balls and theater performances these past few weeks, always playing the gracious host, the canny—albeit secret—politician. It was time to set aside an evening for himself and his own amusement, for once.

No, not mere amusement—*nourishment.* Austria needed him more than ever now. The power structure of all Europe hovered in the balance, waiting to be decided at this Congress, and Francis—behind the shielding figure of Metternich—played a game so delicate it could shatter at any moment if he weren't canny enough to handle it.

If only his uncle could see him now . . .

"*Your Majesty*," Pergen mouthed silently. He bowed deeply, and Francis smiled.

Francis's uncle Joseph hadn't known the half of what his minister of secret police had to offer. Joseph had been too frightened to tackle true power, for all his bluster. Yet he'd held Francis up to public ridicule at court, calling him weak, ignorant, superficial . . .

Old rage seeped up as Francis recalled the countless humiliations he'd endured. But he had been the one to triumph in the end.

Joseph had been so proud of the secret police he'd helped establish, but he hadn't known any of their own secrets. Even Francis's own father, Leopold, in his brief year as emperor, hadn't learned the extent of Pergen's power. For God's sake, Leopold had been stupid enough to dismiss Pergen from his position altogether. He'd even abolished the secret police. If he hadn't died so soon afterward and left Francis to take his place . . .

Francis remembered the night he'd first found out what power the ex-minister of secret police truly held in his grasp.

He had been almost unimaginably young back then, only just crowned at twenty-five years old and overwhelmed by the responsibilities so suddenly thrust upon him. France and Austria were already at war; radical conspirators threatened the empire at every turn. At any moment, a second revolution could explode in Austria itself, and Francis and his brothers would be beheaded just as his aunt and uncle in France had been, half-naked, bound, and helpless against the mob's animal fury.

But that night . . .

He could barely remember what that first girl had even looked like anymore. It had been a girl, hadn't it? Some prostitute, perhaps— or, no, more likely, some inner-city radical's brat. Children were the easiest and best, particularly in their formative years, between eleven and fifteen . . . but he'd only learned that later, under Pergen's patient tutelage.

What Francis had seen for the first time that night was raw power, offered to him without reserve.

Power to be the man he'd always dreamed of becoming, despite all of his uncle's taunts and insults.

Power to protect his empire against the radicals who were always seeking to undermine it. *Undermine him.*

If it hadn't been for Pergen's tireless support through all those terrible years, Austria would have imitated France in its bloodthirsty revolutionary madness decades ago. Even now, Pergen's men reported new plots being hatched in the taverns almost every week.

But when every exposed plot brought Francis fresh nourishment . . . well, that was sweet justice indeed.

Francis remembered this morning's outrage, which had come so close to oversetting him. He nearly laughed at the memory—proof enough that he'd spent too long away from his true center.

Why should he care about some English slut's promiscuity? There were far more important things in life than women and their promises.

Francis could hear the prisoner's breath panting through his hood as Pergen lit the candles in their star formation around him. The sound made Francis's pulse quicken.

It was time.

"*Now*," Francis mouthed at Pergen, and closed his eyes to receive his fulfillment.

She'd never thought it would feel like this.

Power, cold and thrilling, rushed through Caroline's veins. She could have lifted great weights or run miles. Tingles raced across her skin, granting pleasure so intense it could hardly be borne.

But inside . . .

A hole broke open in her chest at her first words. Inside, rising to fill the gap, she felt another presence, as horrifyingly vivid as a nightmare but undeniably real. It rose within her, luxuriating in the transfer of energy, sharing each sensation with her.

She wanted to rip it out to rid herself of the horror. But she would have had to tear open her own skin to do so.

Terror mingled with overwhelming pleasure and choked out a sob around her chanting voice.

What monstrous being was this inside her? And how—how—?

Caroline's mind blurred into a meaningless whirl of incoherence. She couldn't think, could only feel her voice coming out without her will, the sensations roaring through her, and the *thing* within her soaking it all in.

In the back of her mind, a warning sounded.

So much power—too much power—*Charles* . . .

The thing within her shook off the warning.

The chant continued through Caroline's throat, unbroken.

The sky was completely dark now. Twilight had shifted into night as Michael's game shifted its terms around him. Pacing down the Mölker Bastei, Michael caught only shadowed glimpses of Talleyrand's sagging face in the light from the bright windows they passed. The aging politician's weight rested heavily on Michael's arm as his murmured French words streamed into Michael's ears, calmly and steadily telling his fortune.

"If you wish to continue your pretense, it could be arranged . . ." Monsieur de Talleyrand dropped his voice to a bare whisper as they turned a corner on the quiet street. "The Great Powers have no love of justice, for all the English ambassadors' pretense of righteous respectability. But their reputations have yet power over them, particularly with their own people in their home countries."

A group of men stepped out of one of the nearby houses, bound—from the lilt in their raised voices—for either a tavern or more raucous pleasures. Talleyrand nodded with distant civility as they passed and waited until they were a safe distance away before continuing.

"The English Whig journals will be quick to leap on Lords Castlereagh and Kelvinhaugh if they can be seen to promote theft and corruption abroad. Even the Russian nobles themselves are not enamored of their tsar's plans for a reunified Poland."

"No?" The sound of their twinned footsteps on the cobblestones—his own slowed to match the ambassador's gait—rattled an aural accompaniment to Michael's racing thoughts. "But the expanded power it would offer for the Russian empire—"

"Tsar Alexander wishes to impress his old tutor, La Harpe, and make Poland a model of representative democracy, freeing the serfs and granting powers which no Russian peasant may claim . . . and which his nobles will fight bitterly to keep their own underlings from ever gaining. Do you think the great men of Russia will thank their tsar for showing their own serfs such an example so close to home?" Talleyrand's dry voice carried a sting.

"I see," Michael said.

"I should hope so. Because if one man were to take the risk of becoming a lightning rod . . ."

Michael blinked. "I beg your pardon?"

"The Great Powers will never listen to me, or to any of the Continent's lesser powers, by choice. But if they were forced by the pressure of public opinion . . ."

"And how would that come about?"

Talleyrand's lips curved into a half-smile of anticipation. "If a man—a handsome figure of a man, I think, with charm and confidence—were to grant interviews to selected journalists . . ."

Michael took a breath. "I think perhaps you do not know Viennese journalists, Your Excellency. Provocative politics are not exactly—"

"I do not speak, now, of respectable journalists—at least not here, in Vienna. I am speaking of the pamphleteers."

"The illegal presses," Michael said flatly.

Fire, screams, the sound of smashing metal . . .

"Precisely. They are still available, I think you'll find . . . even if they run a significant risk of exposure. And, of course, there is also the English opposition press—they have some representatives here, although they lie low when their ambassadors are present. And the Russians . . ."

"The Great Powers will be furious. Any concessions you hope to gain—"

"Furious indeed," Talleyrand said, "but not with me. No, I shall step in to assuage, to condole with them, to help them soothe ruffled feathers of public opinion." He paused. "And yet . . . I should be grateful. And I believe they would find it difficult, under such pressure, to withhold compensation for Prince Kalishnikoff's famous losses."

Michael's voice came out as a near-growl. "Gratitude might come far too late if the Viennese secret police discovered what I was doing."

"If they discovered it only after the damage had been done, they could do nothing about it. Metternich and his satellites act under stage lights now, watched by all of Europe. They could hardly afford to expel the public's hero from the city."

"But if they discovered it too early . . ."

"Then I would be shocked and horrified, of course, like every other gentleman of principle." Talleyrand shrugged. "It is a risk you alone may choose."

They had completed the circle and arrived again in front of the Hôtel de Ligne. Faint light trickled out of the windows. Talleyrand smiled as he released Michael's arm. The deep, distorting wrinkles in his face further shadowed his expression as he stooped over his cane.

"Well, Prince Kalishnikoff? Shall we shake hands on it, or shall I make your excuses to our host? I am gentleman enough to wait until tomorrow morning before telling what I know to the police." Contempt dripped into his tone. "I'm sure you've developed your own ways over the years of making your way out of a city unseen."

"Indeed I have," Michael agreed tightly. *Hiding in a butcher's wagon . . .*

He'd fled Vienna once already, at the start of his adventures. He'd had time for that when he was fourteen. Time and energy to reinvent himself and start fresh with each new month or week. Michael was thirty-eight now, and he would never have a better chance.

If he wanted a real future and a chance of security in his old age then there was no choice at all.

And as long as he hadn't any good reason to be sensible . . .

A reckless grin twisted Michael's lips. Despite himself, he felt excitement rise, tingling, within him.

After all, when the chips came down and he faced the truth about himself . . .

When had he ever turned down a gamble?

"Why not?" he said, and put out his hand. "Your Excellency . . . Prince Kalishnikoff is at your service."

CHAPTER FOURTEEN

*E*nough.

Caroline bit her own tongue hard to cut off the stream of words.

Silence rushed into the room and swallowed her. She staggered, reaching out blindly for support. Inside her chest, the alien presence yowled protest, trying to force her teeth apart. She clapped one hand over her mouth and whirled dizzily across the room to the closest seat to collapse.

The presence folded and disappeared, leaving her chest to fill with panic.

And energy.

Caroline's vision cleared. Lowering her hand from her mouth, she took a deep, cleansing breath.

She felt ... strong. Strong and capable enough to climb to the top of the Kahlenberg Mountain outside Vienna or waltz all night long in the Great Hall of the Hofburg. She felt strong and also ...

Satiated. Caroline's mind filled in the missing word with bitter accuracy.

Oh God. This was what Pergen had felt each time he'd fed on her or spoken the words to feed his imperial master through himself ...

She was going to be sick.

Caroline stood up, ready to lunge for her bedroom and the chamber pot. Only a faint motion in the corner of her vision stopped her.

Charles. How could she have forgotten? Caroline swallowed hard to hold back the nausea and hurried across the room to where her secretary lay crumpled on the floor.

She blew the candles out around him, breaking the star figure open. "My poor Charles."

He lay facedown against the carpet, unmoving as she knelt beside him. She took his outflung left hand and pressed it between both of hers.

"Charles? Charles, can you hear me?"

He didn't speak. His fingers lay between hers, limp and still. Caroline felt for his pulse. If she had let it go too far . . .

Charles's pulse beat steadily against her fingertips.

Caroline sighed with relief. She sank down fully onto the ground, letting her skirts crumple around her.

"My poor boy. I did warn you what the effects would be, but you would insist, despite everything . . ."

She cut herself off, blinking, as she heard the asperity in her own voice. *Your sympathy is less than overwhelming, Karolina.*

But it was too painful to see him lying there as she had lain so many times. To feel the physical gain in herself that corresponded to his loss and to know it had been accomplished, of all idiocies, by her victim's own voluntary will, after his irresistible, unreasonable pressure.

After all the years she'd fought so hard to escape . . .

Closing her eyes, she took a deep, steadying breath.

For heaven's sake, of course Charles hadn't believed her when she'd warned him of the ritual's effects. He was an alchemist, a seeker after scientific wonders—he would have thought himself a weakling indeed to have been frightened off by a mere woman's stories. She, older and far more experienced, was the one who should have known better. She should have refused regardless of the consequences and thought of some alternate way to retain his loyalty.

Yet she'd been so focused on her own goal, so blind to the dangers he risked, and so flustered by Michael Steinhüller's unsettling presence and her own panic-infused childhood memories . . .

Squaring her shoulders, she reopened her eyes. *Time to face what I've done.*

Charles lifted his head slowly off the floor. His straight brown hair hung over his spectacles. His face looked soft and unformed.

"You're awake," Caroline said. She set down his hand, drawing back to a polite social distance. "Thank goodness. I'll bring you wine and food to restore you. Now that you've seen for yourself what a mistake this was—"

"No!" Charles said hoarsely. He swallowed and shut his eyes. "That—that wasn't a mistake, my lady. That was . . ." He drew a shivering breath.

"Charles, really," Caroline began—just as he looked up and met her eyes.

The avidity on her secretary's face shocked her into silence.

"Really," Charles whispered. "You must teach me how to do that."

"Untie him."

The words pierced Peter's haze. Moaning, he struggled back to full consciousness.

Rough hands brushed against his arms. The ropes around his wrists loosened and fell away. He thought: *I should run.*

The absurdity forced a hoarse laugh up through his throat, shaking his limp body. Run? He wouldn't be running anywhere. He couldn't even walk. Not after . . .

Convulsive shivering swept up through him, overwhelming the laughter. Peter's teeth chattered against each other. His arms tried to reach out to cross his jacketed chest for warmth, but they fell back helplessly against his sides, bereft of strength.

The shivers pushed his shoulders inward, tilted him forward in his chair. He was leaning—losing balance—falling . . .

He landed on the ground, slamming his cheek against the floor. Light flared behind his closed eyes. A gritty, cold surface pressed against his face through the thin hood. *Stone*, Peter thought. But he couldn't make himself care. The chattering of his teeth rattled his skull against the ground.

What use was a cunning escape plan now?

Footsteps walked toward him with slow deliberation. A pause, and then he felt the figure beside him kneel.

"Herr Riesenbeck," the voice said, with soft precision. "I hope you understand, now, what exactly your position is. Tomorrow I'm going to visit you again, to ask you more questions. We'll have to hope—for both our sakes—that your answers then will be more satisfying."

Peter didn't even try to speak.

Cold tears leaked out of the corners of his eyes as large, capable hands picked him up off the floor and carried him out of the room.

He wondered, for a moment, about the performance that must be going on without him, halfway across the city—the Riesenbeck troupe's triumphant debut in Vienna.

After all his months of dreams and preparation, he couldn't bring himself to care.

Michael saw the Prince de Ligne's eyes widen with quickly veiled surprise as he and Talleyrand walked in together to the prince's salon.

It was indeed small, as Talleyrand had warned, and the fire in the grate flickered so weakly as to barely warm the air. The furniture, gathered in a tight circle around the fire, was all sadly out of fashion—even to the point of decrepitude in a few glaring instances. But the people who sat on that furniture . . .

Michael saw a famous French poet, a Viennese playwright, and a Russian archduke all sitting together on one fraying couch. The Comte de La Garde-Chambonas sat beside a distinguished Polish general, while a noted Hungarian diplomat sat on one side of the Prince de Ligne himself, and—Michael's breath sucked in between his teeth at the shock of it—Austria's own Prince Metternich, the orchestrator of this entire Congress, sat on the other.

An excellent assortment indeed for his purposes.

The general conversation continued without a pause as De Ligne rose to greet his newest guests.

"Your Highness, how delightful—and Talleyrand, my old friend . . ." The prince smiled and crossed the room to take their hands. His gaze was searching. "It is a great pleasure to see you both, of course. But did I not see your carriage pull away some time ago?" he asked Talleyrand.

Talleyrand returned his smile. "Your eyesight is as keen as ever, my friend."

"I like to think so, certainly."

The French foreign minister raised his eyebrows in polite rebuke. "His Highness Prince Kalishnikoff was kind enough to accompany me on a stroll around your charming neighborhood. I'd spent too much of today in overheated salons and found that I wanted a bit of fresh air before I ate. Do you mind?"

"Well, you may be certain to find fresh air here, for my butler tells me two new leaks have opened in the roof only today." The prince laughed and turned to Michael. "I trust His Excellency has been a useful guide around the neighborhood? Not only to the buildings but to the schemes buzzing about the Viennese air? I've always thought he knew far more about—well, really, why limit myself to speaking only of Vienna? I'm sure our friend here knows more about everything, everywhere, than we any of us suspect." A warning note sounded in the prince's voice.

"Come now," Talleyrand said genially. "Why so wary, De Ligne? I've always been your friend, you know. Are you surprised that I've cultivated public caution? Only consider, I had to live under Bonaparte's daily suspicion for the last seven full years of his reign."

"Did he truly suspect you for seven years, when he'd known you so intimately for so long? How very curious." De Ligne shook his head. "I've suspected you far, far longer than that, my friend." For a moment, his voice sounded pure steel. Then his smile broadened, as he finished, "If you weren't so clever, after all, you'd be far less charming a companion. Come in, do, and admire our excellent fire. Picturesque, is it not? I always think a fire should look well, even if it has no effect beyond the aesthetic."

"What other effect could ever be preferable?" Talleyrand replied lightly.

With a nod, he slipped past his host to take a seat beside one of De Ligne's daughters. As he passed Metternich, the two ministers exchanged honeyed smiles.

Michael turned back to De Ligne and saw the older man's face alight with interest.

"Excellent," De Ligne murmured, beneath his breath. "Between you and Lady Wyndham, you are stirring up our little society, are you not? Ripples and more ripples ..." His eyes met Michael's with disconcertingly clear understanding. "I take it that my old friend Talleyrand will now treat you for the rest of the evening as a very casual new acquaintance, of no consequence to him whatsoever?"

"I ... can hardly speak for His Excellency, Your Highness."

"I understand." De Ligne grinned boyishly. "I believe I'd better introduce you next to our own distinguished foreign minister, don't you? I am finding this more and more diverting." He paused, though, even as he took the first step. "Was not Lady Wyndham coming with you, though? I thought, as you two are such old friends, you might well share a carriage—"

"Alas," Michael said, "she asked me to pass on her sincere regrets, but she had already formed a prior engagement."

"A pity. She has a sharp wit indeed—I would have liked to hear her use it on our company tonight."

"Mm," Michael murmured politely.

A twinge struck him, unexpectedly, at the thought. As he'd left the house, he'd witnessed Caroline's servants leaving as well. Preoccupied with his own concerns, when Michael had looked back through the carriage windows and seen the stream of exiting servants behind him, he'd noted the oddity without taking the time to think about it. All his wits had been marshaled in preparation for the evening ahead, practicing verbal maneuvers, parries, and defenses.

And yet ... now that he did come to think on it, it was more than odd. Caroline herself had not left the house before him, he was certain of that. Why send away her servants, then? Without a maid, no fashionable lady could prepare herself for an evening out. Without a butler, no visitors could even be ushered in. What appointment could she possibly fulfill?

She'd seemed so distressed—no, more than that, distraught—that afternoon on the stairwell. *"If you only knew what it had led to,"* she'd begun, and never explained herself.

If something were truly amiss, even now, and he had left her alone to face the consequences...

"Your Highness?" The Prince de Ligne was frowning at him, as he gestured for Michael to precede him to the circle of seats.

"Your pardon, sir. I fear I was woolgathering." Michael cut off his misgivings with an irritable snap.

If Caroline were in trouble—*if*—she could have told him. He had asked, after all. He'd done his best, and she had hardly welcomed his concern. If he went racing home now to confirm her safety, she would doubtless find some fresh insult in his action. Why should he feel such irrational childhood loyalty to her when she so clearly felt nothing for him anymore apart from the purest dislike?

And to consider abandoning this golden opportunity to trade jests and companionship with the men who held his future in his hands, only for some paltry qualm...

Guilt gnawed at Michael with the memory of her anguished voice. He banished it, like the rest of his past.

"Please," he said to the Prince de Ligne, and smiled. "Introduce me."

CHAPTER FIFTEEN

There were some mornings, Caroline reflected, when her bed—hers alone, singular and private, buried in thick coverings, with a warming pan at her feet and a fire in the wood stove across the room—seemed the only safe place in the world to be. Mornings when the thought of facing other people, shadowed by her memories of the night before, seemed more effort than she could bear.

Unfortunately, this particular morning she had an early appointment. Groaning, she forced herself up. By nine o'clock, equipped with her public armor of clothes, coiffeur, and careful cosmetics, she was as prepared as she could be for the day ahead . . . and already well into her second pot of strong English tea.

"God, God, God, Lady Wyndham! Why, oh why, did you hire a third-floor apartment?" The Prince de Ligne collapsed dramatically onto a chair as Caroline's butler closed the drawing room door behind him. The prince's blue eyes sparkled with pleasure even as he waved his hat before his face in exaggerated distress. "Have you no pity for a weak old man's bones?"

"I'll summon up pity if you'll show me in return a weak old man." Caroline eyed the prince's bright eyes and unlined face with a mixture of amusement and envy. "Your Highness, have you once had a proper night's sleep since this Congress began?"

"Sleep? What use would sleeping be when the fate of Europe is being decided all around us? Do use your wits, dear lady. Do you think I'd desire any rest at a time like this?"

"I suppose not," Caroline murmured. She restrained herself, with Herculean effort, from yawning.

The unnatural strength and energy that had flooded her the night before had taken their own toll in a buzzing alertness that had kept her awake until dawn . . . awake, wide-eyed, and full of sharpened wits to contemplate all the dire possibilities that might result from her mistake. Each time she'd forced herself to shut her eyes, though, and close her mind to the teaming worries that plagued her, something worse had taken their place.

The memory of another presence within her, using her—feeding through her . . .

Caroline quelled the sickening lurch of memory and forced herself to focus. It might well be the ungodly hour of nine in the morning— an hour most of Europe's aristocratic circle knew only through rumor, rather than by personal acquaintance—and she might have had fewer than three hours of sleep, but there was still no excuse to let her wits wander in company.

Not when she had such an opportunity before her.

"May I offer you refreshments, Your Highness?" she asked. "Or would you prefer to begin our journey without delay?"

"Let us say . . . with very little delay?" De Ligne cocked his head. "I think—ah, yes, I do hear footsteps in the distance."

"Your Highness?" Caroline straightened, frowning. "I don't understand."

"I've invited Prince Kalishnikoff to join us, my dear. We'll have to be a cozy group indeed to fit within my small carriage, but I knew you wouldn't object for such an old friend."

Caroline's jaw tightened, but her smile remained. "Indeed," she said, with brittle cheer. "How could I?"

"A charming fellow. He reminds me of myself, when I was younger." A reminiscent smile tugged at the prince's lips as footsteps sounded in the corridor outside. "Ah, to be that age again and full of wit and fire. When I recall some of my own exploits . . ."

"All of them shocking, I am sure."

"Why, Lady Wyndham." The smile turned into a smirk. "Could you doubt it?"

The drawing room door opened, and Michael stepped into the drawing room. "Your Highness! Lady Wyndham." He bowed sweepingly. "I told your butler I didn't require any announcement. And how do I find you both this morning?"

Michael, Caroline saw with disfavor, looked quite as lively as the prince himself, despite the fact that he hadn't returned to the building until the early hours of the morning. Caroline had had to expand her usual minimal touches of makeup in order to disguise the purple shadows beneath her eyes; Michael looked positively well rested and glowing with energy as he flung himself down onto the sofa beside her. She could actually feel his vibrant heat prickling against her skin through the air that separated them, irritating all her senses . . . and bringing them to tingling alertness.

She forced herself to ignore the sensation. "I trust you both enjoyed your evening last night?" she asked. "I did regret that I couldn't come."

"It was astonishing to witness. 'A school for conversation,' as Monsieur le Baron de Talleyrand rightly called it." Michael raised his hand in a mock salute to the prince. "I believe you took the honors, though, Your Highness. There was some close cross-and-jostle work near the end between a few of the French diplomats and that Prussian countess— oh, yes, and Prince Metternich made a good point or two—but they all retired with honors when you hit them with that final epigram. I was afraid Talleyrand might suffocate from laughing too hard."

"Prince Metternich," Caroline repeated faintly. "Did you share much conversation with him, Prince Kalishnikoff?"

"Why do you ask, my lady?" Michael's eyes widened in mock innocence. "Should I have passed on a personal message from you, perhaps?"

Caroline bit back a sharp retort as she recognized the mischief in his face. Curse him, he knew exactly what she was thinking.

The more he mingled with the head of Austrian foreign policy, the more likely he was to become the object of study by the Austrian secret police. And Caroline, as his publicly acknowledged old friend and landlady . . .

"Our friend here made quite an impression on the assembled

company," De Ligne said. "Although perhaps most strongly with the French side of the diplomatic contingent. I can hardly wait to find out exactly what you and my old friend Talleyrand were scheming about last night, Your Highness."

"Nor can I," Caroline said grimly. "Do tell me, when you can. I'm sure I would find it . . . intriguing, to say the least."

"I am at your service, of course," said Michael. He turned to her, his hazel eyes glinting. "Do feel free to join in my scheming any time."

Caroline stood up, shaking out her skirts with a twitch. "Shall we start out, gentlemen?"

"An excellent idea," Michael said affably. "May I escort you, my lady?"

As the prince walked ahead of them, winking roguishly at the maidservants and exchanging pleasantries with the butler, Michael drew Caroline's hand around his curved arm. He held her back slightly until the prince was a safe distance ahead, then breathed his words into her ear as they walked.

"I wouldn't tease you so often if you weren't so easily provoked, you know."

Caroline sighed pointedly. "What a comfort that is to know. Indeed, how kind you are to mention it, Prince Kalishnikoff."

"I certainly thought so, myself." He grinned as she glared at him. "You see? Easy."

His breath was warm against her cheek as he leaned over her, helping her with scrupulous care into her tight, red Spencer jacket. As she closed the first button of the jacket, she looked up and met his gaze, startlingly close. Close and . . .

Caroline stepped back. Irritatingly, she found herself breathing quickly.

Stupid. Stupid and beyond stupid.

But the expression that she'd surprised on his face, warm and intent . . .

"You needn't overplay your part," she whispered tightly. "I'm not a fool."

Michael stepped back, his expression closing against her. "Oddly enough, I never thought so." A muscle twitched in his jaw. "But I suppose you won't believe that, either."

He waited in rigid silence as she finished. Her hands trembled on the buttons.

It was only exhaustion that made her muscles weak. Made *her* weak.

For just a moment, though—before her wits had stepped in to save her . . .

Caroline lifted her chin and took his arm. The prince was waiting for them at the doorway, his expression alert and dangerously curious. Caroline fixed a smile on her face.

"I'm ready now," she lied.

It was a squeeze, as the prince had warned, particularly as the carriage had been crammed full of wrapped parcels. Caroline exercised all the control of posture that she'd learned in her first years of marriage to hold herself ramrod straight on the seat. Still, her arm brushed against Michael's at every bump in the road, and she found herself irrepressibly aware of his warmth radiating through the half inch that separated them. With every accidental touch, a disconcerting jolt of energy sparked against her skin.

What was it about him that set her nerves so on edge? She'd handled the emperor himself well enough, for all her fears. Compared to the threat presented by Emperor Francis and his minister of secret police, Michael Steinhüller, for all his dangerous knowledge of her past, was still only an exasperation. A cocky, far-too-sure-of-himself exasperation. And even his threats that first night . . .

She sighed, sliding a secret glance up at him. He was listening to the prince with a genuine smile on his lean face, his hazel eyes narrowing with amusement.

Under pressure, she had panicked, but now—too late—she could see the bluff for what it had been.

Michael couldn't turn her identity over to the police or to anyone else without giving up his own disguise . . . and it had been an empty threat from the very beginning. Truthfully, she didn't believe that he would ever give her secrets to her enemies only to hurt her. Provoking though he might be, she couldn't imagine any shred of real malice in him, even now.

No, the real and waiting danger lay not in any intentional betrayal but in Michael's own exposure. This mad game he was playing couldn't last forever, no matter what he thought. And once his masquerade was shattered . . .

She couldn't count on him, she knew that much. He had proven it all those years ago. She knew better than to believe a word of friend-ship or loyalty that came from his lips now, no matter how much some secret, long-buried part of her wanted to break free and rise to them—to believe that, for the first time in decades, she might not be truly alone anymore.

But Michael Steinhüller's friendship only went so far. The moment any true danger arose, he would fly away to safety without a single regret, exactly as he had the last time she had trusted him.

Still, sitting next to him now, listening to his laughing voice trading stories with the prince, and feeling his arm brush against hers with easy familiarity, she found herself as fidgety as a cat.

The carriage veered sharply to the left to avoid an erratic oncoming mail coach. Caroline lurched off-balance, into Michael's side.

"Careful." He helped her sit upright, his hand warm on her arm.

"Do forgive me." She smoothed down the striped skirts of her walking dress, biting her lip with irritation.

The prince sat across from them with his arm laid protectively across a large wrapped package.

"A special gift, Your Highness?" Caroline nodded at the package, glad for a distraction from her thoughts.

"I hope so." De Ligne's lips quirked. "The other parcels all come from my esteemed wife, not from myself. Lace collars, little knick-knacks . . . She feels a grandmotherly tenderness for the boy, I believe—or, at least, for the romantic idea of him. This gift alone I chose myself. I think you'll find that it's appropriate."

"Appropriate?" Caroline murmured. She eyed the bulky package speculatively as she considered the question.

What exactly would be an appropriate gift for the former king of Rome? The three-year-old boy to whom Napoleon Bonaparte had tried to pass on his empire through abdication, before the Allies—combined with his own betraying marshals—had forced him to abandon all hope and give over everything to the returning Bourbons... The boy who had gone from being a doted-upon king and the heir to an emperor to losing all of his titles, all of his potential... and all of his hope.

Caroline had heard that the original plan, as agreed with Bonaparte as a prime condition of his abdication, was for the young boy and his mother to join the former conqueror of Europe on Elba with all speed. Bonaparte had sailed in expectation not only of a generous fixed income—which Caroline doubted he would ever see—but of a speedy family reunion, too.

Now that Emperor Francis had regained control over his daughter and his politically provocative grandson, however...

The carriage drove between two great pillars, each topped by an avaricious double-headed eagle, the symbol of thrusting Habsburg power. As Schönbrunn Palace spread out in golden splendor before them, Caroline measured its capacity... as a prison.

Promises and signed contracts to the contrary, she couldn't imagine that Napoleon Bonaparte's son would ever be allowed to leave.

"And here we are at last." The Prince de Ligne lifted his walking stick in anticipation of stepping outside, even as the carriage wound its way through the busy assortment of carriages, hurrying servants, strolling courtiers, and guards who filled the great paved courtyard between the palace's outstretched golden wings. His keen gaze was already sweeping the crowd. "For all our much-vaunted technological advances, the journey from the city seems to me to grow ever longer, rather than shorter."

"A pity," Michael said. "It is grand indeed for a summer palace." He slid a glance at Caroline and lowered one eyelid fractionally. "It quite dwarfs my own family's small summer residence."

It was too much. "However can you say so, Prince Kalishnikoff," Caroline said sweetly, "when I remember it so very . . . fondly?"

Michael choked back a laugh, his eyes alight. "I think nostalgia may have clouded your memory, Lady Wyndham."

"Hardly," Caroline said. "My memories remain entirely clear."

They had, after all, lived in the same tiny apartment all year round.

Across from them, the prince blinked and refocused his sharp attention on them. "I'd thought you only visited England yourself, Prince Kalishnikoff, rather than ever having our charming Lady Wyndham as your guest?"

Damnation. Caroline hadn't thought to check with Michael on the history he'd invented for himself.

Well, it was his fault, not hers. Let him extricate himself from it. She turned to look at him in simulated surprise. "Did you not mention my own visit, Prince Kalishnikoff? I'm quite offended—it was such a highlight of my youth." She lifted her chin. "Perhaps it was not so memorable for you . . ."

"On the contrary. It remains one of my finest memories—I had only forgotten to mention it yesterday. I can't imagine how it slipped my mind." Michael turned back to the prince. "Lady Wyndham and her husband did visit my humble palace for a month's stay just before my country was invaded."

"Ah. So that would be . . ."

"My second husband," Caroline inserted. Her gloved fingers tightened around her skirts as bleak memory intruded into the game.

It had been childish and absurd to enter such a pretense only to score a point off Michael Steinhüller. He might treat everything as a game, but she should and did know better.

"Indeed," Michael seconded. "A charming fellow. I always wished I'd known him better."

"Mm," said Caroline.

Wyndham wouldn't even have condescended to nod in the street to a "damned Continental adventurer," as he would most certainly have termed Michael on first glance . . . and he would certainly never have allowed Caroline to maintain such a connection.

Her past—and her secrets—had been no part of their bargain.

The carriage drew to a halt, and Caroline turned with relief to the opening door. Waiting footmen laid out the carriage steps, and the Prince de Ligne gestured gallantly for her to walk out first.

The air felt chill and bracing, despite the crowd of chattering nobles emerging from their own conveyances, royal guards marching across the courtyard with glittering dress swords on full display, and busy servants bustling around all of them. Caroline drew a deep breath as she looked across the swarming activity to the palace whose wings enfolded them all.

Schönbrunn's three stories rose in golden grandeur before them, the large side wings bunching toward the great central building. Elegant half-pillars lined the façade in gilded cream stripes, alternating with arched windows against the deep gold walls. Stone spires rose in martial formations atop the roof of the main building; in the very center, above fanned-out swords and shields and the symbols of victory, a Habsburg double-headed eagle spread out its wings in conquest. Caroline felt her chest tighten in response, as if it would squeeze all breath and hope from her.

She had never seen Schönbrunn before, never been held captive here or anywhere else outside Vienna's city walls. But in its elegant architectural assumptions of dominion, it represented all of the smug, unthinking power that had imprisoned her and her father and cared nothing for their fates.

How could she hope to stand against it on her own?

"Lady Wyndham," Michael murmured. He stood beside her, his eyebrows drawing down with concern. "Are you unwell?"

"No, of course not." She rearranged her features to serene lines, drawing away from him. "I'm quite well, thank you."

And not quite alone, she corrected herself. She had been wise enough this time, at least, to hire a valuable ally, in the form of her secretary. Charles was loyal and—potentially—dangerous in his own right, just as she had hoped when she had chosen him.

And yet . . .

She remembered again the avidity in his voice and look the night before. The chill air swept through her thin, waist-length jacket, and she shivered.

Dangerous, yes, Charles could certainly be that. But—if she mishandled him by so much as a breath—dangerous to whom?

She knew better than to ply herself with false reassurances. Still, she was no green girl anymore, to be used and flung away without mercy. Caroline raised her eyes again to the cruel, curved beaks of the Habsburg eagle and set her jaw.

She, too, was a power to be reckoned with now. And she would not allow fear—or anything else—to hold her back.

"Aha." The Prince de Ligne pointed. "I do believe . . ."

Beyond the larger side wings, low arches formed open walkways on each side of the palace, leading to the lines of stables and servants' wings. Through one of the arches, a group of figures moved toward them—a small child flanked by a nursemaid and a tall, stooped man.

The prince strode forward, cutting through the crowd, and Caroline and Michael followed more slowly. Caroline bit back a reluctant smile as she saw the child's impatient attempt at a run cut off by his nursemaid's restraining hands.

"Too young for court manners," Michael murmured, in her ear.

"He's probably been at court since birth," Caroline replied, low-voiced. The sounds of the crowd effectively hid their conversation even from the prince, five feet ahead of them. "Poor boy."

"Fortunate boy, most would say, to be born into that kind of power and wealth."

"Not so much power anymore." Caroline lifted her skirts to step carefully over a pile of horse droppings. "And I wouldn't say fortunate at all to be born into such a life. To be observed on all sides at every moment, forced into strict observances, always held under a magnifying glass of scrutiny and judgment . . ."

"As you are now, you mean?" Michael cupped his hand under her arm to steer her away from a second pile. "You've become one of the great ladies of the English aristocracy. Don't tell me that was a mere accident."

She tensed in his grip. "That . . . is none of your concern."

"Come now," Michael whispered, as they halted, along with everyone else, to make way for the line of marching royal guards, boots clicking and swords shining in the sunlight. "Don't tell me you aren't enjoying any of this. An honored guest at all the great palaces—a wealthy widow, admired by everyone—don't tell me you wouldn't do it all again, in a heartbeat."

"If I could do it all again . . ." Caroline cut the words off with a snap as the last of the guards marched past, leaving the way clear to their destination.

They reached the end of the courtyard just as the Prince de Ligne sank down to one knee on a clean patch of pavement. The boy Caroline had glimpsed before, now revealed to have streaming gold curls and an adult's courtly uniform, twisted free from his nursemaid's grasp and raced across the pavement to land in the prince's outstretched arms.

"Your Highness!"

Napoleon Bonaparte II's chubby arms fastened around the prince's neck. A pang of bittersweet emotion nearly staggered Caroline as she observed their embrace.

To feel such pure trust—such innocent certainty of returned affection, even after so much abandonment and loss . . .

"A charming sight," said the boy's companion, stepping out from the shadowed archway. He bowed. "De Ligne, always an honor—and, of course, any guest of yours . . ."

Caroline's breath stopped in her throat.

Nausea raced sickeningly up her chest as the muscles in her legs gave way. If it hadn't been for Michael's hand on her arm, she would have fallen.

Count Pergen straightened from his bow and smiled directly at her.

CHAPTER SIXTEEN

Michael flinched as Caroline staggered against him. He found himself supporting all her weight in his hand. Only for a moment; by the time the elderly man before them had straightened from his bow, Caroline had recovered herself, her expression cold and distant. Michael kept his own expression affable and open, but his mind flicked into sudden, buzzing alertness.

"Count Pergen," said the Prince de Ligne. He still knelt on the pavement nearby, holding the former king of Rome on his knee. "May I have the pleasure of introducing two new friends? Lady Wyndham, of England, and His Highness Prince Kalishnikoff, of Kernova-as-was."

Count Pergen. Good God. Michael blinked and refocused on the man before them.

It was the devil of his childhood made flesh. Emperor Joseph's hated minister of secret police, reviled by every pamphleteer and printer . . . every one of them, that was, who hadn't already been arrested, beaten, and imprisoned by his men.

It was Pergen who had convinced the Enlightened emperor, Joseph II, to change his reforming laws, retract all his promises, and take away the freedom of the press less than a decade after it had been introduced to Austria for the first time in history.

Michael had never imagined that he would actually meet the devil . . . nor that Caroline would recognize him, when he did.

Pergen bowed over Caroline's hand, smiling thinly. "Lady Wyndham. I've heard much about you already, from the most varied sources."

"I thank you, sir." Her voice sounded chillier than Michael had ever heard it.

He wondered whether she knew that she was leaning into him.

"And Prince . . . Kalishnikoff?" Pergen's eyes narrowed as he turned to Michael. "I am, of course, honored to meet you."

"As am I. It is a great pleasure, sir." Michael smiled widely as he clasped the man's hand. "My late father was always full of praise for your methods."

He met Pergen's gaze and felt his own smile falter in shock.

There was something dreadfully wrong with Pergen's eyes. At first, Michael couldn't place what it was. They were sunken, truly, into the bone, but more than that, there was something wrong—something unnatural . . .

"And I hope you agreed with your father?" Pergen asked, raising his thin eyebrows. His hand felt cold as ice in Michael's grasp.

"Oh, I was never foolish enough to disagree with my father," said Michael. "That would have been terribly impolitic."

There. He had placed it.

There was no color around the pupils of Pergen's eyes. The irises were a solid black. And more than that, when Michael looked closely—as closely as he could, while still maintaining discretion—the lines in Pergen's eyes, which should have formed a faint tracery of red . . . those, too, were black. Even the whites of his eyes were faintly smudged.

It was as if the man were leaking darkness.

Michael felt an involuntary shiver sweep through him. He released Pergen's hand before the other man could sense it.

Too late. "Cold, Your Highness?"

"The chill in the air." Michael shrugged, forcing a laugh. "I fear I spent too many years in the East during my exile from my homeland. I've grown accustomed to warmth year-round."

Pergen's eyes narrowed. "So you spent those years in Turkey?"

"Among other pleasant spots." Michael held his fixed smile with an effort. How widely spread was Pergen's network by now? Could it really stretch so far as the Ottoman Empire to research Michael's history? Surely not within the next month or so . . . or could it? He revised his imaginary history rapidly as he spoke. "And Persia, of course, for a year or two. I spent a few months in India, too, five years ago, but I didn't find it suited me."

"No? Many of Lady Wyndham's compatriots have been making great fortunes there."

"On the sweat of near slave labor," Caroline said coolly. "It is hardly an achievement to boast about."

"Indeed. And your own late husband's fortune . . ."

She tightened her lips. "Is no longer invested there, you'll find."

"How delightful to meet a woman of principle."

There was an undertone to Pergen's last word that Michael caught, though he could not interpret it. Whatever it was, it made color flare in Caroline's cheeks.

Michael pressed her elbow lightly, still smiling. Whatever her game might be, it could do neither of them any good to offend Emperor Francis's retired spymaster.

The former king of Rome's high, childish voice broke into the tense air as he jumped out of the Prince de Ligne's arms, his face alight with excitement.

"You have? Truly? Where are they?"

"Ah," Michael murmured, and turned with relief to the distraction. "I believe we have come to the matter of gifts."

He drew back, pulling Caroline with him, as the Prince de Ligne summoned his footmen to bring the wrapped packages that had accompanied them on the drive. The boy viewed and discarded the gifts of clothing with disdain, then seized upon the largest package.

"This one?" he asked.

"That one," De Ligne agreed. He stood, brushing off his breeches, and watched with indulgent interest as the boy tore open the wrapping.

"Ohhh . . ."

Michael blinked with controlled surprise, even as the child let out a sigh of wonder.

The "appropriate" gift was a highly detailed set of wooden soldiers, carved in wondrous detail.

"A squadron of Uhlans from Flanders, my homeland. They'll move in whichever direction you choose," De Ligne said. "Only set them on their wooden platform—you see?—and pull the lever, and they'll march to your command."

"They're *perfect*," the little boy breathed. "Oh, thank you, Your Highness! Thank you so much!"

"Perfect," Michael echoed softly. He watched Napoleon Bonaparte's son gaze down in open-mouthed delight at his miniature army, and he shook his head ruefully.

Perhaps blood did tell, after all.

"Why don't you set them up in your rooms," the prince suggested, "and I'll join you there shortly to help you lead them in maneuvers."

"Oh, yes! I certainly will." The boy gathered up the package and ran at full tilt toward the closest palace door, followed by his sighing nursemaid.

Pergen regarded the prince with his head slightly tilted, like a snake judging whether to attack. "An interesting choice of gift, Your Highness."

"Do you think so?" A faint sneer lifted de Ligne's upper lip. "Myself, I thought it was traditional for every boy of rank to play at soldiers. Has he no other such toys to occupy him?"

"A few gifted by his own close relations, yes. And yet . . ."

"Then I see nothing in it to distress you." De Ligne turned away, frowning. "Is his mother here today? I have a message or two to pass on to her as well."

"The Archduchess Marie Louise has left for a tour of Switzerland," Count Pergen said.

"Another? Good God, I thought she'd only returned from some such adventure."

"Mm. The emperor has appointed her a new equerry, Count von Neipperg."

"Ah. The very dashing Count von Neipperg." The prince's expression was difficult to read. "I understand. There's been no more talk of joining her husband on Elba then, I take it?"

"The archduchess is quite content, now, to remain in her father's palace, with . . . journeys of pleasure to while away the time."

"I see. Well." De Ligne wiped his hands against his trousers, as if wiping away a stench. "It's all for the best, I suppose."

The corners of Pergen's lips lifted in a small, satisfied smile. "The emperor is certain of it."

"Quite. Well then . . ." The prince took a breath. "I'd best be off to help the boy with his maneuvers as I promised."

"I'll watch, if I may," Pergen said smoothly. "I am certain I will find it fascinating."

"My friends?" De Ligne looked past him at Caroline and Michael.

Michael glanced sidelong at Caroline's cold, set face. "I think not. If you'll excuse me, Your Highness, I've spent too long sitting in a closed carriage. Will you join me, Lady Wyndham, for a stroll around the parkland?"

"Yes." Caroline's voice sounded half frozen; she turned like an automaton under his guiding hand. "Yes, I think that would be best."

It wasn't until they were far from the palace, strolling through rows of tall, protective hedges, past grand circles of flowerbeds and fountains, that she spoke to him again.

"I . . . thank you." The words sounded constricted, as if she'd had to force them from her throat.

"It was nothing." Michael shrugged, watching the tall hedges around them.

There were no gardeners foolish enough to be caught working at this time. The emperor himself might choose not to reside in Schönbrunn during the winter months, but royal etiquette demanded that the gardens appear at all times to be a work of nature rather than effort. The squadron of gardeners would have to do their work when there was no chance of being stumbled upon by casual visitors or their own imperial masters.

Still, Michael kept a wary eye on the hedges and the pathways beyond . . . just in case. He didn't think the emperor would bother to set spies in his own gardens, but then, he hadn't expected to meet with the former minister of secret police here, either.

"An odd companion for a small boy," he mused aloud, low-voiced. "I wouldn't have thought there would be any danger around the lad where he is, hidden out here with only a few selected visitors allowed to see him."

"The more Count Pergen notices him, the more danger he'll be in," Caroline said flatly. "And God help him if Pergen decides he poses a real threat."

Michael glanced down at her and received his second shock of the morning. Her expression was more open than he had seen it since his arrival in Vienna . . . and she was terrified.

"You speak as if you knew him personally," he said.

She bit her lip and looked away. "Everyone knows of him."

"But you recognized him before he was introduced—and he didn't recognize you."

She shrugged and started to pull away. Michael held her back.

"Tell me," he said. "Tell me how you know him. And how he failed to recognize you in return . . . *oh*."

Realization clicked into place with the force of a closing lock. His hand loosened on her arm.

"You knew him as a child, after everything went wrong," Michael said. "Didn't you? That's why he doesn't recognize you now."

"You know nothing about it." Caroline's breath came quickly, in short pants. "What were *you* doing in the years after they came for us? Where were you?"

"The truth?" Michael shrugged. "I was traveling around Bohemia, learning how to live. I worked for an actor's troupe in Pressburg for three years—I started out as the lowliest assistant, but I moved up to take on principal roles for a time." His lips curved in reminiscence. "I learned how to disguise myself, how to take on a new character, a new face . . . For a year or two I fell in with Count Cagliostro himself on his Eastern tours, and then I joined another, less famous pseudo-alchemist—a complete fraud, like all the rest of them, but he was a fine teacher, and it was entertaining enough to pretend at magic, so . . ."

He stopped, shocked at the change in her face. "What's wrong? What did I say?"

"*Entertaining?* To pretend at magic?" Caroline was spitting her words, now, though her voice never rose above a whisper. "If you knew what I was going through while you were playing at adventures a hundred miles away, never even caring what you left behind—"

"Tell me, then! Tell me, or stop blaming me for not knowing." Michael stared at her, his mind working furiously. "You were ... you said you didn't go to an orphanage. When the police burned down the shop and took your father away—"

She turned her head sharply away, clamping her lips together. Still, he thought he heard a muffled sob escape.

"Oh God," he whispered. "They took you, too, didn't they? That's how you recognized Pergen." He stepped back, his head whirling. "But why? Why would they bother to imprison a child?"

"They didn't," she said. Her voice was a bare thread of sound. "Not in the official prisons. Not in the ones that we all knew about."

"Caroline," Michael drew a deep breath. "Karolina ... Tell me what happened to you. Why you're here. I'll help you."

She laughed. It sounded like breaking glass. "Fine words," she said. "How much trust can I put in them?"

"You can trust me with all your heart," he said. "I swear it."

He realized, with a shock, that it was the truth.

For a moment, everything around him seemed to freeze as if caught in a pane of painted glass, all the colors vividly highlighted in the glow of sunlight.

Caroline's dark, anguished eyes against her pale skin—her shining black hair clustering in loose curls around the clean, strong lines of her face, her hands clenched with anger or fear ...

Something twisted in Michael's chest, a mixture of pain and promise.

"You're only playing a part," Caroline whispered. "That's why you came back here."

"You're right." Michael's voice sounded hoarse in his own ears. "I thought, when I first found you again, that it was a great stroke of luck for my plan." He winced as he admitted it. "I truly was glad to see you alive and well," he added hastily, "but still . . ."

He drew a long, painful breath. "I would have used your friend-ship and left without ever thinking twice," he confessed. "I thought that was only the way of life. It's been the only way I've known for a very long time now." He stepped forward, holding her gaze. "But I won't this time. I swear it. Please, let me help."

Her eyes swept over his face like searching light. She opened her mouth to speak.

"There you are!" The Prince de Ligne's voice called out behind them. "Lovely parkland, is it not?" He waved his cane gaily as he entered the square garden behind them. "Nothing stirs the heart quite like a garden, does it? I could walk out here for hours and never grow tired."

"Never," Michael repeated.

Caroline's face closed itself before him, like shutters slamming shut. The light within, as quickly as it had been revealed, was locked away again.

Any man experienced in gambling could tell when his timing had run out.

Peter pulled himself up to a sitting position against the rough stone wall of his cell. He was still shivering, even after hours of sleep; he felt as if he might never grow warm again.

Think, he told himself. *Focus*. It was . . . who knew what time it was, in this tiny, windowless room? He could barely see his own hands or the chamber pot that sat in the far corner. The time could be anywhere between dawn and sundown, for all that he could tell.

Last night, the guards had carried him down a long set of stairs, through three sets of heavy, locked doors, to a row of underground rooms. Escape would have been laughable, even if he hadn't been limp and shaking with sick exhaustion.

But even if he couldn't escape, he could still think and plan. And with a night's sleep behind him—albeit a night of restless nightmares, interrupted over and over again by his own shivers—Peter was no longer prepared to lie back and wait passively for last night's torture to be repeated.

As it would be, he had no doubt, unless . . . unless . . .

Peter knotted his shivering fingers around each other, fighting the cold, the discomfort, the shadows in the darkness . . . the terror.

He had written dialogue, scenes, even entire plays off the cuff for the company on occasion. He had talked thirteen independent, egocentric, rebellious individuals into joining his acting troupe and taking his direction. He had found a way to bring them all to Vienna, despite every obstacle of finance and practicality.

He could come up with a plan to save himself now.

Hours passed. Peter paced the small square room in the darkness, his shoes making no sound against the thick stone floor. He heard nothing from upstairs, nor from the other rooms nearby. Were they empty? Or full of waiting, frightened prisoners like himself?

There was no use wondering about that. It was a waste of his time. He had to focus.

It all came down to Michael, that first day. Michael, who was, it seemed, an enemy of the state—one of those dangerous, wild radicals Peter had heard of when he was a child. Astonishing that he would have dared come back to Vienna to be recognized after all the famous purges and imprisonments of twenty years ago.

Unless . . .

Peter stopped pacing. His teeth chattered together, but he ignored them.

What his torturer had said, when Peter thought back carefully . . . did it necessarily imply that Grünemann had recognized Michael himself? Or had it been the mere fact of Michael's illicit entry into the city that had judged him suspect and dangerous in their eyes? His illicit entry . . . in combination, of course, with Peter's own mad, reckless impulse to help that girl, the pamphleteer.

Grünemann had only seen Michael from a distance and through a crowd of people. All he would have been able to pick out would have been the basics of hair color, dress, and posture—and a wig and a bit of theatrical training could have accounted for all of those external features. So . . . if they didn't know yet exactly who Michael was . . . if they hadn't actually managed to bring him in—because, perhaps, they hadn't been able to recognize him in whatever new disguise he wore . . .

It was a perilously thin thread of hope to hang his life upon. But it was the only one that Peter could find.

Two days earlier, he would never have imagined himself capable of it . . . but two days earlier, he had been a different man. Now, all he could feel, when he looked for guilt, was the sickening, stomach-churning fear of further pain. No hero, Peter Riesenbeck, when he came off the stage.

Self-knowledge was a bitter pill, but it did not—could not—negate hard truth: he could not endure last night's torture again.

The door finally cracked open, hours later, long after Peter had finally subsided, shivering, into a corner, wrapping his arms around each other to conserve heat. At the first sound of a key turning in the lock, he leaped to his feet.

The quick movement made his head spin. His legs gave way. He caught himself on the stone wall and pushed himself forward, regardless. It might be his only chance.

Two men stepped inside, big, broad-shouldered, and uniformed. The first man held a platter with a bowl of food and a clay pitcher, revealed by the glow of the torch in the other man's hand.

"Please!" Peter said. He hurried forward, propping himself against the wall at every step. His teeth were chattering as he spoke, but he pressed on. "Tell your master, I have a message—"

The second man backhanded him with casual ease. Peter tipped over like a falling tree, his head slamming against the stone ground, his legs sprawling awkwardly before him. The men moved around him, taking the chamber pot, setting down the food.

Peter rolled over, gritting his teeth. He pushed himself back up.

The back of his head burned with a cold fire. He wondered, distantly, if it was bleeding.

He didn't care.

"Tell your master," he gasped. "I have a vital message."

The first man let out a snort of a laugh. The other didn't bother to respond.

They walked through the door. Peter flung himself across the cold floor.

"I can find him!" Peter said. "Tell your master. Please!" As they turned to close the door, he threw every ounce of passionate sincerity into his words: "I can find the man he's looking for!"

CHAPTER SEVENTEEN

Charles was waiting in Caroline's drawing room when she returned to her apartment.

Resignation sank through her as she stepped into the doorway and saw him propped on the sofa with high, unhealthy spots of color in his cheeks. Only the greatest determination could have driven him today, to raise him out of his bed so soon after being drained of energy and spirit.

She turned to Michael, who stood close behind her in the corridor. The Prince de Ligne had dropped them off on his way to the next round of engagements, luncheons, and drawing-room rendezvous. They hadn't spoken on the trip up the long, curving stairs, but she could feel his anticipation thickening the air as he waited for the moment when it would be safe to speak privately again.

"Have you planned a busy afternoon?" she asked now, with careful nonchalance. "If you wish to drive out to the Prater, you may take my chaise, of course. I shall be occupied with my own engagements."

"Caroline," he began.

"Prince Kalishnikoff." She stepped aside, so that he could see into the occupied room.

His eyebrows rose. "Mr. . . . Weston, is it not? Are you ill?"

Charles's eyes blazed in his drawn face. "Not too ill to serve Lady Wyndham." He paused, with a distinct sneer, before adding the words, "Your Highness."

Michael's breath hissed in through his teeth.

Caroline drew a deep breath and closed her eyes for a brief, illicit moment of respite from the simmering atmosphere around her.

If she could order the world, just now, both of the men in her drawing room would simply disappear. There would be no questions from Michael that she should not—could not—answer; no demands from Charles that she couldn't bring herself to fulfill. She fought the impulse to flee to her bedroom and lock herself in for the rest of the afternoon.

But she was an adult, and there were hours yet to go before she could escape from the world's view.

"Your Highness," she said smoothly to Michael. "Perhaps I'll see you again tonight." She kept a discreet eye on Charles and saw his flush deepen as she added to Michael, "Will you join me at the tableaux at the Hofburg Palace?"

Safely surrounded by people, she meant, and he knew it, from the expression on his face.

Michael nodded, his own voice hardening. "Your orders are exquisitely phrased, Lady Wyndham . . . as always. I won't importune you any further."

He bowed and left the drawing room, his posture stiff. Listening to his quick steps retreating, Caroline felt a sudden, unexpected pang of . . . what?

Had she actually wanted him to persuade her into telling him the truth?

Nonsense. She forced the unwelcome emotions away and turned back to Charles with a smile.

"How are you feeling? Poor boy, you must be very weak. Shall I call for refreshments?"

"No. Thank you. Lady Wyndham—"

"My dear Charles." She sat down on the seat across from him, hoping that he would take the hint of the still-open door. "Say what you like, but you look quite shattered. You really ought to return to bed for the rest of the day—your duties can surely wait for another time."

"They could, perhaps. But I—excuse me a moment."

He stood and crossed the room, breathing heavily, his face paling with every step. Caroline watched as he closed the door solidly.

"There." He walked back to her, with a tentative smile. "I believe we can speak safely now."

"You think of everything." She bit back a sigh. It was weakness, truly, to have hoped for anything else. But seeing Pergen again, face-to-face, that morning—hearing his voice, seeing the shadows in his eyes . . .

"Tell me," Caroline said abruptly, surprising herself. "What are the effects on a man of doing alchemy?"

"Effects?" Charles blinked at her from behind his spectacles as he sank down on the sofa. "Well, there are rumors, certainly, of length-ened life, extended vigor—are you referring to the old story of the phi-losopher's stone? I hardly—"

"I don't mean the quest for eternal life—at least, I don't think I do." Caroline twined her fingers around each other, holding onto a sem-blance of calm. "I mean . . ." She took a breath. "I knew a man, years ago, who taught me what I know of alchemy. What I showed you last night. He was taught himself, at first, by another. A creature . . ."

She moistened her lips, remembering. *Do not show fear.* Not in front of Charles. Not in front of anyone. She made her voice as cool as if she were discussing the latest fashions. "It looked like a man," she said. "And it spoke with—nearly—a man's voice. But it moved within a column of dark, twisting shadow."

"An elemental, then?" Charles frowned. "It doesn't quite match the descriptions I've read, but—"

"I don't know!" Caroline heard the vehemence in her own voice and steadied herself. "That is, I used to think it must be something of the sort. But of late, I've begun to wonder . . . You see, I've met that man again—my earlier teacher." She tasted bitterness with the words.

"Really!" He straightened, his eyes widening. "But this is mar-velous. If he is willing to aid us—"

"I think not." Caroline restrained a hysterical laugh. "No, there's no use hoping for anything of the sort. But my point is . . . when I saw him again, he had changed."

"How so?" Charles subsided back onto the couch.

"He . . . leaked darkness. There is no other way of saying it. There was something unearthly, even, in the touch of his skin. And it made me wonder whether his own early teacher could have been a man himself, once. A man who had changed."

"Transmuted himself," Charles breathed. "I've heard such tales but always dismissed them. If such a thing were possible . . ."

"It could hardly be desired," Caroline said sharply. "The monstrous nature of his teacher—"

Charles spoke over her, for the first time since she had hired him. "This would have been at the end of the last century? Or just before?"

"I—yes. In the last decade of the past century."

"There were two or three alchemists who disappeared, then. Everyone assumed they'd all died, or else gone into hiding, but never . . ." Charles shook his head wonderingly. "This man of shadows—did he move as a man? Was he constrained by matter? Or—"

"He appeared or disappeared as he would," Caroline said reluctantly. "He did not seem to require doors."

"Astounding." Charles's gaze turned inward. "If you only knew how it had come about . . ."

Caroline took a steadying breath. "So you have no explanation for it?"

"I hadn't even known it to be possible until now. But I suppose . . ." He leaned forward, gesturing to illustrate his points. "In any act of alchemy—whether mystical or mineralogical—we attempt to pull aside the veil that separates our material world from the world of the aetherial. To reach through it—whether by mystical means, as you did last night, or by formulas and powders. To catch a glimpse of the other side—to feel its power coursing through you—"

Caroline gazed at her secretary's enraptured face and felt a shiver of cold misgiving. *To catch a glimpse of the other side . . .*

But what if something from the other side looks back at you?

A chill crept through her chest as she remembered.

That feeling—no, that *knowledge*, inescapable and precise—of something Other flexing itself inside her—looking out through her own eyes, absorbing her own most intimate sensations—

Something that had slipped through the gap that her words had opened in the veil. Was it by an unexpected, unusual mischance, just this once? Or—was it by exchange? Perhaps it was only by summoning just such a monstrous possession that any man or woman could make use of the unearthly powers that Pergen had harnessed, and that Caroline had experienced last night.

If so . . . how much of that creature's essence was left behind in its host each time? And how much of one's own essence might be lost to it?

Caroline opened her mouth to release the question.

The radiant expression on her secretary's face stopped her words in her mouth. She looked down at her own linked hands, breathing deeply.

It had only been once that she had touched the darkness. Surely no harm could come of that.

"If only you could ask your old teacher for further details," Charles said. "To have so much power so close by—so nearly within our grasp—"

"It's out of the question, I'm afraid."

"Well then . . . Will you excuse me, Lady Wyndham?" Charles pulled himself to his feet as he spoke, using the arm of the sofa for support. "I should like to begin my research immediately. All my books are hidden in my room, so . . ."

"Of course." Caroline stretched her lips into a smile. "Do take time to rest, though, too. I am sure you are in need of it."

"Rest? When such miracles are possible?" Charles flashed a sudden smile of surpassing sweetness. The light from the windows sparkled on his spectacles. "I do thank you for your consideration—but I wouldn't dream of it!"

"Of course," Caroline repeated softly.

She watched him limp across the floor and out the room.

She had touched the darkness only once . . .

But the damage, it seemed, had already been done.

Michael stalked outside onto the Dorotheergasse and slammed the front door of the building closed behind him. He had to take a deep breath before he could start moving again.

Damn the brilliant, goodhearted old Prince de Ligne for interrupting Michael's first honest conversation with Caroline in twenty-four years. Damn that smug bastard Weston, who'd gloried in watching Caroline dismiss Michael as efficiently as any unwanted servant. Damn himself, most of all, for caring and letting her see it.

He hadn't let himself be vulnerable to anyone, man or woman, for over two decades. What was the matter with him now?

Michael released his held breath with a shudder and woke for the first time to the environment around him. Cold air tingled against his face, carrying with it all the smells of the inner city—cooking meat from a nearby apartment window, horse muck and sewage from the cobblestones before him, roasting coffee from the Kaffeehaus next door . . . and, above all, the unmistakable scent of crowds of humanity pressed tightly together.

Michael breathed it all in as he stepped back against the pink outer wall of the building, making room for a group of Russian visitors to pass. The closest woman's parasol brushed against his cheek as their rolling voices swept across and past him. Bright yellow, pink, and blue townhouses pressed plastered shoulders against each other across the street, while carriages rattled noisily past in both directions. Coachmen shouted inventive insults at their counterparts, and the occupants of the carriages yawned and gazed out the windows with fashionable ennui.

Michael felt his shoulders relax as he took it all in: the essence of city life, generic and universal, sweeping around him, even as the uniquely Viennese mixture of accents and smells carried with it the unmistakable message of *home*. It was in cities like this one that he had made his way all his life, throwing himself wholeheartedly into the rushing flood of the crowds, taking on different names and personalities as each day—or moment—called for.

It was in this particular city, until that terrible night twenty-four years ago, that he had learned what it was to be alive and breathing in tune with a quarter of a million other citizens, all jostling against each other in one compressed space.

This was all that truly mattered, when it came down to the essentials: to be alive and playing the game in the heart of a vibrant city . . .

No matter what *anyone* might say to the contrary.

Michael shoved aside the frustration that had driven him out of the building, and—with more effort—the memory of that morning. Those memories belonged to Michael Steinhüller.

He stepped out into the flow of the crowd and became Prince Stefan Kalishnikoff once more.

And what would Prince Kalishnikoff choose to do next, on a beautiful, bright, cold October afternoon?

A man of fashion in Vienna could occupy his time in many ways. He might ride out in the Prater, on horse or in a stylish phaeton, or stroll along one of the park's broad avenues, tipping his hat to old and new acquaintances. He might choose to pay social calls or—like a true Viennese—spend the afternoon flipping through newspapers in his favorite Kaffeehaus.

Or . . .

Michael's steps slowed as he remembered the previous night's conversation.

If he wanted to progress the game, he knew what his next move would have to be: to find the radical pamphleteers of the present day, hidden from the ever-watchful Viennese secret police.

Fire, screaming, the sound of smashing metal . . .

He would not be intimidated by his past. He was Prince Kalishnikoff now, not a frightened boy, and he was in his element.

Michael turned his steps to aim himself toward the ninth district. If he could find pamphlets anywhere, he'd swear it would be in the university district. And so long as the police didn't spot him making his inquiries . . .

He told himself that he wasn't afraid. After all, what was there for Prince Kalishnikoff to fear? At worst, a visiting royal could only face banishment from the city, escorted by determined guards. Nothing worse than that could happen. There was no reason to be afraid.

After more than two decades of disguises and deceptions, Michael almost managed to make himself believe it.

It was even easier than he'd expected.

The student wine taverns hadn't changed since Michael was a boy. They were still dark and full of smoke, and the wine they sold was atrocious. Michael bought a jug of white wine anyway and headed for the furthest tables, toward the foulest back corner, where the rats scuttled around the students as they argued. Smiling amiably, his expression abstracted, Michael listened to every conversation he passed as he navigated a path through the crowded tables.

It would be madness, of course, to debate politics, even here . . . but university students as a species, if not precisely mad, were more than reckless. They were, after all—barring a few charity cases—by and large the sons of Austria's highest families, and some of them as young as seventeen years old. Who among them could truly believe in the reality of danger until it seized them by the throat?

The tavern he'd chosen was located underground, in a stone cellar beneath a Turkish restaurant and a thriving bookshop. Guttering candles lit the impassioned young faces that clustered along the rows of benches. The students' gestures, in furious debate, made their dark robes flap like the wings of crows. Michael walked more slowly, to catch the details as he walked.

The first table was useless to him, engaged in a hot debate on the works of Immanuel Kant. Most of the group declared him the greatest philosopher in the German language; a single brave student laughed them all down in favor of the newest lectures by Professor Hegel, passed on through reports from Berlin.

At the next table, a fierce argument raged over the education of females, punctuated by lewd jokes and bursts of hilarity. Michael peered through the darkness ahead, clouded by smoke. He fixed on the single figure who sat in the furthest corner, alone and hunched over a text carefully hidden underneath the table.

Aha.

Michael's steps quickened. He weaved his way through the last of the crowd and sat down across from the solitary reader, setting the jug of wine on the table with a clatter.

"Good afternoon, my friend," he said, in his most rolling Eastern accent. "We meet again!"

The boy's head jerked up. His hands loosened around his text. It slipped through his fingers and fell under the table. He dived for it . . .

But Michael reached it first.

His fingers closed around a thin pamphlet, made of crookedly cut paper. *Poor work*, he thought. His old master would never have countenanced such a slipshod performance from his own apprentice, much less the hastily done print, which marched along the page in angled slopes full of misspellings.

But Prince Kalishnikoff wouldn't care for such details.

"*Why the Congress Is Deluded*," Michael read aloud softly. He flipped the pamphlet open, placing one finger idly in the middle to hold his place. He smiled gently at the student across from him. "An interesting work?"

"I—I wouldn't—that is, I don't . . ." The boy's face looked suddenly sallow and far younger in the flickering candlelight. "I mean . . ."

"We met the other day, did we not? In the Café Rothmann. You were there with a group of friends."

"I don't—" The boy peered at him, blinking. "Prince Kalishnikoff?"

"Good, you do remember. I am honored. Herr . . . Hüberl, is it not? Please"—Michael gestured to the jug.—"won't you share a glass or two with me?"

"Ah . . ." The boy's eyes were still fixed on the pamphlet in Michael's hands.

Michael laid the pamphlet down in his own lap and leaned forward to pour the wine into clay cups. "Fascinating literature, these pamphlets. Of course, it's not surprising that the government forbids them.

To allow dissent—to permit one's citizens to reach such dangerous, possibly *revolutionary* conclusions . . ."

Young Hüberl swallowed visibly. "Your Highness, I should explain. I wasn't—that is, that isn't even my pamphlet, it was here when I sat down—I was going to report it to the authorities, of course, but—"

"But you thought you'd have a look first and see what the madmen said. I understand completely." Michael pushed the second cup across the table. "Here, have another drink. As I was saying, I understand why the Habsburg authorities have forbidden such prints . . . but I must say, I personally find them most intriguing."

"You do?" Hüberl eyed Michael warily, even as he raised the cup to his lips.

"But of course. After all, I no longer have the responsibilities of government, myself, and I've always cherished the idea of an open mind. Free debate can only be harmful, surely, if a man has something to hide."

Had he gone too far? Not yet, Michael judged, but possibly soon, judging by the nervous look in the boy's eyes—half-enticed but also half-horrified.

It was hard to remember, sometimes, that boys like this, even here in Vienna, hadn't grown up with the institution of a free press as Michael had. They'd grown up with a government terrified by the French revolution, committed to repressing all dissent—to making the act of criticism itself a crime. Even at the university itself, there'd been a purge of professors in the 1790s, and those who'd remained had learned to forget all their inconvenient theories of natural law and social contracts.

Michael repressed a sigh. This was no moment for nostalgia, and he had no one to share it with, anyway. Caroline would remember what those heady days had been like . . . but Caroline, as she'd made perfectly clear, would never agree to discuss the past with him.

He widened his smile and leaned back, sipping his own wine. "Don't worry. I shan't tell anyone that I found you reading this. I understand the . . . confusion that might cause for you."

The wariness in Hüberl's expression disappeared, to be replaced by horror of an entirely different sort. "No! Please, Prince Kalishnikoff, I beg you, don't—"

"I've no desire to cause you any difficulties, sir. Why should I? I'm only here for the duration of the Congress, and when I speak with the emperor himself at the Hofburg tonight..." Michael let the phrase linger in the air for a thrumming moment, before releasing it. "I shall certainly have more important matters of state to discuss."

"Of course." Hüberl slumped, and downed the rest of his wine in one gulp.

Michael looked away from the painful relief on the boy's face, keeping his voice light. "Where would I find more of these, by the way?"

"Oh, anywhere on the campus. Or if you really want..." Hüberl stuttered to a stop, relief turning to sudden chagrin.

"It's of no occasion. But I would like to see all sides of Vienna while I'm here." Michael slipped the pamphlet into the inner pocket of his jacket. "Of course, I could simply keep this one as a souvenir to remember you by..."

He held the boy's gaze for a long moment, fighting down an unwonted wave of self-loathing.

If his old master could see him now... or Caroline...

Hüberl swallowed visibly. "The fifteenth district," he muttered. "Where the Jews and Musselmans live. On Rotringstrasse, above the grocery." His voice dropped to a bare whisper. "Only say you want to buy one of their imported fruits."

"Ah. Clever." Michael snorted softly and withdrew the pamphlet from his jacket. "I thank you for your help, Herr Hüberl. And I promise..." His smile twisted as he dropped his own voice. "I shall remember you. In detail."

Hüberl blinked rapidly. "I... understand."

"I'm glad." Michael passed the pamphlet across the table and stood up. "Enjoy your reading."

He stepped away from the table and walked slowly out of the

room, not letting his steps speed up as they wanted to. His legs wanted to break into a run, to distance himself from the boy he'd left behind and from the feeling that was creeping up on him against his will.

He felt ... Michael shrugged his shoulders irritably as he emerged into the narrow, creaking staircase that led to the upper floor. He took a deep gulp of air—stale, constricted air, of course, but at least it was free of smoke and free of youthful student chatter.

He felt *old*.

Damn it! This should be the greatest game of his life, to be played with all his heart. He should have felt joy in the perfect conclusion of a conversation successfully maneuvered to meet all his ends.

He hadn't.

Michael remembered the boy's stricken face, the battle he'd glimpsed there between terror and outrage. Young Hüberl wouldn't report him to the authorities, of that Michael was certain. But there had been no joy in manipulating such an innocent, unworldly pawn.

And as he'd threatened the boy into compliance, all Michael had seen in his mind's eye had been Caroline's face that morning, pale and drawn with remembered horror.

Weariness settled around Michael's shoulders like a heavy cloak. He pushed open the door and stepped outside.

He wouldn't go to the fifteenth district this afternoon, even if that was the obvious next step. Oh, he could find some fair excuse for putting off the visit—if anyone was watching him, for instance, it would be a poor strategy indeed to lead them directly from his informant to his goal—but that wasn't what held him back, just now.

Michael had festivities at the Hofburg tonight to prepare for. And he found himself wanting more than anything else to take a fiery hot, purifying bath beforehand, to scrub himself free of the combined stink of guilt and fear.

CHAPTER EIGHTEEN

Caroline arrived at the Hofburg palace an hour after full darkness. Smoking flambeaux lit the glittering procession of nobility that made up the emperor and empress of Austria's receiving line. The line wound through two full stone courtyards, past statues of past rulers in heavy robes of majesty and statues of muscular Greek heroes in combat with writhing monsters. The torches cast flickering shadows across the statues' curves, so that at one moment a hydra's head came into view and at the next a stern Habsburg face.

As her carriage—required by fashion, if not by common sense, to carry her the three blocks from her apartment—drove away, Caroline stepped to the end of the line. At least a dozen other guests soon followed, streaming forth from their own carriages. Despite all her resolutions beforehand, Caroline couldn't stop herself from looking back covertly to see if Michael was among them.

"Caro!" Marie, Lady Rothmere, swept across to join her from the furthest group, dragging her tall husband behind her. "What a crush! I vow, I can barely breathe." She inserted herself neatly into the line in front of Caroline. "Tedious beyond belief, don't you agree?"

"Mm," Caroline said. She exchanged a rueful smile with Marie's weary-looking husband as he shrugged apologetically at her. "And how are you both today?"

Marie answered blithely, craning her smooth neck to peer at the line ahead of them. "Oh, fagged beyond anything. George has been off at his tiresome political meetings all day long, of course, leaving me to find my own amusement where I could."

"My dear," Lord Rothmere began, placatingly, "I hardly think—"

"Oh!" Marie spun around, her eyes lighting up. "You wouldn't believe the gossip I heard today in Emmie Kelvinhaugh's salon."

"No?" Caroline gave in. "And what was it?"

It was her own fault, she told herself, for letting herself be distracted. If she had only concentrated on tonight's business, she would never have turned around to look for Michael Steinhüller and thus attracted Marie's attention.

"*Well!*" Marie drew a tingling breath. "Lord Stewart, from all reports, has been engaged in a desperate flirtation with one of the greediest high-flyers in Vienna—"

Lord Rothmere winced. "Marie, really—"

"And your own old friend Prince Kalishnikoff, whom you were showing so much favor the other night, is said to be *quite* the new favorite of that dreadful Princess Bagration!"

Caroline blinked into full attention. "I beg your pardon?"

"Shocking, is it not? Such a well-favored man, as *you* certainly seemed to think, with such undeniably excellent manners." Marie gave a delicate shrug. "But I was told that Lord Kelvinhaugh himself commented on how taken the princess was by your friend. *He* said, if you can believe it, that perhaps the prince might offer her some consolation for her loss of Prince Metternich!"

Caroline forced a smile. "I wasn't aware that Emmie Kelvinhaugh was such a gossip."

"Emmie?" Marie let out a trill of laughter. "My dear, she's far too timid a mouse to pass on such news. Oh no, it was another guest who commented on it, and only asked Emmie for confirmation. Well, she made little noises of distress—you know how she does—but of course, in the end she couldn't deny it, could she, when her own husband had been the one to say so in the first place?"

"I see." Caroline met Marie's bright, speculative gaze and shrugged lightly. "Well, I'm not surprised. From all I've heard of the princess, she is more than a little inclined to charming men."

"Oh, from what *I've* heard . . ."

Marie launched into a new story as the line moved forward, but her gaze remained intent on Caroline's face, even as her voice twittered on in an endless stream of gossip. Caroline kept her expression serene and politely indifferent, nodding at all the right moments.

She wanted to gag. Sickness rose up in her stomach as she stepped forward. She took a deep breath, forcing the bile down.

Fool. Foolish beyond measure, first, to believe any of Marie's malicious gossip—although Emmie Kelvinhaugh, her relentless brain reminded her, was not a gossip by even the most exacting of standards, and if Emmie really had confirmed . . .

But no. The greater foolishness—the unforgivable mistake—was to let the possibility of truth sicken her.

She remembered the look on Michael's face that morning, in the gardens.

"You can trust me with all your heart," he'd said. *"I swear it."*

How could she have even wanted to believe him?

She imagined him turning his charm on Princess Bagration—"the white cat," she'd heard gentlemen call the princess and then laugh in a way Caroline knew how to understand. She'd seen the lady herself from a distance, riding in the Augarten with six white horses. Beautiful, certainly, beyond any denial, and fascinating, from all reports—and, no doubt, a valuable ally for a man in Michael's position. Caroline could all too easily envision . . .

Stop. She leashed her wayward imagination with an effort.

Her smile had slipped. She forced it back into place.

It didn't matter whether Michael had flirted—or even if he had already progressed further—with the princess, or with anyone else. It didn't—couldn't—even matter if he had been trying to play Caroline for a fool that morning.

He had failed.

She knew better than to trust him again. It was a blessing in disguise to be reminded of that now, before she could make any fatal slip.

Caroline hadn't let herself care for the attractions of any man since she was sold at fifteen years old, except—once she was finally old enough and wise enough to rise beyond her fear and rage—to see how they could be used toward her own ends.

How could she have let Michael slip so far past her guard?

There were only eight couples ahead of Marie and her husband now. The emperor, tall and glittering with medals, stood beyond his small, slight wife at the head of the line, kissing the hand of a Russian duchess. Servants hurried up to the closest waiting guests to take the overcoats of the gentlemen and the pelisses of the ladies. Caroline took a deep, steadying breath as she unbuttoned her own ankle-length pelisse and handed it to a bowing footman.

No longer hidden beneath the satin-trimmed pelisse, she wore a gown of sheer French gauze over a deep blue silk slip, low-cut and clinging close to her figure. Sapphires sparkled around her throat. She saw Lord Rothmere's brown eyes widen in appreciation, quickly veiled before his wife could spot it, and she smiled in grim satisfaction. *Well, then.* Caroline raised her chin as she stepped forward in the line.

It was time for work, not gossip, and she would waste no more of it.

Distracted or not, Caroline knew better than to seek out the emperor's gaze as she waited for her turn. While Marie and Lord Rothmere exchanged greetings with the imperial couple, she folded her gloved hands and cast her gaze down modestly. She only looked up when it was her turn to move forward . . .

And met a gaze of unmistakable hostility from the diminutive empress.

"Your Majesty," she murmured, lowering her head as she dipped a deep, respectful curtsy.

"Lady Wyndham." The young empress's high voice was as cold and piercing as an icicle. "A pleasure."

"An honor, Your Majesty." Caroline rose, veiling intense speculation behind a submissive expression.

She had only exchanged a few empty words with the empress at the last ball—and none, surely, that could have led to such blatant imperial anger. Unless . . .

"Lady Wyndham," the emperor said. He took her gloved hand. "Charming, as always."

"Your Majesty." Rising from her second curtsy, Caroline lifted her eyes, letting a warm, assured smile curve her lips.

It faded as she met his eyes. They sparkled with a dangerous, unsettling light. Not attraction—or not only. No, something darker, something she couldn't quite identify . . .

He raised her hand to his lips. "I hope you'll save a quadrille for me, after the tableaux have ended."

"I would never dare disobey an imperial command," Caroline said lightly.

His lips twisted.

He released her hand just before she could lose control and snatch it back. She stepped away more quickly than she should have, swallowing hard.

The other ingredient in his expression, flaring briefly into full view, had been simmering rage.

What folly had she managed unknowingly to commit, to change his mood so drastically in the past two days? The hostility of the empress, perhaps, might be accounted for by the emperor's own warmth of two nights' past. But the emperor's own change of heart . . . that, Caroline could not fathom.

Panic beat a quick flutter inside her chest as she stepped forward into the sparkling throng. Lights blazed from all directions, flashing off tiaras and necklaces. A wind band played a bright, piping march in one corner of the Great Hall. Caroline smiled and nodded to familiar faces across the room.

What had she done wrong?

She took a deep breath, stilling the voice of fear within her.

Enough. The emperor had reserved a dance with her. Therefore, whatever mistake she had made had not been enough to give him a disgust of her. She would exert every ounce of skill she possessed to regain his favor—and she had time enough, beforehand, to think on how to do it. She had hours left before the dancing began, to sit through elegant tableaux, make small talk with only half her attention, and plan her next strategy in detail.

There was no need to panic.

As Caroline turned, she caught sight of the Prince de Ligne's white hair, revealed for a moment across the great hall. Relief released Caroline's shoulders from their tightness. She moved forward, holding her fan and reticule close to her side as she weaved her way through the thick crowd—

—And almost walked into the man who planted himself directly in her path.

"Lady Wyndham," said Count Pergen. His thin lips twitched into a smile. "I have been waiting for you."

The first thing Michael saw when he stepped into the Great Hall of the Hofburg was Caroline. She stood at the head of the line, making her curtsy to the emperor. His breath caught in his throat at the sight.

Light sparked off the jewels at her throat and in her hair, but the colorful gems were only a distraction from the picture she presented. For the first time since meeting her again, he saw her as if she were a stranger, without the veil of her past self and their shared history between them.

She straightened from her curtsy, and her gown clung to her figure. Michael swallowed hard.

Karolina, he reminded himself. She was the same girl he'd known . . . but from a distance, she looked very little like the girl she'd been.

The emperor seemed impressed, certainly. Michael's hands tightened into fists as he saw the emperor's gaze turn blatantly to Caroline's chest.

Then he loosened his fingers and tried to smile.

Well. It appeared that Caroline's plan—whatever it might be—was progressing beautifully.

Good for her, he told himself.

Still, he chose not to watch any longer.

Instead, Michael turned his attention to his neighbors in the line.

The woman behind him was a haughty-looking dowager with a forbidding expression, but the young couple in front of him looked more promising. The girl clung to her husband's arm. Both of them looked half excited, half terrified by the prospect ahead of them.

Bourgeois, Michael guessed. The man would be the eldest son of a wealthy merchant family, invited with his wife to this gathering in thanks for monetary favors to the emperor, perhaps. They would spend the evening in reflected honor but also in isolation, watching the royalty of Europe from close quarters but considered too unimportant to be observed—much less spoken to—by any of their fellow guests.

Michael smiled charmingly at them both.

"Am I the only one to feel a bit intimidated?" he whispered.

By the time the line had moved forward five more feet, he knew both the first names of Herr and Frau Gassmann, half their family histories . . . and he had managed to restrain himself from looking to see in which direction Caroline had gone.

At the head of the line, he waited as the Gassmanns were greeted with distant condescension by the tiny empress. As they moved on to the emperor, Michael moved forward to bow reverently over the empress's small hand.

"Your Majesty." He brushed his lips across her glove. "I am charmed . . . and overwhelmed."

"Prince Kalishnikoff." She repeated the name that had been whispered to her by a waiting servant and smiled up at him as he released her hand. At least twenty years younger than her husband-and-first-cousin, Empress Maria Ludovica was lovely but painfully thin, with pale skin stretched across her fine features and shadows underneath her eyes. Still, the charm that had famously won troops and allies to the Austrian war effort was evident as she spoke. "We are pleased to welcome you to Vienna, Your Highness. Is this your first visit to our capital?"

"Not quite," Michael said. On this point at least, thank God, he had prepared himself. He'd asked the prince that question himself, when he'd first won the ring and deed of signatory off the drunken sot in that tavern in Warsaw, scant hours before the exiled ruler had departed on a ship bound for distant Canada. "I did have the pleasure of visiting Vienna once before, but only as a young child."

"I do hope you enjoy your stay."

"Majesty." He bowed again, as he moved on to the emperor. "A great honor."

"Kalishnikoff." The emperor bit off the name without waiting for his servant to whisper an introduction.

All of Michael's instincts flared into warning as he straightened from his bow and met the older man's narrowed gaze. "Your Majesty."

The emperor's eyes glimmered with a dangerous light. "I hear you're finding great favor in Vienna. In *all* quarters."

"Majesty?" Michael raised his eyebrows, keeping his expression good-humored.

Had he been followed to the university district that afternoon? He'd done nothing illegal while there ... nothing illegal, at least, that could have been witnessed. Could anyone have overheard?

"Apparently, you've become quite the favorite with many of our ladies here for the Congress," the emperor said. "Princess Bagration ..."

"A charming woman, is she not?" Michael smiled to hide his confusion. "The Prince de Ligne was kind enough to invite me to accompany him to her salon yesterday."

"Indeed, the Prince de Ligne." The emperor's voice hardened. "And was it he who introduced you to our English visitor, Lady Wyndham?"

Aha. Michael shook his head. "No, Majesty. Lady Wyndham is a very old friend of mine. Almost a sister, one might say."

The emperor blinked. "Surely the royal house of Kernova is not so closely linked to ... England."

And what word had he nearly used there, before he'd caught himself? Michael shrugged, holding his smile. "Our fathers were old school friends, so we met as children. I've always looked on her as a younger sibling."

"Mm. How very ... enlightening." The emperor's eyes narrowed. "Do enjoy the tableaux, Prince Kalishnikoff."

"I thank you, Majesty. And perhaps I might have the honor of speaking to you again, later in the evening?" Michael asked. "The matter of this Congress, as it relates to my own lost land—"

"Pray, don't speak to me of politics." The emperor waved a dismissive hand. "I know nothing of affairs of state, I'm afraid. My ministers see to all such matters."

And that is the greatest lie spoken yet tonight by either of us, Michael thought as he bowed his farewell.

Smiling and assured, he moved through the crowd and arrived exactly as planned, ten minutes later, at the Prince de Ligne's side.

"My dear Kalishnikoff." The prince stepped aside to make room for Michael in his small circle. "You know Monsieur le Baron de Talleyrand, of course, and my young friend the Comte de La Garde-Chambonas."

"A pleasure to see you both again, gentlemen." Michael tipped his head in a courteous nod.

Caroline was nowhere to be seen.

"How goes your stay in Vienna, Prince Kalishnikoff?" Talleyrand asked. His voice was as languid and uninflected as ever, but Michael did not fail to glimpse the meaning in the French ambassador's heavily bagged eyes.

"Most productively, Your Excellency, I thank you. Why, I've made new acquaintances even this afternoon . . . and acquired directions to several more."

"How gratifying," Talleyrand murmured. "And how very energetic of you. I'm sure it will advance your cause admirably."

"We must hope, eh?" The Prince de Ligne's lips twitched as he glanced between the two, as if following the moves in an old-fashioned duel of swords. "But enough tiresome politicking for one night, eh? Have you heard the results yet of the single most dramatic and anguished issue facing the Congress tonight?"

Michael shrugged. "Ah . . .?"

"The Affair of the Mustaches," the Comte de La Garde-Chambonas pronounced. His plump chest swelled with importance. "No one can speak or think of anything else, even in the very highest of circles!"

"How astonishing," Michael said blankly. "And the Affair of the Mustaches is . . .?"

"Our young friend refers to the tableaux which we are about to view," De Ligne explained. His tone was grave, but his eyes sparkled. "They've run into a desperate predicament, you see. The final picture in tonight's gallery of images is to represent Olympus itself, complete with all mythological divinities. It should conclude the entire evening in the most brilliant possible manner."

"But?" Michael supplied. In the distance, he caught a flash of blue silk. He forced his gaze not to follow it.

"Nothing, as you can imagine, has been neglected to make the execution worthy of so grand a subject. And yet, for the past two days, there have been negotiations far more difficult and delicate in their nature than any others at this entire Congress; and they have been followed, my dear prince, with far more personal interest than any tiresome questions over Poland, France, or any other kingdom's destiny."

"The Comte de Wurbna's mustaches!" the Comte de La Garde-Chambonas interjected. "He is the only man thought fit to represent Apollo in the tableau; the role was offered and accepted days ago—but he refuses to shave off his glorious mustaches!"

"They are glorious indeed," the Prince de Ligne murmured, with wicked delight. "And yet . . . who can conceive the God of Day with the hirsute ornament of a captain of hussars?"

"I perceive the dilemma," Michael said. "And what has been the final decision?"

"But this is the exact situation! It is as yet undecided." The comte's cheeks flushed with excitement. "Shall anyone know the end to the story until the curtain rises? The stage manager has entreated him with pleas and tears to see reason. Rather than give in, Wurbna has taken an oath not to part with the mustaches while alive! But it is rumored that the empress herself has now entered into the negotiations. So perhaps . . ."

Servants pulled open the heavy doors to the next room, rearranged as a theater for the night. The crowd began to move. Revealed for a single moment of clarity, Michael witnessed a vivid but unstaged tableau.

Caroline stood less than twenty feet away from him, facing Count Pergen himself, who smiled as he spoke to her. It was not a pleasant smile. To their left, the emperor of Austria watched her with undisguised hunger. Caroline's own face was hidden from view.

Michael took a deep breath. He prepared to step forward.

"What say you, Prince Kalishnikoff?" the French ambassador asked. "Will young Wurbna give in to the demands of the state, or shall the spectacle be ruined for everyone?"

The crowd closed before them again, hiding Caroline from view. Yet, if he took just a few more steps through the crowd . . .

Michael met Talleyrand's measuring gaze and tasted bitter self-knowledge.

"Why, he'll shave the mustaches, of course," he said. "Like it or not . . ." He turned away, toward the doors to the theater and away from the tableau that did not, could not, concern him now. "We all must learn to put aside our own desires and play the roles assigned us."

CHAPTER NINETEEN

"**Y**ou've been waiting for me?" Caroline repeated. She sought for a social smile; failed. She raised her eyebrows instead, fighting for chilly disdain rather than panic. "To what do I owe this honor, Count Pergen?"

"Need you ask?" He bowed slightly, his smile deepening. "I'm sure you must be accustomed to inspiring admiration, Lady Wyndham. Once first met, how could I help but wish to meet you again?"

Repulsion slammed through Caroline's skin like a physical attack. She swallowed hard to keep from gagging.

Then she met his gaze, cold and intent, as he straightened from his bow, and her mind wrested control back from her panicking body.

If that was truly admiration in his shadowed gaze, then Caroline knew nothing about the desires of men. She took a deep breath and forced herself to think clearly.

Interest, Pergen could certainly feel for the objects of his experiments; the will to power and control, she thought, was probably his truest ruler, in every sense of the word.

But personal physical desire for a woman—or a man, for that matter . . . no. That particular impulse, she was certain, had been cast aside long ago, sacrificed along the road to power. She doubted it had ever been a strong compulsion for him. Pergen's deepest passions lay in other directions.

So, what game did he think to play now? And how, exactly, would it be best to respond to this gambit?

She settled on a slight, haughty smile. There was no point in pretending liking; she could never carry it off.

"You flatter me, sir," she said coldly, and turned to leave.

"Flatter? How could I, when the emperor himself sings your praises?"

Caroline stilled. "I'm certain the emperor has far more important matters on his mind." The rage she'd glimpsed simmering in his eyes . . .

"So I would have thought, as well." Pergen drew closer, dropping his voice. A chill emanated from his skin, mingling with his soft, hissing whisper. "To have captured the emperor's interest would have been novelty and boast enough for an ordinary Englishwoman, even one of rank and title. But for a lady without a past . . ."

"I'm afraid I don't take your meaning," Caroline said, through numb lips. "Are you speaking in riddles now? No one is without a past."

"Indeed not. And yet, you've somehow hidden yours with remarkable finesse."

"What a creative imagination you must have, Count Pergen." She laughed, dismissively, her fingers tightening around the delicate fan she carried. "Why on earth would I have bothered to hide my past?"

"Why indeed, if there is nothing to hide?"

Flicking out her fan to its full extension, Caroline waved it as if wafting away a stench. "You are offensive, sir," she drawled.

"I am loyal to my emperor, Lady Wyndham. And I am deep within his confidence."

Caroline drew a deep breath. Time to move to a different strategy. She raised her eyebrows with cool amusement. "Then you must know that he and I have spoken of my past, and he did not seem displeased by it."

"He knew at that time only my first conclusions," Pergen said. "That you were nothing more than your first husband's whore."

Caroline gasped and jerked her fan up to wave in front of her face, a show of aristocratic outrage that safely hid at least half of her expression. Her pulse was beating rapidly against her wrist, but she kept her voice steady. "You have said quite enough, Count Pergen. I will not remain to listen to more slander."

"No? But that was only my first conclusion, while I still assumed you were essentially harmless. Will you not stay to hear how my mind was changed?"

On the other side of the room, two great doors swung open, leading to the improvised stage. The crowd around Caroline and Pergen shifted and surged toward the opening doors, following the lead of the imperial and royal couples. In the press of people, Caroline stood frozen, head held high.

Stay or leave, stay or leave . . .

All she wanted to do was run. Instead, she snapped her fan shut and looked Pergen in the eyes.

Far better to know the worst immediately.

"Changed?" she repeated, as frostily as possible.

"Now that I have met you myself, Madam . . ." Pergen's dark, smudged eyes narrowed as he regarded her. "Something about you strikes me as oddly familiar," he murmured. "Only the emperor's pride has been injured by your actions, so far. That would be reason enough to banish you from Vienna, so far as I am concerned, and yet . . ."

She recognized that look in his eyes: focused interest, as keen and chilling as a dagger. It was how he had regarded her for four long years, as he'd catalogued the effects of his experiments upon her.

"It is not only the emperor who is intrigued by you anymore," he whispered.

Fury swept through Caroline, overwhelming the panic he'd trained her into years ago.

Never again.

She was no one's victim anymore, and she *would not* give this man the gift of her fear.

"Should I consider myself flattered?" She allowed a sneer to lift her upper lip. "I have never been to Vienna before. If you once visited London and attended the same ball or assembly . . ." She shrugged contemptuously. "I cannot always choose my company. But I have no recollection of any such chance meeting."

"No?" Pergen's lips twisted into a half-smile. "You have forgotten a great deal of your own history, it seems. You have even persuaded everyone in England to share in your selective amnesia. But you are no longer standing on English soil, Lady Wyndham."

The last of the crowd filtered out around them. In the distance, Caroline saw the Prince de Ligne disappear through the doorway, followed by—oh, yes, it was—by Michael, painfully familiar even with his back to her. *Again*.

Alone in the great hall except for silent servants, she met Pergen's shadowed gaze and felt a deathlike chill creep across her.

"No one can escape their own past, Lady Wyndham," Count Pergen said softly. "And I will—I promise you—make it my first business to discover yours."

Peter walked back into the Theater an der Wien through the same back door he'd used to leave it. *Only twenty-six hours ago*. Almost impossible to believe it could have been such a short span of time. It felt as if a lifetime had passed.

It had. He wasn't the same man who had walked out into a dark alleyway, full of confidence and luck, thinking himself the hero of his own personal adventure—ready to tilt against Fate to win his inevitable fame and fortune.

No more heroics, Peter thought as he crossed the threshold. He had to pause halfway through, gasping for breath and clutching the doorway for support.

It was a hard thing to realize, at five and twenty years of age, that he wasn't a true hero after all . . . just a bit player, to be used or else disposed of in the second act. If he'd died, it wouldn't even have been the tragic climax to an epic drama—only a minor after-thought to two other men's great struggle.

Peter had written a dozen plays that killed off innocent bystanders to prove a villain's wickedness. But he'd never thought, until now, to find himself as one of them.

He was still alive though. Alive, albeit no longer innocent. For all the noble speeches he'd written and believed in over the years, it seemed, after all, it might be bitterly preferable to be free and in league with horrors than to be nobly resistant and dead . . . or wishing to be so.

He'd been an actor for eighteen of his twenty-five years of life. Perhaps it was time, at long last, to learn the harsh truths of the world outside the stage.

Peter limped his way through the cluttered backstage area, full of sets for a variety of different dramas, from Turkish harem comedies to Spanish tragedies and the local *Hanswürst* slapstick pieces. Through the thin wall of his own company's backdrop, he could hear the steadily growing murmur of the gathering audience in the seats, like the distant roar of a great beast. The play hadn't yet begun, then. He was in luck—

He jerked his thoughts to a halt, gritting his teeth. The fact that his plans hadn't stumbled *yet* meant absolutely *nothing* for the future. He couldn't let himself fall into the trap of overconfidence again.

One of the theater's young stagehands hurried purposefully off the set. He jerked back, wide-eyed, when he saw Peter.

"Herr—Herr Riesenbeck? Is it you?"

Peter snorted painfully, taking in the boy's expression. "I'm no ghost."

"But they said . . ." The stagehand swallowed his way to an embarrassed silence, glancing guiltily over his shoulder.

Peter sighed and squared his own shoulders. "I can imagine what they said. Let me pass."

The boy slid out of his way with a burst of relief-driven speed, and Peter started down the murky, badly lit corridor that led to the actors' dressing rooms. He thanked heaven now for the narrowness of the corridor, though he'd cursed it only the day before. It let him lean both hands against the peeling, moldy wallpaper for support as he walked with the last remnants of his energy.

He heard raised voices even before he arrived at the first door— Marta's shared dressing room. *Of course*, Peter thought, as Karl's voice rose above the others.

"I told you we couldn't rely on him. He's probably off on some drinking binge, or—"

"Herr Riesenbeck has never been a drunkard," Marta said doubtfully. "Surely, my love—"

"Not that you knew of," Karl said, "but—"

"*Ohhh!*" A well-modulated wail cut him off.

It was Josephine, the second lady of the company—eager to wrest the center stage role from Karl, no doubt. "Where can he *be*?" Josephine wailed.

Peter had never heard a more perfect cue. He grinned widely and swung open the door.

"My friends!" he said. "I'm afraid I was delayed."

Despite every ounce of pain, horror, and disillusionment that Peter had suffered in the past twenty-six hours, he couldn't help feeling the hugest enjoyment as he witnessed the frozen tableau before him. His entire company had crowded into Marta and Josephine's small dressing room. All of them were fully equipped in thick stage make-up and costumes, all of them stared in open astonishment at the door, and all of them—for once—were entirely lost for words.

They hadn't lost all their abilities, though. At least half of them had fallen—unconsciously, Peter wondered?—into the hand-flung-to-brow-or-bosom theatrical pose of Shock . . . although Karl, Peter was glad to note, had managed to restrain himself from assuming an actual Attitude of Horror.

Marta was the first to move, rising from her dressing table with a sweep of lace.

"My dear Herr Riesenbeck!" She advanced on him, holding both hands out to him in appeal. "We have been so distraught—so overcome with worry—so—oh!" She recoiled, one hand flying to her chest. "Your face! You've been bruised!"

Peter stepped forward and caught her hands. "Your sympathy is more than medicine enough, dear lady." He raised her hands to his lips. "My dearest Marta—Josephine—Karl . . ." He smiled gently at the lead members of his company. "What can I say? I knew you would take everything in hand magnificently. And you have!"

"We weren't given any choice, were we?" Karl glared at him. "Where have you been?"

"He's been hurt," Josephine said. "Look at his face! And the way he's moving! Were you set upon by footpads, Herr Riesenbeck?"

"Alas, yes. After my meeting last night, I was on my way back to tell you all of our good fortune, when suddenly . . ." Peter staggered— thought to catch himself—and then decided not to after all. Instead, he let himself sag forward into Marta's fragrant embrace. "Forgive me. My legs are so weak . . ."

"You poor man." She helped him to her chair.

Josephine swept up to help, cooing over him as they settled him into a more comfortable position. Peter let himself enjoy the moment, even as he listened to Karl muttering to himself and the rest of the small cast whispering to one another, all jostling for position in the cramped dressing room.

"I woke up this morning in an alley I didn't recognize," Peter said hollowly. "They had taken all the coins I had on me, knocked me unconscious, and left me lying in the street outside the city wall. I've been walking all day, trying to find my way back . . ."

"Did you think of asking directions?" Karl growled.

"Really!" Josephine snapped. "How can you be so unfeeling?"

"Directions? Of course I did. To the nearest policeman," Peter said.

The others turned looks of blank amazement on him. Peter sighed. Perhaps he was stretching the believable truth too far, now. But now that he had begun . . .

"My missing coins," he said patiently. "Your salaries!"

"Oh, God," said Karl.

Marta took a deep, shivering breath. "And . . . did you have any luck?"

Peter shook his head, his face turning grim. "I'd been given coin in advance last night, which I was planning to distribute among you."

"In order of position, I hope?" Marta said coolly, drawing away from Josephine.

"What?" Josephine demanded.

"Dear ladies . . ." Peter sighed again, more heavily. "The police were of no help. In fact, to tell the truth, I'm not certain they even cared."

"You should have made them care," Karl growled. "If you'd been firm enough—"

Marta raised one hand. "From all I've heard, the police in Vienna care nothing for such matters. Their only true concern . . ." She made an expressive face that spoke volumes.

There was a pregnant pause. Karl heaved a sigh of his own, and his big shoulders finally slumped.

"Yes, well, that's done with, then," he said. "But what's this about our good fortune? And who was the patron, after all?"

Peter looked across the crowded group of actors, all watching him with rapt attention. Despite himself, he felt the familiar tingle of plea-sure at the sight. *It was working.* He had them back in hand again.

"Ladies and gentlemen," he said. "In twenty-four hours' time, we are to perform at the Burgtheater itself!" Slowly, painfully, he levered himself to his feet and stood swaying. He raised his voice, pitching it to carry over all the gasps and eager questions. "The emperor has decided to throw open his palace tomorrow night to host every person of rank in Vienna for this Congress. The royalty of Europe, the flower of the nobility . . ." *And the imposters, as well.*

"They will all be audience to your glory—and all, dear ladies and gentlemen, your devoted admirers tomorrow night. We have been espe-cially invited and requested, by imperial command, to mingle and con-verse with as many of the emperor's guests as possible within the Great Hall of the Hofburg palace, before the performance even takes place."

"Invited by the emperor himself!" Josephine breathed.

Even Karl's face had taken on a new glow of rapt determination. It took no great effort of the imagination for Peter to guess that he was already planning how to attract the emperor's own attention.

Let Karl scheme and fantasize as he would. All Peter cared about was that his new plan worked.

He'd convinced his captor that Michael would have taken on the pose of an aristocrat during his stay in Vienna, just as he had for his travels with Peter's own company—and every aristocrat in the city was certain to attend tomorrow night's gala. Michael, just like all the rest, would step smugly across that glittering threshold . . .

And then I'll have you. Because Peter and his company, too, would be there—and Peter would be waiting, along with Grünemann, to capture the man who'd led him into disaster in the first place.

It was enough—just enough—of a chance and a scheme to have won him his freedom . . . at least for one night.

Had his captor truly been convinced? Or was he merely playing a devilish new game, restoring Peter's life and hope only to reel him back in with even greater satisfaction, one night later, when he failed . . . just as expected?

If this was no more than a game on his captor's part . . .

Peter swallowed hard and kept his brilliant smile for his audience. Whether his captor believed in Peter's plan or not, it *would* work.

He would find Michael among the gathered nobility of Vienna, no matter how effective the man's disguise.

Peter's own life depended on it.

Applause rippled through the audience in the makeshift theater, as the great silk curtain rose to reveal the first tableau of the evening—*Louis XIV kneeling at Madame de la Valliére's feet.* Count von Trauttmansdorff knelt before the Comtesse de Zichy, offering himself to her in a frozen, crystalline moment, accompanied by a swelling orchestral background. The young comtesse's face, as befitted the character she played, was a picture of modesty, fear, and innocence . . . but none of those would last for long, Emperor Francis reflected. He wondered, idly, whether the rumors were true. According to gossip, the comtesse had already surrendered herself to the count in private . . . and with far less hesitancy than she displayed onstage.

"How romantic," Tsarina Elizabeth breathed, on Francis's right.

Her face was rapt with longing as she gazed at the brightly lit scene before them; her auburn hair, left loose and unbound, rippled against Francis's arm as she leaned forward.

"Mm," Francis murmured noncommittally, and smiled gently to hide his thoughts.

If the tsarina hadn't already found consolation for her husband's neglect in the arms of one of the tsar's own closest friends, Francis would have been tempted to give it to her himself out of mere sympathy.

The curtain fell before either of the noble actors could succumb to temptation and rub a nose or sneeze to break the moment. As applause broke out around them, the tsarina turned to murmur to her other neighbor. Francis turned his head slightly and nodded. Although all the candles had been extinguished to lend greater effectiveness to the stage lights, he knew his most trusted minister would see his signal even in the dark.

A brush of cold air signaled Pergen's approach even before he spoke.

"Majesty," Pergen murmured, just behind Francis's high-backed chair.

Under cover of the continuing applause, Francis leaned back and whispered softly, "A curious thing, Pergen. You know Prince Kalish-nikoff, of Kernova-as-was?"

"The gentleman staying in Lady Wyndham's second apartment."

"The same." Francis bit down on rising anger and kept his voice to a bare thread of sound. "He informed me that their fathers were child-hood friends."

Pergen's narrow eyebrows rose. Francis nodded slightly.

"Curious indeed," Pergen murmured. "I shall look into it directly."

"Do," Francis murmured. "See to it."

The curtain rose again, and he sat forward in his seat. As Pergen stepped back into the shadows, Comte Woyna and Princess Yblo-nowska were revealed in a reproduction of a painting by Guérin, "Hip-polytus refuting Phedra's accusation before Theseus." The princess's face bore all the signs, indeed, of passion struggling against remorse;

the comte might perhaps be attempting respectful grief, but he did not quite succeed. A beam of light had somehow arranged itself to perfectly highlight the princess's half-exposed bosom in her transparent Grecian dress.

Who could blame the comte for looking a bit goggle-eyed from his privileged angle? Not Francis, certainly.

"Mm, how lovely," the tsarina murmured, leaning forward.

Her hair drifted over Francis's arm.

"Lovely," Francis repeated, with deep satisfaction.

The first round of tableaux had ended, and the orchestra had played through extracts from symphonies by Haydn and Mozart to accompany the change of stage sets, before Michael finally saw Caroline again. The noble performers had switched to a mixture of songs and pantomimes for this second part of the evening, choosing songs written by royals from all across Europe. Michael could only be relieved that the orchestra, at least, was staffed by professional musicians.

"And here is our Lady Wyndham at last," the Prince de Ligne murmured, as the second song finished. "Do you have any inkling of what kept her so long?"

Michael turned in his seat to look. Caroline must have slipped into the back of the great room with the advent of applause; she was only visible by the crack of light from the door as it closed behind her. He wished he could see her expression.

He wished he knew what Pergen had said to her.

The door closed, and shadows swallowed her figure.

"She must have been occupied with other matters," he said coolly.

Unfamiliar guilt pressed forward, but he shoved it aside. She had made it clear she didn't want his help, hadn't she? And yet . . .

"She'll have to be more punctual for our next evening of entertainment," de Ligne said. "Our great leaders of fashion are already deploring how crowded the Hofburg will be tomorrow night with this grand and democratic fête that's being planned by the emperor. Will you follow their lead and stay away from such an overwhelmingly popular affair?"

"The grandest fête of the entire Congress?" Michael shrugged. The orchestra began its introduction to the next song, and he lowered his voice to a discreet whisper. "How could I miss it?"

"And indeed, how could they?" De Ligne snorted with wicked laughter. "I'll make a wager, if you like, that every salon hostess who's decried this affair with the greatest outrage will be struggling and fighting for first place in the line in front of this palace in twenty-four hours' time. After all, if any of them chose to miss it, how could they then take part in the weeks of heated discussions afterward, deploring how crushed and sordid it had all been? They would be social outcasts."

As the prince finished his sentence, Comtesse Zamoyska and Prince Radziwill stepped forward on the stage and launched into Queen Hortense of Belgium's song "Do what you ought, let come what may." Michael rearranged his face into polite attention as the singers pantomimed noble heroics with all their limited range of emotion.

"Never fear," Michael whispered to the prince, under cover of the music. "I will be there."

CHAPTER TWENTY

Caroline waited until eight in the morning to summon Charles. It was hours earlier than she'd ever required his presence before, and he might well still be asleep—but she had been awake and pacing, her eyes burning with exhaustion and panic, ever since she'd returned at dawn.

Her maid, Johnson, had come in when she'd first arrived, to cluck disapprovingly about her hair and gown, but Caroline had dismissed the older woman to bed without making any moves toward her own repose. She couldn't let herself fall into the false security of unconsciousness until she had taken some real action to save herself and her plans ... no matter how dangerous that action might be.

"Your Ladyship." Charles arrived less than ten minutes after her summons, impeccably presented and—Caroline noted with a twist of rueful surprise—clean-shaven already and showing no signs of sleepiness. It was a far cry from her own disordered appearance, still wearing last night's evening gown and with her hair drifting free of its sternly ordered ringlets. Probably Charles had been up for hours already, doing his own work in the few hours he had free from her commands. Had she really forgotten, after so many years, what it was like not to be one of the cosseted upper classes?

"I trust I haven't kept you waiting?" Charles asked, as he straightened from his bow.

"Hardly. You are invaluable ... as always." Caroline plaited her fingers together and drew a breath. *It was time.* She'd kept him in the dark until now, for reasons of more than ordinary caution. Every instinct in her body warned her that it was a risk to entrust him with her most vulnerable of secrets—especially now, after Pergen's warnings and the events of two nights past. But she had no time anymore to listen to the voice of caution. Pergen had made that more than clear last night.

Caroline tilted her head toward the open drawing room door behind Charles. He caught her meaning, like the invaluable servant she had named him, and moved quickly to close the door. She waited until he'd returned to stand before her chair before she spoke again, in a bare whisper.

"I need your help."

"Anything!" His face lit up. He sank down to his knees before her chair. "Lady Wyndham, you know I'd serve you in any way."

"I know." She smiled into his eyes, carefully overlooking the ardent meaning in his voice. "You are more loyal than I deserve, Charles."

"Lady Wyndham—"

"Shh. Please." She drew another breath, centering herself. What to reveal . . . and how much? "I am in danger," she said, with soft deliberation.

"I knew it." His right hand formed a fist against his knee. "Prince Kalishnikoff—"

"No! It isn't him." She reached out to give his fisted hand a quick, reassuring pat with the very tips of her fingers. "I thank you, but there really is nothing to concern you in that quarter."

He compressed his lips for a moment, visibly suppressing a retort. Caroline felt a whisper of new alarm brush against her as she watched him. She hadn't realized how strong a dislike he'd taken to Michael . . . or was it that he felt himself to be threatened?

That possibility was too disturbing to contemplate, in all its implications. Not now, not without any sleep . . . Exhaustion tugged at her. She wrenched her scattered thoughts back into order. She had to finish what she'd begun and address the true and current danger, rather than letting herself be distracted by idle premonitions.

"It is the minister of the Austrian secret police who has threatened me," she whispered. "The same man who has already placed a spy in this building."

Charles frowned. "Baron . . . von Hager, is it?"

"No," Caroline said. "No. In public, Baron von Hager may be named the minister of secret police, but that is no more true than . . ." *Than my own disguise, or Michael's*, she finished silently. She shook her head. "The real position of authority has never changed since the last century. Count Pergen has been their true leader ever since Emperor Joseph's time, for over thirty years now."

"But why the secrecy?"

"Because . . ." Caroline hesitated. The look in Charles's eyes, only yesterday—*no*. She couldn't let herself think about that. *There was no time*. "He is the man I told you of. The man who now leaks shadows."

"An alchemist. A successful alchemist, for over thirty years." Charles met her eyes. "Your teacher—!"

"Yes." Caroline compressed her lips. "But not by choice."

"But . . ."

She could almost name the questions jostling for precedence in Charles's throat. To him, she'd never named herself any other than an English noblewoman, born and bred—one whose interest in alchemy had been born of aristocratic idleness. She smiled thinly as she met his eyes.

"I know," she said quietly. "There are many things I haven't felt safe to discuss. Particularly here in Vienna."

"I . . . see." His shoulders rose and fell. "I think I see?"

"I'm glad. Because I cannot make it any clearer at the moment. It isn't safe, not with so many spies so close at hand." Caroline brushed her hand over her burning eyes and hoped he took it for a sign of budding, fragile tears, rather than the bone-deep weariness that wanted to topple her. "I shall explain everything to you as soon as I may. Dear Charles."

"Thank you, Lady Wyndham." He looked down at his still-fisted hand for a long moment. "And may I ask exactly what Prince Kalish-nikoff has to do with this?"

"He is an old friend, just as I said." Watching his face, Caroline took the risk of adding, "He does not know the truth of my . . . my training. And my knowledge. You are the only one I can trust with those secrets."

"But how can you be certain that he doesn't report to Count Pergen, himself?"

"Charles—"

"You must listen to me!" Charles leaned forward, nearly shaking with the intensity of his whispered words. "You've spoken of spies. Cannot you see how he fits that description? His coming, by claimed coincidence—maneuvering himself into your confidence, your very home—!"

"Please, Charles." Caroline drew back from his vehemence. "You must believe me when I tell you he has nothing to do with such matters. He is a good friend, and nothing more."

"But—"

"I must insist that you say no more of this." She held his gaze until it dropped.

His words came out in a reluctant mutter. "As you say, Lady Wyndham."

"Thank you. I knew I could trust you." Discomfort coiled through her as she looked at his set face and the barely repressed frustration in the hunched set of his shoulders. *Too great a risk . . .*

But no. Once in, she might as well risk everything. "I need you to find someone for me," she whispered. "It is the sole reason I came to Vienna. I thought I would have more time. I thought I would have months to work." She clenched her hands around her thin, gauzy evening gown. "I thought I might have the emperor's help. But it seems that I will not, after all."

"Your Ladyship?"

"A man was arrested by Pergen's secret police, twenty-four years ago," Caroline said. *Please, God, let the door be thick. Let Charles be trustworthy.* If Pergen ever found this out, he would know her and have her in an instant.

She had to force her voice to form the words around the knot of fear in her throat. "His name was Gerhard Vogl. He was a radical, a printmaker who dared to print and circulate pamphlets that told the truth behind the senseless war against the Turks and questioned the ravaging of civil liberties. Emperor Joseph had freed the press and the public to speak their minds when he first took sole rule, but Pergen convinced him to withdraw all the freedoms he had granted. Pergen persuaded him that every honest criticism was an act of treason." Her voice cracked. "Pergen's men smashed Gerhard Vogl's press, took him captive . . . and he has never been seen again since then."

Charles's eyes were fixed on her, alert and watchful. "This man . . . could he have been executed?"

"No!" She had spoken too loudly. Caroline lowered her voice back to a whisper. "Executions were public and accountable to the courts in those days. But secret imprisonments were not uncommon. Particularly when the prisoners had information that might prove inconvenient for the state." *A missing daughter*.

"Have you searched the records?"

"I have spent hundreds of pounds employing my own spies to do just that for the past six years." Ever since she had been widowed for the second time and finally set free, with a fortune under her own control and no husband to hold the reins of their household, make every significant decision . . . and decree that her past, and her lost father, were of no significance to anyone of worth.

Caroline felt the ache of old frustration as she shook her head. "His imprisonment was never recorded, and he was never freed or banished as all the other printmakers of his time were long ago. He is—he must be still imprisoned. I could swear to it."

Still sitting locked in a small dark room, imagining himself to be abandoned forever, just as she had been abandoned to her own fate . . .

"So, the informants have failed, and the emperor cannot be persuaded. You wish to use alchemy, now, to pursue your search?"

"Is it possible?"

"Mmm . . ." Charles's gaze turned inward and thoughtful. "It's not *im*possible. But whether I can do it is another matter. You've given me his name, but that won't be enough, especially if his prison isn't in the city of Vienna itself. If he's hidden elsewhere in the empire, it will be a long and difficult task to search out his location. Such a task will take time."

"I have no time left!"

They stared at each other for a paralyzed moment. Caroline closed her eyes, fighting real tears of frustration.

"Pergen has sworn to discover who I really am," she whispered. "He has set himself upon my path. I must leave Vienna before he can discover me. But I cannot leave without finding out the truth!"

"I see." Charles sighed. "Then I'll need more than a name. I'll require birth signs, signs of identity—"

"I can provide all of those."

"But I can't swear that I'll achieve success. For a true alchemical search," Charles said, "I would need his blood, to track him by."

"I can give you nearly that," Caroline breathed. She met his eyes and let herself take the greatest risk of all. "We share the same blood," she said to Charles. "I am his daughter. And I can give you mine."

It was time.

Michael stepped out of his room just after he heard the apartment door close behind Charles Weston. He didn't trust Caroline's secretary. More than that, every instinct he'd cultivated in the past two decades sharpened into buzzing, full-throated alertness every time the other man stepped into a room.

Weston had been bristling with territorial suspicion from the moment Michael had first stepped over the threshold of their joint apartment. Michael wouldn't put it past him to act as a spy, even if only in Caroline's interest. It might be amusing to lead the man in circles on an ordinary day . . . but today was no ordinary day, and it would be a fatal mistake to let himself be witnessed by anyone in what he was about to attempt.

If an Austrian spy saw and reported him to the secret police, Michael would be in dire danger indeed. And if Charles Weston followed him and reported on his actions to Caroline . . .

What had she said to him that first night? She'd recoiled when he'd spoken of loyalty, and thrown his own words back in his face. If she found out that he was putting both of them at risk now by visiting just such an illicit press as they had both grown up assisting . . .

Michael shut his eyes for a brief moment.

If he didn't follow Talleyrand's orders, his gamble would be lost indeed, and he might as well abandon Vienna and all his hopes without further ado. If he did not stay and fight for the rights of "Prince Kalishnikoff," he would never win the money he needed to buy himself a true home for the rest of his life and achieve security at last. He would be on the run forever . . . and sooner or later, his luck would finally run out.

Against that bleak prospect, Caroline's reaction—the hurt, the betrayal—could not be allowed to matter.

And yet . . .

He set his jaw, hard.

He would simply have to make certain that she didn't find out.

Michael strode down the stairs with careful nonchalance and exited the building into the bracingly cold morning air. Even at eight in the morning, the Dorotheergasse was crowded. At this hour, all of the nobles were still abed, but their servants were already hard at work, and the inner city—for this brief span of hours, at least—was entirely their own. They filled the narrow, cobblestoned streets, bustling through with baskets of shopping and calling out greetings to their fellows. Michael side-stepped a plump duo of housekeepers in mid-gossip and weaved through a crowd of busy maidservants and Turkish salesmen. They drew back far enough to let him through but looked at him with far more curiosity than respect.

And no wonder. His clothes might place him in the aristocracy, Michael realized, but his behavior in stepping out among them at such a time was more than enough to tinge social awe with outright irritation. He wondered if he ought to have attempted a footman's costume, the better to blend into the background . . . but no. If Weston had spotted him in such an outfit, there would have been no escape. All he could do was hope that the servants' own interests, during their rare hours of freedom, would be strong enough to overbalance the oddity of his appearance in their midst.

He walked a meandering route toward the fifteenth district, stopping at every block to gaze through a shop or café window and take a discreet look at the reflections of the crowd around him. Any repeated face, from block to block, could be a danger; any figure always spotted at the same distance, who might be following on another's orders . . .

Michael spotted nothing and didn't know whether to be relieved or alarmed. Every foreign noble would be watched by the police, he was certain—and the emperor's personal dislike had been more than evident the night before. Perhaps the imperial spies themselves were still abed. Perhaps they were simply too good to let themselves be spotted.

Michael wished he knew which option was more likely.

Perhaps, if he waited until later . . . No, he was only looking for excuses. He took a deep breath and strolled forward at a leisurely pace, taking a side path onto the Ringstrasse for distraction's sake.

Half an hour later, holding a newspaper he had bought from an urchin on the way, Michael finally arrived at the grocer's shop on Rotringstrasse that young Hüberl had described to him the day before. He stood on the street outside for a moment, looking in.

The shop itself was a typically dark little space, overflowing onto the street outside with baskets of vegetables and fruit and the imported foods popular with immigrants in Vienna. Sacks of coffee beans mingled with bags of flour, freshly baked flatbreads that smelled of exotic spices, and baskets of colorful fruits from a warmer climate. Groups of cheerful, chatting Muslim women, their heads and faces discreetly covered, were already involved in picking out the best of each.

Michael drew a deep breath and released it. He looked truly out of place in this neighborhood, and he knew it. If he stood unmoving for too much longer, the residents would start to worry.

Warning bells sounded in his own head. He could still turn away, walk back . . .

But he recognized no faces in the crowd around him, and it was far too late to give into faintheartedness.

This gamble was all or nothing, after all.

Michael pasted on his most charming smile and straightened his shoulders. He tipped his hat to the women he passed as he stepped into the dark, spicy confines of the shop.

The shopkeeper rose from the stool at the back of the room. The man's bow drew a shadowy, blurred arc in Michael's vision as his eyes adjusted to the sudden darkness.

"May I be of any assistance, your honor?"

"I certainly hope so." Michael shut off the voices of warning in his head, and spoke the code words Hüberl had given him: "I'd like to buy one of your imported fruits."

"Ah." The shopkeeper stilled. As Michael's vision sharpened, he saw a dark-skinned face prematurely lined by hard work and weariness, focusing now into sudden taut worry.

It was a risk for the shopkeeper, too, of course. If Michael were a spy for the government, only waiting for evidence to take the man into custody or decree exile for him and his family . . .

Michael reached into his pocket, holding the other man's gaze, and gave a small, respectful nod. "I've come on a friend's recommendation," he said. "I have no ill intent, I promise."

He slipped a coin into the other man's hand without breaking their held gaze.

The shopkeeper sighed. "Yes, sir." The expression on his face was bleak, but the coin disappeared into his broad trousers as he shrugged. "You'll want to take the back stairs," he said.

"You won't regret it," Michael told him. *I hope.*

A new group of women stepped into the shop, and the shopkeeper hurried forward to greet them, abandoning Michael with visible relief. Under cover of their conversation, Michael crossed the sanded shop floor and slipped through the curtain at the back of the shop. He found himself at the base of a set of narrow, rickety wooden stairs set beside a closed door. The warm, familiar smell of baking bread drifted through that door. But from upstairs . . .

Michael sniffed the air. *Aha.* Now there was a smell far more familiar—and, in his youth, even more comforting: the distinctive smell of a printing press.

It wasn't comforting any more. It summoned up the memories of fire, smoke, screams . . .

Too late now.

Michael started up the stairs to play out the next move of the game.

CHAPTER TWENTY-ONE

Michael knocked on the door at the top of the stairs. A sudden paralyzed silence replaced the sounds of conversation and bustling activity within.

He knocked again. Quick footsteps approached the door.

"Who's there?" It was a woman's voice, sharp with tension.

"A friend."

Michael stifled a sigh as the waiting pause continued. Surely even the rankest novice would know better than to expect visitors to shout out names and titles on command?

Hissing whispers sounded faintly through the door as the occupants of the room engaged in some dispute. Finally, the lock rattled, the door swung open, and Michael stepped into one of the most crowded rooms he had ever seen.

A giant printing press hulked in the back corner, filling at least a quarter of the tiny room, along with its assorted accoutrements—inky templates and boxes of replacement letters stacked on top of one another in untidy piles and spilling over onto the floor. Next to the boxes, a small table and three spindly legged chairs jostled for space under vast piles of uncut, printed broadsheets. More paper filled the air, as newly printed pages hung from half a dozen clotheslines attached to the ceiling, waiting for the ink to dry. As Michael stepped inside, a tall, painfully thin young man with a prominent hawk nose and a wild shock of brown hair rose from one of the chairs, interrupted in the task of cutting yet more papers into shape.

Michael's old master would never have countenanced the mess in the room. Half the uncut papers had already slid off the chairs and table onto the floor, where they mingled with the bound books and pamphlets that filled the rest of the room. Crooked shelves had been nailed to the walls by an amateur carpenter, but they could barely contain a small fraction of the literature that flooded the compressed space, rising as high as knee-level at some points.

Where was the older and wiser mentor in this venture?

Michael stepped carefully over the closest pile and closed the door behind him, glimpsing for the first time the young woman who had let him in.

"My friends," he said genially, and divided his nod between the pair.

Brother and sister, he would guess; they were roughly of an age—nineteen and twenty, perhaps?—and they shared the same curling brown hair and dark eyes, although there was more determination in her face and greater fear in his.

The young woman was the first to reply. She stepped forward, darting a reproving look at her brother.

"Can we help you?" Her gaze passed over his outfit, and her eyebrows rose. "If you're in search of literature to read . . ."

"Not today," Michael said gently. "But I thank you for the offer." His eyes picked out a familiar spine in the shelves; he moved closer to confirm his guess. "Ah, you do have some old treasures here. I didn't think that one would be in print any longer."

"*On the Corruption in the Secret Police?*" The young man spoke for the first time, his expression becoming eager. "It hasn't lost its relevance, sir, I can assure you. Have you read it?"

"You could say so."

Michael felt a sharp pang as he turned away. Had the pamphlet been reprinted by some brave soul, or was it really one of the original copies? All he had to do was pick it up to answer his own question—he would recognize his master's typeface anywhere—but he found that he didn't really want to know.

"You could buy it for twenty florins," the young woman said sharply, behind him. "But only if you're not working for the police yourself."

"Me?" Michael turned with deliberate slowness to meet her fierce gaze. "Quite the contrary, I assure you. But I'm not here to buy your wares today."

"Then perhaps you ought to leave."

The young man coughed. "Aloysia—"

"Shh." She kept her gaze on Michael. "Well?"

Michael sighed. "Forgive me. I'm not handling this as well as I ought."

It was true . . . and it was completely senseless. This could be the most important move in his entire game. He ought to be savoring it, charming them both, playing the idealistic émigré for all he was worth.

But ever since he'd stepped inside, the past seemed to have risen like a dizzying fog around him. He had to concentrate to force himself to focus on their faces, in front of him here and now, instead of seeing faces from long ago and hearing the voices of people he had loved . . . people he had forced himself to forget.

His old master, Caroline's father, gently directing Michael's hand with his own larger, ink-stained fingers, as he led Michael through the motions of using the printing press for the first time . . . He had seemed old to Michael in those days, though he'd likely been no more than five and thirty—younger than Michael himself was now. A sobering thought.

Gerhard Vogl had been soft-spoken and reserved in person, despite the passion that had poured out in the pamphlets that he wrote and printed. One would never have guessed his radical politics from his sober appearance. He had dared take in a homeless young street-thief as his apprentice, though, for all the head-shaking and tutting that that had provoked among his more sensible friends. And his face had broken into a rare smile each time Michael had mastered a new challenge.

That last night, when Michael had left with his friends for an evening's pleasure, his master had clapped him on the back and folded a coin into his hand.

"For your good work today, lad," he'd said. *"Enjoy yourself tonight. Tomorrow we'll begin something new."*

Tomorrow . . .

Michael staggered, only half playacting. "Forgive me," he repeated. "May I sit down?"

"Of course," the young man said. He tugged out one of the other chairs, scooping a pile of papers off it to make space. "Can I find you a drink? Beer, coffee—"

"Kaspar!" Aloysia said.

"No, thank you." Michael ducked beneath one of the low-hanging clotheslines of papers and sat down. The chair legs were uneven beneath him. He had to rest his weight on his right leg to keep himself upright. He waved away the offers. "I only need to rest. I've had a difficult past few weeks, and now . . ."

Kaspar sat down across from him, listening eagerly, while Aloysia stood watching from across the small room.

"Who sent you here?" she demanded.

"I don't think he would wish me to use his name," Michael said. "But he told me this was a place that would print honest truths."

"It's what we do," Kaspar said. He leaned forward. "What's amiss?"

Michael almost choked at the hopefulness in the younger man's eyes. How old were these innocents? Young enough to be idealistic, even in this day and age, apparently. Young enough . . .

Young enough to be fools, he told himself, and throttled guilt before it could properly form.

He'd been innocent and idealistic once, too. It hadn't lasted. He'd have to hope, for their sakes, that they received no ruder an awakening than he had.

At least the girl had enough sense to be wary of strangers, if nothing else.

"I was once the prince of Kernova," Michael began, "until . . ."

He told the story with all the passion and conviction he could muster, hoping that the exhaustion in his voice sounded only that of desperation.

He'd been running from his past for twenty-four years. It felt bitterly appropriate now that he should have to return almost exactly to the site of his most painful memories in order to tell the tale of his most fantastic invented history yet.

At the end of it, Kaspar shook his head. "But—*all* the countries were invited to the Congress! It was in all the treaties. And—"

"But there were other, secret agreements," Michael said wearily. "And, it appears, only the desires of the Great Powers are to be given any consideration. Bonaparte has been defeated, but the lands that he devoured are apparently never to be freed . . . only to be turned over in turn to his squabbling victors."

"Shocking," Aloysia said. Even she had been drawn over to the table by his recitation; she sat now between Michael and Kaspar, watching Michael closely. "But not surprising," she added, deliberately.

"No?" Michael blinked. She was more discerning than he'd hoped—which, perhaps, might be the answer to how this little press had survived for any time at all. He raised his eyebrows. "I must admit, I was surprised. Foolishly, perhaps . . ."

Aloysia sighed and wiped back a stray loop of brown, curling hair from her disordered chignon. Her hand left inky stains on her cheek. Kaspar's own face was flushed with indignation, Michael noted, but the young man held his tongue while he waited for his sister to speak.

A problem, that; Kaspar himself might be easily duped, but he was apparently sensible enough, at least, to put great store in his more practical sister's opinions. Michael appreciated the wisdom of it, from an objective point of view, but found it a pity nonetheless. It would make matters more difficult, if nothing else . . . and he hadn't the time, at this stage in the game, to waste time searching for easier prey.

Prey. He swallowed a bitter taste at the truth of it. He'd never preyed on his own before. He'd lied and cheated his heart out, yes, but only to those who could afford their losses. What guilt could he feel over swindling a greedy merchant out of a smidgeon of his fortune, or tricking an avaricious baron eager to illicitly augment his own vast estates? Michael had never thought to put genuine innocents into danger.

But Talleyrand's orders had been more than clear. If Michael was not to abandon all of his own hopes for the future, he had no choice but to endanger theirs.

"All they care about is power," Aloysia said. "Their own and nothing else. It's the way of the world."

Michael's lips twisted. "You have a cynical eye, Fräulein."

"We wouldn't have to sit hidden up here if it weren't true," she said. "Do you think we'd gladly put our lives in danger if we didn't have to? If our emperor and his ministers cared for the good of the people, not only the security of the throne—if those who ruled cared ever to *listen* to the voices of the poorest souls, instead of outlawing protest and refusing to take notice of hunger and misery! Did you know that the chancellery is pouring fifty thousand florins per royal guest into this infamous Congress every day?"

"I . . . had heard that, yes."

"Fifty thousand florins!" Aloysia repeated, hammering on the table to give the words emphasis. "Fifty thousand apiece for balls and tableaux and mock tournaments, when half the men in this empire are *dead* and the lands wracked with misery from twenty years of war and the emperor's war taxes!"

"Twenty-six," Michael corrected her, automatically.

"Pardon?" She blinked.

He sighed, cursing his own slip of the tongue. "Twenty-six years of war," he murmured. "Emperor Joseph's Turkish war began in 1789 and ended only just before the wars against France began."

"You're a historian," Kaspar said.

Aloysia's eyes narrowed with sudden suspicion.

Michael shook his head. "I lived through it," he said flatly. "Do you expect me to forget? There were hunger and high taxes in the war against the Turks, as well, and there were riots in Vienna over the cost of bread. News of it reached us even in Kernova. There were pamphleteers then, too, though they were already forbidden in the Habsburgs' dominions."

It was time to take the upper hand. Michael let his voice sharpen into a whip. "Have you learned nothing from history, yourselves? Do you think it so virtuous to sit back and care nothing for the squabbling of the Great Powers over the powerless smaller nations?"

Color flushed Aloysia's cheeks, but she set her jaw. "What does it matter which Power gains control? They're all the same."

"Not to the people who live there. Perhaps you've lived so long in the capital of a great empire that you've forgotten—or never even imagined—what it might be like to be a smaller state amalgamated by a Great Power that cares nothing for your history, your culture, your language, your religion . . . your future. Nothing but what it can wrest out of your land and your people's resources to feed its own coffers, back in Vienna or St Petersburg."

"Sir," Kaspar began. "That is, Your Highness . . ."

Michael kept his gaze on Aloysia's face. "Do you genuinely believe that the poor and the hungry of Kernova will be better served by governors who live two hundred miles away and have never set foot on the soil that they tax—for their balls, their tableaux, and their mock tournaments?"

Aloysia bit her lip and looked down at her ink-stained fingers.

"And will you outlaw pamphleteers in Kernova?" she asked, finally.

Tension flooded out of Michael's shoulders so quickly that he nearly lost his balance in the uneven chair. He looked from Aloysia to her brother and let triumph overwhelm his guilt.

"Never," he said sincerely. "I swear it."

Michael walked out the front door of the grocer's half an hour later, armed with the sweet certainty of his own success.

Within five days, pamphlets would spread across Vienna, deploring the hypocrisy and shamelessness of the Great Powers who planned only to turn tyrants in Bonaparte's place . . . and using the case of Kernova as a prime example. Within a week and a half, if he worked hard, he could have copies of the pamphlets translated and slipped into the hands of the English Whig journalists in Vienna, who were all too eager to find evidence of their Tory ambassadors' wrongdoings. Within two weeks, Michael might even be a cause celébrè on the streets of distant London, and the English—key financial players in all of the Great Powers' decisions—would be forced to press for the opening of their private ruling circle.

All he had to do was stay in the game for another two weeks, and he would be untouchable. The government and the police might be furious, but they would never dare touch a figure at the center of an international moral outcry.

Two more weeks of balls, operas, tableaux, and mock tournaments . . .

Michael shook his head with rueful chagrin and turned to glance into a nearby bakery window, seeking distraction from the twinge of guilt. Fresh pastries were stacked in steaming array in shelves just through the glass windows; Michael could vividly remember their glorious tastes from his childhood.

And why not? Why shouldn't he celebrate his success?

He stepped inside and waited behind a stream of excited small boys, apprentices on their single morning off. They must have saved up all their pocket money for the past several weeks to afford that morning's feast; the number of pastries each of them ordered could have choked an ox. Michael watched them with idle pleasure, remembering his own past, for once, with more affection than pain. When it was his turn at the counter, he ordered a juicy Krapfen for old times' sake.

It was still steaming from the oven. He bit into it as he stepped away from the counter, and powdered sugar scattered across his gleaming shirtfront. Just as well that it was still early morning—he would be safe from meeting any new acquaintances until he'd had a chance to change his clothes in the apartment. He tasted the sweet jam inside the Krapfen's center and closed his eyes for a moment of pure appreciation.

When he opened his eyes, he saw Peter Riesenbeck, the actor, staring directly at him through the bakery's clear glass window.

CHAPTER TWENTY-TWO

Peter had been walking since dawn. *Anything to escape.*

The night before, he'd lain down with the blissful expectation of a long, deep, healing sleep. Instead, nightmares had swept him staringly wide awake well before the sun rose. He could have fallen back to sleep if they'd been mere fantasies of his imagination, but they had been far worse. They had been unvarnished memories.

And every time he'd closed his eyes, he'd felt the walls of his cell close back around him.

At first light, he gave up. He slipped out of the silent guesthouse and begun to walk, desperately and relentlessly, ignoring his aching, still-weakened limbs.

He'd walked through the fashionable center of Vienna on his first night here, dreaming of future successes at the Burgtheater itself. Now that he was scheduled for an actual performance there, he couldn't even force his steps back to the city center. That would have meant walking too close to the Hofburg palace and the hidden rooms inside.

The rooms, and the monsters that lurked within.

Peter struck out in a different direction this time, through the outskirts of the walled city. As the sun rose, and he shut his mind to the thoughts that wanted to bombard him, he turned his attention instead to the theater around him, forcing himself to become an audience instead of an actor, for once.

He watched street cleaners set off from their own filthy, narrow streets for their work in the wealthier parts of town. As the hours passed, he watched immigrants from all over Europe and the Ottoman

Empire start their days. Limping through the streets without pause, he passed Russians and Turks, Poles and Croats, many of them dressed in colorful native dress and all of them talking in a stream of different languages that passed meaninglessly through his ears.

Perhaps he ought to have been taking notes for future roles, stage sets, and costumes. But the future felt too amorphous and threatening to let himself imagine. Instead, Peter focused his eyes on the images around him and forced his feet forward, letting the effort and the images take the place of any rational thought.

His fate was coming for him soon enough. He wouldn't waste what freedom he had left.

He was in the fifteenth district when he glimpsed a familiar gesture in the corner of his eye.

Peter lurched to a halt, blinking. He didn't even know, at first, what had caught his attention so strongly. Something to his right . . .

He turned slowly, focusing his bleary eyes. A bakery stood on his right, the glass windows transparent for the sake of temptation. The baker himself stood behind the counter, a massive figure. A group of small boys hurried out the door, scattering past Peter, as he frowned at the two customers left inside.

A woman stood at the counter now, ordering with quick, irritable gestures. Before her, stepping away from the counter, was an aristocrat in full morning-dress, tall and lean, with silvering brown hair, looking as out of place as an exotic animal in this humble neighborhood. His face was turned away from Peter, but even so, Peter was instantly certain that this couldn't be any of the noblemen he had known in Prague. Yet something about the way this man stood . . .

The man turned, half-smiling, and lifted his pastry to his mouth.

Peter staggered. He knew that rueful smile and that easy bearing. *Michael.*

The clothes and the hair color had changed, but the mobile, intelligent face was exactly the same.

Peter's breath battered his aching chest. He'd barely believed in any chance of success for his own mad, desperate scheme. But now . . .

He glanced quickly up and down the street. There were no visible policemen here on the immigrants' side of town. If he were to run back to the Hofburg, by the time he convinced anyone of his credibility Michael would be gone. Peter couldn't summon official help or even hope to overpower Michael himself in his current state.

But if he hid and followed Michael back to his hiding place . . .

He looked back into the bakery just as Michael looked up and met his gaze.

Recognition flashed in the other man's face.

"Hellfire!" Peter muttered.

No choice.

He turned to run.

Michael cursed and dropped his half-eaten Krapfen. It fell to the bakery floor in a puff of powdered sugar, scattering against his polished boots as he leaped for the door.

It jingled as he threw it open. Outside, the street was nearly full of people by now, with boys selling newspapers and street cooks hawking savory Turkish *Böreks*, sweet Viennese *Palatschinken*, and roasted almonds to passersby. The grating noise of a knife grinder buzzed through the sounds of the crowd as Michael scanned the colorful, moving groups of people. Finally, he caught a flash of Peter Riesenbeck's blond hair— just as it disappeared around the closest street corner.

There was no good reason for Riesenbeck to turn tail and run at the sight of his old traveling companion. No reason at all, if Riesenbeck still believed the story Michael had spun him.

If he thought Michael such a horror-inducing danger that he would run to avoid meeting him again, then Michael could think of only one explanation that fit: Vienna's secret police had found the actor.

Michael's heartbeat thudded in his ears as he gave up discretion and leapt forward, pushing past paper boys and ignoring the loud protests of the street cook whose ingredients he knocked over on his way.

Elbows caught him in his side, knocking the breath out of him, but he didn't stop running. He didn't dare.

The other man might be heavier built than Michael, but he was also more than ten years younger and fitter . . .

And yet, oddly, he seemed no faster. Michael thudded onto the side street in time to see Riesenbeck less than a block ahead of him, far closer than he'd anticipated.

Michael didn't stop to savor his luck. Instead, he put on a burst of speed. Riesenbeck swerved into an alley, cutting past a veiled woman and six children who formed a happy, noisy family group that effectively blocked the alleyway for a full twenty seconds. Michael could have snarled in his frustration, but any further commotion would be fatal. He waited, cursing inwardly, for them to pass, then finally lunged behind the last bouncing child to skid into the narrow alleyway.

. . . Which was empty.

Damn, damn, damn!

Michael thudded to a halt at the other end, his chest burning with effort. The narrow alleyway ended in a side street lined with taverns of the lowest sort. This early in the day, only a few men wandered down the street, already staggering from too much liquor. The actor was nowhere to be seen.

Michael tipped his head back against the closest stone wall, reeling with disappointment.

He could walk up and down the street, peering into every tavern he passed, but in this neighborhood, every tavern would have half a dozen secret exits. The search would be every bit as bitterly futile as a hunt for any of the "lost" inheritances of the French Revolution that Michael had sold to gullible magnates across Eastern Europe in the past twenty years.

Worse yet, by the time he had searched four or five of the closest taverns, Riesenbeck might well have returned to this street with a policeman in tow. All that Michael could do now was turn around and make his own way, as secretly and swiftly as he possibly could, back to Caroline's apartment to pack.

Heaviness sagged through him.

There was no other choice. Wealth, luck, a guaranteed future . . . they might all beckon to him with a siren song, but Michael had been a professional gambler for nearly all of his life. That was more than long enough to recognize the change in the wind that signaled oncoming disaster. He knew when to stay in the game and when to cut his losses before it was too late.

He would have to leave Vienna.

Peter slipped out of the tavern's back entrance after five minutes of skulking in the darkest corner of the room. The back entrance led into another alleyway, filthy and deserted except for the busy chittering of rats rooting through the tavern's discarded chamber pot slops and rubbish.

His panting breath shuddered through his weakened body, and his one chance at capturing Michael this morning was gone . . . but even as he breathed in the stench of the alleyway around him, he savored the sudden, glimmering shard of hope that cut through his chest, sharp and bright and painful.

A single glimpse of the other man's attire had been more than enough to confirm everything he'd claimed to Grünemann.

He would find Michael again at the Hofburg tonight, just as he had promised.

And then Peter would never have to play the role of victim again.

Caroline followed Charles down the stairs, her breath coming faster with every step closer to his apartment . . . closer to the ritual that awaited her.

This is a mistake, her mind whispered, even as she forced her feet forward. They turned the curve in the stairs, and perspiration broke out on her forehead. The muscles in her chest felt as tight as if she were running rather than walking forward at an even, ladylike pace.

Nothing could be a mistake if it brought her father back to her. Not after twenty-four years of misery, guilt, and loss.

She couldn't turn back now.

Charles bent over the door to his apartment, jingling the keys.

"Your Ladyship." He opened the door and gestured her forward.

Caroline nodded graciously and swept through the doorway, careful not to brush against him on the way.

She'd never stepped inside her secretary's apartment before. *Michael's apartment, too, now.* She found herself glancing inquisitively for the door that might lead to Michael's own chamber. It was a foolish impulse, of course—he would keep nothing there of value; nothing that meant anything about the man himself, hidden underneath his many layers of disguise.

If anyone ever found out that she'd stepped, unchaperoned, into the apartment of two bachelors, her reputation would be besmirched beyond repair.

If . . . But, of course, it was far more than a mere possibility. The emperor's spies would certainly report today's expedition to him. *Never mind.* She was past worrying about that now.

She couldn't dismiss all of her servants from her own apartment at a moment's notice. *That* would cry out suspicion to anyone who cared to look, including—especially—the spy already placed in her household by the emperor. There would be no servants left in Charles's apartment, though, after Michael's breakfast had been attended to, the apartment cleaned, and Michael himself safely departed for the day.

Caroline and Charles had waited a full half hour after the last of the maids had finally finished their duties in the apartment below. There would be no one to witness what happened next. And if any rumors did spread that she had lowered herself so far as to have a liaison with her own secretary . . .

Caroline imagined Marie Rothmere's poisonous satisfaction and winced.

Well, she had never cared for the opinion of high society before, so why should she begin to care now?

"This is my bedroom," Charles said. He hesitated in front of a gold-colored door, flushing. "I . . . that is, it might be wise . . ."

"I understand." Caroline's lips twisted in a humorless smile. "We will certainly be safest in your own room, without fear of interruption."

"Quite." He coughed and turned away quickly. "So." He opened the door and let her step inside before him.

Charles's room was high-ceilinged, if not large, and it might have felt spacious if it hadn't been so filled with clutter. Books, magazines, newspapers, and even—surprising Caroline—scattered shirts, jackets, and cravats covered the floor, the zebra-wood secretaire, and the cabinets, all of the clothing tossed aside with far less care than she would have expected from her efficient secretary.

"Goodness," Caroline said lightly. "I must keep you busier than I'd realized."

Charles hurried ahead of her to clear a space. "Nothing secret is visible," he said, "but I thought it might be just as well to deter any spies from looking too closely underneath."

"So you've filled your room with distractions for them. Very sensible."

Caroline gazed politely out the window as Charles conducted his own search through the rubble that he'd created. The sky was clear and bright—it must be a sunny day outside.

On sunny days when she'd been a girl, her father had sometimes taken pity on her restlessness and released Michael from his other duties to take her to the Prater. They would wander through the public paths hand-in-hand, and she would eat warm Palatschinken bought fresh from a street cook, with sweet apricot jam dribbling down her chin . . .

"Now," Charles said, and drew a curtain across the window.

Enough sunlight still trickled through the dark curtain to let her see Charles's silhouette as he sat down on the cleared patch of floor before her. He struck a tinder, and light flared to life on a squat candle. He set it before him and looked up, shadows flickering across his spectacles.

"Your Ladyship?"

On the floor beside him, Caroline glimpsed the glint of a silver knife.

She took a deep breath and sat down across from him, smoothing down her skirts.

"Yes," she said. "I'm ready."

Michael trudged up the stairs to his apartment. Plans swarmed through his head, but his feet felt too heavy and slow to keep up with them. He had to pack and leave, that much was certain . . . but now, in daylight, or after nightfall?

He didn't know. For the first time in years, he couldn't see his way forward.

His instincts should all be leaping into top form now to carry him safely out of the city and into his next adventure. They had done so a dozen times in the past five years alone. But now . . .

Michael imagined Caroline's face when she realized that he was gone.

. . . And that he had abandoned her again, leaving chaos and disaster in his wake.

Again.

He straightened his shoulders with an irritable jerk. He could only protect her by leaving now. With luck, even if any policemen tracked him here and arrived to question her, they would assume she'd been taken in as completely as the rest of them. He *should* leave now, for her sake as much as his own—perhaps even leave her a note that would act as protection, for her to show any accusers and prove her own aggrieved innocence. And yet . . .

That was the difference, he realized, between this and every other quick escape he'd made over the last two decades. Before this, he'd never cared whom he'd left behind. Not since the first time, when Karolina's screams had haunted his nightmares. After that, he'd taken care never to let himself grow too attached to anyone he met in his schemes.

Oh, he'd had pleasant affairs along the way, with women he'd respected and liked who'd enjoyed the game as well as he did—but he'd never left behind anyone whose absence would truly pain him.

Until now. *Again.*

Karolina's old loyal, unquestioning adoration of him was long gone—Michael almost laughed at the understatement—along with the innocence that he'd once associated with her. But something else had taken their place in the adult Caroline—a strength of character that resonated irresistibly within him.

Perhaps it was the fact that she'd spent so much of her life effectively alone, just as he had. Perhaps it was the raw truth of their shared past, which cut through all the layers of illusion they'd both cultivated over the years—or the twin spirit that he could sense buried underneath her disguise, despite all her horrified denials. The passionate intelligence that had led her to play her own staggeringly successful gamble against the British aristocracy for so many years.

Or the fact that, after all of that, she still *cared.* She might try to hide it beneath her polished demeanor, but her sheer intensity of feeling cut through all his polished shields, straight to the boy he thought he'd buried long ago.

Whatever the reason, he'd been a fool. Now he remembered why he'd held himself so carefully apart from his companions all these years. Leaving Caroline today would feel like ripping out the last honest feeling inside him and leaving himself maimed and hollow.

Michael had just enough self-possession left to be silent as he opened the door to his apartment. For all he knew, Charles Weston would be inside, and there was no one he wanted less to observe his actions than Caroline's disapproving English secretary.

Michael stepped softly into the front room and slid the door closed behind him. He crossed the room and stepped into the passage that led to both bedrooms. Holding his breath, he listened for any rustle of papers or cough that might signal Weston's presence.

Instead, he heard something he had not expected.

Through Weston's door, too soft to be understood, but instantly familiar, he heard Caroline's voice.

Shock froze Michael into immobility. He heard Weston murmur something in return, followed by an unmistakable gasp from Caroline.

So. Michael realized his hands had clenched themselves into fists. He loosened his fingers and drew a silent breath to release the knotted muscles in his back.

So. He had wondered what special value Weston had for her, that she would spend a fortune on renting him a first-district apartment so intimately close to her own.

Now he knew the answer.

Michael's clenched jaw throbbed as he slipped open his own door and closed it behind him. He glanced unseeingly around the impeccably neat room—the room of a man who had never truly existed.

How long . . . ?

No. Caroline's affairs were her own concern.

He ripped open the chest of drawers and tossed his few garments into his gleaming new satchel. He needed nothing else. His own secret stash of money and last-minute resources (a forged will of inheritance, a "diamond" ring made of glinting crystal, a deed of signatory to a non-existent plot of land in the south of France) was kept in a secret purse next to his own skin, always.

Of course, it would be wisest to wait in his room until the apartment was empty again before he left.

Wait here while they . . .

No. That, he could not bear after all. Michael picked up the satchel and started for the door. If they caught him leaving—well, what then? Caroline would be relieved to see him go. And Weston . . .

Michael bit back an unprofitable surge of rage, as irrational as it was violent.

He would make no noise.

He turned the handle of his door in silence. Thank God for well-oiled doors, every trickster's best friend.

Barely breathing, Michael stepped out into the passageway. For one long, mad moment, he stood outside Weston's door. He heard Weston's voice, murmuring in low urgency. The door handle seemed to grow larger at every moment in Michael's funneled vision.

He wanted to turn the handle, throw the door open, say something unprintable . . .

But he had done enough damage to Caroline already in his life. If she had found true happiness now, it would be a poor friend who interfered with it.

Michael closed his eyes, trying to dismiss the visions summoned up by his over-vivid imagination.

He would never see her again.

Opening his eyes, he walked steadily toward the apartment's front door. One step, two steps, three . . .

Behind him, Caroline's voice rose in a sudden cry of pain.

Michael dropped his satchel, spun around, and leaped for the closed bedroom door.

CHAPTER TWENTY-THREE

Michael threw open the door and found himself in a scene from a fever-dream. Caroline and Weston sat on the floor in the middle of a wilderness of scattered books. The candle between them sent shadows leaping across their faces. With one hand, Weston held Caroline's bare left arm poised above a metal beaker. With the other . . .

Michael's gaze slipped from the silver knife in Weston's hand to the blood that dripped from a long cut in Caroline's pale inner arm into the waiting beaker.

"What in God's name are you about?" Michael lunged forward, stumbling on the cluttered floor. He grabbed Caroline and swung her up off the floor and behind him in one quick movement. With her safely shielded behind his back, Michael glared at Weston. "You bastard! I'm going to—"

"Prince Kalishnikoff!" Caroline's voice came out breathy with shock, but her grip on his shoulder was firm as she tried to pull him aside. "Calm yourself. Charles isn't—"

"Don't tell me to calm myself. He attacked you!"

Weston glared back at him, holding the beaker protectively close to his chest. "Perhaps you should listen to what Lady Wyndham has to say. *Your Highness.*" He spat out the final words like an insult.

"You—!" Michael wished he was wearing a glove to slap across the other man's face. Then again, in his latest guise, he wouldn't be allowed to fight a duel with a servant.

Just as well. He'd hate to put off the satisfaction for that long, anyway.

Michael fisted his hand, swung forward—

And Caroline pulled him back with a hard yank, even as Weston leapt away, hugging the beaker close.

"Stop!" Caroline said. "I can explain. I swear it."

Weston let out a choked sound of protest. "Lady Wyndham!"

"Charles..." She paused, biting her lip. Her face was bone-white, Michael saw, and pinched with pain. He looked down at her arm, and his stomach roiled.

"You're still bleeding."

"I . . . yes, I am. Of course." She took a deep breath, as Michael yanked out a handkerchief from his pocket and passed it to her. "Charles," she said calmly. "You have what you need. I know I can trust you to do the rest without me."

"Yes, your Ladyship. But—"

"Thank you. I'll meet you upstairs in my drawing room as soon as possible. Wait for me there. Prince Kalishnikoff..." Her dark eyes met his, as she pressed the folded handkerchief against her skin. "Come with me," she said. "Please."

Michael hesitated. Weston was still hugging the disgusting, blood-filled beaker to him like an infant. Every one of Michael's instincts told him to snatch the damnable thing away and punch Weston in his smug face.

Caroline tugged at his arm. "Please," she repeated. She swayed slightly and reached out for balance.

Michael slipped one hand behind her back for support. As Caroline turned toward the doorway, Michael met Weston's glare for one last moment.

"Later," he promised softly.

Weston's eyes narrowed. He darted a swift glance at Caroline's turned back and then dipped his chin to Michael in silent agreement. Michael felt the secretary's venomous gaze on his back as he and Caroline picked their way across the floor, until they finally closed the door behind them.

Caroline hesitated in the passageway. Her cheeks were still deathly pale, and Michael watched her with concern. How much blood had she lost to that leech?

"I don't know where—"

"My room," Michael said. "It's the only safe place. You don't want your servants to see that wound."

"No," she agreed. "Not until I've thought of a good reason for it."

Michael's teeth set. "There is no good reason." He guided her into his room and closed the door. "Let me see."

He raised her arm, lifting away the handkerchief, and took in, for the first time, the seriousness of the wound. It was only a narrow slice down the skin of her forearm, but it oozed blood at a worrying rate, without any signs of slowing. Michael set his teeth together.

"I am going to kill him."

"Don't be absurd." Caroline pulled her arm back and pressed the skin together. "I'm sure he didn't mean to cut so deeply. I only need a proper bandage."

"I'll find one for you." Michael turned around—and bit back a curse as he surveyed his empty bedroom.

Of course, he had nothing left here to bandage her arm. All of his possessions were sitting in the front room, in his packed satchel. *Brilliant.*

"Just wait here a moment. Sit still and keep your arm raised above your chest."

She sighed. "You don't need to speak to me as if I were a child."

Michael gritted his teeth and hurried out into the passageway. He scooped up the packed satchel from the drawing room floor just as the door to Weston's room opened and the secretary stepped out.

"You're leaving?" Weston asked.

"You're not so fortunate."

Michael brushed hard past the other man, heading down the passageway. He heard the front door of the apartment open and then slam shut with an unspoken message of resentment.

When he stepped back into his own room, he found Caroline sitting on the edge of his bed.

"Did you know—?" she began. Then her gaze fixed on the satchel in his hand, and her eyes widened. "You're leaving." It was a statement, not a question.

"Not at the moment," Michael said curtly. He tugged out a clean silk shirt from the satchel and ripped it neatly in two. "Hold out your arm."

She shook her head, still staring at the satchel he'd dropped to the ground. "You were going to leave without even telling me, without—"

"I said, hold out your arm." He dropped down to his knees in front of her.

"You—"

"Pay attention." He met her gaze. "Do you want to bleed to death?"

"It's not so deep a wound."

"It's too deep for my liking." Michael folded the first half of the shirt into a thick pad and pressed it against the open wound. "Hold this here for me," he said.

Caroline did, but glared at him. "You can stop giving me orders now." As her voice regained its strength, it took on a cutting edge. "You're hardly in a position to command."

"No?" Michael wound the other half of the shirt around her left arm, careful not to tie it too tightly. "I'm still waiting for you to explain exactly what madness was going on in there. Weston's gone, so you needn't worry that he'll overhear you. I want the truth."

Her eyes narrowed. "You have no right to expect any such thing from me! You were on your way out, without any warning, any word of—"

"I would have told you," Michael muttered. He tied the final knot and looked up at her, releasing her arm. "I intended to tell you. Originally."

"But—?" Her face, only inches away from his, had settled into haughty unapproachability. Was he only imagining the hurt hidden behind the anger?

"But," Michael continued steadily, "I heard your voice in Weston's room as I came into the apartment."

Caroline blinked. Confusion pierced her mask of aristocratic hauteur. "What on earth would that have to do with anything?"

Michael shook his head and gave in to the disaster he'd been trying so hard to escape.

He'd spent twenty-four years trying to forget her. It had never, ever worked.

"What do you think?" he asked.

He leaned forward, careful not to brush against her injured arm, and kissed her.

Caroline froze, eyes wide open.

Michael's lips felt warm against hers. *So warm.* They moved gently, tentatively, against her mouth. He tasted faintly of powdered sugar, but mostly of himself, an indefinable, irresistible essence, like coffee or rich, dark chocolate. With a breath, she could push him away.

She ought to push him away.

Caroline hadn't kissed a man for pleasure since . . . *Wait.* Had she ever kissed a man just because she wanted to? Because it felt like this?

She'd kissed men because she'd had to. She'd kissed men because she'd wanted to, because it had been her key to survival.

But Caroline had never kissed a man with nothing to gain and everything to lose. She'd never kissed a man who truly knew her.

She had never kissed Michael.

Caroline closed her eyes and gave in to temptation.

Just for a minute. I'll push him away in just a minute.

She reached up to touch Michael's face lightly, caressingly, as her lips moved against his. His skin felt warm and already faintly rough against her fingers. The feeling of that light stubble sent tingles racing across her palm. She curved her hand around his cheek and threaded her fingers into his soft, short hair. At her touch, she felt him suck in a breath.

She opened her mouth and leaned into him to deepen the kiss.

Just one more minute . . .

He tasted bone-deep familiar and utterly intoxicating. She fell into the kiss like an ocean wave, letting it sweep away all reason and common sense, carrying her far from where she'd meant to go. Michael's strong hands came up to hold the back of her head and the nape of her neck.

Caroline slid forward onto the floor beside him, pulled inexorably closer to his warmth.

She had been cold for so, so long . . .

When she pressed herself against him, he sucked in a gasp through their kiss. She shivered with the shock of it, and the pleasure.

Being with a man wasn't supposed to feel this way. It was a chore that she had learned to accept, because there were no other choices. She had forced herself, years ago, to turn it into a talent, to save it from feeling like utter degradation. She'd developed careful skill but always held herself removed while her body played out the set moves of the ritual.

Now, though, she could have melted straight into Michael's skin. His chest felt warm and solid against hers, and his arms wrapped around her back as if he could hold her safe forever. The tops of his thighs pressed intoxicatingly against hers as she half-lay across his lap.

She wanted to crawl inside him and lose herself.

Caroline wriggled even closer, reaching out to catch her balance—and her bandaged left arm hit the sharp edge of the cabinet just behind him.

"Ahh!" She jerked back and fell against the bed.

"Are you all right?" Michael loosened his hold around her. "Your arm—"

"I'm fine. It was only . . ." Caroline drew to a halt, staring at him. She was gasping for breath—and so, she saw, was he, his eyes half wild.

Their legs were still tangled together, warm and close.

What in the world was she doing?

"Don't," Michael said. He drew a ragged breath. "Please. Don't move away." His lips twisted into a half-smile, but he looked physically pained. "I can actually see you considering it, you know."

Caroline swallowed, her gaze trapped by his. "You see too much."

"I love you," he said.

Caroline's whirling, disordered thoughts went completely still.

"Wait." Michael winced. "Forget that I said that, please. Pretend I didn't?"

"So it isn't true, then?" Caroline asked. Her voice seemed to come from a long way away.

"No, it is. I hadn't realized it until now, but . . . it's true." Michael's eyes were wide with what looked like panic, his linked hands held very still against her back. "But you don't want to hear it yet, do you? So I shouldn't have said it."

"I don't . . . I can't . . ." Caroline drew a deep breath. Pain throbbed in her left arm, a beating reminder. "I have to stand up," she told him.

"Don't," Michael said. He dropped his hands to his side, freeing her, but kept his searching, hazel gaze intent on hers. "Stay," he said softly. "Please."

Caroline stood up, carefully disentangling herself. Once she was upright, though, she found her head whirling too much to do anything more than collapse down onto the bed. *Michael's bed*, she thought, and then cursed herself.

"This is madness," she said. She looked down at her bandaged arm to avoid looking at Michael. Her eyes felt drawn to him with mesmeric force. Her eyes, her hands, her mouth . . . She cut off the all-too-enticing train of thought. "This is only a whim—a moment of madness—"

"Not on my part," Michael said quietly. "I wish I could dismiss it so easily, for my own peace of mind."

"Perhaps you ought to try harder," Caroline said.

"Never." Michael moved to sit on the bed beside her, keeping a careful hand's breadth of distance on the narrow mattress. The heat from his body reached out to brush, temptingly, against her skin.

She could have pinched herself with irritation at the words that somehow escaped her mouth: "And Princess Bagration?"

"What?" Michael stared at her. "What has she to do with anything?"

Caroline closed her eyes, burning with self-contempt. She shouldn't care, she didn't care, she—

"Marie Rothmere said that you were her latest paramour." Caroline pressed her lips together tightly to hold back any further revelations. Where had her self-control gone? It must have deserted her at the same moment as her common sense, when she'd first been foolish enough to kiss him back.

"Do all of the lady's romantic affairs consist of a courtesy kiss on the hand and a few polite compliments from her guests?" Laughter warmed Michael's voice. "It would be a sad lack of passion to wish on anyone, I fear."

"Really?" Caroline opened her eyes. "But—"

He was smiling at her with the same rueful, affectionate grin she had known since childhood. It had charmed her then, as a naïve, impressionable girl. Now . . .

"Princess Bagration is an admirable hostess and politician," Michael said, "but she hasn't a tongue sharp enough to cut her enemies into slivers and a heart fierce enough to light them on fire afterward. She's not the one with the courage and the wit to climb out of poverty and disaster, create a new history for herself, and play a role in front of all society for decades." His smile dropped away as his voice dropped to a bare whisper. "Princess Bagration is not the woman I admire and desire with all my heart."

"I would have hated it if she had been," Caroline confessed, and felt her last defenses drop away.

His mouth was warm and familiar and absolutely right, first against her lips, and then trailing soft, tingling kisses down her neck. She shuddered at the intensity of it and pulled him closer.

They fell back onto the bed together. Caroline kissed his stubbled cheek and pulled off his cravat to kiss his throat. There was too much between them, suddenly, too much blocking her hands and her skin. When she tugged at his fitted dark green coat, he pulled it off willingly and tossed it onto the floor beside the bed. His white silk shirt felt soft under her hands, fitting close to his strong, lean arms. His scent dizzied her.

If she let herself stop and think, she'd remember all the reasons she couldn't do this, not now, not ever. So she didn't let herself think about it.

Caroline unbuttoned his silver waistcoat instead, cursing the difficulty of the tiny gilt metal buttons, and pressed her hands into his shirtfront, soaking in his warmth.

Michael's chest moved with ragged breath against her hands. She looked up and met his eyes.

He started to say something—shook his head—then laughed.

"If you had told me this morning that this would happen, I would have thought—"

"Don't think," Caroline said. She tugged down the puffed short sleeves of her gown and felt the cool air brush against her exposed shoulders.

Michael's eyes darkened. He replaced her hands with his own on the edges of the gown's bodice.

"May I—?"

"Don't stop!"

Michael tugged down the dress until it fell to her waist in a crumpled mass of blue silk and gauze, and only her thin, cotton stays supported her breasts.

"Look at you," he whispered. "Karolina Vogl. In my bed. You are so very beautiful."

Caroline could barely breathe. The intensity of his gaze mingled with the tingling heat in her skin. *Michael.*

Michael Steinhüller.

Looking at her.

She formed his name with her mouth but couldn't speak. Instead, she leaned wordlessly forward, wrapping her hands in his hair and pulling him forward.

His lips traced her skin, from her throat down to her breasts. She gasped with pleasure—

And the door to the bedroom crashed open.

CHAPTER TWENTY-FOUR

Charles stood in the doorway, his face ravaged with shock.

"Charles!" Caroline struggled up, pulling at her crumpled gown. "I thought you were upstairs . . ." Her voice trickled hopelessly to a halt.

Oh, God. The look in his eyes sent dread lancing through her. There had to be something she could say or do, if only she could think of it. Something . . .

Michael pushed forward to shield her from the door. "What the devil do you mean by bursting in here, Weston?"

"I apologize. Your Highness." Charles bowed stiffly. His voice came out as a near croak as he turned away. "I won't disturb either of you again. I promise."

"Charles, wait—!" Caroline began.

The door fell closed. She heard his footsteps turn into a run, hurtling down the hallway.

Caroline pushed Michael away and leaped off the bed, working her arms back into the tiny puff sleeves of her gown with excruciating awkwardness. Every moment lost . . .

"Caroline," Michael began.

She lunged for the door. "Charles!"

She emerged into the corridor just as the apartment door slammed shut. She hurtled down the corridor, through the outer door and down the stairs. If anyone saw her—shoeless, her hair uncovered and disheveled, running as fast as she could—they'd take her for a madwoman.

The bleak fear in her stomach told her there were worse fates, and she was already courting them.

She pushed open the door onto the street.

Sunlight glinted off the windows of the elegant carriages that rattled down the Dorotheergasse. Strolling gentlemen paused to stare at Caroline through their quizzing glasses as she emerged into the cold, fresh air. Ladies whispered to each other. Derisive laughter sounded in Caroline's ears.

Charles was nowhere in sight.

Caroline sagged against the doorway. She heard familiar footsteps running down the stairs behind her. Her feet felt as heavy as millstones as she stepped back and let the door fall shut, closing off the light and air. *And hope.*

She'd ruined everything.

"Caroline." Michael took her arm and turned her to face him. He was fully dressed again and looking unfairly polished, in sharp contrast to her own appearance. "What on earth—?"

"Don't touch me!" Caroline jerked away. "Do you have any idea what a disaster has just occurred?"

"Disaster?" Michael shook his head. "It was unfortunate, it was ill-timed . . ." His mouth relaxed into a smile. "*Most* ill-timed. But I'd hardly call it—"

"You know nothing about it." She set her jaw and started up the stairs.

"Then tell me!" He caught up with her half a second later. "So your secretary saw us in a compromising position. What of it? He's hardly a social arbiter."

"Be quiet," Caroline hissed. "The door upstairs could be open. There are spies—"

"Everywhere. I know." He dropped his own voice to a whisper. "And how much joy do you think they took in watching you tear after him so desperately, just now?"

She sucked in breath between her clenched teeth. "A charming description."

"Charming for me, too." Michael's face was tense with anger. He threw open the door to his apartment and gestured her inside with exaggerated courtesy. "Would you care to explain?"

If she didn't, he'd doubtless follow her up to her own apartment to pester her. Giving in, Caroline swept past him with all the dignity she could muster and waited for him to close the door before she turned on him.

"I don't have to explain anything to you."

"No? What of your relationship with your secretary, then? You must care about him a great deal to let all the emperor's spies witness you running after him like a woman lost in love."

She let out a half-laugh that bordered on hysteria. "I am not in love with Charles!"

"What other reason could you possibly have?"

"You fool," Caroline said, and felt all her resolution break into the release of pure despair. "Didn't you understand *anything* about what you saw earlier?"

Michael rubbed his hand over his eyes and dropped his shoulders back against the green wallpaper as if all his boundless energy had finally deserted him. "Just this once, could you answer a simple question for me? Please?"

"Certainly," Caroline said, and felt clear, clarifying coldness flood through her body. "Charles is not only my secretary."

"Hah."

"Charles is an alchemist. *Al-che-my*," she added, enunciating each syllable with precision. "You do understand what that is, I presume?"

"Alchemy? Oh, let me think." Michael closed his eyes. "Half-mad experimenters dabbling in chemicals and trying to transmute lead into gold, perhaps. Or extremely accomplished tricksters who convince the gullible of their deep magical prowess. Several of whom I worked for when I was younger. Give over, Caroline!" He opened his eyes to glare at her. "I'm not a fool to be fobbed off with children's stories. I can't see Weston fitting either type."

"That's because you don't understand anything about it." Caroline bit out the words. "Alchemy is no fraud, nor is it as simple as turning lead into gold. Not for everyone."

"And you would know this because . . .?"

"Because I had the knowledge thrust upon me." She turned away from him, looking sightlessly out the drawing room windows. "You think of alchemy as a children's story?"

"Well..."

"Then think of this story," Caroline said. Anger seemed to have released her, until she was floating above herself, listening to herself speak words she had never planned to say. "Imagine an eleven-year-old girl being taken by the police when her father was arrested and their house set aflame."

She heard Michael's indrawn breath behind her, but she didn't pause. "Children of criminals aren't typically arrested, you might think. They are sent to orphanages, or to foster homes, or let loose into the streets. But sometimes they disappear. And who is there to notice, when the only person who *might* have cared had already run away to save himself?"

"Caroline..."

She moved toward the window. "And so this girl, who was only eleven, was taken away and put into a tiny room, underground. And when the door to the room opened..." She reached out to rest the flats of her hands on the cool glass windowpane, drawing in the cold to infuse her body and protect herself against the memories. "*You* might not believe in alchemy, but Emperor Joseph's minister of the secret police did, and he needed practice to better his skills at it. Who better to experiment on than a girl nobody else would miss? She could be drained—hurt—used..."

"Caroline." Michael was standing behind her suddenly, his hands on her waist, his voice taut with suppressed anguish. "I'm so sorry."

"*Four years,*" Caroline said. She didn't turn around. Instead, she spoke into the window, looking out at the bustling life of the street below. It was a reminder: *I have escaped.* "Four years in a tiny, windowless room, first in one of Pergen's own houses and then ...

"He moved me into the Hofburg, after Francis came to power. Because"—she paused, fighting to control her voice—"because Francis wanted to help. He was Pergen's pupil. In every way."

"Dear God." Michael's breath ruffled her hair. "Does he know—?"

"Who I am? Not yet." She held herself still in his embrace. She couldn't let herself relax back into his arms. If she did, the cold she'd hoarded within would melt into warmth, and all her frozen tears would melt with it. "He—they sold me when I was fifteen. Every so often, Francis would show me off as part of his collection of curiosities to a few men he trusted. Wealthy, discreet visitors. He was younger then, of course. Less practiced in politics. Now he'd never dare reveal the secret. But then . . ."

"He showed you off," Michael repeated tonelessly behind her. "And?"

"One of the visitors was English. A wealthy alchemist himself. And he . . . wanted me. So they sold me to him, and he took me to England." Caroline breathed deeply, steadily, controlling her voice. "He would show me to his friends sometimes, too. And he had one friend—a marquis, very eccentric—who took a fancy to me. He even shocked convention by marrying me, although he kept me hidden on his estate, of course. And he gave me a new name. *Caroline*. He died a year after that, and then one of his friends, Lord Wyndham . . ." She stopped. The broken pieces inside her were too close to the surface for safety. She shoved them down again. "It doesn't matter."

"And you raised yourself from that to become one of the most powerful women in English society," Michael said softly. "You are remarkable."

"Haven't you been listening to me?" Caroline twisted around to meet his gaze. "Don't you understand anything? I was Pergen's prisoner. I was *nothing*. I was his experiment! I tried every single day to escape. I did everything I could, and nothing worked. *Nothing ever worked*. Every day, I swore I wouldn't let the alchemy work against me, and every single day that he chose to visit . . ." Tears stung behind her eyes. She gritted her teeth and held them back.

Michael captured her cold hands and held them between his own. Warmth leached into her skin, persistent and inescapable. "You survived," he said, "and you didn't stop fighting."

"It didn't do any good."

"If you think that, then you're the one who hasn't been paying attention," Michael told her. "You're the strongest person I've ever known."

Caroline shook her head numbly, even as she met and was trapped by his intent gaze. Intent and unmistakably sincere.

The frozen cold within her shivered and creaked under his warmth. She opened her mouth, searching for protection, drawing on all the methods of grim self-defense that she'd mastered over the years.

"I would give anything to change the past for you," Michael said. "*Anything*, Caroline. But I would change nothing about you now."

The ice cracked. Caroline almost choked on the painful, gulping sob that forced its way up her throat against her will. She knew better than to lean on anyone. She couldn't trust anyone, ever, no matter how much she was tempted.

Her legs melted underneath her, and she collapsed into Michael's embrace as sobs ripped up from her chest, overwhelming her.

Michael wrapped his arms tightly around Caroline, holding her as she wept. Every wrenching sob was a knife blade thrust into his chest.

What could he have done differently, indeed. How many times had he used that excuse to himself over the years? It rang poisonously false to him now.

Perhaps he couldn't have saved her, truly.

But he could have tried.

Michael had never sacrificed his own good to help anyone else after his long-ago flight from Vienna. It had been the strongest and most vivid lesson he'd learned from that night of fire and terror: never again to let himself care about anyone or anything but his own safety and advancement.

What lesson had Caroline learned, when she'd watched him turn away from her that night?

No wonder she'd lashed out at him with such anger when they'd first met again at the emperor's masked ball. He could barely believe that she was letting him hold her now.

Caroline's sobs gradually slowed and stilled. She sniffed and took a breath against his damp shirtfront. Michael held his arms still around her, hardly daring to breathe and break the moment.

"That was why they didn't let my father go," she whispered, so softly that he wasn't sure he'd heard her correctly.

"Your father?"

"All the other printmakers from Joseph's reign were released by the turn of the century. Except for him."

"Oh." Michael met her upturned gaze and swallowed. "*Oh*. I see."

If Pergen and his emperor wanted to avoid uncomfortable, public questioning...

"That's why you came back," he said. "Isn't it?" He barely needed her nod of confirmation. "That's what you want from the emperor." *The emperor...*

Realization of the risk she ran squeezed his chest with sudden panic, worse by far than any he'd felt for himself. "If they recognize you—"

"They almost have. Pergen told me..." She paused, taking a deep, shivering breath. "He told me last night that I seemed strangely familiar. And that he would make it his first priority to find out who I really am."

"We have to leave." Michael would have stepped away if he could have forced himself to let her go. "I've already packed. If you gather your things, we can—"

"I can't leave! Don't you understand? I haven't found my father yet."

"If Pergen finds out the truth—"

"If I run now, I'll never find him," Caroline said. "It's my fault he's imprisoned."

Michael's sharp bark of laughter hurt his chest. "Your fault? You were a child! It was Pergen who—"

"My father has no one else but me. He's been locked in a prison for twenty-four years now. Twenty-four years!" Tears shone brightly in

Caroline's eyes, but Michael recognized the thread of steel in her voice. "I *will not* abandon him. I cannot leave until I find out where he is."

Michael swallowed a groan. "And what does Weston have to do with it?"

"I brought Charles with me . . . as a safeguard against the alchemy I knew to be waiting here for me." Her voice turned level, expressionless. "And then, if nothing else worked, to use alchemy myself, as a final weapon."

"So what I saw this morning—"

"Was my last plan. My final hope. I asked Charles to find my father, using my own blood."

"So Weston knows—"

"Almost exactly who I am." She nodded. "Now do you see why that moment downstairs was such a disaster?"

Michael bit back a foul curse. Every instinct in his body told him to flee. *Now.* Without waiting even long enough for Caroline to pack. He'd escaped barely in time from discoveries and retribution in a dozen cities in the past two decades, relying on those well-honed instincts. None of those situations had promised the sheer horror that he could feel roaring toward them now. But the stubborn, set look on Caroline's face expressed more clearly than any words that logical arguments would be futile.

He should be making his excuses, now. He should grab his satchel from his room and slip out of the building before it was too late.

Just as he had last time.

"Of course you don't have to stay." Caroline's face stiffened as she stepped back, pulling free of his arms. "It's not your battle." Her lips twitched, attempting a smile that didn't quite work. "There's no reason for you not to leave now and save yourself."

"I am not leaving you again," Michael said, through gritted teeth.

He must have gone mad. Even as her expression softened into startled hope, he wondered where his sense of self-preservation had gone.

It must have abandoned him back in that damned bedroom. Or maybe it had flown away at that first moment when he had recognized her adult face underneath her English bonnet and his life had shifted, insensibly and irrevocably, in its path.

"But," he added reluctantly, "I should tell you that I'm in danger too."

"Well, of course, if they discover my—"

"No," Michael said. "Not because of you. A troupe of actors smuggled me into Vienna from Prague. The Riesenbeck troupe. I fobbed them off with a story of lost inheritances, a tragic romance, powerful families, danger—"

Caroline's laughter startled him—and herself as well, judging by the surprise on her own face as laughter broke out of her mouth. She raised one hand wonderingly to her lips, but she didn't stop laughing. "You are incorrigible. Even when we were children, the stories you used to try to fool me into believing—"

Michael captured her hand in his, smiling despite himself. "Quiet. I'm telling you something important."

"Fine. What name did you use with them?"

"Count Michael von Helmannsdorf."

"Hmm." Her lips quirked into a mischievous grin. Her face, open with laughter, looked suddenly younger, echoing the carefree girl she'd once been.

"I saw the leader of the troupe again this morning," Michael told her. "He saw me and recognized me, even without the disguise."

"And?" Caroline raised her eyebrows. "What did you tell him?"

"Nothing. He ran the moment he saw me. I chased after but couldn't catch him."

"Oh." The amusement drained out of her face. "*Oh*. So—"

"So he must have known that I wasn't who I'd claimed. Otherwise, he wouldn't have run. Which means—"

"The secret police," Caroline breathed. "He had already been questioned."

"At the very least." Michael kept his firm hold around her hand. "That was why I packed to leave."

"I see." Her eyes narrowed as she thought. Her fingers tightened around his.

Michael watched her, waiting. Something felt odd, itchingly unfamiliar . . . *ah*.

His decades of travel and adventuring and avoiding real attachments had saved him from all the dangers of loss and regret . . . but it had also meant that he'd never had a partner he could trust. Someone who would listen to his own declaration of risk without immediately severing ties and betraying him for their own self-preservation, if that was what the moment called for.

Just as he would have done in turn . . . until now.

Caroline hadn't returned his unexpected, involuntary declaration of love when he had blurted it out and shocked them both. But that stubborn loyalty, which had already sent her back into unholy danger, was at the core of who she was, beneath all those layers of disguise and self-control. And as their fingers wrapped tightly around each other, Michael *knew* that the bone-deep connection he felt to her was not one-sided.

"He didn't see where you went, afterward?" Caroline asked.

"I don't think so."

"Then you're safe for the moment—at least, until you leave the building again. If he wanted to find you, dressed as you were, it would be obvious for him to look in the first district, among the nobility."

"Exactly."

"But if he is an actor, he'll be engaged in the evenings with his own performances. Do you know where his troupe is employed?"

"The Theater an der Wien. Every night," Michael added, remembering their boasts.

"Well, then. You should be safe in the evenings. Tonight." She drew a breath. "Tonight is the gala festival at the Hofburg. We should go."

"If Weston has gone to the secret police himself—"

"Then I'll be lost indeed. But if he hasn't, if he only walks the streets for a few hours and turns the matter over in his head and wonders what to do and drinks more than he should before he makes any decisions . . ."

"As many a man his age has done in the past, truly," Michael admitted.

"Then we'll be safe until tomorrow, at least. And I only have one last chance, tonight."

"Which is?"

"To go to the emperor and confess everything," Caroline said. "And to beg him to release my father. For my sake."

Michael's grip tightened convulsively around her hand. "What could possibly persuade him to have pity, in such a case?"

"I can offer him tens of thousands of English pounds for the chancellery. Money that he desperately needs to fund the rest of this Congress."

"And if that isn't enough to persuade him?"

She set her jaw and met Michael's gaze. "Do you have to ask?"

Michael's chest burned as he remembered the look of hunger on the emperor's face the night before. "Caroline . . ."

"Twenty-four years," she said softly. "For twenty-four years, my father has been locked in a small, dark room, alone. Isn't it worth anything I can do to rescue him from that at last?"

Michael closed his eyes to shut out the expression on her face . . . and the memory of strong, sure hands directing his own on a printing press: the hands of a man who had taken in a fatherless street-thief instead of leaving him in the cold. "The emperor won't say yes," he said, desperately. "It would be a mad bargain."

"Then we'll leave tonight from the gala, immediately, before he can speak to Pergen and call for our arrest. I'll have my carriage packed and waiting in case the worst should occur."

Not the worst. That wouldn't be the worst.

But Michael didn't say the mad, irrational words that burned in his throat.

"I . . . understand," he said instead, nearly choking.

"And you'll come with me?" She swallowed, showing a first visible crack in her composure. "I don't think . . . I don't know if I could bear to go alone, tonight."

"Then I'll come." Michael tried to smile reassuringly. He couldn't, even after all his years of training in illusion.

He had no right to forbid her anything, to claim the privilege of a commitment she had never made to him. He couldn't stop her from making her own choices . . . or even argue with her reasoning this time.

But the words he was so carefully, rationally restraining felt like ground glass in his throat.

"Good." She let out a sigh. Her face was still flushed from her tears. She wiped off the last dampness as she turned. "Before we do anything else, though, I have to retrieve something from Charles's room. For safety's sake."

Michael followed her back into Weston's darkened bedroom and shoved his way through the layers of clutter. He jerked open the curtains to let in the sunlight. As Caroline searched through the room, Michael stared out the window at the blue sky outside. It seemed too bright and clear for a day such as this.

He turned around when he heard Caroline's indrawn breath.

"What is it?"

"The beaker," she said. The color had drained from her face. She held up the beaker he'd seen earlier, when it had been filled with her blood. It was empty now. "He must have transferred the blood into a sealed case. And if it isn't in this room . . ."

"Well?" Michael frowned. "You'll have to explain it to me. I know nothing about the kind of alchemy that actually works."

"In proper alchemy . . ." Caroline moistened her lips, looking ill. "Blood is the most powerful signifier there is. It can locate a person or anyone in his or her family. It can be used to affect a man's health or energy . . . or cause his death."

"So, if your blood isn't here in this room—"

"Then Charles carried it with him," Caroline said. "And he holds my life in his hands."

CHAPTER TWENTY-FIVE

"**N**o announcements?" Marta stared at Peter from behind her husband's muscled shoulders.

They stood with the rest of the company on the stage of the fabled Burgtheater. In the midafternoon, on a day with no matinee performance, it was only an empty theater, albeit one of more than ordinary magnificence. Its white and gold boxes flanked and surrounded the wooden stage. The sound of stagehands' voices bled through the thin backstage wall; cleaners in the auditorium swept out the public stalls with stoic indifference to the drama being enacted on the stage before them.

But then, Peter thought ruefully, this was the same stage that had showcased the best of French and German theater for the past hundred years, from Molière to Mozart, Goethe, and even the great Beethoven's new opera, which had played here only the night before. How could his own troupe's far-from-original melodrama hope to hold the cleaners' attention after such rich fare?

The thought made him smile for a moment...which was a mistake.

"How can there be no announcements of which troupe has been invited to perform?" Marta's voice rose to dangerous heights of power, until she could have blasted straight up to the theater's highest tier. "Did you negotiate *nothing* to our benefit?"

Peter winced as the rest of the company murmured restlessly around them. "The emperor desires to present his guests with an unexpected treat. Part of the entertainment for this evening will be their opportunity to guess which troupe of players they will see, and then—"

"And then they'll think themselves disappointed to see unfamiliar faces in a troupe straight from the provinces," Marta said acidly. "Because they weren't prepared for it properly, with signs and advertisements that quoted all our best reviews. How could you have been so thoughtless as to agree to such a plan?"

"Did you expect him to struggle for our benefit?" Karl snorted, crossing his arms. It was Karl, of course, who had brought the news to Marta and the rest of the troupe after scouring not only the outer walls of the Burgtheater itself but also all the streets around it for any signs advertising their coming performance. "He didn't even have the courage to argue the Theater an der Wien into paying for our accommodations. How did you think he would stand up to the emperor's representative?"

"Actually," Peter began, but he was cut off by Josephine, who looked nearly ill with panic.

"They won't even realize what our names are, if there are no signs to tell them!"

Peter sighed. "We will announce all of the players' names, at both the beginning and the end of the performance."

"But all they'll hear will be the names of the leads! None of the reviewers will be able to remember—"

Marta rolled her eyes. "There's no need to worry about that, dear, really. They wouldn't have bothered to comment on your performance anyway."

"You spiteful cow!"

"It's not too late," Karl broke in, stepping between the two women. "As our respected leader has fallen short in his duties—much as I'd expected he would, else I wouldn't have bothered to look in the first place"—his glowering gaze swept over Peter's face—"I'll simply arrange the matter myself. I'll take two stagehands with me, and between us, we'll have the entire first district plastered with theater bills by the end of the afternoon."

"Oh, darling, you are a genius," Marta said. "But the bills themselves—"

"You'll have to mention *all* of our names on the bills," Josephine inserted, her face set mulishly.

Peter managed, at last, to draw a ragged breath through the horror that had nearly choked him. "You will do no such thing!"

"I beg your pardon?" Karl turned to him with exaggerated courtesy. "You wish to instruct me, perhaps, on how to negotiate a deal? Or how to look out for our company's best interests? Or—"

"If a single sign is posted, we will forfeit our contract and all of our payment." Peter had to clench his jaw shut to keep himself from losing all control and simply leaping for Karl's thick neck. He forced the words out through his teeth. "The emperor made his conditions quite clear."

"How would he even know? He'll be occupied in public functions all day. He'll never—"

"*You damned stubborn fool,*" Peter gritted.

The rest of the company fell into a shocked silence.

There. It's out.

Peter had never spoken in that tone of voice to any member of his company before. He had danced around Karl's simmering jealousy and resentment ever since the first week he had formed the troupe, three years ago, never speaking an angry word in return. He had never needed to. He'd had his silver tongue and self-confidence to fall back on, to keep the company balanced well under his thumb.

Dramatic heroes didn't lower themselves to abuse or aggrievement, and Peter had always been a hero, setting off on an epic journey to success.

But no longer. Now his hands trembled with the force of his anger. He kept his voice to a hoarse whisper, because otherwise his shouts might lacerate his throat and keep him from playing his proper part tonight . . . quite possibly, the last part he would ever have a chance to play.

He had nothing to fall back on anymore except his rage.

"Do you have *any idea* what I went through to secure this performance?" he asked. "Do you? You're such a keen critic of my work, aren't you, Karl? Always writing your own reviews, saying how I should have done it all differently. Well, you weren't there to see what happened! No, nor in Prague either, when I had to beg the theater manager to let us play out our last week, despite the drop in ticket sales."

"Herr Riesenbeck," Josephine began, timidly.

He ignored her, his attention on Karl's broad, reddening face. "You think I should have talked the Theater an der Wien into paying for our accommodations, do you? And how, precisely, do you think that would have worked, when I'd already had to pay them nearly the last of my own savings only to bribe them into taking us on in the first place?"

There was a moment of horrified silence onstage as all the other actors stared at him. The only noises in the theater were the steady rustling of the cleaners sweeping out the stalls, and the creaking of sets being wrestled into place backstage.

"What madness is this?" Marta breathed.

Peter's voice came out gravelly with rage. "Your husband told me he thought the whole company deserved a pay rise when we came to Vienna. A charming thought, when the Viennese managers laughed in my face at the mere idea of inviting a provincial company that couldn't even manage to pay off the bills with the scanty audiences they'd managed to summon in their own city."

Karl's voice sounded hoarse. "You said—"

"We never had problems with the theaters in Prague," Marta said, voice throbbing. "Never!"

"No? That would be because I paid them the difference in their funds to make up for the sales they lost by hiring us." Peter gazed with bitter satisfaction at the blanched faces of his company members. "And you think I could have done better by you than I did? It took the persistence and the persuasiveness of a devil to find us paying work at all!"

"But—you said—" Karl began.

"I said what you all needed to hear." Peter shook his head. "Would you have performed at your best if you'd known the truth? If you'd known what the theater managers truly said of you to me when you couldn't hear? Would you care for me to tell you the details?" He paused, waiting. "No? I thought not."

"But . . . but . . ." Marta swallowed, raising a hand to her throat without any graceful fluttering, for once. "We saw the reviews. The critics, they said—truly, they *did* say—"

"'The best small company in Prague,'" Peter quoted, from memory. "'Best acting and direction. A company to watch.' Yes." He drew a deep breath, releasing the tension from his shoulders. "They said it because it was true. And they were right. That was why it was worth throwing everything into this trip. Making it possible. Giving us all a chance."

Karl blinked owlishly. "Your savings—"

"Gone. For good, unless we make ourselves a success." Peter set his jaw. "Which we *can*. That's why I threw everything into buying us this chance to be seen in the center of the empire. No matter what it took."

Of course, if he'd realized at the beginning just how much it would take . . . Peter dismissed the thought before it could settle onto his shoulders and crush him. He couldn't afford to think that, not now. Not ever.

He met Karl's eyes evenly. "Are you going to throw away this single chance I've won us only to suit your sense of pride?"

Marta made a small sound of distress. She put one hand on her husband's arm.

Karl didn't bother to look down at her. His jaw firmed. "No," he said. "But after all this—if it doesn't succeed—"

"Then you'll be free to think on what would be best for yourselves. And if that means leaving this company for a different one . . ." Peter shrugged heavily. "I won't hold you to your contracts. Not after tonight."

Karl nodded, his expression grim. Low whispering started up behind him in the rest of the company. In a moment, all would descend into chaos.

Peter's head throbbed. All he wanted to do in the time he still had left was to curl up in a dark corner—or, no, better yet, a well-lit corner. Where no shadows could lurk, and no voices either, and no effort, no outsized energy would be required of him.

Instead, his voice sliced straight through the whispers. "We have one chance to impress the gathered nobility of Europe. One chance alone. If you don't wish it to be wasted . . ." Peter stepped back, raising his chin to disguise his weariness. "It's time for us to rehearse."

Charles Weston pushed his way through the crowds on the Graben. A fine lady cried out in aristocratic outrage as he knocked her aside. He shrugged away from her and her inanely twittering companions.

Half a dozen different languages streamed past him as he staggered down the crowded street. He recognized them all from years of study and rigorous self-improvement.

What a goddamned bloody waste.

What was the native language of betrayal? Perhaps there was none. Could it be common to all countries?

He choked at the thought and nearly crashed into the blazing oven of a street cook. Strong arms pulled him away just in time.

"You are careless, Monsieur Weston," a cool voice said beside him, in French.

Charles shrugged the arm off, not bothering to turn around. "Leave me alone."

His spectacles were smeared with spattered oil from the street cook's griddle. He pushed his way forward, half-blinded, bulling his way through the crowd.

"Now, now." The voice had caught up with him again. A firm hand took hold of his arm and pulled him to a stop. "This is no way for a sensible man to behave."

"No?" Charles spun around, panting, to glare at the stranger. "And what the hell would you know about it?"

The man facing him was small and nondescript. *Like me*, Charles thought bitterly. But even more so than a discreet secretary, this man seemed almost designed to fade into a crowd. Indeed, Charles could see the gazes of the passersby flit past his companion without a moment's interest. The only curious looks were the ones that landed on Charles.

Under the scrutiny of quizzing glasses and sidelong glances, Charles became reluctantly aware of the anomaly he presented: an aristocrat's proper secretary, standing panting and disheveled in the middle of Vienna's most fashionable street, with smeared glasses and an oddly shaped bulge in his disordered jacket.

The realization only intensified his glower.

"What the devil," Charles said, in precisely articulated French, "do you mean by accosting me in this fashion?"

"There's no need for indignation, sir." The man smiled placatingly as he released Charles's arm. "I'm only here on behalf of my employer, who asked me to seek you out."

"For what?" Charles shook his head even as he finished the question. "Never mind. I'm not available for discussion at the moment." He started forward.

"Nor for new employment?"

"New . . ." Charles took a breath, as pain pierced him, starting a throbbing headache.

He wouldn't, he would not torture himself by remembering—

But he couldn't force away the image: Lady Wyndham and that insinuating bastard. She couldn't even claim he'd forced her. Charles had seen the look on her face, before she'd realized he was there.

The pure, sensuous enjoyment.

The bitch.

He was almost sobbing. In public. Damn it.

He gritted his teeth and blinked back humiliating, boyish tears. It was a good thing his glasses were already smeared. Perhaps the madman before him might even miss the telltale sheen of water in Charles's eyes.

"I understand you are the most highly valued secretary of an Englishwoman? Lady Wyndham?"

"She has been my employer," Charles acknowledged evenly.

But not for long. By God, he wouldn't let himself be used and discarded like this. She'd played him for a fool. Begging for his help, telling him he was the only one she could trust . . .

Charles's fingers clawed themselves into fists.

He would make her pay. He didn't know how he could do it yet, but he would. No matter what it took.

And then, maybe—possibly—afterward, when she'd been forced to admit she was wrong, when she had really suffered and he'd seen her pain . . . His short fingernails pressed into his palm with stinging force. If she begged him, afterward . . .

Then, perhaps, if he was feeling generous, he would give her another chance.

But until then . . .

"Let me buy you a drink," the man before him said. "It really will help, I promise you."

"You don't know anything about it," Charles muttered.

"No? You might be surprised." The other man leaned forward. His voice lowered to a whisper. "The uses of alchemy have never been forgotten in this city, Monsieur Weston. Nor have we forgotten how to honor those who are accomplished in its practice."

Charles blinked. Five conflicting thoughts tried to take shape in his mind all at once, and canceled each other out to leave it blank. "Who are you?" he asked, finally.

"My name is Vaçlav Grünemann, and I've been watching you for some time. My employer is most anxious to make your personal acquaintance. Shall we?"

Grünemann gestured to a narrow side street. Charles found himself following the other man, trapped by bewildered fascination.

"Very good," Grünemann said calmly. "You have made the right decision, sir. But then, my employer thinks that you show great potential."

Emperor Francis II viewed his reflection in the mirror with dissatisfaction.

Tonight would be the greatest fête of his Congress, and everything was prepared. He would charm and flatter the tsar and his Prussian toady as he must throughout the evening, and then—at last, the culmination of all his maneuverings—as soon as the theatrical performance was over, he would finally seal his secret pact with England, for an endless supply of English gold and the power it would bring him to stand against the Russian empire as an equal.

After all his years of endless humiliation, he would have his triumph at last.

Francis's cravat was tied with crisp elegance, in preparation for the evening's entertainment; the Orders of Knighthood pinned to his claret-colored tailcoat gleamed in the soft candlelight. Everything was in place. And yet . . .

His face looked positively sunken. And his eyes . . .

It was a trick of the light, no more. Candlelight was known to cast odd shadows. It was only his own weakness that summoned up a tinge of supernatural dread, to see the shadows form in his own eyes.

"More light," Francis snapped. In the mirror's reflection, he saw his personal valet jerk to sudden attention at his words, while the uniformed footman at the door kept his own gaze directed firmly ahead in professional disinterest. Francis felt a sharp stab of annoyance. "I can barely see myself!"

He waited, tautly, as the valet lit more candles around him. With each added flame, more shadows disappeared from his cheeks, taking away the look of hollowness, and—yes—removing the shadows from his eyes as well.

Francis let out his held breath in a sigh. *There.* No need to fear, after all. Pergen protected him from that fate, as from so many other potential dangers in his empire.

As if he'd summoned his chief minister only by thinking of him, a knock sounded on the inner door of his apartments. Francis nodded graciously, and the footman swept the door open.

"Your Majesty." Pergen swept a deep bow. "If I might have a word . . ."

Francis shrugged. "As you will. Leave us," he added to the others, and the two servants filed out of the room. As the door closed behind them, he turned away from the mirror.

"Well?"

"All is prepared for tonight."

"I knew I could count on you." For once, Francis couldn't summon up the interest that catching a new subversive deserved—but for such a loyal servant as Pergen, it would be ill-done indeed not to offer well-earned praise. And perhaps afterward . . . His breath shortened with sudden anticipation. "Do let me know if I can help in any way."

"But of course. Your Majesty would be most welcome."

"I could use some fresh distraction." Francis directed a look back at the mirror and twitched the lapels of his coat a fraction more even. Where was the triumphant glow he should have exuded, at the anticipation of his greatest success?

"Ah," Pergen said. "Perhaps I can help even now, in that case."

Francis blinked and turned his attention to his minister. "Yes?"

"I have recently made a discovery which, I believe, you may find quite interesting," Pergen said. His thin lips curved into a smile of fierce satisfaction. "Let me tell Your Majesty what I've only just learned of Lady Wyndham's true identity . . ."

CHAPTER TWENTY-SIX

Blackness pressed inexorably against the glass windows of Caroline's carriage. Only the flambeaux borne by the link-boys before and behind the carriage sent occasional streams of light across the windows and the sides of the buildings nearby. *The same buildings, every time*, Michael noted, sighing. The carriage had moved less than a foot in the last half hour. With every visitor of noble birth invited to the emperor's gala celebration, the inner streets of Vienna were as tightly packed as cards in a closed deck.

And, for once, Michael had no idea who had stacked the cards.

Sitting above the carriage, Caroline's coachman and her personal maid were already bundled up in traveling clothes, in case they had to flee directly from the gala itself, without stopping back at the apartment for any of their cases first.

Within the carriage itself, only the faintest flickers of reflected light revealed scattered glimpses of Caroline's face—the edge of her strong cheekbones, her closely pressed lips, her gaze fixed ahead in focused determination—or was that obsession? *Too late to worry about that now*. Michael took a deep breath, rolling out his tense shoulders. If they were to have any chance at all of success in the evening ahead, he could allow no fear or self-doubt to mar his performance. The only way to win at the very riskiest of gambles was to show your opponents a face of unblemished confidence.

But this was a gamble he would never have accepted on his own behalf.

"Is everything—?" he began.

Caroline hadn't spoken for the past ten minutes. Now, she rattled off her words at a breakneck pace: "Everything is packed and ready. I have enough money in my reticule to take us halfway to France, and the rest can be sent to me there within a day."

"Good. We—"

"I have a bribe set aside for the guards at the city walls. If they question us, I've just received word of an ill uncle in Sussex, possibly on his deathbed, and I cannot wait until morning to begin my travel. You're escorting me to protect me on the journey. You don't have your papers with you because we left in such a rush, but our bribe will ensure they don't stop us for it. They're always less fastidious with visitors who wish to leave the city than with visitors coming in."

"I understand. But—"

"We can change carriages in the mountains. I left a second carriage and horses stabled there on my way in case of emergency. That carriage doesn't carry my crest or any other signifying mark, so—"

"Caroline." Michael took hold of her hands. "You've made excellent preparations. Clearly." His lips twitched. "You needn't convince me of anything."

Her clenched hands opened in his grasp. Caroline let out a choked laugh, hardly more than a puff of breath.

"I . . ." Her words trailed off. "I've tried to plan everything," she whispered. "But I can't stop remembering how it felt to be a prisoner there."

"I understand," Michael said. The carriage jolted forward suddenly, as space opened up in the line, and he jerked at the surprise of it. Still, he didn't release her hands. "It's different now," he said. "This time, you're not alone."

"No," she whispered. Her dark eyes were hidden in the shadows, but her fingers tightened around his. "Neither are you," she said. "Not anymore."

It all felt like a dream, Peter thought.

The Great Hall of the Hofburg Palace was lit by magnificent chandeliers that cast reflected flames in a hundred mirrors set about the hall. Smothering heat rose from the press of a thousand bodies, despite the frosty chill outside. Peter had played princes, counts, kings, and dukes on stages all across the eastern edges of the Habsburg Empire. Now he mingled with all of them in truth, breathing the same stifling air and sipping at the same expensive champagne.

He was too nervous to swallow any of it.

Through the crowd, he caught a glimpse of Marta, her head tipped back in affected laughter, flirting outrageously with a silver-haired man in Prussian uniform. Peter wove through the shifting mass of bodies, trying not to bump any lightly held crystal glasses. The cost of a single shattered glass would doubtless rival his own salary from a successful night's performance.

Marta ignored Peter's arrival beside her as the Prussian nobleman finished what was obviously the cap of a long-set-up joke.

"... And then she said: 'In that case, Your Majesty, I'll have another!'"

Marta's trilling giggles mingled with the Prussian's own roar of laughter at his own wit.

"My goodness, Count." Marta raised her painted fan high to peek demurely at him above its edges. "You do have a way with words."

"Might I have a word with you, Frau Dujic?" Peter asked. He nodded to the nobleman as he took Marta's arm. "Just for a moment . . ."

She stepped away from him with a twitch of twice-turned imitation silk. "Perhaps later, Herr Riesenbeck?" She cast him an irritated, sidelong look behind her raised fan and mouthed the words: *Not now*.

"Marta," Peter began, under his breath.

The Prussian glared at Peter. The military medals on his uniform glittered in the light from the chandeliers. "I believe the lady wishes to remain exactly where she is . . . sir."

"Apparently so," Peter muttered . . . but refrained from clicking his heels together in submission, as the other man would clearly have liked.

Belatedly, his good sense returned to him, shouldering its way past his buzzing nerves. *Take hold of yourself*. As a struggling director,

Peter could hardly afford to offend any powerful men, no matter how abstracted he felt from such mundane considerations at the moment.

"I do beg your pardon, Frau Dujic. And yours, Count." He bowed, restraining any hint of irritation from his tone. "But Frau Dujic ... should you happen to recognize an old friend in the crowd tonight, would you do me the favor of letting me know? Preferably, before the gentleman himself sees you?"

Her eyes narrowed in calculation. "Whom are you speaking of, exactly?"

Peter shrugged, conscious of the Prussian's impatient glower fixed on him. "An old traveling companion of ours," he said lightly. "I'd like to see him again, nothing more."

Peter moved aside before she could pursue the point. Not that he had to worry about that, he realized a moment later, as he saw her lean closer to her companion, drawing her fan across her face in the motion that signaled *deep interest*. Peter wondered what spot Karl had chosen to monitor the progress of his wife's professional flirtation.

It was just as well that he couldn't see Marta's husband in the crowd. Peter had no intention of asking Karl the same favor he'd asked of Marta. That could lead to far too many sharp-edged questions, especially with Karl's pride still raw and sore from the afternoon's confrontation.

Peter tossed down half his glass of champagne in a single gulp. Normally, he'd never drink before a performance. Tonight, he needed all the help he could muster.

Clenching his fingers around the fragile stem of the glass, he set off through the crowd to begin his search.

By the time Caroline's carriage finally drew up outside the Hofburg, her nerves were jangling more harshly than any Janissary band. She accepted Michael's hand as she stepped out of the carriage, less for any physical support than just for the warmth she drew from the momentary contact.

The line of glittering guests that led through the stone entryway into the Hofburg's inner courtyards looked like a procession of buzzing flies, walking blindly into a waiting spiderweb. And at the center of the web . . .

Caroline dismissed the fancy with an effort, even as she released Michael's hand.

She knew better than anyone else—even Michael, for all the protective fears he'd been trying so hard to hide from her—exactly how deep was the danger she faced tonight. She knew the secrets at the heart of the Hofburg and Emperor Francis's government. If she let herself, she could remember exactly the way Pergen's experiments had felt— and the coldness of the stone floors against her skin afterward, as she'd lain sobbing and alone.

But this time she wasn't alone. She held onto that fact like a candle to carry with her into darkness.

Michael stepped onto the stone paving slabs beside her, looking as elegant and distinguished in his evening clothes as if he truly were the Eastern prince he claimed to be. At a word from the coachman, the horses moved forward, carrying the carriage away to make room for the next party of guests.

"Lady Wyndham?" Michael murmured.

"Prince Kalishnikoff." She met his eyes in the flaring light of the footmen's torches.

"May I?" He offered her his arm.

Caroline lifted her chin. "Of course," she said, and laid her hand across it.

Father, she promised silently, *we won't fail you.*

Together, they joined the line of guests.

Michael's senses tingled with alertness as the line moved at a snail's pace across the first of the Hofburg's inner courtyards. Caroline's hand was steady on his arm, but he felt the tension in her grip. The night air snapped with frost against his skin, a promise of the frigid winter to come. The flaming torches held by the footmen to light the way cast flickering shadows across the faces of their fellow guests, creating images as distorted as any mask. In the deeper shadows behind the torches, Michael thought he spied watching faces, contorted and malevolent—only to have them revealed, in his next step forward, to be nothing more than crannies in the ornamented stone walls.

As they crossed into the second courtyard, they stepped into the light that spilled out of the open doors leading into the Hofburg's Great Hall. Michael drew his lips into a genial smile, nodding at the familiar and unfamiliar faces suddenly revealed before them. Heat poured out of the Great Hall, along with the gathered chaos of music and a thousand voices. As they stepped inside, Michael felt a sudden twinge of discomfort. He'd glimpsed a movement in the corner of his eye, something familiar and yet unexpected, something he couldn't quite pin down . . .

Michael turned his head smoothly, maintaining his courtly smile even as his muscles tensed.

But whatever he had seen was gone.

Even as Michael turned away, a soft hand grasped Caroline's arm from behind.

"Caro!"

She shouldn't have been surprised, Caroline thought wryly. After all, what else could make this evening worse? She arranged her lips into a smile and turned.

"Marie. How lovely to see you here."

"Well, how could I miss it?" Marie squeezed her way into the line ahead. The ostrich plumes in her piled hair fluttered in the wind from the open doorway. "George was hideously boring and insisted on arriving far too early so that he could conduct some tedious political business, but I wouldn't hear of being so unfashionable—especially as we're only to be rubbing shoulders with anyone and everyone tonight, not any *true* elite." She raised her eyebrows meaningfully as she tilted the edge of her fan backward, toward the couple who stood behind them. "But now that I am finally here . . ."

Marie's bright gaze landed on Michael as he turned back from whatever had distracted him. "Why, Prince Kalishnikoff." Her lips curved into a smile of pure delight. "How absolutely marvelous to see you again. And together with Caro again, tonight."

"Lady Rothmere." Michael bowed as the line moved forward. "A pleasure."

"I've been hearing talk of you everywhere," Marie purred. "Who was it . . . oh, yes. Princess Bagration, so I hear, has named you the handsomest gentleman at the Congress."

Caroline felt her jaw tighten, even as she maintained her smile. She saw Michael's lips twitch with barely restrained mirth. If he teased her about this later, she would have to throttle him.

"An honor indeed," Michael murmured. "The princess is too kind."

"So all the gentleman say, certainly." Marie sniffed. "I wouldn't know, of course."

"No?" Michael's voice was as soft as silk. "What a pity for you, Lady Rothmere."

"I beg your pardon?" She blinked at him.

Amusement restored Caroline's voice. "I believe we're being invited to the retiring room, Marie," she said, nodding to the gesturing footman beside them. "Prince Kalishnikoff . . ." She met his warm gaze and let herself smile, even knowing that Marie was watching. "I'll see you again shortly, I hope."

"I shall look forward to it." He lifted her hand to his lips.

His kiss tingled against her skin, shooting warmth up through her arm. She almost stepped back to keep herself from revealing her feelings too publicly, but then she remembered. Her final duty . . .

Under Marie's interested gaze, Caroline said carefully, "I know you haven't been feeling well, Your Highness. If you should need to leave before me tonight . . ."

Michael's brows drew together into a frown. Caroline finished as lightly as possible.

"My carriage is waiting on the Bankgasse, and I've instructed my coachman, Henry, to follow your commands. Do feel free to take the carriage if you should need to retire early. You'll find everything there that you might need." Should she hint at where she'd hidden the bribe for the customs inspectors? No, he was surely clever enough to find it on his own.

Michael's grip tightened around her hand. "I'm certain that won't be necessary."

"I do hope not." She drew her hand away, keeping her serene expression with an effort. "Shall we, Marie?"

She felt Michael's gaze following her as she led the way to the women's retiring room, where maids waited to unbutton their pelisses and smooth any wind-blown hairstyles before they were presented to the emperor and empress themselves.

"Well, well, well," Marie murmured, as they stepped inside the packed room. "I would never have thought it of you, Caro. After what everybody's been saying, too . . ."

"Have they?" Caroline murmured vaguely.

She raised her chin to allow a hovering maid to begin to unbutton the column of tiny buttons that led from the collar to the waist of her ankle-length pelisse. The smells of the multitude of other women around her, mixing lavender water, powders, creams, and sweat together, was nearly overpowering. She clung to the memory of Michael's words.

That won't be necessary, he had said.

With all the willpower she'd developed in her thirty-five years, she prayed that he was right.

Michael would have given away any of the imaginary fortunes he'd invented for himself over the past twenty years to understand the gleam in the emperor's eye as they met in the receiving line.

"Prince Kalishnikoff." Rather than glaring at Michael as he had the night before, the emperor graced him with a glittering smile of amusement. "How fortunate that we have you here tonight."

"Fortunate for me, certainly," Michael said, as he bowed. "A magnificent event, Your Majesty. As always."

"Ah, well, my wife handles all such matters. Of course." The emperor's smile deepened. Rather than nodding for the next guest to approach, he leaned closer to Michael. "Don't you find that women are generally the best at arranging social niceties? And social stratagems, as well?"

"Ah . . ." Michael paused. "Alas, I've never been a married man, Your Majesty."

"And yet, I would be surprised if you had not . . . but never mind." The emperor shook his head, as if restraining himself from sharing a private joke. "Do enjoy the evening's entertainment, Your Highness."

"I thank you, Majesty." Michael moved on, keeping his smile fixed even as his mind whirled with suspicion.

The emperor's amusement could forebode nothing good. Of that, at least, Michael was coldly certain. Thank God the carriage was ready and waiting for them. Even if it weren't for Caroline's mad plan, he would have insisted on leaving Vienna directly after tonight's gala.

Michael moved away from the receiving line, directing his gaze in a casual sweep of the crowd. With luck, it would appear that he was merely looking for the closest drink rather than searching for potential escape routes.

"Prince Kalishnikoff." A familiar voice spoke behind him. Michael turned to find the French foreign minister regarding him with cool appraisal.

"Baron de Talleyrand." Michael swept a bow. "I'm delighted to see you again. I trust you are well?"

"Perfectly. And you?" Talleyrand raised his eyebrows within his sagging face. "I was surprised not to hear from you today."

"I've been much occupied, I'm afraid." Was that—? Michael stiffened as he heard a disconcertingly familiar trill of female laughter nearby. Familiar, and yet not readily identifiable. Where had he heard it before?

"Profitably, I hope," Talleyrand drawled.

"I beg your pardon—that is, yes. Very profitably indeed. I hope you'll agree with me when you see the results." Michael fought to gather his scattered thoughts under the French ambassador's heavy-lidded gaze. This was no time to let his nerves run away with his tongue.

"I hope so too," Talleyrand said softly. As the crowd shifted around them, the two men were pressed closer together, and Talleyrand's voice dropped to a whisper. "And do you have any notion just when I might be impressed with those results?"

When you find I've disappeared, tomorrow morning? Michael thought.

The too-familiar female laugh sounded again, closer this time. Tension tightened into a warning knot between Michael's shoulders. He smiled. "Very soon, Monsieur. Perhaps within five days."

"I am pleased to hear it." Talleyrand's face retained a look of indifferent courtesy, but his low voice was cutting. "If it took much longer, I'm afraid my interest, and any small influence I possess, might be strained to their very limits."

"I'm certain that won't be a problem," Michael said smoothly. He bowed, already backing away. "If you'll excuse me . . ."

He turned as soon as courtesy would allow to search for the source of that disturbingly familiar laugh.

But the crowd had shifted into new formations, and Michael did not hear it again.

Caroline's chest tightened with every step she took in the receiving line. Each step took her closer to the promised confrontation . . . and to her ultimate goal.

Tonight, she would save her father. She told herself that with every breath.

As one person after another stepped to the front of the receiving line, Caroline became more and more conscious of the emperor himself, as if he possessed a tangible magnetism that reached out toward her. He was in an expansive good humor tonight; his sharp laughter reached her ears, and she caught glimpses of fierce, flashing smiles.

Perhaps Pergen had already fed him on some poor creature's spirit tonight. That had always . . .

Caroline wrenched her thoughts away from that direction. She would not be able to go through with the evening ahead if she let herself remember that.

Her feet moved forward of their own volition. She found herself facing him, only inches away.

She took a breath and dipped a low curtsy. "Your Majesty."

"Lady Wyndham." A smile played at the corners of his mouth as he raised her hand to his lips. "I am honored. Of course."

His lips brushed against her fingers. Caroline fought down the impulse to pull her hand away.

The rage she'd seen in his eyes the night before had unnerved her. But the glee she saw in his patrician face tonight . . . *That* made her almost numb with fear.

"I wonder . . ." Caroline slipped a sideways glance at the empress, who was absorbed in conversation with a Russian noblewoman. She forced herself to play out her lines as she'd prepared them, her eyelashes demurely lowered. "Might it be possible for me to speak to you more privately, Your Majesty? Tonight?"

His fingers tightened around her hand. When he spoke, his voice sounded as smooth and rich as cream. "My dear Lady Wyndham, you've taken the very words from my mouth. I was about to make the same suggestion."

"You were?" Caroline looked up involuntarily and met his triumphant gaze.

"Soon," the emperor murmured. "As soon as I can escape this duty. I'll seek you out, never fear."

Caroline forced herself to smile. "I can hardly wait."

CHAPTER TWENTY-SEVEN

Peter walked through the crowd, all his senses alert.

It had been an hour since he had arrived at the gala celebrations. In another hour and a half, he would need to leave for his final performance of the evening.

Seconds ticked away in accompaniment to his rapid heartbeat.

Through the crowd, he glimpsed a familiar face: Vaçlav Grünemann, the spy, here to help Peter in his mission . . . or to take him prisoner once again, if he failed. Peter looked away, wincing, but not soon enough. In the corner of his vision, he glimpsed Grünemann's cool smile and nod of recognition.

A liveried footman approached, offering Peter a new glass of champagne in exchange for his empty one. Peter paused a moment, his hand hovering above the silver tray, then shook his head as common sense asserted itself. He moved on, still clutching his empty glass and listening intently for any echo of a familiar, lying voice.

French conversations blurred in his ears, blending with scattered German, English, Russian, and other languages he couldn't recognize. Whenever the closely packed crowd allowed, Peter tried to scan the line of new arrivals streaming in from outside. All he managed to see were glimpses of military medals, fans, and outrageous hairstyles. Twice, he thought he recognized Michael's lean build. He pushed his way through the crowd—and found only unfamiliar faces before him.

An hour and a quarter left. Peter elbowed past the people in his way, ignoring the laws of courtesy and logic. If he shoved past the wrong man, he'd find himself challenged to one of the lethal duels that the nobility so loved.

He didn't care. A far worse fate awaited him if he failed.

Just over an hour left. Sweat streamed down Peter's face. He was nearly running now.

He broke through a gap in the crowd—and tripped.

The Prince de Ligne stood out even in this packed room. Caroline glimpsed his gleaming white hair and felt herself relax for the first time in nearly twenty-four hours. She disentangled herself from the group of Englishmen who had gathered her up after her arrival and slipped through the crowd toward the prince's erect figure.

It was only a rest, not a rescue from what lay ahead. But still she found herself smiling with genuine pleasure as she swept toward his circle of admirers.

"Lady Wyndham." The prince bowed with an elegance left over from the last century and stepped aside to welcome her into the circle. "Tell us, have you made up your mind yet on the most burning issue of the day?"

"Your Highness?" Caroline raised her eyebrows as she stepped into place beside him. The Comte de La Garde-Chambonas stood on De Ligne's right; beyond the comte stood Michael. She nodded to both men and tried not to let her gaze linger too long on Michael's face. Still, his half-smile warmed her even as she turned back to De Ligne's look of wicked delight.

"Why, how shall you describe this evening in your letters home—and indeed in your own book of memoirs?" De Ligne used his champagne glass to gesture at the press of people around them. "Is it to be named an insufferable crush? The most tedious gathering of the entire Congress? Or an awe-inspiring event to remember for the ages, an unprecedented gathering of all the greatest and most glittering personages from across the Continent? You must make up your mind soon, you know—descriptions are already flying about the room, and you wouldn't wish to be last in registering to the world how terribly, terribly sophisticated your appreciation was."

"Mine?" Caroline shook her head. "I'm afraid I am no author, Your Highness. I'll leave all memoir-writing to the comte and yourself."

"Surely you underestimate yourself." De Ligne regarded her quizzically. "I suspect you possess hidden depths, my lady, which you don't choose to reveal to the world at large. If you were ever to sit down and write your own perspective on this Congress—"

"Then we should all be astonished and scandalized, no doubt," said a familiar voice behind them.

Caroline's fingers tightened around her fan. She forced herself to relax as the emperor stepped up between them.

"De Ligne." The emperor nodded affably. "Preparing for another of your own publications? You'll show this one to me ahead of time, I hope?"

"I? Why, I am only a harmless old man," said the prince, with wide-eyed innocence. "What danger could my poor words possibly possess?"

"Oh, it's never too late to surprise everyone," said the emperor. "Lady Wyndham . . ."

Caroline felt Michael's gaze upon her. The smile had faded from his face. She turned to the emperor, raising the fan high against her own face. It was a flirtatious gesture; better yet, it gifted her with a mask.

"Might I have a word?" the emperor asked.

"Of course," Caroline murmured. "I would be honored."

She took his proffered arm and gave a nod and smile of farewell to the circle of watching men. Together, Caroline and the emperor walked away, leaving the prince, the comte, and Michael behind them.

Michael's left hand throbbed with pain. He recognized the sensation a moment before he realized its cause: his hand had fisted so tightly that his fingers had cramped and his short nails had dug reddened semicircles into his palm. He shook his fingers out discreetly and forced his gaze away from Caroline's retreating back.

He found the Prince de Ligne watching him with keen blue eyes. "A fascinating woman," De Ligne murmured.

"Mm." Michael nodded and took a sip of champagne. A moment later, he couldn't even recall the taste.

"Twenty-four years . . . isn't it worth anything I can do?"

He couldn't have stopped her. But he wanted to kill the emperor of Austria with his bare hands, and not only for the hell the bastard had already put Caroline through.

Calm. De Ligne was speaking again.

". . . feels she has an intriguing story behind her, don't you agree?"

"Intriguing indeed," Michael agreed, and drank again.

"I shall certainly be describing her at length in my memoirs!" the Comte de La Garde-Chambonas announced. His plump face was flushed, whether from the heat or from the champagne, Michael could not tell. "She is the most elegant woman in Vienna, beyond compare. Perhaps . . ."

He rambled on, but Michael didn't follow. He had lost sight of Caroline in the crowd. He turned slightly, scanning the sea of heads. Perhaps . . .

"But perhaps Prince Kalishnikoff could tell us more of that," De Ligne said gently. "As such an old friend of Lady Wyndham."

Michael blinked and turned back to the other men. "I beg your pardon?"

De Ligne's brows drew together, but his voice remained courteously pitched. "We were only wondering how long Lady Wyndham plans to stay in the city."

"Well . . ." Michael shrugged. "I cannot answer for her, of course, but I'd expect several months at the very least. After all, who would choose to leave Vienna at such a historic moment?" He attempted a charming smile. It felt stretched and false. Where had all his training gone? "But what of tonight's entertainment?" he asked, too quickly. "Has anyone heard a hint of which theater troupe it is to be? And which play—or opera—we're to enjoy?"

"The matter of 'enjoyment,' of course, is rather dependent on the answers to both your questions," De Ligne said dryly. "But from what I've heard . . ."

The prince broke off as a commotion disrupted the crowd ahead. A clumsy figure—intoxicated already?—stumbled into two different men, knocking them apart. Cries of irritation sounded around him. The figure half-tripped and caught himself on a noblewoman's arm. His face was hidden as he leaned over her, but Michael saw blond hair above a solid, compact figure that was dressed far more modestly than any of the other guests.

Sudden suspicion stole Michael's breath. He stepped backward, fighting for rationality. There was no logical way it could possibly be—

The noblewoman shoved her assailant's hand aside with a gasp of outrage. Straightening, the man turned toward Michael's group.

Michael met Peter Riesenbeck's gaze for the second time that day.

Even as he met Michael's gaze, Peter realized that his challenge had only just begun. Grünemann stood half a room away, separated from the drama by hundreds of nobles of different nationalities. For all Peter knew, there might not be a single secret policeman closer than forty feet away—and in such a crowd, forty feet might as well be three miles.

If he didn't convince his audience immediately, he could lose his only chance.

Peter's eyes widened in horror. He raised one trembling finger. He pointed it straight at Michael.

"Traitor," Peter breathed. And then, in the actor's voice that he'd spent his life developing, he projected his words throbbingly through the aristocratic crowd: "Traitor and revolutionary!"

A shocked and avidly listening silence spread in widening circles around them, punctuated by gasps and whispers. Michael looked at

Riesenbeck's theatrically wavering finger, felt the horrified eyes of the crowd upon him . . . and smiled dazzlingly in response.

"A fine performance indeed," Michael said. He lifted his glass to toast the other man. "And far better than the earlier version I saw last week in Prague." He turned to share his amusement with the onlookers. "Ladies and gentlemen, I believe tonight's mystery has at last been solved! May I present Peter Riesenbeck, head of the excellent Riesenbeck theatrical troupe, which is currently touring to Vienna from Prague . . . and, I presume, playing for us tonight in the Burgtheater." He gestured with his glass. "I think he merits our applause, don't you?"

Approximately a third of the company began to clap, with varying degrees of enthusiasm; the other two thirds settled back into their conversational groups, a few with looks of active disgust at the nature of the interruption. Riesenbeck had to raise his voice again to be heard.

"Don't listen to him! He—"

"Am I wrong?" Michael asked. "Do enlighten me—are you not performing tonight, after all?"

"Did you meet in Prague, then?" the Prince de Ligne asked. He nodded with courteous condescension to the actor as he waited for Michael's response.

"You don't understand," Riesenbeck said. He turned to look around, his eyes wild. "He—I know him! He's—"

"I am honored to be remembered, indeed, after meeting so briefly when I congratulated you after that performance in Prague." Michael met Riesenbeck's eyes with cool amusement. "I know I promised you future patronage, months ago, but I'm afraid you can't call in my debt quite yet—my own fate is yet to be decided at this Congress." Was it worth trying—? Oh hell, why not? He added, casually, "That offer still holds true, by the way. I would be happy to take on your company's interests in the future, when I have the capability to do so."

Riesenbeck stared at him. He opened his mouth to speak, and then stopped. Michael felt the tension in his shoulders begin to ease.

"A fine promise indeed," the Prince de Ligne said. He raised his own glass to the actor. "I look forward to watching the Riesenbeck company perform tonight, after such a recommendation."

"I beg your pardon," the actor muttered.

He turned around and struck out through the closely pressed crowd, pushing his way across the room.

Damnation. Michael's heart sank as he watched Riesenbeck's blond head move through the crowd. Unaccustomed panic made his fingers tremble around the stem of his glass.

He felt the Prince de Ligne's watchful eyes upon him, waiting for a reaction or explanation, but for once Michael's brain refused to conjure up an appropriately light remark. All he could think of was the unpalatable truth that faced him.

He had to escape now, without delay, or else prepare to give himself up to the emperor's secret police.

Caroline focused on keeping her fingers relaxed and still on the emperor's arm as they crossed the Great Hall. When she slid a sidelong look up at his face, she saw his blue eyes hooded and his face unapproachable. She made no attempt at small talk, and neither did he.

If she turned, now—if she begged a sudden sick headache, a nervous indisposition—she could still escape and signal Michael. Within half an hour, at most, they would be together in her carriage. An hour later, and they'd be safe outside Vienna's city walls, and then—

Caroline took a firm grip on her rebellious nerves. She had been preparing for this moment for years. She would not shame herself or her father now by failure.

They reached a closed door flanked by expressionless footmen. At the emperor's nod, the door swung open.

"Your Ladyship?" The emperor gestured her forward.

Caroline lifted her chin and swept through the door.

She found herself in a narrow corridor, wide enough only for one person and lit by a single wall bracket of candles. Six feet ahead of them, the corridor curved sharply, hiding the end from view.

"Your Majesty?" Caroline kept her voice light and questioning.

"My apologies for the inconvenience," the emperor murmured. "This is a passageway particularly designed to give access to a private meeting chamber, separate from my public gatherings." His lips twitched. "You might be surprised by some of the meetings I've held here, while dances and banquets took place in the hall outside."

"I'm sure I would." Still, Caroline hesitated. If only she could see the end of the corridor . . .

"Well?" The emperor shrugged. "It was my understanding that you desired a private conference. I do have a fair number of duties to attend to, though, if you've changed your mind."

"No," Caroline said. "I haven't changed my mind."

She walked forward at a steady pace. Five steps, six, seven . . .

She turned the corner.

Five more feet of narrow corridor ran ahead of her, ending in a closed door.

"Do step through," said the emperor, behind her. "I'm afraid there are no servants to open doors for us here. I prefer to keep my private meetings as secure as possible."

"I understand." The door handle felt cool and smooth in Caroline's hands. She took a deep breath and opened it.

The small, octagonal room was empty. Caroline let out her held breath and stepped inside, onto a floor tiled in black and white. Ornately detailed Japanese panels lined the walls. A single settee of black velvet sat against one wall, supported by rosewood carved into muscular lion's legs; across from it, a lacquered table held a decanter of red wine, two glasses, and a long bracket of candles. Only one of the candles was lit; the emperor crossed the room to light the rest, working quickly.

Caroline looked past him to the two empty glasses. "You were expecting me."

"I had hoped to have your company tonight, I must confess. Of course, I really ought to be doing my duties as a host outside, rather than attending to my own private pleasures. But after such a flattering request..." The emperor turned, smiling, and lifted the decanter. "How could I refuse?"

"I'm glad." Caroline waited while he poured out two glasses.

A cool breeze stirred the back of her neck. She jerked around.

She saw only lacquered black panels on the wall before her. No fireplace warmed this room or let in air from the outside.

So where had the breeze come from?

"Lady Wyndham?"

She turned back to the emperor. Deep red wine swirled in the crystal glass he offered her. Caroline accepted it with a forced smile.

"Excuse me, your Majesty. I was only admiring your panels."

"Mm." His lips twitched. "I am fond of them myself." He raised his own glass. "To your health."

"And yours," Caroline murmured. She lifted her glass to her mouth.

Peter charged through the crowd.

He'd made a mistake, challenging Michael on aristocratic ground while surrounded by the man's powerful friends. But it still wasn't too late.

He shoved past diademed ladies, ignoring gasps and sharp words. He had to get to the other side of the room, where—

There. Through the crowd, he caught a glimpse of the man he was seeking.

Vaçlav Grünemann stood in a corner, sipping champagne and listening to an elderly dowager's complaints with every appearance of bland attention. A moment later, the movements of the shifting crowd had hidden him again. That momentary glimpse was all that Peter had needed. He redoubled his efforts with grim determination.

One man, at least, was fated to torture and imprisonment as a result of tonight's actions. Peter was determined that, this time, it would not be him.

"That was an odd fellow," the Prince de Ligne said, as Peter Riesenbeck shoved away from them. "Is he smoother-spoken on stage than in company?"

"One can only hope," Michael said absently. Riesenbeck's head had disappeared from view. *Damn.* Now he couldn't even track the man to gauge how much time he had left.

"'Hope'?" the prince asked. "But did not you say you'd attended—"

"Pardon me," Michael said. "I'm afraid—that is, I think I see, across the room—" *Who? What*, to explain such rudeness? He couldn't even formulate a proper excuse. Panic was running too thickly through his blood.

"Prince Kalishnikoff—" De Ligne began.

"Forgive me, I must go." Michael stepped away, moving quickly. He was breaking every law of courtesy, but he hadn't time to worry about that now.

The wisest option was to leave. No—the *only* option was to leave.

He had to find Caroline first.

Michael moved in the direction the emperor had led her, slipping discreetly between groups of people. Caroline was a tall woman, he told himself, as he scanned the crowd. He ought to spot her dark head, even at a distance.

If she was still there. If she was still in the crowd, talking to the emperor in a private corner, Michael could simply tap her on the shoulder and draw her away. And if they walked briskly out of the palace and then ran the rest of the way to her waiting carriage . . .

There was still a chance. He told himself that, repeating the phrase the way he'd repeated the titles of the pamphlets and the newspapers he'd hawked as a child, over and over again as he'd waved them through crowded streets and Kaffeehäuser. *Still a chance, still a chance, still a chance . . .*

There were too many people crowding in his way. Light from the chandeliers flashed off women's diamonds and sapphires and off the gold Orders pinned to men's coats. Michael walked faster and faster, searching...

Until a familiar head of blond hair appeared in the corner of his vision.

Michael spun around. Peter Riesenbeck was striding toward him through the crowd, followed by another man in courtly dress. The expression of grim determination on Riesenbeck's face spoke for itself. Michael didn't recognize the other man, but he didn't need to.

He turned and ran for the door.

Caroline nearly gagged on her wine as another chill brushed against the back of her neck. She forced herself not to turn around in search of the source. All she had left to fight with now was the impression of self-confidence.

Caroline lowered the glass and met the emperor's eyes.

"Your Majesty, there is something I must tell you."

"Really? I must confess, I am intrigued." The emperor stepped closer, his fierce gaze intent on her face. "Would it be about this marvelous gift you're offering to our chancellery? The financial salvation you are so eager to grant us?"

"Yes," Caroline said steadily. "But first..." She lowered her voice to a soft, seductive murmur, shifting her wineglass into her left hand. "I believe we spoke, the night we met, of sharing secrets."

"Ah. I remember." The emperor's eyes narrowed. He stepped closer yet, until his breath whispered against her face with his words. "And are you finally ready to share your secrets with me, madam?"

Caroline hardened herself to smile without flinching. "I am," she whispered, and reached out to him with her free hand.

"Excellent," murmured the emperor. He stepped back, leaving her outstretched fingers touching only air. "Pergen? You may come out now. I believe your moment has arrived."

CHAPTER TWENTY-EIGHT

Caroline spun around. The black lacquered panels on the wall shifted before her eyes and slid apart.

Count Pergen stepped through the gap. A chill swept with him into the room—the same deathly chill, Caroline realized, that she had felt before, leaking through a gap in the hidden doorway.

Pergen's thin lips curved into a smile as he bowed with mocking grace.

Caroline raised her chin and wrenched her gaze from the horror of Pergen's shadowed eyes to the emperor beside her. "What, precisely, is the meaning of this?" she demanded, in freezing tones. "I had understood this meeting was to be private."

"You seem to have understood a great many things, Lady Wyndham," the emperor said. "You will have to forgive me for being slightly less gullible than you had assumed."

"Your Majesty—"

"Come now," Pergen murmured. "This meeting is still private enough by any man's standards. The outer doors are guarded, no one can see us or hear a word we say . . . and after all, we two are old friends. Are we not, *Karolina*?"

Peter cursed as he saw Michael suddenly lunge forward. He'd already been luckier than he'd expected, for the other man to stay this long after their first confrontation; but apparently his luck had run out.

He dropped back briefly to speak to Grünemann. "Call out the guards!"

"Not tonight," Grünemann said briefly. "Too much noise. It would distract the guests."

"But—"

Grünemann raised his eyebrows quellingly. "Just hurry!"

Peter gritted his teeth and set off. The line of incoming guests seemed never-ending, swelling the crowd even though the emperor and empress had long since abandoned the receiving line. Sweat poured down Peter's neck as he pushed his way through the packed bodies around him, ignoring gasps, insults, and even snarled threats.

A group of diademed archduchesses passed in front of him, and Peter lost sight of his prey. He started forward to push them aside. Grünemann's hand clamped down on his arm and pulled him back.

"No noise," Grünemann snapped.

"What do you mean, no noise?" Peter rounded on him, ready to erupt. "Do you want to catch him or not?"

"To be perfectly frank . . ." Grünemann shrugged, looking maddeningly at ease. "I'll find him sooner or later, now that you've pointed him out to me."

"But if we don't catch him tonight—!" Peter stopped as the truth hit him.

If they didn't catch Michael now, Grünemann would simply catch Michael tomorrow . . . and imprison Peter tonight. By God, Grünemann would probably prefer it that way.

It was up to Peter.

He waited, seething, until the last of the archduchesses had passed, then ran. This time he didn't wait for Grünemann to follow.

Ahead of him, he saw Michael disappear through the open doorway. *Outside.* With all the winding streets of inner city Vienna to choose from . . .

Peter hadn't thought he could run any faster, with his body still tired and weak from the torture of two nights before.

He'd been wrong.

Bitingly cold air hit Michael's face with the force of a slap as he emerged into the Hofburg's inner courtyard. It nearly brought him to a halt after the suffocating heat of the Great Hall. He sucked in a freezing lungful and kept running, past the line of incoming guests, through the archway that led into the next courtyard, and toward the street outside.

Frantic calculations streamed through his mind as he ran, weighing risk versus reward. If he could first lose his pursuers in the tangled maze of narrow streets in Vienna's inner city, he could leap into Caroline's waiting carriage with no fear of his conveyance being noted and reported to every border guard in Austria. But if he failed and they caught him before he could reach the carriage . . .

Michael hurtled through the last archway, onto the crowded, well-lit square facing the Burgtheater, and lurched to a halt. Hovering indecision held him in a vise. If he ran directly for the carriage, only a few blocks away, he had a decent chance of climbing into it and taking off before his pursuers could catch up with him. He would escape the city of Vienna within the hour. If he was to escape all of Austria unhindered, though, he should do anything and everything to keep his pursuers from seeing the carriage that he took.

And yet, and yet . . .

God help me. Michael closed his eyes for an anguished moment. For the first time in his career, he couldn't think. He couldn't even choose a gamble. *Caroline* . . .

Would she be surprised to find him gone when she finished her meeting with the emperor? Or was it only what she had expected of him all along?

And she herself . . .

The sound of pounding footsteps brought him to his senses. With a curse, Michael lunged to the left, straight down the far-too-well-lit Herrengasse, aiming directly for the Bankgasse and Caroline's carriage.

For all he knew, there could be a dozen armed guards chasing him by now. He couldn't afford the risk of trying to lose them all in the inner city.

Even as he ran for the carriage, though, Michael had a sinking feeling that, for the first time in his career, his instincts might have failed him.

Peter lunged through the Hofburg's final archway just in time to see Michael's lean figure disappearing into the crowd to his left. He would have sent up a prayer of thankfulness if he'd had any breath or energy for it.

He had no idea why his nemesis would choose to stay on a main street instead of disappearing into the warren of smaller streets that twisted through the city center, but he thanked all the saints for the other man's bad judgment.

While the nobility's carriages clattered through the street itself, the pavements of the Herrengasse were filled with middle-class couples promenading between cafés and theaters, groups of elegantly dressed young women engaged in discreet solicitation, and flash young men of the upper classes, already half-tipsy and out for a night on the town. Peter plunged into the mix, gasping for each burning breath and marking his way by the occasional glimpses of Michael's elegant dark green coat flashing in the crowd ahead.

It felt all too familiar. Only this morning Peter had been the one being chased. If he let himself stop running now, he would collapse onto the filthy cobblestones to be trampled by a carriage horse. *And good riddance.*

But what would become of his company if he let himself give up? Who was to say that Grünemann's employer wouldn't decide to punish them for his failure? Peter's head throbbed with the effort of it, but he pushed himself forward relentlessly.

Intersecting streets created a sharp corner, two blocks ahead. Peter rocked back, realizing he had lost sight of Michael. No matter how hard he peered, he couldn't see the other man anywhere in the crowd ahead . . .

Aha. A motion to his left caught Peter's eye. He turned and spotted Michael's tall form loping down a line of standing carriages on a quiet side street.

Carriages. Revelation curdled Peter's stomach.

No wonder the man had chosen the main street for his escape.

Peter lurched into a sudden, desperate burst of speed.

Michael raced past the darkened palaces that lined the Bankgasse. The buildings themselves were mostly empty tonight, but the street itself, as one of the closest side streets to the Hofburg, was lined with carriages waiting to return for their owners at the end of the evening. He didn't dare slow down to seek out any details; he had to hope he would recognize Caroline's embossed crest in the darkness.

If he even made it that far.

He couldn't help it. He slid a quick look backward as he ran, cursing himself for his own weakness.

Peter Riesenbeck was barely half a block behind him, gaining quickly. And behind Riesenbeck . . .

Michael jerked his gaze back to the pavement ahead of him, biting down on self-loathing.

There were no armed guards. No inescapable force swept toward him in pursuit. He couldn't even see the other man who'd been with Riesenbeck earlier—together, Michael and Riesenbeck must have out-paced him.

In other words, Michael could have lost both pursuers in five minutes if he had chosen the inner city.

So be it. It was too late now to change the past. If he could do that, he would have refused to come with Caroline tonight at all. He would have kept her from attending the gala by any means at his disposal, no matter how dishonorable. He'd known better than to agree to her mad plan even when she first came out with it. Only his cursed guilt had kept him from acting on his instincts. If he could change the past . . .

There. A familiar crest. Michael aimed himself like a perfect shot in a game of billiards. He had always saved himself from dire conse- quences and catastrophes before, no matter how inescapable they had appeared. In twenty-four years, he had scored a perfect record. He wouldn't break it now. Only fifteen more feet until . . .

Peter Riesenbeck barreled into Michael from behind and sent him flying forward. Michael didn't even have time to throw out his hands for self-protection before he crashed onto the ground.

Peter landed on top of Michael's back. The older man had fallen facedown, with an impact that must have scraped skin raw. But he was surprisingly agile; before Peter could even catch his breath, Michael twisted around, pushing himself up from the muck-covered cobblestones and fighting to pull away from Peter's hold.

Peter had just enough energy left to slam his knee into the small of Michael's back. With a grunt of pain, Michael went limp beneath him. Peter found himself grinning fiercely, almost laughing with elation. He'd only fought in stage-fights since he'd been plucked from the streets of Prague by Paul Périgord. Apparently, though, not all of his childhood skills had faded. Peter leaned forward to push Michael down hard against the filthy cobblestones, even as he slid a quick glance backward. All he had to do was hold the older man down until Grüne- mann caught up with them, and then . . .

Michael's elbow jerked up in a fast, angled arc. Peter doubled over in agony.

The older man twisted free in one quick motion. He shoved Peter aside and scrambled to his feet.

Tears of pain stung Peter's eyes, but he threw himself forward. With all his strength, he grabbed hold of Michael's closest leg and jerked. Michael's arms windmilled as he flailed for balance and lost. He crashed back down to the cobblestones. Grunting with effort, Peter lurched forward and grabbed the other man's hands, pulling them behind Michael's back at an excruciating angle. He heard a gasp of pain hiss out of the older man's lips.

"There," Peter panted. "There! Are you repentant yet for what you did to us?"

"Repentant?" Michael's voice sounded thin and cracked with pain. He took a strained breath, and Peter braced himself to withstand pleas, curses, and even bribes . . .

But what emerged from Michael's throat instead was something Peter hadn't expected, incongruous but impossible to mistake: laughter.

Michael gave himself up to hopeless laughter as he took in the earnest drama in the younger man's tone. "Repentant?" he gasped. "Good God, man, of course I am. What else did you expect?"

"Well . . ." Riesenbeck sounded chagrined. "I should hope so."

"You have me pinned down, I'm about to be taken away to suffer God only knows what tortures—"

"That's your own fault!" Riesenbeck said, so quickly that Michael knew he must have touched a nerve. "You chose to put us in danger to follow your own ends, and now you're only facing the natural results."

"And you wonder whether I'm feeling repentant?" Michael shook his head in disbelief as his laughter finally trailed off in the darkness of his final evening as a free man. "What do *you* think?"

"You're bluffing," said Riesenbeck. "But I know better than to be taken in again by any of your stories."

"So what exactly do you expect from me now? A villain's speech of rage, cursing everyone in sight before he jumps off the cliff or the castle tower?" Michael sighed and lowered his head to the ground. The cobblestones should have been rough against the raw, reddened skin on his cheek. Luckily—or unluckily—they were so covered by slippery mud and horse muck that they were almost soft. If it weren't for the stink he would hardly even mind being there.

Now that it was all over—now that he'd lost the gamble, lost everything—Michael found himself oddly calm. Twenty-four years had been a good, long period of escape from the secret police in his home city, hadn't it? He'd had a good run between the night he found his master's shop in flames and this night, when he'd rubbed shoulders with the rulers of all Europe.

And he'd told Caroline he loved her, a braver act than he'd performed in a long time—ever since that first night of escape and abandonment. Lying here in the muck on the cobblestones, he was glad to remember that he had at least done that.

Better yet, he hadn't even revealed to Riesenbeck which carriage had been his aim. Caroline could still escape unharmed tonight as soon as she realized he had gone. All in all, this was a far better night than that first one had been.

Still, it seemed a pity to close a glorious adventure with a scene of cheap melodrama at the end.

Michael lifted his head from the filthy cobblestones and strained to turn until he could see Riesenbeck out the corner of his eye. "I'm not really a villain from one of your plays, you know. I was only trying to survive, as you are now."

"By using my company."

Michael nodded painfully. "I used what was available. But I do genuinely regret that you've been drawn into all of this. I thought I'd been careful not to be spotted. You should never have heard of me again."

Riesenbeck shook his head, his voice grim. "Nothing you say could convince me to let you go."

"I didn't expect it would," Michael admitted. "But I've been realizing, lately . . ." He tried to shrug, but failed. "I wanted to apologize, regardless. For my own sake."

Riesenbeck looked back searchingly. His words, half-whispered, reached Michael's ears. "If you knew what awaited me if I'd failed tonight . . ."

"I have a fair idea, I think." Michael remembered Caroline's choked-out story of the hell her childhood had become. *Because of him.*

How many people had suffered because of him? Exhaustion swept through him at the thought...and at Riesenbeck's jerk of astonishment.

"In case you wondered," Michael added wearily, "I didn't know any of that when I first came here. Even I am not so ruthless that I would have knowingly put you and your company at risk of supernatural tortures."

"But..." For the first time, Riesenbeck's voice softened, as confusion crept into it. "How do you—?"

"They certainly aren't common knowledge, it's true." Michael snorted. "Even the most radical pamphleteers never dreamed of that. If we had..."

"So you *are* a pamphleteer!" Riesenbeck said. "That's what ...*it*...told me, but I wasn't—"

"I used to be a pamphleteer." A bitter twist pinched Michael's mouth. "Back when I still had ideals to publish."

"I met a pamphleteer, my first night here," Riesenbeck said. "She wasn't what I'd expected. The most amazing curling dark hair and big, dark eyes—what?"

"Nothing," Michael said. But he smiled wryly, against the filth on the ground.

It was good to know that Aloysia had made a conquest.

Oh Lord, Aloysia and Kaspar. Two more loose ends he'd left on this trip. With luck, when he didn't come to check the pamphlet in two days as promised, they would be sensible enough to assume the worst. Aloysia probably would, anyway. She—

"I saved her from the police," Riesenbeck said. "I didn't realize who she was, but they took that as proof that I must have been your accomplice."

"Ah." Michael sighed. "I see." *Not such an amusing twist, after all.*

"That was when I learned better." Riesenbeck's voice turned from wistful to grim. "You may not be a villain, but I'm no hero. I can't afford to be."

"Who can?" Michael gritted his teeth as burning cramps added to the pain in his pinned-back arms. "Do you think you might let me stretch my arms for just a moment?"

"I'm no fool." Riesenbeck's head turned away again. "I'm only waiting for the policeman who was with me. I don't know why he's taking so long..."

"Perhaps he doesn't care." Michael tossed out the words flippantly but was startled by the sudden jerk Riesenbeck gave to his arms—as if all of Riesenbeck's muscles had tightened at the thought. Blinking, Michael automatically played the new hand he had suddenly been dealt. "He certainly didn't bother to put much effort into the chase, did he?"

"*He will come.*" Riesenbeck spoke the words with the intensity of a prayer. "He will!"

"And then?" Michael said. "What have they promised you for capturing me? Privileges for the rest of your company? A contract for—"

"I'll be free," Riesenbeck gritted. "They'll let me leave Vienna."

"Knowing what you do?" Michael let out an involuntary choked laugh. "Good God, man, don't you know anything about life offstage?"

The hold on his arms tightened to sheer agony. "You know nothing about this!"

"I take it you've met Count Pergen—"

"Who?"

Michael rolled his eyes. Between the pamphleteers this morning and Riesenbeck tonight, he was feeling his age far too acutely. "The former minister of the secret police," he said patiently. "And, despite official statements to the contrary, still their leader. He also happens to be an alchemist."

"Oh." Breath hissed out of Riesenbeck's clenched teeth. "It—he—kept me masked. I never heard his name."

"Regardless. You've been exposed to horrors that would shock the rest of the empire and all the members of this Congress. Are you really such an innocent that you think they'll let you go free after tonight, to spread the word of what you've gone through?"

He felt Riesenbeck shiver. "They *will* let me go. That was the agreement. That—"

"Oh, and you can certainly trust an agreement with a power-mad alchemist who's tortured you once already." Michael rolled his eyes. "How foolish of me to even suggest otherwise."

"You bastard!" Riesenbeck's voice trembled. "You don't know anything about it."

"Perhaps not," Michael agreed. "But if I were you, I wouldn't simply hand myself over to them. I would at least make an attempt to escape."

"Some of us care about other people," Riesenbeck said tightly. "Some of us have responsibilities we can't walk away from as easily as you."

"Fair enough," Michael said. "And yet—"

"Here he comes."

"Ah." Michael sighed and laid his head back down on the cool, slippery muck. "Never mind. I might have known."

He hadn't really expected to win over Riesenbeck at this late stage in the proceedings. Persuasion had only been a reflex he couldn't seem to stifle after so many years. Perhaps he'd still be trying to shift the situation to his own advantage even as he was thrown into a prison cell . . . or worse.

The thought made Michael's chest tighten with a flutter of sudden, animal panic. He quashed it with an effort.

It was too late for any new schemes or hopes of escape. There was no point wasting his precious final moments in contemplating future horrors that he couldn't prevent. The only thing he could do now was focus on the fact that Caroline would escape.

That was enough. It had to be.

Riesenbeck stood up and yanked on Michael's pinned-back arms to pull him off the ground. Michael gritted his teeth at the pain as he clambered awkwardly to his feet. The muck still plastered against his raw face felt excruciatingly cold in the chill breeze. Still facing the line of carriages, he couldn't see the man who approached them, but he heard Riesenbeck's voice behind him, hoarse with anxiety.

"What took you so long? I thought you'd never arrive."

"You don't seem to have required me." Footsteps approached, and then the voice spoke again, closer. "Let me see his face."

Riesenbeck pulled Michael around, necessitating an awkward shuffling of position that left Michael facing the policeman in the faint illumination from the nearest carriage lamp and Riesenbeck standing behind him, his hands clamped around Michael's wrists. Michael set his jaw and met the policeman's gaze in the darkness without expression.

"Well." The policeman smiled blandly. "Here he is, indeed. A pleasure to meet you, Herr...?" He trailed off invitingly. When Michael didn't answer, he shrugged. "Never mind. I'm sure we'll discover your identity soon enough. Come on." He spoke over Michael, aiming the words at Riesenbeck. "Let's take him around to the back quarters and stow him in a cell."

"But..." Riesenbeck's voice faltered. "Aren't we taking him directly to your master? Finding him was the whole purpose of—"

"It may have been your whole purpose, Herr Riesenbeck, but it certainly wasn't his." The policeman's smile tightened. "He may have been pleased to gift the emperor with a talented troupe so desperate they would work for free at tonight's gala, to save His Majesty's coffers and capture a revolutionary in the bargain... but for himself, at the moment, he has rather more important prey in mind than one more minor seditionist."

"But—"

"He is on the emperor's business tonight, and I can assure you: he wouldn't relish any interruption."

The emperor's business.

Nausea rose in Michael's chest, gagging him. His cloak of detachment dropped away in an instant of hideous revelation.

"It's too late for riddles," Riesenbeck said, behind him.

"It's not a riddle," Michael said. His voice came out cracked, like all his comforting delusions. Had he really been fool enough to believe they could be true? Or had he somehow known the truth all along? "I know exactly what he means."

Caroline.

She had been trapped inside the palace with the emperor and Pergen, while Michael had run. And failed. And abandoned her again.

CHAPTER TWENTY-NINE

Caroline directed a freezing stare at Count Pergen. "I haven't the faintest idea what you're talking about, but I don't care to find out, either. I'm leaving now." She turned, head high, and stalked toward the door. Two steps, three steps . . .

"I think not." The emperor's voice brimmed with quiet satisfaction. "Perhaps you didn't notice, Lady Wyndham, but I locked the door behind us when I entered."

Caroline came to a halt, staring at the door handle. She hadn't faced the emperor as he'd entered; he could have locked it all too easily. If she tried the door and it was locked, she'd look a fool and forfeit the appearance of cool confidence; but if he was lying and she didn't even make an attempt . . .

She pressed her lips together and crossed the last few feet in two quick steps. The handle refused to move beneath her hand.

"Very sensible," Pergen approved in German, from across the room. "But then, you were always my brightest subject, Karolina."

"Enough." Caroline turned to face them both. Cold panic bubbled up within her chest, but she kept her voice steady, her left hand gripping the stem of her wineglass. "I demand to know the meaning of this strange prank you've chosen to play. You cannot imagine the British embassy will tolerate such mistreatment of a peeress of the realm."

The emperor's narrow eyebrows rose. "Mistreatment of a peeress of the British Empire? Indeed, no one would ever dare take such an act lightly. But the arrest of an Austrian native citizen on suspicion of conspiring against her true government? Well, *that* is an action no ruler could condemn in these perilous days. Particularly . . ." He smiled and toasted her with his wine glass. "Particularly when it can be proven that she's lied to all her English acquaintances these past twenty years at least, and no doubt taken in her poor deluded husbands as well."

Caroline stared at him. "Are you mad?"

"Mad? I think not. I believe when the facts of the case are disclosed to the public, your government will be both grateful and deeply relieved by our actions . . . particularly as the possessions and wealth of a known traitor are invariably surrendered to the Crown. Your former friends, of course, will no doubt be shocked and horrified—but only by your outrageous audacity and their own gullibility in accepting you as one of them."

Caroline tried to speak. No words would emerge from her throat.

The emperor regarded her quizzically. "Do you not agree with my assessment, Lady Wyndham?"

Caroline gathered up her scattered wits. "If my lands and wealth are turned over to the British Crown, you'll have none of them for yourself. Why forfeit a fortune only to exact some paltry revenge?" She stepped closer, fighting to keep her tone as sweetly reasonable as the emperor's own. "If you release me now, I'll leave Austria within the day. You'll be safe from any schemes of mine, and your treasury will be the richer by tens of thousands of pounds. Why—"

"Your concern is touching," the emperor said, "but sadly misplaced. I cannot imagine the British government being any less than generous when we relieve them of such an embarrassment. I feel confident they will agree to share your wealth with us quite willingly."

"But—"

"Moreover, you seem to hold an entirely false impression of me." The emperor stepped close to her and breathed his last words directly into her ear. "Why on earth would I desire you to leave Austria?"

Caroline stared into his triumphant face and felt her rippling panic stilled by cold certainty.

There would be no chance of negotiated escape. She had lost . . . and she would be forced to pay, over and over again, for the wound she'd inflicted to the emperor's precious pride.

"I'm sure you'll find a way to accept your fate, in time," he whispered.

Caroline gathered up the last of her shattered confidence. She reached up to stroke his cheek caressingly. He leaned forward . . .

And she spat directly in the emperor's face.

"You are worth even less than your lackey," Caroline snapped in the Viennese German of her youth. "Pergen is a monster, but you ride on his back to enjoy his leavings. What exactly do you think that makes you?"

The emperor staggered back, scooping a handkerchief from his pocket. He wiped off the spittle from his nose and cheek, still staring at her. His thin lips worked, but no sound came out. Had no one ever dared speak so to him before?

Pergen stepped forward, and a wave of cold air swept around him, brushing against Caroline's skin. "That," he murmured, "was most unwise of you, Karolina."

The emperor shook himself and stepped away, his narrow face contorted with anger. "You know how to deal with her," he told Pergen. "Lady Wyndham . . ." He jerked a mere caricature of a bow. "By the time I see you later, you *will* be ready to apologize. Of that I have no doubt."

Caroline only looked at him. Her whole body was trembling with rage and fear, sending rippling waves through the red wine in her glass, but she met his glare with a gaze of icy indifference.

She had never given up in all her years of imprisonment. She would not give him the satisfaction of witnessing her surrender now.

The emperor paused, his face working. "Perhaps . . ." He flung a glance at Pergen. "I hear you came to Vienna looking for your father. Is that correct?"

Caroline's breath caught in her throat. She steeled her spine and closed her lips to keep any words from spilling out.

The emperor smiled as if he'd received response enough. "Well, then. You may be interested to learn that he died of influenza ten years ago, in a prison cell outside Pressburg. Apparently it was a particularly cold winter that year . . . and his radical fervor wasn't quite enough to keep him warm after all."

The world compressed into a shimmering bubble around Caroline. She couldn't make herself take a breath.

The emperor's final words seemed to come from a great distance. "Pergen's men researched his fate for me this afternoon. A pity that you should have come all this way for nothing, is it not?"

❧

Michael's vision blurred as the enormity of it struck him.

Caroline had walked into a trap. And he . . .

He could have resigned himself to his own failure, with her escape as consolation. But he would not walk into captivity without a fight, knowing that she needed him.

He would not abandon her again.

Michael relaxed his arms within Riesenbeck's grasp. Slowly, carefully, he linked his fingers together into a double fist.

"I don't understand," Riesenbeck said to the policeman. "What are you both talking about?"

"He seems to know the answer." The policeman nodded at Michael. "An interesting point, that. I'm sure we'll find out more about it later."

Nearby, the closest carriage horse shifted and let out a muffled snort. Michael slid a sideways glance.

The coachman, inured to urban life, hadn't shown a jot of interest in the fight that took place beside his carriage. Whether that reflected cynical wisdom or pure lack of interest, Michael couldn't even guess.

However, there was one other man on this street, only fifteen feet away, who might actually come to his aid—who had been instructed, in fact, to follow all of his orders. Earlier, Michael had been unwilling to risk giving away Caroline's identity to his pursuers.

Now, though . . .

"Come." The policeman jerked his head. "We should start off. I'm needed back at the gala, and you . . ." His lips twisted into an unpleasant smile. "You'll need to prepare for tonight's performance, Herr Riesenbeck."

"Very well," Riesenbeck muttered. "But don't think I'm going to—ah!"

Michael gave a sudden jerk of his arms, pulling his captor off balance. Then he smashed one booted heel down onto the actor's toes, grinding down with all his strength.

Riesenbeck's grip loosened for barely half a second, as he let out a muffled grunt of pain.

It was enough.

Michael was already shouting as he yanked his hands free. "Henry! Lady Wyndham needs you *now*!"

What the hell was the man shouting about in English? And *why?*

Peter lunged to recapture the slippery bastard just as Michael leaped at Grünemann, knocking the policeman backward onto the cobblestones.

Caught off-balance, Peter hit midair instead of solid flesh and flailed for balance. The wrestling bodies lurched across the cobblestones and knocked into Peter's feet. He stumbled backward, panting. He couldn't tell who was winning in the scuffle at his feet, or how to help Grünemann without getting in his way.

Perhaps—

A heavy weight slammed against the back of Peter's head. Consciousness fled, and his half-formulated strategy vanished with it.

Michael let out a groan of sheer relief as the policeman suddenly slumped against him, his fingers falling away from Michael's throat.

"Thank you for that." Michael struggled out from beneath the policeman's limp body, grunting with effort. He massaged his bruised throat as he stood to face Caroline's stocky, solidly built coachman. "You're a good man in a fight."

"Thank you, Your Highness."

The coachman regarded Michael steadily, still holding his whip half-coiled in his hand. The head of the whip was solid bronze—a handy feature indeed. Michael wondered whether Henry had chosen it for that purpose. Whether or not the whip was a mere tool for driving, Michael had a strong feeling that Caroline had chosen the man himself for more than his ability with horses.

"And what does Your Highness want done with these gentlemen?" asked Henry, apparently imperturbably.

"Hmm." Michael glanced down at the cobblestones. "We can't leave them here, certainly."

"Do you want me to dispose of them?"

"Dispose—?" Michael blinked. "Ah, no. Not yet." He took a breath.

Perhaps he wouldn't inquire too closely into the other man's background, after all.

Henry coughed. "I only meant, Your Highness, to drive them out and drop them on the outskirts of the city. It would take them a few hours to walk back, and if you need to buy a bit of time for Lady Wyndham . . ."

"Ah. Yes, that is a good idea." Michael gathered up the wits that had scattered in the fight. "Thank you, Henry." He nodded with just the right degree of royal condescension. "We'd better tie them up first, though, just in case they wake up at an awkward moment."

"That one already is." Henry jerked his chin at the actor, whose head was shifting. Riesenbeck mumbled something unintelligible, and Henry asked, "Shall I give him another tap?"

Michael opened his mouth to agree, but a sudden stab of reluctance startled him. It was the tug of his instincts, and he paused to think the impulse through.

It would be another gamble, certainly—and at the most dangerous possible moment. If it was only his newfound and highly inconvenient guilt that pressed upon him now, he might well be sacrificing his only sliver of a chance. Yet, when he weighed up everything he knew, and tallied it against the odds . . .

"Not yet," Michael said. "I want to talk to him first."

Caroline put all her effort into holding herself upright and not letting herself faint as the door closed behind her. The emperor's words rang through her head, repeating themselves over and over again until they merged and became only one word, inescapable and without end.

Died ... died ... died ...

"You look unwell, Karolina."

Pergen's voice pierced the fog, but she could barely see him as his footsteps approached. Her vision refused to focus on the room around her; only his blurred outlines appeared before her, even as his chill surrounded her.

Died ...

"I hope you haven't turned missish in the years since you left this country. The girl I remember wouldn't have fainted away when things went badly. She would have been screaming and fighting by now, no matter how futile she knew it to be. Aren't you even going to make one last escape attempt?"

Escape? Caroline almost laughed. If the laugh had escaped her lips, she thought it might have contained blood.

Michael had been right. She had been mad ever to think that her plan could have worked. That she could still save her father after all these years.

So many years ... all the years of her two marriages, waiting for her independence. Then the long years when travel between England and the Continent was blocked by the endless war, and she had been forced to wait and wait, gathering her plans, hiring informants and throwing all her frustrated energy into scheming for this moment. *This moment*, when everything she'd gone through, everything she'd chosen or been forced to do over the years, would all be redeemed and made worthwhile ...

And her father had been dead these past ten years.

"Can you even hear me right now, I wonder?" Pergen sounded distantly amused. "Never mind. I imagine you'll wake up soon enough."

What had Caroline been doing when her father died shivering and alone? Had she been writing letters in her warm, cozy morning room in her elegant London townhouse? Or had she been staying at a glittering country house party full of innuendos and falsehoods, hailing the blanket of snow outside as a charming Christmas touch?

"I'd thought it might be difficult to subdue you enough to be carried to your cell," Pergen murmured, "but perhaps I misjudged you after all. I wonder, if I simply steered you by the arm, would you walk quite quietly back to your old cage?"

Caroline didn't answer. She couldn't. The chill that emanated from Pergen wrapped around her completely now. It felt right. It felt like the cold that had killed her father, years before she had even managed to cross the English Channel on her way back to him.

It had all been so hopeless. When Pergen's thin fingers closed around her arm, Caroline didn't even attempt to struggle.

There had been no point in coming here tonight. Michael had been right, but she'd been too driven by need to listen to him. Now that it was finished, though, and she had failed . . .

Michael. Horrified realization lanced her body, breaking through the fog.

Michael didn't know what had happened to her. He might wonder, but it hadn't been long enough since she'd left the Great Hall for him to be certain that her meeting with the emperor had gone wrong. And the emperor would know—*must* know, by now, as he knew who Caroline was—that Michael himself was a fraud.

The emperor, whom she had spat on and insulted, who had left the meeting room seething with rage.

When he found Michael waiting for Caroline . . .

Caroline's vision focused into painful clarity. The little room closed in around her—five steps to the door, six steps to the opening in the wall through which Pergen had first emerged—and Pergen's hand was firm on her left arm as he turned her toward that dark passageway. Caroline staggered, as if overcome by faintness, and red wine sloshed out from the glass she still held.

"I have to—I must—" She drew a ragged breath.

"Take a moment to compose yourself, certainly," said Pergen. "We have all the time in the world, now, you and I."

Caroline closed her eyes and raised her free hand to massage her forehead, pulling Pergen's hand with her arm. He released her, and she stumbled back a pace. She stopped there a moment, leaning her head forward into her hand, then raised her other hand—and mimed surprise as her cool wine glass touched her face.

"I forgot—I really ought to . . ." Trailing off, she staggered the last few steps to the table where the half-full wine decanter sat, its facets sparkling in the candlelight. She set her own glass down carefully beside it, shadows shifting on the wall beside her.

"You have grown over-nice in your habits," Pergen said. "The servants would have carried it back, have no fear."

"I don't," Caroline said. She straightened, and managed a wavering smile. "I am coming now. I only—" She broke off again, raising her left hand back to her forehead. "I feel—I feel as if I might swoon, if I move even a step."

"Then allow me to assist you." Asperity tinged Pergen's voice as he started toward her. "But I beg you not to imagine that these delaying tactics are going to do you any good."

"Oh, I don't," Caroline said. "Truly."

She waited, poised, her left hand limp against her forehead, as he crossed to her. Two steps . . . three steps . . .

Now. Caroline grabbed the heavy glass decanter with her right hand and swung it against Pergen's face with all her strength.

CHAPTER THIRTY

The decanter smashed into Pergen's face, and he fell to his knees. Caroline swung it again, and the thick glass shattered as it hit the side of Pergen's head. Pergen toppled, red wine showering around him. Caroline dropped the last shards of broken glass and raced for the door.

It was too late to escape, but she didn't need to escape to alert Michael and save his life. If she only made it out into the Great Hall, she would be witnessed by the entire gathered, gossiping crowd, her long white gloves stained with her own blood from the shattered glass, as she was subdued and taken prisoner on the emperor's command. Michael would see or be told about the spectacle as rumors swept the crowd, and he would suffer in the knowledge, yes, but he could run, as he'd been running all his life—as he should have been running tonight, if she hadn't stopped him—and he would be free.

Michael, run! Don't wait for me this time.

The door handle turned beneath Caroline's bleeding hand, pushing even more tiny fragments of glass through her thin gloves. Ignoring the sharp bites of pain, she pulled it open. The cool air of the outer corridor brushed against her skin . . .

And a hand closed around the back of her dress, yanking her back into the room.

"Now, *that* is the Karolina I remembered." Pergen's smile cut through raw, gaping wounds. It wasn't his smile, though, but the wounds themselves that made the bile rise in Caroline's throat as he kicked the door shut behind her.

Ragged cuts from the glass covered Pergen's sunken face and head, but they did not bleed red blood. Instead, dark shadows leaked through the cuts, swirling past his skin and hair into the air around him. They trailed through the air toward Caroline, and she flinched away, struggling to escape. Pergen's hand held her firm as the shadows brushed against her skin, burrowing against her cheeks as if seeking a way inside. A moan escaped Caroline's closed lips as the shadows wiggled against her nostrils and crept up her face toward her eyes.

What monstrous new development was this?

"Afraid?" Pergen asked. His voice had calmed into the scientific detachment he'd always assumed when beginning a lecture to the emperor or one of the other rare observers of his experiments on her. "The shadows themselves cannot harm you, having no mind or purpose of their own. However . . ." Satisfaction overcame the detachment as he reached into his waistcoat. "I must thank you for giving me the opportunity to carry out a new experiment. I was afraid you had become too docile to need it after all."

Caroline clenched her jaw to hold back a sob as shadows wriggled into her nose and worked their way up inside her.

Pergen's hand reappeared in her line of sight. "Do you recognize this, Karolina?"

Caroline blinked rapidly, trying to focus through the raw fear.

It was a small silver tube, etched with unfamiliar markings and sealed at the top with a flat cap. Caroline had never seen it before in her life.

"No?" Pergen shrugged. "Perhaps a familiar face will remind you."

Still holding her arm, he turned his head toward the dark, inner passageway through which he'd first emerged.

"Mr. Weston? You may come out now."

As Peter opened his eyes, Michael's face swam into focus. His lips were moving, but it took a moment for his words to penetrate the pain in Peter's head.

"Can you hear me?"

Peter started to speak, then stopped as the pain intensified. He pushed himself up as far as his elbows. Nausea overwhelmed him. He closed his eyes, fighting to keep the bile down.

"Let me give you a hand."

Peter opened his eyes and found Michael reaching out to him. It hurt too much for Peter to scowl. He accepted Michael's outstretched hand and pulled himself painfully to his feet. Grünemann's crumpled body lay nearby.

"There you are," Michael said. "The pain will wear off soon, I promise. You can trust me on that, by the way—I've had it happen to me too many times to count."

"I can't trust you on anything," Peter said. He dropped Michael's hands and stepped back . . . and bumped into a solid figure.

"Ah, that's Henry, who saved me," Michael said genially. "He doesn't speak German, I'm afraid, but I'm sure he's pleased to meet you, too."

Peter turned and met the measuring gaze of a toughly built, middle-aged man wearing a coachman's multi-caped coat and holding a bronze-handled whip in his right hand. Peter had never seen that whip before, but his throbbing head made immediate and excruciating connections.

"And now that you've made each other's acquaintance . . ." Michael turned to the coachman and pointed to Grünemann's limp figure.

Peter couldn't understand the stream of English that came next, as the two men argued over something, but it was only too easy to read the suspicion on the coachman's face as he glanced at Peter and gestured with his whip.

Michael waved off the other man's protests, though, and flashed Peter a grin. "We don't want that fellow waking up here to turn us *both* in to his employers, now, do we? So it's really better to stash him somewhere safe."

Peter didn't smile back. He was well aware of the real meaning behind Henry's reluctance to leave right now, and it had nothing to do with Grünemann . . . and everything to do with leaving Peter unguarded. The fact that Michael was treating him as a comrade now, rather than as a prisoner, only made him more uneasy.

He didn't move away, though. As the coachman dragged Grüne-mann's limp—but still breathing—body away, Peter kept his eyes on Michael. The pain in his head was slowly subsiding, leaving room for his wits to revive.

Michael didn't mean to harm him, it seemed . . . or, at least, not yet. That had to mean that he wanted something else. Peter narrowed his eyes as he studied the other man's body language, gauging the messages that it sent with a director's eye—all easy friendship and fellow-feeling, drawing them together.

So, Michael had devised another scheme, and he had made the decision, once again, to use Peter to help himself. Was he mad, to believe he could trick Peter again so soon? Or full of such overweening arrogance that he couldn't even see the inherent flaw in his plan?

Regardless . . . Peter shifted, letting his weight balance evenly on his legs. It was a pose he'd perfected in his training as an actor; it let him move rapidly in any direction. At the same time, he took control of his wayward expression, forcing open suspicion to metamorphose into mere confusion—the face of an easy dupe.

He couldn't overpower Michael here, where he was outnum-bered. And if he let his nemesis go free, Peter would give up all his own chances at life, freedom, and the safety of his company. That left only one remaining option.

Peter would have to agree to Michael's plan, whatever it was . . . and wait until the first available moment to turn on him.

"Charles?" Caroline whispered.

Held within Pergen's grip, she could turn only her head to look toward the secret passageway, her vision half-blocked by Pergen's shoulder. But the figure she saw in the dark opening was instantly recognizable.

"Lady Wyndham." Charles Weston gave a stiff bow. His face was deadly pale.

Caroline forced the words out of her suddenly tight throat. "How much did Pergen offer you?"

"Oh, we didn't need to bribe Mr. Weston with money," Count Pergen murmured. "You needn't fret yourself imagining that a mere rise in pay would have secured his loyalty."

"I rather thought I had that already." Caroline fought to keep her voice light. "What did you offer him instead, then?"

"Knowledge," Charles said. "Power."

"And revenge," Pergen added. "Don't be shy, Mr. Weston. She might as well know the full truth at the outset."

"Revenge on me, you mean?" Caroline asked.

Pergen's head tipped in a nod, trailing shadows.

Charles's face twisted. Perhaps he meant to look nobly defiant, Caroline thought. To her eyes, it looked like the grimace of an angry child.

"You tricked me!" he said.

"Perhaps," Caroline said. "But you also tricked yourself." She met his gaze and held it. "Was it truly worth such a betrayal as this?"

Charles looked down, his expression mutinous. Pergen answered for him.

"I've already found Mr. Weston an apt pupil. And a useful one. This tube, for instance . . ." Pergen turned it gently from side to side. "Your own blood, he tells me. And I find . . ." He glanced pointedly at the visible bump beneath her left glove, where a discreet white bandage was still wrapped around her forearm. "I believe him. Shall we attempt an experiment?"

"Charles?" Caroline stared at his downturned face, searching for any sign of recognition. "Are you really going to help him with this?"

Charles looked back up and met her gaze. His face was hard and set.

"I will," he said. "And I'll enjoy every moment of it."

❧

Unease trickled down Michael's spine as Riesenbeck's face softened into a frown of simple confusion. Open suspicion had made sense, after the actor's earlier experiences; to show signs of softening so soon, before Michael had even attempted any persuasion, hinted at either a lack of common sense or else something more sinister.

Still, it was too late to turn back now.

Michael began to put on his most confident smile, then stopped. Nothing would do now except for utter sincerity . . . the one thing he hadn't had much practice at, over the years.

"We've both been left in the same straits," he said, without preamble. "You heard what that policeman told you. Catching me was no one's priority but yours—and you were being used like a puppet on a string, to reel me in as an added bonus before being locked up again yourself."

"Why would they do that?" Riesenbeck asked.

"Why? You could probably tell me better than I could guess myself, having spent only five minutes in conversation with Count Pergen. But from what I've been told of him . . ." The memory of Caroline's broken voice choked him for a moment.

What Caroline might be undergoing even now . . .

Michael's voice flattened with the effort of holding back his panic as he repeated the information she had given him in the hours before they'd left for this evening's disaster. "Count Pergen feeds on fear," he said. "Or . . . something within him feeds upon it, at any rate. I haven't seen it happen myself, but I understand that it's part of how he draws out your spirit, for his own use or for another's."

Real vulnerability flashed across Riesenbeck's face for a moment, before it was suppressed. "That—does fit with what I experienced."

"Mm?" Michael paused, waiting to see if Riesenbeck would expand upon it. After a moment of taut silence, Michael continued. "To reel you inexorably back into his clutches, fresh with energy from a few days' grace, but even more frightened this time for having come so close, as you'd thought, to escaping . . . That sounds to me like what he might consider excellent fodder for his needs."

Was it only pretense that sent such mixed emotions shifting across Riesenbeck's face? Michael forged forward, his chest tightening. *This has to work.*

"If you try to escape, you'll have abandoned your company, and you might not even be allowed out through the city walls."

"And you?" Riesenbeck met his eyes squarely. "Why not escape now in your fine carriage? They wouldn't know to turn you back. I couldn't even give them the name that you're using."

"I . . ." Michael drew a deep breath. It was time. Time to drop all the protective layers he'd built throughout the years and give in to the inevitable.

"I can't leave," he said. "Not until I rescue someone who's being held captive now, just as you were before."

"What?" Riesenbeck stared at him. "You can't think to break into those cells below the Hofburg. The guards, the stone walls—"

"I couldn't do it with a sword," Michael agreed. "But I could do it with words, if they were the right ones."

"You . . ." Riesenbeck shook his head, letting out a pained half-laugh. "You think you can talk the imperial guards and the secret police into releasing your friend, only to please you?"

"No," Michael said steadily. "I think I can rescue my friend, you, *and* your entire company . . . but only if you're willing to help."

As Peter listened to the other man's plan, his thoughts whirled as quickly and uncontrollably as a flight of pigeons rising from Prague's Old Town square.

He had been an actor all his life, and he could swear Michael wasn't acting now.

No, Michael was going back for love, not for profit. He was willing to run the greatest of physical and supernatural risks, purely to save someone he cared about from torture and death. To choose to face that creature himself . . .

It was the most heroic thing Peter had ever heard of in real life. It was genuinely worthy of a play.

Perhaps it was a ruse, after all. And yet . . .

Peter remembered a cold room and a voice hissing into his ears through a muffling hood. Every bone in his body wanted to freeze in terror at the memory. He'd thought he could never risk going back to that—and that no one else could ever know, or understand, how it had felt. How it had melted away every other consideration but self-preservation, turning all the high ideals he'd ever acted out onstage into mere words and empty gestures.

But now . . .

Peter could have dismissed promises of a fortune or bribes of fabulous appointments at foreign courts. No matter how strong the ring of truth, he could even have dismissed Michael's suspicions of the minister of secret police's motivations.

But it seemed, after all, that there was one thing in life that Peter couldn't resist, no matter how hard he tried.

"I swore I wouldn't try to be a hero anymore," he said.

Michael's shoulders slumped with relief. He smiled crookedly at Peter. "Think of it as your greatest role."

"Mr. Weston, why don't you place her . . . ah, there. Yes, that should do nicely." Count Pergen pointed at the black settee that was set against the wall.

Caroline braced herself for the handover. She couldn't escape pain or even death—not while Pergen kept her blood—but she might be able to escape this, at least. Better to die three blocks from here, and free, than be a helpless prisoner again. The moment when Pergen passed her to Charles would be the one chance she would have. She counted down as Charles crossed the room toward her, his face full of guilty defiance.

Three . . . two . . .

"I should add," Pergen added calmly, "that she always tries to escape, no matter how impossible the circumstances. Do make certain you have a very firm hold on both her arms." He kept his own grip as tight as an iron vise around Caroline's forearm as Charles grasped her from behind.

"I have her," Charles said grimly. His hands clenched around her upper arms, fingers digging into flesh.

"No, no, that leaves her hands free to attack you, Mr. Weston. Clearly, you haven't had much experience dealing with recalcitrant subjects."

"I'll learn," Charles said.

His hands felt damp with sweat. Caroline shifted slightly, testing his grip, and he clamped his fingers around her wrists with excruciating pressure. She forced back a gasp of pain.

"There," Pergen said. "That looks far better. Now."

He released Caroline's arm.

Now.

Caroline lunged sideways, throwing all her weight into the move— even if it broke her wrists, anything for freedom. She felt Charles lurch off-balance behind her. She kicked his shin, hard, and he shouted with surprise and pain. His hands loosened. She started forward—

And Pergen's fist smashed into her face, knocking her backward. Charles's arms closed bruisingly around her.

"As I said," Pergen murmured. "She always tries. I don't know why. She's quite bright in every other way." He nodded to the settee. "Set her down there, and we'll begin."

CHAPTER THIRTY-ONE

It took a teeth-grittingly long fifteen-minute detour to find a spot to wash the filth from Michael's face, hair, and clothes. In the end, though, he was dripping but reasonably clean as he slid into the glittering crowd that surged across the square between the Hofburg and the Burgtheater.

"Prince Kalishnikoff." The Prince de Ligne raised his eyebrows as Michael fell into step beside him. His keen gaze took in Michael's disheveled appearance, but he only said, "Are you quite well, Your Highness? You were called away very suddenly, it seemed." His tone was courteous, as ever . . . but unmistakably lacking in warmth.

"I'd like to tell you the truth of it, actually. And you as well, sir," Michael added to the Comte de La Garde-Chambonas, who walked on De Ligne's other side. "Might I beg a moment of time from both of you gentlemen, before we enter the theater?"

"Well . . ." De Ligne's eyebrows rose skeptically. He glanced at the comte, who frowned.

Michael smiled ruefully, smoothing down his wet hair. "I can imagine that you might be reasonably reluctant after the absurd figure I must have cut in the Great Hall. But I should like to explain that to you both."

De Ligne regarded him through half-lidded eyes. "I didn't see you return to the Great Hall after your . . . ah . . . curious manner of departure."

"No, you did not," Michael admitted. "Nor . . ." He lowered his voice. "Nor did you see Lady Wyndham again, I believe."

De Ligne's eyebrows drew down into a frown. He came to a halt, leaning on his walking stick. Elderly or not, the ferocity of his military reputation was suddenly mirrored in his expression. "And what exactly do you mean to imply by that statement, sir?"

The Comte de La Garde-Chambonas edged closer, letting the rest of the crowd pass him by. Not only avidity for gossip but also genuine concern showed on his plump face. "Is something amiss with Lady Wyndham?"

"That," said Michael softly, "is exactly what I'd like to discuss with you."

"There you are!"

Peter entered the Burgtheater's backstage and found his gathered actors awaiting him.

"My friends!" Peter bowed splendidly. "Did you all enjoy your grand evening of socializing?"

"Oh, so much," Marta murmured. Her lips curved in a satisfied smile. Josephine and the other actresses chimed in their own agreements, while Karl shrugged his reluctant satisfaction.

"Good, good. I certainly heard admiration for all of you flowing in from all directions! In fact . . ." Peter drew out the pause. "In fact, you were so very admired . . . that I've agreed on your behalf to take on a challenge."

"Challenge?" Karl scowled. "What sort of challenge?"

"A challenge of skill, my friend. Certain royal visitors pointed out to me that the play we've planned to present to them is one we've already performed in the Theater an der Wien for merchants, newspapermen, and any drunken lout from the street who could afford to stand in the stalls. To repeat it tonight, unaltered, would be to name the collected royalty and nobility of Europe as worthy of no more than the table scraps left behind by their inferiors."

"But we've only rehearsed—" Josephine began.

"*My* actors," Peter said, "can improvise. You've performed tragedies, comedies, and romances. You have memorized and embodied the words of the greatest playwrights of the age. And now, tonight—"

"It would have to be based on the play we meant to perform," Marta said thoughtfully. "To give structure to the drama."

"You've taken the very words from my mouth," Peter said. "That was my own idea as well."

"We only have fifteen minutes before the play is to begin," Karl snarled. "How many changes do you expect us to make?"

"Only a very few," Peter said. "But you're quite right to ask that, Karl, as your character will be the most affected. In fact, you'll need to think hard about whether you can manage it at all, for I foresee . . ." He drew a breath, letting the moment linger. "An entirely new scene for him, full of supernatural vileness and cruelty, at the very beginning of the play—and complete with a new, added monologue of rage."

"A . . . new scene?" Karl repeated. He blinked, twice. "With an entirely new monologue to be *improvised*?"

"Indeed," Peter said. "But do, please, understand, my friend, that you can tell me now if it's too much to ask of you. After all . . ." He sighed sympathetically. "It would add at least fifteen minutes to your character's time on stage."

"Oh, my dear," Marta breathed. Her face lit up with a mixture of loving pride and blatant envy.

Karl's harsh face did not break into a smile. But Peter could have sworn he saw a glow begin underneath the skin.

"Of course I can do it," Karl said curtly. "And if it pleases the royal audience . . ."

"It is the particular desire of His Highness Prince Kalishnikoff of Kernova-as-was," Peter said. "And he assures me that the entire audience will be most struck by his idea. Let me tell you exactly what he proposes . . ."

Only a few aristocrats still lingered in the street outside the Burgtheater as Michael finished his story. The Comte de La Garde-Chambonas let out scattered gasps and exclamations of horror throughout; the Prince de Ligne said nothing at all, but in the shadows, he looked suddenly stooped with age and weariness.

At the end, De Ligne took a deep breath and spoke for the first time. "I suppose you haven't any proof to present to us?"

"Other than the fact that, as you know for yourself, the emperor returned from their meeting and Lady Wyndham did not . . . no. Peter Riesenbeck can corroborate, if you ask him, but I expect we won't be able to find him now until the end of the play. And if you don't choose to assist me . . ." Michael tasted bitterness. Never before had so much rested on a single gamble. "Then he and all his troupe will undoubtedly be arrested for their performance at the end of it, and I will have sentenced them to horrors for their loyalty."

The comte shook his head, like a dog shaking off water. "You cannot expect us—no. No! Such a story could not be true! Oh, everyone knows the secret police of Vienna are a fearsome force—one knows better than to speak of politics where others can hear, or else be deported from the city . . . and of course there are spies everywhere . . . but this—that the emperor himself would employ so vile and unnatural a force—! Even if one believed it could work," he added hastily, "which is evident nonsense and superstition, but—"

"Oh, it could work," the Prince de Ligne said softly. The other men both turned to him, and the elderly prince's lips twitched in a smile of bitter amusement. "You are both of you—yes, even you, Kalishnikoff— too young to remember the days when alchemy was an accepted—and respected—facet of Viennese society, before our current moralizing era."

The comte said, "Well of course there were natural philosophers of the last century who may have *called* themselves alchemists, but—"

"The demonstrations I saw, in the grandest Viennese salons and country houses, were convincing," De Ligne said heavily. "To say the least. I had thought . . . I had hoped . . ."

"Yes?" the comte prompted.

De Ligne expelled his breath in a long sigh. "I am not at all surprised." He shook his head slowly. "I saw Pergen push old Emperor

Joseph further and further from his Enlightenment doctrines into paranoia and rage and fear of his own populace. And if you had seen the mad way Joseph taunted Francis as a youth, calling him a weakling and a fool, not fit even to be trained as emperor ... Francis must have been ripe indeed for Pergen's flattery and persuasion ... on this as well as so many other fronts." De Ligne's lips compressed. "Our Emperor Francis has always most desired to be proven strong."

"Yet you stood up to him once before," Michael said. "Lady Wyndham told me how you published letters that criticized him for his policies and gave him the kind of critique all nobles were once allowed to offer their emperor, before these days of public silence and submission."

"I did," De Ligne said. "And I came very close to losing my position at court entirely. I lost many chances for financial advancement through that reckless act ... which is more than I confessed to Lady Wyndham, I'm afraid."

Michael thought back to his own visit to the Prince de Ligne's house—the surprisingly poor array of food, the furniture that seemed ready to fall apart at the slightest touch—and stifled a groan. Bitter reality, crashing against his plans ... He'd wondered at the time how a field marshal of the Austrian Empire could have been allowed to sink into such genteel poverty despite international fame, proven loyalty, and public bravery. Now he knew.

Still ... Michael moistened his lips. There must be another angle he could use, another gamble he could play. There had to be. With every moment that he wasted, Caroline might be suffering torments he could barely even imagine. If he could only think of another way ...

"If you don't help her, she will die," Michael said finally. It was too blunt—it had no courtly polish—but he found that he had none left to give. "She is already a captive. She may already be undergoing torture." He met the Prince de Ligne's eyes. "If you, too, turn your back on her now ..."

"But what else is there to do?" The comte's face shone with perspiration and distress. "Of course one would like to help her. But to speak open criticism of the emperor's actions—to stand against him—!"

"Then you'll be asked to leave the Congress and go back to France, or Switzerland, or one of your numerous other homes," the Prince de Ligne said dryly. "A tragedy indeed. And yet . . . perhaps exactly what your memoir needs, my friend, to supply a proper sting? And to be devoured by every possible reader, all across the Continent?"

Michael closed his eyes for a moment of relief so acute it was nearly a physical pain. When he opened them again, he found the Prince de Ligne regarding him with a small smile.

"Touché," the prince said. "I am an old man, Kalishnikoff . . . or whatever your true name may be."

"Steinhüller," Michael said, on a sigh. "Michael Steinhüller."

"Sir." The prince inclined his head in a stately nod. "The turn of the century has been anything but a rousing success for myself and my family fortunes. I've lost my family home, my wealth, and nearly everything else. If I am not to lose my self-respect as well . . ." He sighed and gestured a graceful invitation in a turn of the wrist that Michael recognized from century-old paintings. "You may tell us what plan you've devised. But first . . ." His keen eyes narrowed. "I believe there is one other person who might find your story of profitable interest."

Michael gave a return nod as grave as the prince's own. "I had thought of that as well."

The galleries of the Burgtheater, alight with thousands of candles, rose dizzyingly high above the stage, showcasing level upon level of the aristocrats and royalty of Europe. Crammed together in the thin, tall building—the most cramped theater Peter had ever performed in, as well as the most glorious—their glittering tiaras and golden Orders of distinction joined the blaze of the candles. The light they flashed blinded Peter for a moment as he looked up at them through the crack in the thick velvet stage curtains.

He didn't look away, even as his vision blurred. He didn't want to lose even an instant of appreciation.

He stood on the stage of the Habsburgs' own Burgtheater, at the center of the empire. Even Périgord himself had never achieved such a goal. But Peter stood here with his own company gathered behind him, waiting for him to give the signal.

And—it had to be said—he was playing the role of a lifetime. Quite possibly it would be the last role of his lifetime. If it was . . .

Peter's vision cleared, adjusting to the glare, and revealed the massed glory before him.

"Don't confuse yourself with the heroes you play onstage." His old master had snarled that at him so many times that Peter had finally come to believe it.

But they had both been wrong.

Peter stepped through the curtains, and the entire theater hushed for him.

"Your Majesties and Highnesses," Peter declaimed. He heard his own voice roll through the auditorium, pitched to carry all the way to the highest gallery. "My Lords and Ladies. Ladies and gentlemen. May I present the Riesenbeck troupe at your most humble service."

He sank into a deep bow as a thousand pairs of hands clapped applause.

Paul Périgord might never know the truth of Peter's final success, but Peter found that, somehow, that no longer mattered.

He had already won.

Michael raised one hand to hold back the men who stirred restlessly behind him. The sound of applause rippled through the Burgtheater, bleeding through the thin walls of the royal boxes before them.

"Not yet," he breathed.

They stood in the narrow outer corridor that ran behind the central boxes on the second floor. With the doors to the crowded, brightly lit boxes shut, the corridor itself was dark and silent, lit only by a single brace of candles. All the rest had already been extinguished in preparation for the performance about to begin.

"Dare I ask," the French foreign minister murmured, sotto voce, "if there is in fact any compelling reason for us to wait any longer? Realizing that the further into the performance we wait, the harder it will be to extract the emperor from his company without raising any number of eyebrows and suspicions in the rest of the audience?"

The Prince de Ligne sighed but remained silent, leaving all direction to Michael, while the comte watched with wide, interested eyes—taking notes for his memoirs, no doubt.

Michael gritted his teeth. "Have faith," he whispered. "There is a reason, but I haven't time to explain it now."

"Oh, indeed, I imagined there must be a reason of some sort. And yet . . ." Talleyrand paused delicately. "You will forgive me, *Prince Kalishnikoff*, if I wonder whether faith is necessarily as sensible an option as—"

The applause died down, and Talleyrand was forced to break off or else be heard through the thin walls. The ambassador subsided with a meaningful glare. The near silence was broken only by the dull roar of audience murmurs. Then a deep voice spoke, rising from a low growl to a dramatic torrent of rage.

Karl. Michael relaxed. "It's nearly time," he whispered. "Only a few more minutes left. But the emperor must see this first scene performed."

Seated in the imperial box between the tsarina of Russia and his own intermittently coughing wife, Emperor Francis had to grit his teeth to hold back his seething rage. His fingers tapped a rapid drumbeat against the sides of his chair until his wife reached across and stilled his hand.

He glared at her in return until she looked away. But it was not Ludovica's face that he saw in his mind's eye.

"You are worth even less than your lackey."

No one had ever dared speak such words to him. The contempt in her voice . . .

His fingers were beating against his chair arm again. He stilled them himself, before his wife could give another one of her pointed hints.

She didn't seem to have noticed, though. Francis realized that Ludovica's focused attention was, for once, entirely caught by the action on stage, rather than the more vital social action that went on within the boxes of the theater. The more impressionable tsarina, on his other side, was nearly hanging over the railings in her eagerness for the drama. Even Tsar Alexander, who was half-deaf and had little fondness for the theater, was watching the action with a slight frown.

"I can harness the darkness for you, my king," the actor onstage said, in insinuating, slippery tones. He leaned over the crowned actor. "No one will ever know."

Francis blinked. He leaned forward, focusing his attention.

"Then let us use prisoners and street children," the other actor—the king—responded. "No one will care what becomes of such as them."

"But of course. Your wisdom shall be our guide. And if ever any man dare question you or whisper the truth about your rule—"

"Then he shall be the first to be arrested," the king declared. "And I shall feed from his life force, with your help."

His advisor bowed deeply. "Your wish is my command."

Francis jerked back in his seat, dragging the heavy chair backward across the carpeted floor. His vision had gone strangely blurry in sudden panic.

"Francis?" He felt a hand on his arm—his wife, he realized only after he had pulled away from her. He forced himself to focus on her frown. "What's amiss?" she whispered.

"Nothing! Nothing. I only—" He looked back to the stage. A new actor had been dragged on, his head covered with a sack. The actor-king prepared to draw energy from him, using his advisor's dark powers.

Francis twisted around in his seat, almost toppling it. "Damn it, where's a footman?"

His wife gestured, and one hurried toward them. "What—?" she began.

"I want those actors arrested," Francis snarled to the footman. "Now. All of them!"

Ludovica gasped. "But Francis—"

"What have they done?" the tsarina asked. Even she had turned at the news. "Good heavens, it's only a play. A rather strange play—unusual, truly—but quite fascinating. If—"

"You seem most distressed, my friend." Tsar Alexander turned his frown to Francis. Confusion mingled with the dangerous beginnings of suspicion in his heavy voice. "What is it about this play that has had such an effect upon you?"

Francis shook his head, forcing a smile. "Nothing. I merely . . . this play does not amuse me."

"Then you needn't hire these actors again," the tsarina said. "But surely—"

"You cannot seriously intend to arrest them merely for putting on an unamusing play!" A hacking cough overcame Ludovica, and her slight frame shook, but she stared at him, eyes wide, as she bore through the interruption. "In heaven's name, Francis, what has come over you?"

"Nothing!" Francis said. "It was only a jest. I meant nothing by it. In God's name, would you *all stop haranguing me?*"

With a sudden jerk of horror, he realized his voice had risen to a shout. Not only his own companions but everyone in the boxes around them was openly staring at him now. Even on stage, the actors had stumbled in their lines.

Francis stood up, shoving his chair aside. "I need fresh air!" He shouldered past the footman and out of the box, into the narrow, darkened corridor outside. He slammed the door shut and leaned back against it, drawing a shaking breath.

A footstep sounded nearby.

It was only then that he realized he was not alone.

Michael stepped out in front of the others. "Your Majesty." He bowed, minimally.

"You!" The emperor scowled. His gaze skated past Michael to the men who stood behind him. "What—?"

"I trust you've been enjoying the performance?" Michael kept his voice soft with an effort. Looking at the emperor's long, arrogant face, all Michael wanted to do was lunge for the man's throat and throttle him until he let Caroline go free.

Calm, he told himself. At the emperor's first cry, the corridor would be flooded with guards and outraged guests, and all of Caroline's chances would be lost. Violence wouldn't solve anything now. Words, on the other hand . . .

"*You* arranged that performance?" the emperor breathed. He was staring at Michael as a man would stare at a venomous snake.

"I believe your minister of the secret police arranged this particular performance, actually," Michael said smoothly. "I did, however, suggest a few changes to the play itself, to make it more appropriate for its audience."

"You—!" The emperor cut himself off abruptly, looking at the men who stood behind Michael. "De Ligne. Talleyrand." He ignored the comte. "What are you doing here with this man?"

"Supporting him, Your Majesty," said the Prince de Ligne. His face was ramrod-stiff, his posture rigid with military precision. For the first time since meeting him at the Congress, Michael saw not the charming old bon vivant and raconteur, but the man who had been a prince of the Holy Roman Empire and a field marshal in a dozen Austrian wars. Sorrow tinged De Ligne's face as he spoke, but his voice was firm. "For the sake of our empire."

"And what, precisely, is that supposed to mean?" The emperor whirled around before De Ligne could answer, turning on the French foreign minister. "Talleyrand? Do you care to explain yourself?"

"I am here for my own king, Your Majesty. And for the good government of Europe," Talleyrand added gently.

"'The good government'—!" The emperor broke off, nearly sputtering. "Good God, have you all gone mad?"

"We have only just managed to remove one tyrant from his throne, at the expense of millions of lives," Talleyrand said. "This Congress was intended to restore harmony to Europe . . . but, in order to do so, it must possess the good faith of the people. Should it be revealed that one tyranny has merely been exchanged for another . . ."

"Is that meant to be a threat?" The emperor turned from one man to another. Receiving no response, he jerked back to Michael, pointing a shaking finger. "Are the rest of you aware that this man is an imposter? He's no more a prince of Kernova than I am!"

"Less, no doubt," Michael agreed. "For, unlike yourself, Your Majesty, I am Viennese by birth. I spent my childhood in this city, unlike you. And I saw the lives that were ruined by you and Count Pergen together."

"This is absurd." The emperor reached for the door to the box. "I'll—"

"Did you enjoy the scene you just watched in the play?" Michael advanced toward the emperor inexorably, while the others maintained a watchful silence. "Did it bring back fond memories, Your Majesty?"

"I don't know what you're talking about," the emperor rasped. His hand dropped away from the door, but he did not turn.

"No? The men beside me do. And unless you release Lady Wyndham and retire Count Pergen in truth, as you retired him officially so long ago, then every other man in Europe shall know it too, within the week."

"You must be mad," the emperor whispered. He turned around slowly. His burning gaze met Michael's. "You wouldn't dare—"

"Your Majesty, you might be able to silence Prince Kalishnikoff," said De Ligne, "but you will not be able to silence the rest of us so easily."

"You wouldn't dare—"

"By midnight tonight, letters will go out to every statesman and gossip in Europe." Michael held the emperor's gaze. "By the end of the week, all the English Whig papers will be printing their own furious articles about the ungodly and tyrannical practices of the Austrian Empire. How long do you think the English diplomats will be able to maintain ties of alliance with your government once their people have taken to arms?"

The emperor sucked in a sudden hiss of breath through his teeth.

Michael watched the other man's face as he continued. "Without the wealth and power of England on your side in the Congress's negotiations—"

"It is not only England that will move against you, Your Majesty," Talleyrand added, in his dry monotone. "My own king may not have been invited to join your alliance of Great Powers, but the tsar of Russia is a deeply religious man, who would be horrified by such blasphemous practices. And more than that—his boyars have been urging him at every opportunity to take over the gap in power left by Bonaparte's defeat. He has only been searching for an excuse to seek out more land and power for the Russian Empire and for his desired puppet state in Poland. Had he that excuse to give the international public . . . the excuse you will have so obligingly handed him in the public outrage sparked all across the Continent . . ."

Talleyrand shrugged, a faint smile tugging at his lips. "Russia is an uneasy ally—but a deadly enemy. And, of course, your own Habsburg holdings do happen to sit so conveniently on her borders . . ."

Michael held his tongue. All his attention was focused on the emperor's furious expression.

"And my memoir!" The Comte de La Garde-Chambonas's voice came out as a near-squeak, but his face was defiant. "Everyone of consequence will read my memoir and know the truth of this discussion!"

Red color splotched the emperor of Austria's hollow cheeks. He spun around to face Michael.

Applause flooded through the thin walls of the boxes as the first scene of the drama ended outside.

"At the end of this act, an announcement will be made," Michael said. "It will either state the truth of this drama, and your own identity within it . . . or not." He shrugged. "All hangs upon the message I give."

"You fool," the emperor breathed. He straightened, squaring his narrow shoulders. "You're nothing. You haven't a drop of noble blood in your veins. You're no more than street scum. I could—"

"You could crush me in an instant, certainly," Michael agreed. "You could order me killed and satisfy your pride. Or you could choose to hold your power, reputation, and empire secure for the rest of your reign. Which will it be?"

Michael held his ground as the emperor advanced on him. "Will you be the infamous tyrant of the moment, despised by all the rest of the world, from the greatest rulers to the lowest readers of the penny papers in London? Or will you swallow your pride, let go of revenge and alchemical deeds, and be respected as a sovereign for the rest of your reign?" He kept his voice pitched low, but in a piercing whisper.

Every gamble in his life was held in the balance now, in this moment of uncertainty.

Michael took a deep breath. "The choice is yours to make, Your Majesty."

The emperor of Austria looked from one man to another. Through the walls of the boxes, the applause went on and on.

His shoulders sagged. He spat out the words. "And your terms, gentlemen? Exactly?"

Talleyrand's voice was firm. "France's inclusion in the meetings of the Great Powers, on an equal basis with Austria and the rest."

"The dismissal of Count Pergen," the Prince de Ligne said, with icy precision. "There is to be no more dark alchemy practiced in the heart of this empire."

"Absolute amnesty for all the actors who performed in tonight's play," Michael said. "They are free to go, they will be allowed to perform elsewhere in the city, and they will be allowed out of the country afterward, with no retribution at any point."

"And Prince Kalishnikoff's freedom as well," the comte added. He lifted his chin proudly as he met the emperor's eyes. "If he is arrested or even said to have disappeared, we will all know how to take it, and we shall respond accordingly."

"I thank you," Michael said to the comte. "But most importantly . . ." He clenched his fists to keep his fingers from shaking now and revealing his full vulnerability at this last, most vital moment.

"Lady Wyndham is to be released instantly. Unharmed and free to leave the empire."

"Fine! Take her, if you must. Good riddance to her—and to you, if you're fool enough to be taken in by the slut." The emperor shook his head. Michael was alarmed to see a smile twist the corners of his narrow lips. "Unfortunately . . ."

"What?" Michael heard his voice rise, but for once, he couldn't stop the raw panic from breaking through. "What have you done to her this time?"

"I? Nothing at all. I left her half an hour ago, entirely unharmed. However . . ." The emperor's lips curved into a full smile of malevolent satisfaction. "I left her in Pergen's able hands, with instructions to punish her in the way he best knew how. That may have been only half an hour past, but from my intimate knowledge of Pergen's skills . . ."

An icy chill swept through Michael's body as he absorbed the emperor's final words.

"I doubt you'll find much left of her to rescue."

CHAPTER THIRTY-TWO

C harles pushed Caroline back onto the settee, and she landed hard, the back of her head hitting the wall. Her face burned with pain from Pergen's blow.

She had sworn she would never be a prisoner again. *Never again.* The words repeated themselves in her head as panic swirled through her, too rapidly for reason to reassert itself.

Her common sense told her to grit her teeth and endure it. She had been here so often before as a girl—not in this room but in this situation—too many times to count. She'd learned, then, how to wait out the pain and fear, how to numb herself to the distress. If she only stayed as calm as possible throughout, using the control she'd learned as an adult to restrain herself from useless struggling, she could marshal all her efforts for a rational state of alertness, seeking out any potential means of escape once her jailers were finally certain of her and had lost their wariness.

Rationality be damned. She couldn't bear it.

Not again, after so many years. Not now.

Caroline's clenched right hand throbbed with pain. She glanced down, relaxing her fist. Warm, slippery blood pooled beneath her glove. The glass decanter of wine had cut her hand as it had smashed into pieces. Most of the fragments had been tiny, no more than pinpricks, but a few shards had cut into her skin so deeply that they hadn't even hurt at first. Now that the numbness had faded, the pain was becoming a dull accompaniment to her thoughts—and the bleeding showed no signs of stopping.

She would have found that worrying, under normal circumstances.

Now, she sought for the first hints of dizziness and found herself hoping that the blood loss would make her swoon. She'd gain at least an hour's respite from her torture if that happened—a full day, even, if she was lucky.

Unfortunately, her head remained maddeningly clear. She saw Charles turn away to confer with Pergen in low whispers. He still kept one wary eye on her, though. Running for the door would do her no good.

Caroline remembered the look on Charles's face when she had performed the transference of power upon him, only a few nights before—the sick pallor, glistening behind the look of greedy excitement.

She had been such a fool to give him that first taste of darkness. She had allowed her own need for him to blind her to his thirst for power. *Just like Pergen's.* And she had brought him here to Vienna herself, giving him training and incentive to aid her enemy against her.

Just as she had shown him.

Caroline drew a deep breath. Desperation stilled her whirling panic.

Think.

She'd tried to run, and it had failed. Pergen had been right: it always failed. And yet she had never stopped trying as a child, and even now, as a grown woman. Imprisoned again, she'd reverted to her childhood mindset, helpless to think beyond her old patterns of mindless terror and flight.

But she was no longer a child. She'd heard every dry, scientific explanation Pergen had given to the witnesses of her pain and degradation, all those years ago. And two nights ago . . .

Caroline recalled the feeling of a hole opening inside her chest: darkness opening within her.

She had more power than she had realized . . . or wanted to believe.

All the candles were on the other side of the room, set in a bracket on the table; even as she thought it, she saw Charles walk across to retrieve them. Pergen drew a tinderbox from his coat pocket as Charles returned.

Caroline didn't need any candles. She had something more powerful, if she only dared to use it.

Drops of her blood were scattered across the floor in the area where she had struggled with Pergen and along the path that she'd been dragged by Charles. They already formed a half-circle around the two alchemists. All she had to do . . .

Caroline half-closed her eyes and slipped from the settee to the floor, pulling off her blood-stained glove along the way.

Charles turned. "She's fainted."

"I think not." Pergen's voice was dry. "You'll become more familiar with her ruses soon enough, Mr. Weston. I believe she's only trying to buy time for herself at this point—but just in case, do stand ready to catch her if she runs for the door. In the meantime, if you'd be so kind as to light those candles for me . . ."

As the two men bent over the bracket of candles, Caroline raised her right arm with painful slowness. She couldn't afford to draw their attention too soon.

One drop, two drops, three . . . She inched forward, holding her breath. Four drops of blood, five . . .

Tinder struck, and light flared in the corner of her narrowed vision.

"Now," Pergen said. His voice was rich with satisfaction. "Set these around her, Mr. Weston, if you please."

Caroline flung out her arm. Drops of blood flew out, scattering across the floor . . . and closing the circle.

Charles turned. "What—?"

Before he could step forward, Caroline spoke.

She spoke the first words of the invocation while still lying flat on the ground, looking up at them. She saw Pergen's shadowed eyes widen in sudden shock. He glanced down at the floor, and recognition dawned in his face. He tensed and lunged forward in a leap. Charles followed close behind.

Pergen hit the edge of the circle of blood and was flung backward as if he had bounced off a wall. The silver vial flew from his hand as he fell to the ground.

Caroline didn't dare halt in the invocation. Words poured through her mouth as she watched the path of the vial that held her blood. The ritual wasn't working as quickly this time as it had before. Why hadn't it affected the two men inside the circle yet? She fought back panic, searching for reason even as the words left her mouth. Drawing power from two people must be a greater endeavor, and she had never done it before. Who knew how long it might take this time to have a real effect? Even now, if Pergen acted quickly enough, before it was too late . . .

She saw the same thoughts pass across Charles's face. He stumbled forward, reaching for the silver vial as it flew through the air. It hit the invisible wall and rebounded, flying back toward Pergen. If it reached him . . .

Caroline's breath caught in her throat, and she stumbled over the words she spoke.

Charles grabbed for the vial. He was going to catch it . . .

His hands knocked against the vial at just the wrong angle. It flew in the opposite direction and hit the floor with a crack that knocked off the stopper. Red blood slid out across the black and white tiles. Charles let out a groan of frustration.

Relief pulled Caroline up to her knees, still chanting. The words flowed easily now, as she watched the blood stream safely across the tiles. Pergen couldn't use it against her anymore, even if he had the strength. And soon . . .

She met his eyes with bitter satisfaction. She had sworn never to perform alchemy again after her experience two nights ago. But as she looked at the man who had destroyed her childhood, she felt no regret. Even if it hadn't been her only defense against him, she would have been glad to do it anyway. Glad to show him exactly how it felt.

Even as she thought it, darkness fogged, then overwhelmed her vision.

Power flooded through her in an icy wave that knocked her backward. She thought she might have landed against the settee, but she couldn't tell. She couldn't see, though her eyes were open. She couldn't stop the words that formed themselves in her mouth as a hole ripped open inside her chest.

A dark presence formed, squeezing itself through the hole. It stretched luxuriantly and reached through her.

An opening in the veil, Charles had called it, when she'd asked him before. Every act of alchemy opened the veil. That opening functioned from both sides.

But this time it was even worse . . . because this time, it felt familiar. And she knew, with sudden, bleak certainty, that the recognition, like the opening itself, worked in both directions.

This was how Pergen had transformed.

The presence settled itself within her, this time with the casual ease of familiarity. She felt its hunger and its satisfaction as clearly as she felt—*oh, God*—her own.

No, she thought. *No!*

Caroline reached out blindly, searching for something—anything— to anchor her. Her fingers only scraped against the cold, tiled floor.

The power she'd tasted the first time had been nothing to this. The strength of it was overwhelming. But the difference was not in strength alone.

Caroline felt the presence inside her chime in resonance to something within Pergen's body. Even as strength and energy flooded into Caroline, something else flooded into the creature within her. She tasted the edges of it like a physical flavor—bitter, smoky, and intense. The creature within her swelled and grew with every mouthful. With every mouthful, it settled more firmly within Caroline's chest.

It had been long enough. Surely, it had been more than long enough to subdue Pergen and Charles for her escape. They couldn't be any danger to her now. But Caroline couldn't close her mouth. Her lips moved inexorably, controlled by the creature within her.

Caroline flung her own hands to her mouth. It didn't help. Her lips moved behind her hands, and the sound escaped between her fingers. She pressed her hands into her mouth with all the new strength that was flooding into her.

The creature within her flexed with casual ease, and her hands fell away, turning numb.

The smoky, bitter flavor faded away. That had to mean something, Caroline knew; something dangerous. But it paled in significance compared with the more pressing realization.

The power was slowing in its path, as if it were trickling to a halt. Yet, the creature inside her was only gaining more and more control. If it were still in control of her—if her lips were still moving in the chant when the other two had been completely drained of energy and life— what would happen then?

It might choose to leave of its own volition. But Caroline knew better.

How does the man merge with the shadows? she had asked Charles. Now, she knew the answer.

She had to stop before it was too late.

Caroline flung herself to the side, until her face was pressed into the cushions of the settee. It didn't help. Her lips kept moving, and the words escaped into the air. She tried to close her throat. The creature within her pushed it open.

The power had slowed to a thin stream now.

She tried to scream. No sound would escape around the words.

Pergen was either dead or dying. For years, she had dreamed of killing him for all that he had done to her. Now, the act brought her only fear.

If she didn't stop in time, she would lose herself forever.

When had it first happened to Pergen? When had the shadows formed behind his eyes? Had it frightened him, too, as he lost control to the power he had always sought?

She'd never thought to feel pity for her enemy.

The trickle of power slowed. It was only a dribble now. And soon . . .

Caroline wanted to sob. The creature within her wouldn't let her. She felt its triumph as it readied itself. Her willpower was slipping away, along with her consciousness. Only another minute, and then . . .

A sudden sound caught her attention—the slamming of a door, in the distance. The incongruity of it gave her a moment of strength. She flexed her hands. If she could only wrest control away for even a moment—

She heard the door to the chamber crash open. Footsteps halted a moment, than hurtled toward her.

"Dear God, Caroline!"

She knew that voice.

Michael. Thank God for his arrival—the surge of emotion she felt at the sound of his voice gave her renewed determination, pulling her back into clarity. If she could only choke off the words for one moment . . .

Even as she struggled, strong hands grasped her shoulders and turned her around. She couldn't see through her darkened vision. She could only faintly hear the angry, frightened words Michael spoke to the companions who had followed him.

But she felt it when Michael's warm lips settled on hers. He kissed her with the passion of overwhelming relief.

His kiss sealed off the words. Her lips moved irrepressibly against his, but the words they formed couldn't escape into the air.

The creature inside her howled with protest as the invocation was finally broken.

The opening within her chest shrank and closed and pulled the struggling creature out with it. As the opening sealed itself, Caroline's vision cleared.

Beyond Michael's head, she glimpsed the Prince de Ligne kneeling by a fallen body, his expression grimly satisfied. She heard the Comte de La Garde-Chambonas's high, agitated voice asking question after question while more footsteps sounded on the tiled floor of the secret chamber. Michael's arms pressed her against his chest as if he would never let her go again.

Caroline closed her eyes, wrapped her arms around Michael's warm, familiar shoulders, and kissed him back with all her strength.

She had tasted the darkness, but this time it hadn't won.

After twenty-four years, she was finally free.

CHAPTER THIRTY-THREE

Twenty-four years ago, Michael Steinhüller had fled Vienna, crouched and shivering in the back of a butcher's wagon, leaving everyone he loved behind him. This time, he rode through the city walls in a gleaming, aristocratic carriage, with his oldest and dearest friend at his side. The customs inspector bowed and let their carriage pass without question, requiring no paperwork beyond the affidavit signed by the emperor himself.

As their carriage rolled away from the customs checkpoint, Michael opened the window to wave a last farewell to the travelers behind them, heedless of his royal dignity. Peter Riesenbeck leaned out of the open window of the Riesenbeck company's own traveling carriage to wave back at him.

"Come see us perform in Berlin for the Prussian king next month!" he called. "We'll give you both free tickets!"

"Empty promises!" Michael called back. "You'll have no tickets left to give away."

Riesenbeck's grin lit up his face. "From your lips to the Almighty's ear," he said. "As always!"

Shaking his head, Michael closed the window.

"Better?" Caroline asked. He heard the smile in her weary voice.

"Better," he agreed, and took her hand, still craning his neck to watch the actors' inspection. Their affidavit should be enough to see them through, but . . . "Thank you for having the patience to wait while I saw everything sorted."

"We don't leave anyone behind." She leaned her head against his shoulder, visibly relaxing her guard. It only ever happened when they were alone, and each time it felt to him like a rare and precious gift. "Have you finally finished now?" she asked.

"I have," Michael told her. "It's a strange feeling, you know. I've never done that before—actually cleaned up the messes I left behind me. But I think I've managed it this time."

The actors weren't the only innocents he'd deceived in Vienna. Before leaving town, he'd sent a discreetly coded note and parcel to a room in the fifteenth district, where two young pamphleteers worked above a fruit and vegetable shop. All of Prince Kalishnikoff's political pretensions had ended forever the night before, leaving no necessity for the printing of angry pamphlets that could put Kaspar and Aloysia in further danger . . . even under a police regime that was finally free from alchemy.

It was too late for him to save his old master. But perhaps it wasn't, after all, too late for some redemption. And with luck those two young idealists would use the signet ring of Prince Kalishnikoff—or rather, its proceeds, when they sold it off—to perform more good than he ever could have managed with it.

The Riesenbeck carriage rolled safely away from the customs inspection, and Michael turned in his seat to meet Caroline's eyes.

For himself, he could only feel a fierce gratitude for the deaths of the two men who had held her in that ungodly chamber two nights ago. For Caroline, he knew, more complicated emotions were at stake.

Now, her right hand was thickly bandaged, and her pale face was drawn with exhaustion as well as deep new lines of grief . . . for her father, most of all, but even for her damned traitor of a secretary, who had died at her hands. It would take a long time, he thought, for all of her sorrow and her guilt to fade.

But for the first time in years, they both had all the time they needed . . . and neither of them would have to face their demons alone anymore.

As Caroline looked at him now, her expression was open and unmasked. She reached forward to trail her left hand lightly across his cheek, smiling ruefully.

"Well, Prince Kalishnikoff?" she said, in the lilting Viennese German of their youth. "Do you think you'll find a mere English country house exciting enough to please you, after all your years of adventuring?"

Michael captured her hand with his own and kissed it. "We'll just have to risk it," he said.

HISTORICAL NOTE

I usually feel at least a little bit guilty when I make real historical characters the villains of my stories—but I have to admit, I felt no guilt whatsoever about making Emperor Francis and Count Pergen the villains of this book. Nearly every academic historian I read in the course of my research referred to Pergen as "the sinister Count Pergen" or "the notorious Count Pergen"—a very atypical description in those otherwise dry and scholarly tomes!—and the truth is, Pergen's real actions as the creator and head of Vienna's infamous secret police, from the end of the eighteenth century onward, were more than horrifying enough for any villain, even without any alchemy being involved.

My own academic specialty was limited to Vienna between 1765–1790, under the reign of Emperor Joseph II, but that's a deeply depressing historical arc for any modern historian to watch, as the "Enlightened Emperor" was persuaded by Pergen into authorizing all the (non-magical) actions described in this book, including nighttime raids on "radical" printers, the smashing of their printing presses, burning of their shops, arrests, beatings, and disappearances. Emperor Leopold, Joseph's brother, immediately dismissed Pergen and abolished the secret police after Joseph's death, but when Leopold's son Francis took the reins only a year later, Pergen came into full power . . . and a city where politics had been freely debated in the famous coffee houses for years became a place where people were terrified to express any political opinions for fear of being reported to the secret police by their many informants.

Francis's paranoia, his general personality, and his relationships with his uncle Joseph and with Pergen are all described as accurately as possible in this book . . . with the obvious proviso that in real life, of course (I assume!), no alchemy was involved, and Baron von Hager was the true leader of the secret police by the time of the Congress of Vienna, rather than merely serving as Pergen's proxy. As well as monitoring all the prominent visitors to the Congress, Von Hager's informants scoured the visitors' fireplaces and rubbish, searching for any incriminating information, and the secret police delivered daily reports to the emperor, exactly as described in this book.

Caroline, Michael, and Peter are all fictional characters, but Michael's former mentor, Count Cagliostro, was very real, and all the various cons mentioned in Michael's backstory were based on actual cons that were successfully performed by various charming and persuasive con-men across Europe in the late eighteenth century. I created the principality of Kernova in the long tradition of imaginary Eastern European kingdoms that hearkens back to *The Prisoner of Zenda*, but all of the other political maneuvering described in this book really did happen at the Congress of Vienna, including the Polish Question and Talleyrand's brilliant and successful disruption of the Great Powers' original plans to leave France out of any decision-making. (In real life, of course, he used different methods of persuasion than those described in the climax of this book.)

The Prince de Ligne was a real and fascinating person, as was Princess Bagration, and as were all the other royals and political figures described in this book except for Marie Rothmere and her husband. The Comte de La Garde-Chambonas was also real, and he wrote an entertaining and opinionated memoir of the Congress (translated into English as *Anecdotal Recollections of the Congress of Vienna*) that I found incredibly useful in my research. You can buy the book in paper, or you can find it digitized online in various historical archives, along with many other memoirs and letters written by visitors from across the Continent, all competing to give their own spin on Vienna and the famous Congress.

If you'd like to read more, and you want a vivid and colorful introduction to the Congress, its various personalities, and its political wrangling, Harold Nicolson's *The Congress of Vienna* is a fabulously fun place to start. And finally, if you'd like to find out more about the Prince de Ligne, there's a wonderful biography of him that I'd strongly recommend: *Prince of Europe: The Life of Charles-Joseph de Ligne*, by Philip Mansel.

ACKNOWLEDGMENTS

Thank you so much to everyone who critiqued all or part of *Congress of Secrets* for me: Patrick Samphire, Justina Robson, Lisa Mantchev, David Burgis, Sarah Prineas, Jenn Reese, and Leah Cutter. I really appreciate your help!

Thank you so much to Patrick Samphire and Ben Burgis for reading first-draft chapters as I wrote them and cheering me along. Thank you to Justina Robson for saying at a crucial moment: *Send it!* And thank you to David Burgis for sharing my obsession with Habsburg history and trading wonderful research books with me over the years.

I owe an enormous thank-you to my parents, Richard and Kathy Burgis, for making it possible to edit this book at the same time as moving house. I genuinely could not have done it without you! And thank you so much to my husband, Patrick Samphire, for taking time in the middle of that house move to read and critique this book yet again. I appreciated it so much.

Thank you so much to my wonderful editor, Rene Sears, for believing in this book, and for helping me to make it stronger. Thank you to Lisa Michalski, my fabulous publicist at Pyr, and to Nicole Sommer-Lecht, who has created such beautiful covers for my books. Thank you to Sheila Stewart for the careful copyediting that's saved me from my own mistakes so many times, and a huge thank you to my agent, Molly Ker Hawn, for representing this book so beautifully! I can't imagine any better partner in publishing! I definitely owe you lots of chocolate.

Chocolate is also owed, along with profuse thanks, to Carly Silver, research goddess, who answered my last-minute cry for help on a particular historical detail and came up with the right answer within minutes. My book and I both thank you!

This is going back quite a way, but still, it really does have to be said: I am so grateful to the Fulbright Commission for sending me to spend a year at the University of Vienna, where I fell even more in (complicated) love with the city, after spending a six-month exchange program there two years earlier; and to my late grandfather, Emil Bauman, who encouraged me to go to Vienna in the first place, and who passed on his own Austro-Croatian father's deep love of the city. That particular branch of my family may have had to flee Vienna in the early part of the twentieth century, but the emotional connection has held strong across the generations.

And, of course, I am deeply grateful to the Arts and Humanities Research Council here in the UK for supporting me in a two-week research trip back to Vienna, years later. I was meant, at the time, to be researching a doctoral thesis on Viennese opera and politics, and I promise that I really did do that research, in lovely long hours spent every day in the National Music Library, with the smell of lilacs floating in through the open windows . . . but in my off-hours, I wandered the streets of Vienna's first district and planned out the staging of this book with deep pleasure. Thank you so much for giving me that opportunity!

ABOUT THE AUTHOR

Stephanie Burgis grew up in East Lansing, Michigan, and was a Fulbright scholar in Vienna, Austria, where she studied music history, attended the opera as often as possible, and ate far too much apple strudel. After spending three years as a doctoral student studying the opera and politics of eighteenth-century Vienna and Eszterháza, she moved into the more practical side of opera studies by going to work for an opera company in the north of England. Nowadays, she lives in a small town in Wales, surrounded by castles and coffee shops, with her husband, fellow writer Patrick Samphire, and their two sons. She is also the author of *Masks and Shadows*, as well as the *Kat, Incorrigible* trilogy and over thirty short stories in various magazines and anthologies. You can find out more at her website: www.stephanieburgis.com.

Photo by Patrick Samphire